Books by Jonathan Kellerman

FICTION

ALEX DELAWARE NOVELS

Motive (2015)
Killer (2014)
Guilt (2013)
Victims (2012)
Mystery (2011)
Deception (2010)
Evidence (2009)
Bones (2008)
Compulsion (2008)
Obsession (2007)
Gone (2006)
Rage (2005)
Therapy (2004)
A Cold Heart (2003)
The Murder Book (2002)

Flesh and Blood (2001)
Dr. Death (2000)
Monster (1999)
Survival of the Fittest (1997)
The Clinic (1997)
The Web (1996)
Self-Defense (1995)
Bad Love (1994)
Devil's Waltz (1993)
Private Eyes (1992)
Time Bomb (1990)
Silent Partner (1989)
Over the Edge (1987)
Blood Test (1986)
When the Bough Breaks (1985)

OTHER NOVELS

The Golem of Hollywood (with Jesse
Kellerman, 2014)
True Detectives (2009)
Capital Crimes (with Faye
Kellerman, 2006)
Twisted (2004)

Double Homicide (with Faye
Kellerman, 2004)
The Conspiracy Club (2003)
Billy Straight (1998)
The Butcher's Theater (1988)

GRAPHIC NOVELS

Silent Partner (2012)
The Web (2014)

NONFICTION

With Strings Attached: The Art and Beauty of Vintage Guitars (2008)
Savage Spawn: Reflections on Violent Children (1999)
Helping the Fearful Child (1981)
Psychological Aspects of Childhood Cancer (1980)

FOR CHILDREN, WRITTEN AND ILLUSTRATED

Jonathan Kellerman's ABC of Weird Creatures (1995)
Daddy, Daddy, Can You Touch the Sky? (1994)

MOTIVE

JONATHAN KELLERMAN

MOTIVE

AN ALEX DELAWARE NOVEL

BALLANTINE BOOKS

NEW YORK

Motive is a work of fiction. Names, characters, places, and
incidents are the products of the author's imagination or are
used fictitiously. Any resemblance to actual events, locales, or persons,
living or dead, is entirely coincidental.

Published in the United States by Ballantine Books,
an imprint of Random House, a division of Random House LLC,
a Penguin Random House Company, New York.

BALLANTINE and the HOUSE colophon are registered trademarks
of Random House LLC.

Library of Congress Cataloging-in-Publication Data
Kellerman, Jonathan.
Motive: an Alex Delaware novel/Jonathan Kellerman.
pages   cm
ISBN 978-0-345-54137-6
eBook ISBN 978-0-345-54138-3
1. Delaware, Alex (Fictitious character)—Fiction.   2. Forensic psychologists—Fiction.
3. Sturgis, Milo (Fictitious character)—Fiction.   4. Police—California—Los Angeles—Fiction.
5. Serial murder investigation—Fiction. I. Title.
PS3561.E3865M68 2015
813'.54—dc23   2014038686

Printed in the United States of America on acid-free paper

www.ballantinebooks.com

2 4 6 8 9 7 5 3 1

First Edition

To Faye—of course

MOTIVE

CHAPTER

1

My closest friend, a homicide lieutenant, refuses to add up how many murders he's investigated, claiming nostalgia is for losers. My rough guess is three hundred.

Most of those have been a sickening mix of tragic and mundane.

A pair of drunks pounding the life out of each other while equally besotted witnesses stand around hooting.

An errant knife-flick or gunshot putting the period on a domestic spat.

Gangbangers, some of them too young to shave, wielding firearms ranging from explode-in-your hand .22s to military-grade assault weapons, as they blast away through the open windows of scruffy compact cars.

It's the "different" ones that bring Milo Sturgis to my door.

Katherine Hennepin's homicide easily qualified but he'd never mentioned her to me. Now he stood in my living room at nine a.m. wearing a dust-colored windbreaker and brown poly pants from another era, his olive vinyl attaché dangling from one massive paw. Pale, pockmarked, paunchy, black hair limp and in need of trimming, he sagged like a rhino who'd lost out to the alpha male.

"Doctor," he grumbled. He uses my title when amused or depressed. That covers a lot of ground.

I said, "Morning."

"Apparently it is." He trudged past me into the kitchen. "Sorry."

"For what?"

"Offering you a tall glass of warm skunky beer." Stopping short of the fridge, he sank into a chair, rubbed his face, clicked his teeth, and avoided eye contact while unlatching the green case. Out came a blue binder identical to so many others I'd seen.

Hennepin, K. B. had been opened two months ago.

"Yeah, yeah," he said, still looking away. "Didn't think I needed to bug you, 'cause it was obvious." He growled. "Don't take any stock tips from me."

He waited. I read.

Katherine Belle Hennepin, thirty-three, a bookkeeper at a mom-and-pop accounting firm in Sherman Oaks, had been found in the bedroom of her West L.A. apartment, strangled and stabbed. The blowup of her driver's license photo portrayed a thin-faced, fine-featured woman with shoulder-length light-brown hair, a sweet smile, and freckles that managed to assert themselves with the DMV camera. Sad eyes, I thought, but maybe I was already biased.

I knew why Milo had included the shot: wanting me to think of her as a person.

Wanting to remind himself.

Rosiness and pinpoint blood dots around the ligature mark but far less pooling and castoff and splotches than you'd expect with thirty-six stab wounds suggested the killer had choked first, slashed second.

A few blood drops and a tamped-down section of carpeting indicated the murder had begun in the hallway just outside the kitchen, after which Katherine Hennepin had been dragged to her bedroom.

The killer then positioned her atop her twin mattress, lying faceup, head propped on a pillow. She was found covered, head-to-toe, with a blanket taken from her linen closet.

The pose the killer had chosen—arms pressed to her sides, legs close together—suggested peaceful repose, if you didn't consider the gore. No obvious sexual positioning and the autopsy confirmed no sexual assault. Milo and Detective 1 Sean Binchy had gone over the apartment with customary thoroughness and found no evidence of burglary.

An empty slot in a knife-block in the kitchen fit the heaviest butcher blade in the set. The dimensions of that high-quality German utensil synced with the coroner's description of the murder weapon. A careful search of Katherine Hennepin's apartment and nearby garbage bins failed to turn up the knife. The same disappointing result followed a canvass of the quiet, middle-class neighborhood where the victim had paid rent for two years.

No fingerprints or blood were lifted that couldn't be traced to Katherine Hennepin. The lack of foreign blood was another letdown; knife-murderers, particularly those engaging in overkill, often lose their grips on blood-slicked hafts and cut themselves. Despite the apparent frenzy of this attack, there'd been no slip.

I turned the page to a new set of photos.

In the dinette off the kitchen, the table was set with dinner for two: a pair of lettuce side-salads, later determined to be dressed with olive oil and vinegar, plates bearing grilled salmon fillet, rice pilaf, and baby string beans. An uncorked bottle of medium-grade Pinot Noir stood to the right of a small floral centerpiece. Two glasses held five ounces of wine each.

Everything about the crime scene—no break-in, theft, or rape, obvious overkill postmortem attack, shrouded victim, opportunistic weapon—suggested a killer well known by the victim, and driven by nuclear rage.

Milo's interview of Katherine Hennepin's employers, an octogenarian pair of CPAs named Maureen and Ralph Gross, uncovered a stormy relationship with a boyfriend, a chef named Darius Kleffer.

Someone with excellent knife skills.

I read on.

Katherine was described by the Grosses as "lovely," "sweet," and "shy." Ralph Gross termed Darius Kleffer a "damn maniac" and his wife concurred. Twice the ex had "barged in" at the office "ranting at poor Katherine." The first time, he obeyed the Grosses' command to leave. The second time he didn't, hovering around Katherine, trying to convince her to leave with him. The Grosses called the police but "the lunatic" left before the black-and-white arrived.

Research into Kleffer's background revealed two arrests for battery on fellow drinkers in Hollywood clubs, both charges eventually dismissed. His volatility, the notion of a chef cooking dinner for two, and the fact that Kleffer had lived close by in North Hollywood seemed to wrap it up and I understood Milo's confidence in a quick close.

He drove to Kleffer's apartment, but Kleffer hadn't lived there for three months and had left no forwarding. A week of searching failed to locate him and Milo was surer than ever he'd targeted the right quarry.

Obvious.

Until it wasn't.

I got up and poured my third cup of coffee. The first two had been savored at six thirty a.m. with Robin, before she took our dog to her studio out back and resumed carving a guitar top. I offered a cup to Milo.

"No, thanks."

"All of a sudden you're into self-denial, Big Guy?"

"For Catholics it's a genetic trait," he said. "Atonement must at least be attempted."

"The big sin being . . ."

"Failure."

I said, "I would've come to the same conclusion on Hennepin."

"Maybe."

"I digest facts the same way you do."

He didn't answer.

I said, "You can beat yourself up all you want but Kleffer looked perfect."

"Until he didn't."

I pointed to the blue folder. "There's nothing in here about why you scratched him off."

He said, "Haven't done the paperwork, yet." His smile was sadder than tears. "Okay, I'll sum up . . . confession being good for the soul and all that. I'm looking for him everywhere, no dice, finally his name pops up as a little yellow stripe on a Google search. He was on a video, pilot of a show that never actually ran called *Mega-Chef.* Working on the team of some Michelin-star Chinese genius. The filming was in Lower Manhattan, and months before that, Kleffer was living in New York. No airline has a record of him flying out of there, same for car rental companies. Borrowing a friend's wheels is a possibility but I never found evidence of that. Amtrak was also a consideration if Kleffer paid cash for his ticket, except that for five days before the murder and three days after the murder, he's verified present and accounted for, taping. Nights he bunked at a hotel where the show put up contestants. One of those dorm situations, three roommates who didn't like him but still vouched for him. So did the show's producers and everyone else I spoke to. This guy's got an army of alibi-confirmers."

I said, "Did you speak to Kleffer himself?"

"I tried, got no callbacks. I know that's weird, his girlfriend is slaughtered and he's not curious. But unless you can find some way to alter the laws of physics, he's not my guy."

"Does he have any evil friends? Someone in L.A. who'd do him a favor?"

"I thought of that but so far, no pal willing to do something like that comes up. No one who considers themself Kleffer's friend, period. He is not Mr. Popular."

"Unlikable and a knife pro," I said. "How often have you seen thirty-six wounds with no slippage?"

"I know, I know . . . any further insights?"

"Even if the killer wasn't Kleffer, the crime scene's still worth reading."

"Someone else she knew."

"And planned to have dinner with. Any idea if she prepared the meal?"

"No evidence of cooking in the apartment but it could've been cleaned up. You're thinking she had a thing for chefs, followed Kleffer with another culinary psychopath."

"Or just one of those guys who likes to impress women by cooking for them. A new man in Katherine's life would explain why Kleffer showed up at her work irate."

"Mystery boyfriend? I checked and rechecked with the neighbors, and Kleffer's the only man anyone ever saw. Binchy and I went through the place and you know how OCD Sean is. We found no indication of romance in her life."

"When's the last time she and Kleffer talked on the phone or emailed?"

"Way before the murder—he left for New York six months ago and they stopped talking before that. The rest of her records didn't say much, either. Mostly she emailed her employers about work-related stuff—a lot of it after hours, poor thing was a diligent type, they really loved her. The rest of her calls and emails were to her family. Lighthearted stuff, happy birthday, anniversary. She's from a big clan in South Dakota. Parents, grandparents, a great-grandmother, five sibs, nieces, nephews. A whole bunch of 'em came down to take care of the body and to get educated by me. There I am, facing a room full of well-mannered, decent folk and giving them zilch. And they were nice about it, which made me feel shittier."

He raised his arm and brought his fist crashing toward the table.

Stopping just shy of contact, he dangled his fingers a millimeter above the surface. "If there is no secret boyfriend, maybe you're right and a buddy of Kleffer was dispatched to carve her up." He got to his feet. "Okay, thanks for the coffee."

"You didn't drink any."

"It's the thought that counts." He paced a few circuits, returned. "What do you think about the meal being staged postmortem? Some sort of sick joke?"

I thought about that. "Sure, why not? If Kleffer did contract the killing, a mock meal could be a way of putting his stamp on it."

"I cooked for you, you dumped me, now you're dead meat."

"You do have a way with words."

He rubbed his face, like washing without water, loped to the cof-feemaker, poured, took a sip, dumped his cup in the sink. "Nothing wrong with it, sorry, my gut's raw."

I said, "How many Hail Marys for wasting caffeine?"

"Add it to the tote board. How's Robin?"

That sounded obligatory. A kid trained to say the right things.

"She's great."

"The pooch?"

"Charming as ever. How's Rick?"

"Putting up with my foul temperament since I began working Hen-nepin." Dropping the murder book back in the green case, he left the kitchen, paused at the front door. "I should've come to you sooner. Don't know why the hell I didn't."

"I haven't come up with much," I said.

"Maybe if you'd been to the scene—"

"Doubtful."

"Whatever. See ya."

I said, "Hope something develops."

Nothing did.

Two weeks later, he phoned to say the case was officially backburnered, no trace of anyone or anything linking Katherine's death to Darius Kleffer, no other suspects.

I didn't hear from him for another twenty days when he phoned, sounding adrenalized.

"Progress on Hennepin?"

"New case, amigo. This time you're on it from the git-go."

2

The crime scene was the bottom level of a subground Century City parking lot. Eighteen-story building on Avenue of the Stars. One of the older ones, built before developers managed to convince zoning boards that genuine skyscrapers made sense in seismic territory.

Easy drive from my house atop Beverly Glen and by the time I arrived the body was covered with a white cloth and the techs were finishing up photographing and scraping blood from the splotches spreading under the cloth. Red spray speckled a pillar to the left of the victim's silver Jaguar sedan.

A white lizard-skin purse and a set of keys, including one bearing the snarling feline Jag logo, lay on the ground near the corpse. Loops of tire tracks crisscrossed the concrete, creating an overlay that defied interpretation. All the coils and swirls I could see looked dry and grayed by time. Not a single fresh oil spot, no sign of a skid or a sudden stop.

Milo, gloved up and wearing a brown suit and skinny black tie, stood away from the forensic activity. He held a small white rectangle in one hand, pressed his cell phone to his mouth with the other.

The area smelled of gasoline. Dusty frigid air forced from overhead ducts turned the tier into a meat locker. I stood around until Milo nodded at the unseen person on the other end of his phone conversation, clicked off, walked to the body, squatted, lifted the cloth, and drew it back gently.

You are hereby invited . . .

The woman had fallen facedown. Her hair was the blond of raw oak, styled in one of those bobs cut high in back to reveal the nape of the neck. Long smooth neck. She'd probably been proud of it.

No wounds to the back of her tall, slender frame. She wore fitted jeans with spangled seams, a red leather jacket that ended mid-buttocks, medium-heeled white pumps. Her right leg twisted awkwardly, partially dislodging its shoe and offering a view of the pump's interior. Manolo Blahnik.

Platinum and gold glinted at two knuckles on each of her hands. The ear I could see was graced by a sizable rose-gold disk surrounded by pinpoint rubies.

Milo motioned to a male tech who looked like a high school junior, the kind of eager introvert who'd volunteer for Audio Visual Lab. "Okay if I flip her partially?"

The kid said, "C.I.'s come and gone and we're finished, far as I'm concerned you can flip her completely."

Milo shifted the woman as if she were made of spun sugar, lifting her just enough to give me a view of what had once been a lovely face: full-lipped, heart-shaped, clean-jawed. Expertly made up but no attempt to hide the fine lines earned by experience. My guess was early to midforties, extremely well tended.

Underneath the red jacket she wore a black silk blouse. A gold link necklace punctuated every two inches by small square diamonds circled a smooth neck. A bullet hole marked the sweet spot where the necklace met the center of her clavicle. Another entry wound marred her left cheek, an inch or so beneath the eye. That one had distorted her expression into something hard to categorize: confusion, helplessness, terminal dismay.

Faint stippling around the holes said the shooter had been six inches to two feet away. Two clean shots to the windpipe and the brain said death had probably been quick. No exit wounds in her back made small caliber likely, a pair of .22s or .25s bouncing around inside her, ravaging tissue.

"Casings?"

Milo shook his head. "If there were, they were taken. There's a thousand bucks and change in her purse as well as a Lady Rolex that isn't working, maybe she was planning to take it in for repair. Plus a whole bunch of platinum cards and the bling she's wearing. Need to see more?"

I studied the face for a second. All that cared-for beauty brought to this. "No."

He rolled the body back, covered it up. "Thoughts?"

"She was probably targeted and followed on foot. Unless you've spotted fresh tire tracks that I missed."

"Nope."

"How many security cameras are in the lot?"

"Ready for this? Not one in the actual parking areas."

"You're kidding."

"Wish I was. There's a unit above each elevator door and at the main entrance to the lot, plus a couple at the front and rear doors of the building."

"Why nothing down here?"

"You tell me."

"Who found her?"

"Another woman walking to her car. Poor thing was so shook up I had to back her Mercedes out for her. Took a while to calm her down for a statement, hence the relative quiet by the time you got here. What do you think about it being a frontal attack?"

"Shooting her from behind would be easier," I said. "So maybe whoever did it wanted her to know who was killing her. Or the plan was to get her from the back but she heard footsteps and turned. Who is she?"

He handed me the small white rectangle.

California driver's license of Ursula Corey, forty-seven years old, blnd/blu, five eight, one twenty-nine. Address in Calabasas.

"I mapped it," he said. "Horse country. Fits an affluent lady."

"Any idea what she was doing here?"

"Matter of fact I do. It was her housekeeper I was just on the phone with. Señora Ursula had a meeting with her lawyer, maid's not sure what his name is, something with an 'F,' maybe Feldman or Fellman. Any other ideas? If not, I'm ready to check the directory."

The lobby was half a football field of gray granite and brown marble under a thirty-foot coffered ceiling centered by a six-foot-wide Venetian glass chandelier. Bank of four elevators on each side. People in suits and business casual hustling back and forth. Plenty of gravity on some faces but no shortage of workplace levity—smiles, jests, bouncy strides. The news of the murder hadn't made its way up from the basement.

I wondered if Ursula Corey had begun her final elevator ride feeling chipper.

Most of the tenants listed on the directory were law firms, the rest sounded like outfits that moved money around for fun and profit. Hundreds, maybe a thousand attorneys. The way people sue one another in L.A. you could probably develop an entire city occupied by legal types. But what masochist would take on the job of law enforcement, let alone toxic cleanup?

Milo and I scanned the F's. A Feldman and a Feld were listed, both business managers.

He said, "Maybe to the housekeeper anyone with an office is an *abogado,*" and copied the suite numbers in his notepad. Dropping his eyes he stopped. Pointed to the spot where I'd just arrived.

Grant Fellinger. Law offices of Weintraub, Harrow, Micziewski and Fellinger. The entire south wing of floor seven.

"Best bet, right, lad?"

"Definitely," I said. "Let's give the housekeeper credit for knowing who's an *abogado* and who isn't."

"There you go again," said Milo. "Wanting to see the good in everybody."

The lift was souped-up, barely audible, let us off seconds later facing a glass door backed by an inner wall of black slate. The law firm's name was etched so discreetly you could barely read it. Maybe one of those *if-you-have-to-ask-you-don't-belong* deals.

The young woman behind the reception desk was a pretty, bright-eyed Latina in a tasteful black dress and pearls. Serious mien. Terrific posture. Sitting that straight all day implied self-discipline. Milo's badge evoked no change in expression.

"What can I do for you, Officers?"

"Is Ursula Corey a client of Mr. Fellinger?"

"One second please." Deft fingers pushed buttons on a panel faster than I could follow. Handheld devices may have damaged attention span but they've done wonders for fine-motor coordination.

Half a minute later a tall man in his thirties wearing jeans with rolled bottoms, a tiny-collared white shirt, and a red paisley tie appeared. Longish dark hair was combed to look careless. Black-rimmed glasses and red-brown saddle shoes added up to hipster, not corporate lawyer.

His voice was soft, as if eager not to offend. "I'm Jens Williams, Mr. Fellinger's paralegal. How can I help you?"

Milo repeated his question.

Jens Williams said, "Um, may I ask why you're asking?" New England in his accent.

Milo smiled. "I'll take that as a yes."

Jens Williams's return smile was lopsided. "Okay, yes, sir. Ms. Corey is a client. I'm just not at liberty to . . ." He shrugged. "She was just here, as a matter of fact."

"How long ago?"

"I'd say . . . an hour ago, give or take. Why?"

"She was here to see Mr. Fellinger?"

A beat. "This is above my pay grade. Um, can you tell me what it's about?"

"Ms. Corey was just found dead in the parking lot."

Jens Williams's hand shot to his mouth. "Oh my God, a car hit her?"

Milo said, "What kind of law does Mr. Fellinger practice?"

"Family and business litigation—my God, I just *saw* her." Williams looked at the receptionist. One hand worried her pearls. Her jaw had dropped open and her posture had gone to hell.

Milo said, "We need to talk to Mr. Fellinger."

Jens Williams replied, "Yes, yes, of course you do, I'll go check, please hold on."

He hurried away.

The receptionist said, "This is horrible. She *was* just here."

Milo turned to her. "Sorry to deliver bad news."

She shook her head. "That place is crazy dangerous."

"The parking lot?"

"Don't quote me but all those turns where you can't see around the corner? Are you kidding?"

Milo said, "Scary."

"I can't tell you how many times I nearly got run over on the employee level."

"Which level is that?"

"Second before the bottom."

One above the death tier.

The receptionist said, "Did the person stick around or was it a hit and run?"

"No trace of the offender," said Milo.

"God, that's evil! Maybe now they'll do something about it."

"They?"

"The management company."

"What should they do?"

"Like—I don't know. Something. I mean look what happened."

A voice said, "Gentlemen?" Jens Williams was back, standing ten feet behind the reception desk, crooking his thumb to the left.

We followed him up a long hall hung with generic abstractions. A short, stocky man emerged from an office midway up the corridor and stood with his arms folded across his chest. Fifty or so, he wore a pink shirt over blue pin-striped slacks held in place by leather-braid suspenders, a mint-green tie patterned with orange French horns, brown calfskin loafers.

Black hair combed straight back and thinning at the top was probably tinted. Bushy eyebrows topped a shelf-brow. His face was full, somewhat simian—more chimp than baboon. Clean-shaven but already blue in the beard zone by late morning.

Jens Williams said, "Mr. Fellinger, these are the police—"

Grant Fellinger silenced him with a hand-slash. A deep voice with an odd echoing quality emerged from plump but narrow lips: "Do me a favor and go down to the café and get me a white jasmine tea. Make sure they leave the flower in."

"Plain, one Splenda?"

"Plain, no Splenda. I'm not feeling particularly sweet given the circumstances."

Peevishness but no anxiety.

Williams said, "Done," in a faint voice and hurried off. Maybe his was a job that required aerobic training.

Grant Fellinger kept his arms folded as he studied us. Everything about him was thick—flat nose nearly as broad as the bud-lips below it, banjo-earlobes sprouting a few dark hairs, bull-neck, sturdy wrists, stubby fingers, sloping shoulders.

As if a sculptor had applied an extra layer of clay.

Milo introduced himself.

Fellinger nodded. "Ursula run over? I can't believe it, she was just here, Jesus." He gnawed his lip. "Forty-five minutes ago, she's on top of the world. Now this. *Jeesus.*"

A finger swiped at the corner of one eye. "*Damn.* Did you get the moron who did it? If he didn't have the decency to stick around, it should still be easy because there's a surveillance camera above the exit."

Milo said, "Ms. Corey left here forty-five minutes ago?"

"Give or take," said Fellinger. "And not that much take, maybe five minutes, so check out who left the lot during that period and you've got your bad actor."

Milo said, "Appreciate the information, Mr. Fellinger. Unfortunately, Ms. Corey wasn't hit by a car."

"No? What, then?"

"She was shot."

Grant Fellinger's head thrust forward, as if ready to butt reality. "*Shot?* Jens said it was an accident."

"We gave him no details so he assumed."

"Great," said Fellinger. "He does that a lot—jumps to conclusions, I'm always telling him about it. Yale, no less. Shot? By who?"

"We don't know yet, Mr. Fellinger."

"Shot," Fellinger repeated. "Shot? Ursula? Jesus Christ." His meaty arms dropped. Both hands were hirsute fists. He punched a palm. "This just knocks the stuffing out of me."

"Anything you can tell us, sir—"

The attorney's cheeks hollowed as he sucked spit, creating a bubbling noise. He threw up his hands. "You'd better come in."

◆

His office was surprisingly modest with a sliver of sky barely visible to the east. Plain wooden desk and matching credenza, oversized black leather chair, three functional chairs. A tweed sofa and glass coffee table created a conversational area near the rear wall. Fellinger moved behind his desk and motioned us toward the hard-backed chairs.

The grass-cloth wall above the credenza sported diplomas from the U. and its law school, supplemented by certificates in family law and arbitration. Photos hanging askew portrayed Fellinger with a pleasant-looking dark-haired woman and two boys at various stages of development. In the most recent shots, Fellinger's sons were sullen teenagers. His wife had aged conspicuously.

Milo said, "You do family law. Was Ms. Corey involved in a nasty divorce?"

"They all have the potential to be nasty," said Grant Fellinger. "If you've got two crucial ingredients."

He waited.

I said, "Kids and money."

"Bingo. Ursula and Richard had both but the kids weren't an issue, they're almost adults. It was all about dollar signs. Tweaking their settlement took five years, three of them after the decree."

"They came back for more."

"Fine-tuning," said Fellinger. "We finally arrived at a mutually beneficial settlement. By we, I mean myself and Richard Corey's attorney."

"Who's that, sir?"

"Earl Cohen. He's old-school."

I said, "Someone wanted rematches?"

"Both of them wanted rematches. Every year or so. For all my experience, it was a weird situation. One day they'd come in looking like best friends, saying the right things, willing to do anything to smooth things out. They'd leave looking cozy. Affectionate, even. I'd see them like that and wonder why the hell they divorced in the first place."

Fellinger leaned forward. "This was *not* a situation where the lawyers kept it going to churn fees. Earl and I are both busy. This could've been the exception—smooth sailing, genuine amicability, move on and have a nice life."

I said, "The Coreys didn't see it that way."

"They moved on, all right. Then they'd retrench. What made it a royal pain was that Earl and I would take them at their word and proceed accordingly. Several thousand bucks of billable hours later, we'd both get irate phone calls, all bets are off, back to the trenches. The impetus never seemed connected to a specific event. Nor did they ever seem hostile when they showed up. It was as if they'd saved up their energy and were ready to reenlist. Last go-round was a year ago."

Milo said, "Anyone walk away angry that time?"

Fellinger stared. "Could Richard do something like this? Good God, I hope not. I mean that would be disgusting. That would make me doubt my ability to judge people. No, Lieutenant, there was no anger from either side. In fact, they seemed genuinely settled." His eyebrows rose. "Was Ursula robbed? Because she likes her jewelry, was wearing plenty today."

Milo said, "No evidence of robbery."

"You're sure? I saw a whole lot of diamonds on her, maybe something's missing."

"We removed and cataloged three rings, Mr. Fellinger, along with a necklace, two bracelets, and a pair of ruby-and-gold earrings. Plus there was an expensive watch in her purse."

Fellinger's tiny mouth rotated. "That sounds about right. So you're considering Richard a suspect? I guess the husband's always where you start and Lord knows I've seen plenty of spouses I'd consider prime suspects if anything happened. But I don't know about Richard. It really doesn't fit."

I'd been an expert witness on scores of divorce cases, couldn't recall a single one where the opposing lawyer defended the enemy.

I said, "Richard's a good guy."

"Honestly?" said Fellinger. "He doesn't have a winning personality but he's always seemed to be decent and honest. Five years is plenty of time to dig up dirt and, believe me, I dug. So did Earl—fishing around about Ursula. In fact, last year we met for drinks and had a laugh over it. All those hours spent trying to make each other's clients look bad with zero success."

"But they kept fighting."

"Not fighting," said Fellinger. "What I said, tweaking. Voices were never raised, they just wanted to nip and tuck their finances. To get an accurate accounting."

Milo said, "If the divorce was resolved, why did Ursula come to see you today?"

"That," said Fellinger, "brings us right back to the jewelry. Which is probably why I thought about it. Ursula's got a lot of bling, expensive stuff she's been buying for years. With divorce issues out of the way, she began thinking about her daughters, wanted to specify who got what. I don't do that much estate work anymore but I agreed to handle it if it didn't get too complicated. It turned out to be simple: two girls, fifty-fifty. It made Ursula feel better putting it in writing."

"Codicil to her will," said Milo.

Fellinger looked at him. "Did she sense something bad was going to happen? Not that I saw. Just the opposite, she was in a great mood. It's what affluent people do, Detective. They think about their toys, fine-tune, try to feel in control."

"Where did the affluence come from?"

"The business she and Richard built together. Import–export."

"Of what?"

"Cheap crap," said Fellinger. "Their description, not mine. You know those rubber sandals you get for two bucks in Chinatown? They'd bring them over in pallets from Vietnam at ten cents per unit."

Milo said, "Nice profit margin."

"Cost them twenty, twenty-five cents when you factor in shipping and transport, they wholesale out at seventy-five cents to a buck? I'd say that's a fantastic profit."

"What was their working arrangement?"

"Ursula did the purchasing. She was familiar with the Far East, her father had been some sort of diplomat. Richard's the numbers-cruncher, manages the day by day. He's also done a good job of investing their money."

"In what?"

"Blue chips, preferred stock, bonds."

"Conservative."

"Extremely," said Fellinger. "There's also a rental property on the water in Oxnard."

Milo said, "How large of an estate are we talking about?"

Fellinger's eyebrows rose again, startled caterpillars. "Does that matter?"

"At this point, sir, everything matters."

"Well . . . I suppose you could always access the family court records, numbers have been bandied around for five years." Fellinger sat back, tented his hands over his firm, round gut. "Last accounting, their total net worth was between fourteen and fifteen million and there's no debt to speak of."

Milo whistled.

"Let me temper that a bit, Detective. Three and a half million is the appraised value of the main house, it's a big spread in the West Valley, the daughters are into horses. That came out of Ursula's half. Richard received the Oxnard condo, which he uses as his residence. Appraised value there is considerably less, around one point five, so Richard received another two million in stocks and bonds. Everything else was divided evenly."

"Including Ursula's jewelry?"

"No, sorry, that was also factored into Ursula's half but it's not that much, maybe five, six hundred thousand. Admittedly not piffle, but measured against an estate that size it wasn't a big deal."

I said, "Are any commercial properties owned by the business? Warehouses, offices?"

Fellinger shook his head. "Urrick, Ltd.—that's the name of the company, amalgam of both their names—operates lean and mean. It's just Richard and Ursula, not even a secretary or a receptionist. They use typing services when the paper piles up and both of them work out of home offices. When merchandise arrives at the docks in San Pedro, one of them is there to facilitate direct shipment to the customer. When inventory needs to be stored, they rent warehouse space east of downtown, a sweetheart lease they signed during the recession—that's Richard, nose for a bargain. That's the beauty of their business, no need to stockpile for long, they're middlemen, essentially get paid for moving goods from one place to another."

"What was in dispute for five years?"

"Urrick, Ltd.'s worth if they ever did decide to dissolve the company. Ursula saw it as more valuable, Richard's more of a glass-half-empty type."

"What was the discrepancy?"

"It varied from tweak to tweak," said Fellinger. "Usually around two million, give or take. What made it crazy was that neither of them was ever *interested* in splitting or selling. They were just talking theoretically and last year was their best ever, they moved in a big way into the religious market—Buddhist combustible paper." He smiled. "Never heard of it, right?"

Milo and I shook our heads.

"Me neither, until they educated me. Apparently, when some Buddhists want something from their god, they burn a small paper replica on an altar. If it's cash they're after, they offer up what looks like Monopoly money. If it's an automobile, they burn a little paper car. Et cetera. Last year, Ursula and Richard made a big investment in religious paper and it paid off."

I said, "Why do you think they kept coming back to tweak?"

"Was it financial?" said Fellinger. "So they claimed but frankly, I thought it was a way for them to have contact outside of work without admitting it."

"Ongoing chemistry."

"Must be."

Milo said, "Did either of them have any bad habits? Drugs, gambling?"

"Never."

"What about love affairs? Jealousy?"

"It was always about money, Lieutenant."

"Every year or so, they wheel in for a tune-up, meanwhile the business keeps running?"

"Harmoniously. I told you it was strange."

I said, "Who initiated the divorce?"

"Even that was mutual." Fellinger threw up his hands a third time. "Being objective, I'd have to call them a little nuts. In most cases litigants are out to grind each other down. In this case, they ground Earl and me down." He laughed. Stopped himself. "And now Ursula's dead. I'm assuming you'll be notifying the girls and Richard. Because I sure as hell don't want to."

Milo said, "We'll handle it, Mr. Fellinger. And we ask that you don't talk to anyone about this conversation or the murder, in general."

"Sure, I get it."

"What's Richard's address and phone number?"

Fellinger consulted his computer, rattled off the information.

"The two daughters are the only children?"

"Ashley and Marissa."

"Where can we reach them?"

Before Fellinger could answer, a knock sounded on the door. He shouted: "Busy!"

From the other side: "Your tea, Mr. F.?"

"Oh. Fine. Bring it in."

Jens Williams entered bearing a silver-handled glass teacup on a crimp-edged pewter plate. The cup held pale amber liquid. A white, anemone-like blossom sat on the bottom.

Fellinger said, "The café is using glass?"

"This is ours, sir. I transferred it from Styrofoam."

Fellinger inspected the tea. "Kind of a dinky flower, that's all they had?"

"Unfortunately," said Williams.

"Okay. Now please get me addresses and numbers for the Corey girls."

"Shall I bring them to you or use the intercom?"

"Just bring it in."

"You bet." Williams left.

"You *bet,*" said Fellinger. "Like we're pals. I had to talk to him about using my first name soon after he started but compared with the last assistant I had, he's Einstein. That one covered up during the interview but the day she starts she's in low-cut and low-back, you can see her ass-crack, talk about a clueless generation."

"Changing times," I said.

"Better than stagnation? Sometimes I wonder."

Another knock. Jens Williams scurried in and handed a slip of paper to Fellinger. "The younger one's in college, sir, we don't have her dorm in our records. The older one lives at home, I wrote down the address."

Fellinger crooked a thumb at the door. "How are things out there in the real world?"

"A few callbacks on court dates but nothing frantic."

"Good. I'll get to everything, these gentlemen are leaving."

3

The building's Operations and Security office occupied a corner of the ground floor, a few steps past the café and the public bathrooms. Windowless space set up with three untended workstations, the rear wall a grid of closed-circuit TV monitors and recorders. Metal chairs were lined up for easy viewing. Screens flickered; gray people and cars doing their thing.

The director of security was a black man named Alfred Bayless wearing a black blazer, gray pants, and white turtleneck. He'd come down to the crime scene just as we were leaving.

Milo asked to see security tapes.

Bayless said, "This is a disaster. Okay, let's go to my place."

On the ride up, Bayless said, "Worked auto and burglary at Hollenbeck, sixteen years. Thought retirement would be quiet." He looked at me.

Milo said, "This is Dr. Alex Delaware, our psych consultant."

"You think this was a nut-job?"

"It's not run of the mill, could be anything."

The moment we arrived at Bayless's office, he copied several disks, placed them in paper sleeves, handed them over.

"Thanks. How much time do these cover?"

"From seven a.m. when the lot opens until just before you called me."

Bayless led us to the wall of monitors and fooled with one of the recorders. A blank screen at the bottom lit up then filled with a steady parade of incoming vehicles. Bayless pushed a button that shifted the view to outgoing traffic. Clear view of machines but not of the drivers. If a car didn't move too quickly you might make out a license plate.

"That's it?" said Milo.

"Yeah, I know, nothing in the parking tiers." Bayless shook his head. "Disaster, nothing like this has ever happened before."

"Hopefully it won't happen again."

"You work the bodies and still believe in luck?"

"Only the bad kind."

"Ain't that the truth," said Bayless.

"Listen, I don't want to ask but I have to—"

"Yeah, yeah, *why* no cameras in the tiers." Bayless motioned us out of the security room, continued a couple of steps up the hallway, dead-ended at a door marked *Utility,* looked around.

Milo said, "You're being surveilled yourself?"

Bayless smiled. "You never know. In answer to your question, you want the official reason or the real one?"

"How about both?"

"Officially, we've got state-of-the-art surveillance and safety, hardware and software as well as top-notch expertly trained personnel. Reality is we're bush league. One of the first things I *suggested* when they hired me eight months ago was cameras on the parking levels. I mean where does bad stuff happen? Not in the damn lobby."

He scanned the hall. "But the wise men who manage this place saw no reason to take on the expense, this is Century City, people don't come to Century City to do bad things."

"All those lawyers and it's a shrine to virtue?"

Bayless managed a snorting laugh. "Anyway, those are yours to keep. I hope some of that bad luck converts to mediocre."

Back down to the parking lot under discussion. I'd parked my Seville on the top tier, my name on a list allowing me access to a section guarded by a uniformed cop. Four spaces away sat Milo's current unmarked, a bilge-green Impala.

We stood near my driver's door and he called Moe Reed, told him he'd be bringing the CDs to the office, Reed should copy and go through every second. "Exit'll be soon after the murder but entry could be anytime after seven. Run any plate you can decipher. Look for anything that stands out."

"Will do, L.T."

Clicking off, he placed his hand on the Seville's forest-green hood. "Shiny. You take it to a detailer?"

"Did it myself last Sunday."

"Talk about dedication. I could use some shiny, you get to drive, I'll come back to get mine."

"Where are we going?"

"To the ex-husband slash prime suspect and if we can't find him, the daughters."

"You didn't buy Fellinger's character testimony on Mr. Corey's behalf?"

"Sticking up for the enemy? Yeah, that was different, wasn't it?"

"So were Fellinger's kind words about Richard's lawyer."

"One big happy family. Except that the Coreys have been shelling out legal fees for five years and now one of them got executed. No, I'm not buying it. I'm thinking Fellinger just bullshat us shamelessly and I want to know why."

"Maybe you should talk to Richard's lawyer, see if the love really is mutual."

"Before we see Corey and the girls?"

"If he's close enough and available."

"Sure, why not?" Milo looked up Earl Cohen, attorney-at-law. Roxbury and Wilshire, Beverly Hills. Ten-minute ride.

He phoned. Cohen gasped when he heard about the murder. When Milo asked if he had time to chat, Cohen said, "Yes, of course."

The brass plaque on the walnut door made Earl Cohen, Esq., the senior partner in a three-lawyer firm. Second in command was Beverly Cohen, number three was Rajiv Singh.

Smaller setup than Fellinger's but similar geometry, including the use of hardscape behind a receptionist/gatekeeper, this wall, travertine marble.

This woman sat typing. No need for her to break her stride because Earl Cohen stood in front of her, motioning us in.

Richard Corey's legal rep was eighty or close to it, thin and narrow-shouldered in a beautifully draping mocha suit, a blue shirt with a high, starched Eton collar and a yellow tie that had to be Hermès. Mesh loafers tinted somewhere between orange and brown revealed a hint of aqua-and-orange argyle sock. His hair was thick, long, snow white, swept back. The right side of his neck was hollowed out; surgery to remove a parotid or salivary tumor. Bright-blue eyes dulled to gray at the edges.

He said, "Hello, policemen. Come in, please," in a soft, raspy voice.

Cohen's personal office was enormous, with French oak walls and deep-pile burgundy carpeting. Grant Fellinger subjected his guests to hard seating; Earl Cohen indulged them with cushy leather club chairs.

The old lawyer's desk could've been swiped from the White House attic—a carved Georgian piece, the one discovered to be too large for the Oval Office. Crystal decanters, designated *Gin, Whisky,* and *Brandy* by silver badges on silver chains, sat atop a brass cart. Windows facing Roxbury Drive were blocked by oak shutters and tie-back brocade drapes that could've been sliced from an Aubusson tapestry. Soft light issued from a blue-and-gold dragonfly-patterned chandelier that was probably real Tiffany.

Cohen's paper was from Harvard. His own collection of certificates shared space with photos of himself with senators and every governor since Reagan, as well as multiple shots of a blond woman who could've been an actress when Reagan was an actor. One child reappeared progressively, a blond daughter who favored her mother. In one picture, Cohen handed her a degree, both of them decked out in crimson caps and gowns.

"Sit, please," he rasped, lowering himself with discomfort. The scar tissue on his neck bore the gloss of long-ago intrusion. Not a recent incision; something else was bothering him.

Near his pen set was an ebony humidor from which he took three claros. "You fellows smoke?"

"No, thanks."

"Then I won't either," said Cohen. "Maybe it'll extend my life by five minutes." He looked at Milo. "You're the one I talked to."

"Yes, sir."

"And you . . ."

"Alex Delaware."

"I know that name," said Cohen. "Unusual name. American Indian?"

"Supposedly that's part of the mix."

"There's a psychologist with that name, does custody work."

"That's me."

Cohen's stare was long and appraising. "Small world. You were recently recommended to me as someone who doesn't take guff from shysters. Fortunately, the case settled and I didn't need to test that hypothesis."

"Lucky break," I said.

"Oh, boy, it sure was," said Earl Cohen. "When I started out, I took every client that came my way, such ugliness, such vitriol. When I turned sixty-five, instead of retiring, I decided only to take cases where a high degree of animosity was unlikely." His chuckle was faint, a puff of dust. "Those I inflict on my daughter. She's young, her cardiovascular system can take it."

"The Coreys were low risk."

"Cut to the chase, eh?" Cohen turned to Milo. "Might I inquire why a psychologist is here?"

Milo said, "We sometimes consult Dr. Delaware."

"This isn't child psychology. The Corey girls are older. One's a legal adult."

"We use Dr. Delaware on cases that are unusual."

"I see. Actually, I don't."

Milo said nothing.

Cohen said, "Okay, no sense dillydallying, you're here to learn about poor Ursula. Not my client but a lovely, lovely woman, nonetheless. They don't come more gracious. Brits of a certain class learn manners in a way we don't."

"You represent her husband—"

"And I still have nice things to say about her? That's my point, fellows. I consider myself an arbitrator, not a warrior, and the Coreys fit that perspective. They disputed issues from time to time, but it was all about working things out, not drawing blood." He blinked. "Unfortunate choice of words. *Vey, vey,* this is terrible—how did you come to know about me?"

"Ms. Corey was killed in the parking garage of her lawyer's building."

"Fellinger's building?" said Cohen. "He sent you to me?"

"We inquired and he gave us your name, Mr. Cohen."

"Let me guess: Grant's take was he and I are best friends, ready to pack off on a cruise together."

"He did speak highly of you, sir."

"Look," said Cohen, tilting back and lacing his hands over his belt buckle. "I don't want to be perceived as ungracious, but the truth is I tolerate Grant because he's been tolerable."

"For five years."

"That's misleading, Lieutenant. True, the Coreys' divorce was initiated five years ago and finalized after two, but most of the serious negotiation was accomplished within the first year. We are not talking about five years of constant litigation."

"Just on-and-off engagement."

"Fine-tuning. So, yes, I'm able to take Grant in intermittent doses. And frankly, the fact that Ursula was his client was a factor. Such a lovely woman. May I ask how she was killed?"

"Gunshot wound."

"*Vey iz mir.* In the parking lot? A mugging?"

"No signs of robbery."

"Then what?"

"That's what we're trying to ascertain, Mr. Cohen."

"A gun. Dreadful. It's hard to imagine Ursula gone. She was a vibrant woman. Creative—she was the creative force in the business."

"Tell us about the fine-tuning, sir."

"In that regard," said Cohen, "I'm severely limited by confidentiality. Unlike Fellinger, my client is alive."

He rolled a cigar between his palms. Same mannerism Milo adopts with cheap panatelas. "Let me ask you this, Lieutenant: What did Grant tell you about his work on Ursula's behalf?"

"The Coreys divorced but continued to work together amicably. Occasionally financial disputes came up, mostly regarding the value of Urrick, Ltd."

Cohen remained silent.

"Is that your view, Mr. Cohen?"

"You're not hearing me debate anything, Lieutenant."

"Must've been an odd situation, sir."

"What was?"

"Exes continuing a business relationship."

"It happens more often than you'd imagine," said Cohen.

"With positive consequences?"

Cohen suspended the cigar between his forefingers. "Not usually, no. In a perfect world, a business can be divided up equitably with the parties free to pursue their own interest. Sometimes I'm able to do that. If those interests are independent."

"The Corey interests were intertwined. They needed each other."

Cohen smiled. "Did Fellinger explain what they do?"

"Import–export of cheap goods from Asia."

"Flowers of the Orient," said Cohen. "Yes, trashy *tchotchkes*."

"And now your client gets everything from stem to petals."

"Poetic," said Cohen. "But the truth is, I'm not sure Richard will be able to continue."

"Ursula being the creative force."

"Exactly. Without Ursula, I'm not sure there'll continue to be a business."

"So your client has no motive."

"Not that I see."

I said, "Mr. Fellinger said the latest conflict arose around a year ago."

Cohen shrugged.

I went on. "Mr. Fellinger also said he was optimistic about the issues finally being laid to rest."

Cohen laughed.

Milo said, "You disagree?"

"I'm an old man, Detective. My powers of prediction have waned. Why was Ursula meeting with Grant today?"

Milo smiled.

Cohen said, "No matter," and rested his cigar in an onyx ashtray. Bracing himself on the desk, he rose to his feet, tottered, took a deep breath. "Obviously, you'll be talking to Richard if you haven't already done so. What he chooses to tell you is his prerogative but I can't say any more."

He held the door open. "Beautiful, elegant woman. How are the daughters handling it?"

"They don't know yet."

"You'll be informing them soon."

"Part of the job, Mr. Cohen."

"Don't envy you. Will you also be informing Richard? Because I'd prefer not to."

"We prefer the same thing, sir. Please don't call him or talk to any-one about the murder."

"Murder," said Cohen. "Snap of the finger and we're gone." Sway-ing, he gripped the door frame, took several more deep breaths. "If there's nothing else, gentlemen, I have a doctor appointment."

In the lobby of Cohen's building, Milo said, "Ursula's mouthpiece sticks up for Richard and Richard's mouthpiece thinks the world of Ursula. Next, I'm expecting a van full of hippies distributing daisies."

"Peace and love," I said. "Meanwhile, Ursula's in a van on her way to the morgue."

He stared at me. "Isn't cynicism *my* gig?"

"A little sharing never hurt anyone."

"Know what Oscar Wilde said about cynics?"

"They know the price of everything and the value of nothing."

"Silly of me to ask. Now what's the atomic weight of molybde-num?"

"No idea."

"Thank God for small blessings."

CHAPTER

4

I'd parked the Seville in a Beverly Hills metered lot, found myself looking for cameras. I picked out a few but plenty of blank spots remained.

I pointed that out to Milo.

He said, "Ursula's killer staked the place out beforehand?"

"I would."

He laughed.

I started the engine. "Where now?"

"The station to drop off the surveillance disks, then Richard Corey's condo . . ." He consulted his notes. "Jamestown Way, Mandalay Bay. Unless I arrest Daddy first, it'll be his job to tell the daughters."

He alerted Moe Reed, and the young detective, blond and pink as ever, big arms threatening to burst through his sleeves, was waiting outside the station to take the CDs.

"Have fun, Moses."

"Movie night?" said Reed. "Maybe I'll call out for pizza."

"Beer, too," said Milo. "In case you find nothing and your mood drops."

"I'm used to that, L.T.," said Reed. "Beer doesn't sound bad, though."

West L.A. to the beach towns above Malibu is an hour minimum. I hit some clog on the 405 prior to the 101 transfer, compensated with fast-lane lead-footing, made it in sixty-five minutes. Milo had slept through most of the ride. As I rolled into Oxnard, he sat up, knuckled his eyes, and groaned and muttered something about surfing.

I said, "Ever try it?"

"You've got to be kidding," he said. "Sharks eat walruses."

Oxnard is one of Ventura County's toughest towns, an often hardscrabble place rimmed at the outer borders by agribusiness and truck yards. Next come layers of trailer parks catering to seasonal farmworkers and modest tracts occupied by multiple generations of blue-collar families. A notable Latino gang presence proclaims itself with angular graffiti. Crime rates are among the highest in the region.

A whole different Oxnard appears when you cruise past miles of high-end industrial park and head west toward the ocean. A whole different planet appears when you reach the harbor: luxury hotels, tourist piers offering seafood and whale-watching tours, recreational marinas crowded with sleek white yachts that occasionally leave their berths.

High-end developments cluster along the inlets carved into the city's western rim. Mandalay Bay was one of those, a finger of serene blue water lined with fresh-looking single dwellings and condominiums, many equipped with docks and boat slips.

As we approached the apricot-colored, side-by-side duplex Richard Corey called home, a vee of pelicans soared overhead and brine itched my nose. Corey, R./Urrick Ltd. was the northern unit.

The man who came to the door was bald and rangy, with a pointy white goatee roughened by random errant hairs. He wore a faded navy polo T-shirt and yellow paisley shorts. His feet were bare, his arms and face tanner than his legs. Half-glasses perched low on a long, fleshy nose. His eyes were small, brown, watery. The portion of face not taken up by the chin beard was coated with two or three days of stubble.

"Yes?"

"Richard Corey? Lieutenant Sturgis, Los Angeles police."

"Los Angeles?" Corey adjusted his spectacles and read Milo's card. "Homicide? I don't understand."

"May we come in, please?"

Corey blanched. "One of the girls? Oh God—don't *tell* me that!"

"Your ex-wife, I'm afraid."

Corey staggered. The card fell from his fingers. He made no effort to retrieve it. "Ursula? No way. I just spoke to her this morning."

"I'm so sorry for your loss—"

"My loss?" said Corey. "What about the girls—we have daughters." He gaped. "Do they know?"

"Not yet, Mr. Corey. May we come in?"

"Oh, God, how am I going to tell them? Ursula? What happened?" Corey's breath caught. His mouth remained open, streaming sour breath. "How could this happen? Where did it happen?"

"Could we come in to talk about it, sir?"

"Come in? Of course, you need to come in, sure, yeah. My God!" Corey stepped aside. Both of his cheeks were tear-streaked.

A lot of detective work is accomplished over the phone. Some D's even notify telephonically. Milo had come in person because, among other things, he wanted to study Richard Corey's initial reaction. Psychopaths, skillful as they are at manipulating others, have trouble with emotional regulation and generally screw up at either extreme: theatrical histrionics or cold stoicism.

To my eye, Richard Corey's behavior revealed nothing. I glanced at Milo as we entered the condo. Detective stoicism.

Corey trailed us then sped up and walked ahead, collapsing on a sagging brown fake-suede sofa and burying his face in his hands. The space was expansive and well laid out: open floor setup with a slick chrome-and-teak kitchen, high beamed ceilings, glass instead of plaster wherever feasible, exposing gorgeous views of the inlet and the ocean beyond.

But years after his divorce, Corey hadn't done his bachelor pad justice. The place he'd chosen to sink a million and a half dollars into remained as sparse and sad as a newly single man's temporary crib: blank walls, unadorned wood floors, just the one sofa and two metal-and-black-vinyl folding chairs for seating, a forty-inch plasma screen set up on cinderblocks and bottomed by a pasta of wires, a flimsy-looking treadmill to the right of the hallway leading to the sleeping area.

Blocking the bottom half of the best view—French doors leading to an empty deck—was an off-kilter plywood desk topped by a laptop, a cell phone dock, and a laser printer. More wire-snarl coiled to the floor. Stacks of paper covered a good third of the floor.

The place smelled of ocean and stale food and inertia.

We stood by as Richard Corey sat on his sole piece of upholstery and cried silently.

Finally, he muttered, "Sorry," and looked up. Sniffing, he crossed to the kitchen, fumbled in several drawers, and returned with a dinner napkin that he used to dry his face. His knees knocked against each other. He tugged at his beard. "What the hell *happened*?"

Milo said, "I'm sorry to have to tell you, sir, but Mrs. Corey was shot in the parking lot of her lawyer's office building."

"Fellinger's building? That's Century City. What, a mugging? Someone jacked the Jag?"

"Doesn't appear that way."

"Then what?" said Corey. "This makes no sense!"

"That's why we're here, sir. To try to make sense."

Corey didn't move or speak. We sat down on the folding chairs.

"Fellinger," Corey repeated. "She told me she'd made an appointment. That's what I meant by we just spoke."

"When was that, sir?"

"This morning, maybe eight. We had some business issues—we run a business, a shipment was held up in Thailand. While she was on the phone she said she was going over to Fellinger's. But nothing about the divorce, she wanted to make sure I knew that."

"Did she tell you the reason for her meeting with Mr. Fellinger?"

"She wanted to divvy up her jewelry for the girls. I told her that was morbid, she was young, healthy."

Richard Corey sucked in air. "What the fuck did I know? Oh, God." He began to sob, caught himself. "So what exactly the hell *happened*—" Panic tightened his face. "Oh, no, I need to tell the girls soon."

"Sir, if we could—"

"How do I do it? You're the expert. How do you tell your kids something like that?"

"After we talk a bit, we can help you with that." Milo's eyes drifted to me. *Your mission, should you choose to accept it.*

Richard Corey rocked horizontally. "This is *vile.*"

I said, "So Mrs. Corey told you this morning she was going to be meeting with Mr. Fellinger."

Nod.

"She didn't want you to worry—"

"We were divorced three years ago but went back for a few negotiations. She didn't want me to think it was more of the same."

"Sounds like you two remained friendly."

"Friendly?" said Corey. "Far as I'm concerned we broke up legally but not spiritually—oh, man, I need a drink."

Hurrying back to the kitchen he removed a half-full bottle of Bombay Sapphire from a cupboard, poured a couple of fingers into a juice glass, swigged half at the counter. Pouring enough gin to refill and then some, he plopped back down on the couch. Liquid splashed on one knee. He wet a finger with the gin and licked.

Milo said, "You and Mrs. Corey—"

"Never Mrs., *Ms.,* Ursula was all about independence. She's bright, capable, a great mom—what the hell am I going to tell the girls?"

"It's never easy but we can guide you, if you'd like."

"I would," said Corey, slumping and covering his face with his hands. "I am *lost.*"

"Soon enough, sir, but I do need to ask questions."

Corey looked up. "Sure, yeah, I get it, this is business for you. Fine. What can I tell you?"

"You and Ms. Corey have been divorced for three years but you don't feel you broke up spiritually."

"I'm speaking metaphorically. From here." Corey patted the polo player logo on his shirt. "There was a special bond between us. I never stopped loving Ursula and I believe she never stopped loving me. It's been that way since we met."

"Where'd you meet?"

"Twenty-four years ago, business seminar in Scottsdale, bunch of Wall Street types offering the pathway to riches. Total bull, Ursula and I both realized it soon and bonded over skepticism. Once we learned about each other's backgrounds and talents, we decided to explore starting a business. The other stuff came later."

I said, "The personal stuff."

Corey nodded. "We're not Buffett but we built a great business. And yes, it got personal pretty soon. Like half a year in."

He gazed out at the water.

Milo said, "What were your backgrounds?"

"I'd worked in garment wholesaling. My training's in accounting." His shoulders dropped. "Basically high-level bean-counting but no company I ever worked with wasn't profitable. Ursula had a degree from the London School of Economics—she's English, lived all around the world but mostly in Asia, her father was a military attaché in a bunch of different places. When I met her, she'd never run a business but she was creative and understood about the Asian submarket here in the U.S. We made a fantastic team."

"What do you do?"

Corey's face crumpled. "Without Ursula, I don't know what's going to happen . . . can we do anything?"

Milo waited.

Corey said, "What was the question?"

"Your business—"

"We import consumer goods, mostly from Vietnam and Thailand. Ursula handpicks everything, I've never been to Asia, Ursula's been there probably fifty, sixty times, she's the inside person, spots bargains that we then sell to retailers—who the fuck would *do* this to my *girl*!"

Emptying his glass of gin, he began to rise.

Milo stepped forward and blocked his way. "If you don't mind, sir, we'd prefer to talk to you without any more alcohol in your system."

Corey looked at him, chastened. "I'm able to maintain."

"I'm sure you are, sir—"

"Fine. You're doing your job, I don't envy you." Corey sank back. "What else do you want to know?"

"Please don't be offended, sir, but I need to ask. Where were you between nine a.m. and noon today?"

"I was here doing paperwork."

"Did anyone see you?"

"Did anyone—you're kidding. No, I guess you're not. Okay, I get it, I've seen those crime shows, the husband is always the first suspect, I get it, no offense. Unfortunately I don't have any sort of alibi. Which I would have if I'd planned to do something criminal, right? I mean, the last thing I thought I'd need when I woke up this morning was an alibi. Like I said, Ursula called me around eight, I was already online, trying to work out snags with the shipping agent in Bangkok, and I stayed right here doing just that. Haven't left the place in days, if you want to know. Okay?"

"Okay, sir. Thank you."

"So what now?" said Corey. "I'm a serious suspect? No problem, do your thing, I have nothing to hide. But it'll only take time out from your investigation."

"I'm sure, sir—"

"Hey," said Corey, holding up a finger. "I just *thought* of some-thing." Angry laugh. "Maybe I *do* have an alibi. Those shows, they say cell phones can be traced. From the towers. Is that true?"

"We are able to pinpoint—"

"Then pinpoint away. When I wasn't on the computer—which you can also check—I was on the phone. The towers will tell you I was right here. Never moved my ass."

Reaching around, he scratched said body part. Did the same for his beard. Dandruff floated onto his chest.

"That would be helpful," said Milo. "If you give us permission to—"

Corey jumped up, strode to the cheap desk, touched the screen of his laptop. "C'mere."

He logged onto his email, scrolled slowly, giving us a clear view of sixty or seventy messages over the three-hour time frame. Nearly every correspondence sounded like business: All Star Fashion Imports, Ya-mata Home Decorating, Paradise Gifts of Chinatown, two pages of correspondence from Bang-Buck Superior Goods and Lading of Bang-kok, Ltd.

Only one exception that I could see: ashleycee@westrnmail.net had written twice.

"My younger daughter," said Corey, opening the first message.

Hi daddy, had no classes went to give Sydney a workout. Still on for dinner next Th? Xoxo A.

"Sydney's her horse." Corey moaned and logged off.

Milo said, "Busy morning."

"No different from any other, welcome to my life," said Corey. "Ur-sula's the artistic one, I do the boring stuff and there's plenty of it. So can we put it to rest—my need for an alibi?"

Men in his tax bracket often delegated. Being home and occupied didn't rule out a hired killer.

Milo said, "Sorry to offend you, sir, but like I said, we need to ask difficult questions." He motioned toward the sofa. Corey seemed to balk at complying but ended up shrugging and sinking back into the depression he'd created in the cushions. Placing his hands on his bare knees, he sat rigidly, staring straight ahead.

Milo said, "I know this is a tough time, Mr. Corey—"

"No need to preface, ask what you want."

"We've already spoken to Mr. Fellinger and Mr. Cohen and they've given us a basic history but couldn't get into details. Apparently you and Ms. Corey returned to your lawyers to dispute financial issues—"

"Not to dispute, to tweak," said Corey. Same word everyone used.

"Could you give us an idea what you and Ms. Corey tweaked?"

"Details, minutiae."

"Such as?"

Corey sighed. "I don't see why it's relevant but fine. We found ourselves disagreeing at times about what the business was worth. In case we ever decided to retire and sell and split the proceeds. Which we didn't. But we were both i-dotters and t-crossers. A trait we shared, that's one reason why we've been so damn successful. But now? Oh God, now I probably will have to fold my tents. Just as the economy is ticking upward, isn't that ironic? I mean everything was looking up, Ursula and I were planning to have our best year. Now? Goddamn, what the hell *happened*?"

"Can you think of anyone who'd want to hurt Ms. Corey?"

"Absolutely not—so those two gave you a basic history, huh? Fellinger and Cohen."

"Actually, Mr. Fellinger did. Mr. Cohen protected your confidentiality."

"Bully for him," said Corey, voice grown ragged. "Did they also inform you they slept with Ursula?"

Milo blinked. "Sir?"

"Fellinger did for sure. I can't prove Earl but I'd put money on it. Nowadays even mummies have access to Viagra."

"You're saying you believe—"

"I don't believe, I know." Corey let out a bizarre giggle. "Ursula made no attempt to hide what she did. A couple of years ago, during one of our go-rounds—in Fellinger's office, as a matter of fact— I picked up a vibe. Fellinger sitting too close to Ursula. Looking at her in a personal way. When I asked Ursula about it, she came right out and admitted it. I made some snarky comment about Fellinger giving her a discount and she pretended to be offended, made like she was going to slap me. Then she cracked up and we had a good laugh. She said nude he looked like a monkey."

"But she—"

"Yes, she did, guys. Came right out and said it, that was Ursula. Independent. Not when we were married. At least I don't think so. But afterward? It was like she was making up for lost time."

"It didn't bother you?"

"Did I say that? Sure it bothered me, I loved her. And the image of her with that ape—not exactly pretty but what could I do? And frankly the fact that Ursula was so open about her behavior kind of . . . reduced it. Trivialized it."

I said, "The fact that it meant nothing to her emotionally."

"Exactly," said Corey.

"And you think she also might've slept with Earl Cohen?"

"The old scrotum? She never said but, again, I was pretty attuned to Ursula's nonverbals and one time we were in Earl's office, he's my lawyer but I'm getting the distinct vibe he'd rather be Ursula's lawyer. After we left, I made a crack about that but she just laughed. Still . . . my bet is she was aggressively promiscuous after the divorce."

"Are you aware of anyone else—"

"Not by name but my daughters intimated she was dating pretty heavily."

"How did you feel—"

"Initially it hurt, but I realized that wasn't rational, we were divorced, I had no claims on Ursula. So rather than eat my guts out, I learned to live with it. Told myself it was like learning to live with an alcoholic or an addict or a hoarder if you cared about them. I mean, let's face it, everyone's got quirks, that was hers."

He studied the bottom of his empty glass. "I know you guys are judging us but I loved her and wanted her happy, so you can believe me or not, I don't care."

I said, "Did you and Ursula continue to—"

"From time to time," said Corey. His eyes fluttered, closed, reopened at half-mast. Looking at his glass with yearning, he said, "With me she made love. With everyone else it was sex. Once I was able to stop thinking of it as betrayal, to consider it like having lunch with friends, I was okay."

He put the glass down. "This is going to sound brutal but did you attend Ursula's autopsy? Detectives do that, right?"

"It's a bit early for that, sir."

"Well," said Corey, "here's a prediction for when you do attend: They're going to remove Ursula's clothing—tight jeans, right?—and find out she wasn't wearing any panties. How do I know? Because after the divorce Ursula told me her new motto: 'Ready for action.'"

I said, "Adventurous."

"Like a gun cocked and ready to shoot."

If the metaphor gave him pause, he didn't show it, began turning the glass between his palms. "Trust me, guys, that's what's going to solve it. She went overboard and slept with the wrong guy. Some scumbag she thought she understood but didn't. I mean you can only engage in high-risk behavior for so long before it bites you, right?"

Milo said, "Why did the two of you get divorced?"

Corey crossed a thin leg. "Because Ursula wanted to and at that point I couldn't find a reason to tell her no."

I said, "She'd brought it up before."

"Constantly. Whenever she was in a low mood or stressed about something, she'd start in on three topics: running off to a remote place to find a slower pace of life, moving back to Asia because even though she didn't believe in God she admired the Buddhists and their ability to move on."

Retrieving the glass, he gazed toward his kitchen.

I said, "What was the third topic?"

"Pardon?"

"You said she talked about three things when she was—"

"Divorce," said Richard Corey. "As in she wanted one, sooner the better. No reason, no warning, nothing I'd done. I guess all three added up to the same thing: She was feeling trapped and wanted out. Was it hurtful? At first, but then she'd drop it so I basically tuned her out."

I said, "What changed that?"

Corey shifted his weight. "I need to talk about that, huh?"

Milo and I sat there.

"Okay, what changed is that I thought *I'd* found someone so when Ursula started in for the zillionth time, I said sure, let's do it. That really threw her. She got pissed, stomped out. Maybe she figured out I was bluffing when the next day she told me she'd hired Fellinger. I said sounds like a good idea and hired Cohen and the rest, as they say, is marital anti-history."

"The stress points you mentioned—"

"Petty stuff we could deal with. I get pissed because she hasn't sent in all her order forms, she gets pissed because I haven't informed her about accounts receivable. Ridiculous stuff, we'd have a snit, make up, move on. But this was different. I *found* someone. Someone I thought I might develop something with. So when Ursula started doing her bullshit divorce routine and I told her fine, it was like a . . . runaway train. Was it stupid? Probably. But Ursula and I remained friends and frankly that was always the good part of our relationship, the friendship. So getting rid of the other stuff was almost a relief. And the business kept rolling. Better than ever, if you have to know, we had our best years since the divorce."

Milo said, "Speaking of which, where's your place of business?"

"You're looking at it," said Corey. "Both of us worked out of our houses. Cuts costs, keeps us out of each other's hair."

I said, "The person you found—"

"Is no longer in the picture," said Corey. "I realized that soon after." He laughed. "A Buddhist, how's that for irony?"

"Someone you met in the course of doing business?"

He looked at me. "Good guess. But please don't ask me more, she's a good person, I don't want to screw up her life. Now, is there anything else you need to know about Ursula? Because I still have to figure out how to tell my daughters their mother's gone."

All business, now. Eyes Sahara-dry.

Milo said, "We could tell them, sir."

No answer. Corey's face had gone blank.

"Sir?"

"Yeah, I guess so. You actually do that? With kids?"

"When necessary, Mr. Corey."

"I don't want them to think I punted . . ."

Milo said, "Up to you but we can tell them we insisted on notification because it's an open homicide."

Corey scratched his beard. "You think? Okay, sure."

"Soon as we're done, I'll call you and you can come over to be with them."

"You think doing it this way will be easier for them?"

Milo said, "Nothing makes it easy but we're old hands at notification, Mr. Corey. Unfortunately."

"Put it in the hands of the experts . . . like I do with my shipping agents and my drivers—fine, let's do it. Because I have to tell you, guys, I wouldn't take your job on a bet. No offense."

"None taken, sir. Is there anything else you can tell us that would help figure out who killed Ms. Corey?"

"If I knew the names of the guys she dated I'd give them to you. It has to be one of them."

"We'll check it out," said Milo. "You think of anything else, let us know."

We got up. Manly handshakes all around. Corey's palms were as dry as his eyes.

At the door, Milo said, "Oh, one more thing, sir. You verbalized permission to access your phone records. Could you put that in writing, please?"

Corey's eyes slitted. "You're serious? I'm still a suspect?"

"It's not a matter of that, sir. A lot of the job is the process of elimination. Once we clear you completely, we're free to move on. But if it's a problem for you, we understand."

"No problem, hell, why not?" Corey returned to his makeshift desk, scrawled something on a piece of paper, thrust it at Milo. "Okay?"

Milo read. "If you could sign and date, please."

"Oh, Jesus." Scratch scratch scratch. "Here."

Retrieving his glass, he went into the kitchen and poured three fingers of gin. Drank with his back toward us as we saw ourselves out.

We walked to the harbor side of Corey's building. The deck railing was crusted with birdshit and in need of refinishing. Several ducks floated past Corey's slip. Empty slot, no boat. Seagulls hovering above screeched territorially. We returned to the Seville.

Milo said, "Odd fellow, Mr. C. First he cries, then he gets kind of . . . I don't know, matter-of-fact? Maybe a little paranoid, too? Both lawyers screwing Ursula? Unless it's true and he's learned to face reality."

"Calling her a gun cocked and ready to shoot?"

"Yeah . . . so despite his alibi, you don't see him as any less of a suspect than before we met him."

I laughed.

He said, "Thought you might say that."

CHAPTER

5

Ursula Corey's address on Lobo Canyon was a thirty-minute drive from Richard Corey's Oxnard condo.

I said, "Freeway-convenient. The two of them split up but Richard didn't settle far."

Milo said, "Maybe he was telling the truth about staying BFFs."

"Or only he saw it that way."

"He wanted to keep tabs on her?"

"Wouldn't be the first time an ex hung on."

As I raced along the 101, he looked out the window. "I keep thinking about the way he described her sex life. Weird."

"Weird, voyeuristic, and ambivalent," I said.

"Love her madly, the filthy slut."

"One minute he's grief-stricken, the next he's telling us she won't be wearing underwear because she wanted to be ready for action."

"Let's see if he was right." He made a call to the crypt. The body had arrived but hadn't been looked at.

I said, "What's especially strange is telling us she slept with both lawyers. Something we'd never have known. If it's not paranoia."

"Wifey doing the monkey-man."

"Turning it into a joke," I said, "was probably his way of keeping Ursula's sexuality partially under his control. She wasn't abandoning his bed for another man, she was providing amusement."

"So maybe he's one of those guys gets off watching the missus do another dude."

"Maybe, but that's always a risky game. Priorities change, all of a sudden the actress wants to direct. Maybe that was the real reason for the divorce."

"Ursula got too independent," he said. "He did admit she threatened divorce all the time."

"But again, he was out for control: reducing Ursula's threats to impulsive bullshit and claiming the ultimate decision was his."

"Calling her bluff. That's nothing *but* hostility. The more I think about it, the more I'm feeling we just talked to an extremely angry man."

I said, "What if the choice wasn't his and Ursula finally made good on her threats? His alibi doesn't mean much—people at his level hire out. Toss in a few million dollars of additional motive even after estate taxes and you've got something."

"That assumes Ursula willed him her share of the estate."

"As an ex, she might not have wanted to, but as a business partner she could've had no choice. That fits with the two of them repeatedly trying to assess the value of Urrick. If the partnership ever came to an end, both their interests would be protected. But even if Ursula willed everything to the daughters, Richard might figure he could control their share."

"Daddy knows best," he said. "Let him continue to run the business and they enjoy the benefits. Sure, makes sense. The only snag I can see in a financial motive is both Fellinger and Richard told us it took both Coreys to keep the business running."

"Like I said, priorities change. Ursula knew the Asian markets and was creative but what if Richard met someone he felt could replace her? Business-wise as well as romantically."

"His Buddhist girlfriend," he said, rotating his neck. "I'll see what I can learn about that. Meanwhile, let's get to see how Ursula lived. We're lucky, we'll get to meet the offspring created by such a glorious union."

Lobo Canyon was velvety pasture rolling into fog-capped hills, copses of California oak reveling in the dry spots, grass thriving where sprinklers ruled. Impeccable manses were graced by equally impeccable corrals inhabited by beautiful prancing creatures. All that bucolic loveliness topped by a cloudless Delft sky.

This was stunning terrain laid out millennia ago by God or Nature or whoever you chose to give credit, then developed and subdivided for decades. For the most part intelligent progress, with an eye toward preservation. But all that serenity came with a price: Once you were this far from the city, you rarely left.

Back when I saw patients regularly, I encountered plenty of bored West Valley adolescents who'd stimulated themselves with mischief and occasional felonies. I wondered how the Corey girls had fared in Eden.

How they'd cope now, with everything crumbling.

The house Ursula and Richard Corey had once shared lay behind a guard-gated entrance six miles south of the freeway. Iron lettering atop the left-hand gatepost proclaimed *RANCHO LOBO ESTATES: A PRIVATE COMMUNITY.*

The gate was more symbol than barrier, an X of metal set into a wooden frame, the spacing more than wide enough to admit a large man. The road beyond the gate snaked quickly out of view, a narrow S of decomposed granite shaded by sycamores native to the region and eucalyptus, once Australian interlopers, now granted amnesty as resident aliens.

The guard was a stout, middle-aged woman in a blue gingham shirt with western-style pearl snaps. As we idled next to her booth, she continued reading *Modern Equestrian*. I thought Milo did a great job of simulating patience.

Finally, he cleared his throat. Loud.

The woman blinked but her attention remained fixed on the page. "Who're you here for?"

"The Coreys. Don't call ahead."

She turned to find Milo's badge in her face. "Is there a problem?"

"Not on this side of the gate."

She waited. He stared her down.

Finally, she said, "That's good," and pushed a button.

A wooden sign ten yards in warned against speeds above five mph. I dared to tackle the granite road at fifteen, the Seville's tires playing a crunch sonata as we passed estates ranging from generous to vast.

Most of the properties were named: *La Valencia, Cloudburst Ranch, El Nido, StraightWalker Farms.* Grass was as green as it could ever be, dirt was uniformly cream-colored and raked smooth, fencing was stark white when it wasn't burnished pine.

The beautiful beasts confined to the corrals flashed flanks groomed to sateen and sported manes and tails so composed, they might have been blow-dried.

When people accompanied the horses—riding, walking, pampering—they were always female and, with the exception of one woman cantering in a maroon dressage uniform, attired in snug jeans and tailored shirts. More English saddles than Western. Trim bodies abounded, as did jewelry glimmering at the same body parts as Ursula Corey's corpse. I pictured her alive, turned out perfectly, riding or leading a mount around the ring or just enjoying the quiet.

Her homestead was the ninth property past the main gate, closer to generous than vast. Two, maybe two and a half acres hosting a low-slung tile-roofed Spanish Revival house and three outbuildings of similar style, including a two-story barn.

With most of the acreage fronting the residence, the view was an unobstructed swath of terraced lawn, privet-hedged flower beds, swooping meadow, and impeccable corral. Choice lot, backed by an outcropping of granite and set high enough to block the scrutiny of neighbors.

Two horses occupied the riding ring, both statuesque and dark brown with black manes and tails and white ankles that suggested gym socks. They circled slowly, bearing the easy weight of slender young women. Finally a break in the dress code: This pair wore form-fitted T-shirts tucked into their jeans, one red, the other yellow. Loose hair the color of clarified butter streamed in the breeze. The sound of laughter sailed through the high, dry air.

No need to disturb the reverie yet; entrance to the property was a coast under a white-painted arch crowned *Aventura.* Easing onto an asphalt patch, I parked in one of four slots delineated by white paint.

The T-shirted girls brought their horses to a halt.

Milo said, "Here we go. Damn."

Two years separated the Corey sisters but they could've been twins. Tall, leggy, effortlessly svelte, their faces were smooth bronze ovals graced by symmetrical features. Narrow hips, tight waists, and generous shoulders suggested athleticism. Straight blond hair flowed past the belt line of the girl in the red tee. Luxuriant waves fanned the shoulders of Yellow.

Both girls remained straight-backed on their horses as we reached the railing of the corral, pretty mouths set firmly, blue eyes watchful.

Milo said, "Ashley and Marissa?"

Wavy said, "I'm Marissa, she's Ashley," in a husky voice. "Who are you?"

"Lieutenant Sturgis, L.A. police. We need to talk to you, please."

"Cops? L.A.?" said Ashley Corey in an even throatier tone. Once upon a time, their mother probably had a sultry voice.

Marissa Corey said, "Agoura sheriff's in charge and we already told them we had nothing to do with it."

"With . . ."

"Laura's car. We knew totally nothing about it and the sheriff finally believed us so only Laura has to go to court so I don't know what you think—"

Ashley squeezed her sister's arm. "Fellinger said you shouldn't even be talking to them, Rissy."

Milo said, "I'm glad the thing with Laura worked out, but that's not why we're here. Now, if you could please get off your horses, girls."

Marissa said, "This is exercise time."

Ashley said, "We don't stop because you say."

"It's important, girls. Really."

Ashley tossed her own mane, frowned, and formed silent words that looked nasty, but she complied. When her boots touched ground, her sister followed suit. The two of them left the corral, Ashley locking it behind her. Both girls were over six feet in polished riding boots—snakeskin for Ashley, something that looked like elephant hide for Marissa. Each T-shirt read *Look a Gift Horse* above a cartoon of a wide-open mouth.

Marissa folded her arms across her chest. "Okay, what?"

"I need to talk to you about your mother."

"Mom?" By the end of the syllable her voice had shot up half an octave.

Ashley's eyes narrowed. "What about Mom?"

Milo did his best to be gentle but there's no way to mute the horror, no way to prevent yourself from becoming yet another survivor's worst memory.

Ashley and Marissa Corey shrieked in unison then began shouting "No, no, no" in a syncopated rhythm that smoothed out to a cataract of grief.

Marissa's arms dropped. She began punching herself in the chest. Ashley wrung her hands and drummed her own forehead. Tears gushed.

Both girls slammed against each other, remained locked in a terrible embrace.

Milo chewed his cheek and tapped his foot and wiped his face so hard with one hand that he raised a pink splotch where his left eye met his temple.

We continued to watch and wait and feel useless as Ursula Corey's daughters began gulping and wailing something that sounded like *youyouyouyou.*

It took a long time for that to taper to downcast sniffling and involuntary shudders. Milo was ready with tissues that were ignored.

Marissa said, "No, no, no," and shoved waves of hair away from her tear-soaked face.

Ashley said, "Why would anyone hurt her?"

Milo said, "Don't know that yet, Marissa."

"When? When did it happen?"

Milo said, "This morning."

Ashley said, "It wasn't Daddy. I'll tell you that for sure."

Her sister looked at her. An instant passed before she said, "Shit, no, it wasn't Daddy."

Milo said, "Let's go inside and talk."

Bawling, the girls stumbled toward the house. Milo and I followed, giving them a four-step lead.

Mourners always head the line.

When they reached the house, Ashley shoved one of the limed-oak double doors and it swung open silently.

Unlocked. The Corey girls had grown up assuming safety.

From now on, they'd never feel completely safe.

Milo and I continued to trail as they staggered, sobbing and clutching each other clumsily, past a flagstone rotunda topped by a wrought-iron chandelier. The fixture was crusted with beautifully forged songbirds and set up with mock candles tipped by LED bulbs. A niche to the right hosted a crudely fashioned Virgin Mary, the kind you can get all over Tijuana. The girls continued into a huge, high-ceilinged great room backed by windows and walled in rough-hewn granite. The furniture was expensive, perfectly placed, determinedly casual: distressed buckskin sofas and love seats, iron and glass tables, kilim throw pillows, straw-backed chairs painted the color of summer-dried sage.

The Corey sisters collapsed together on the largest sofa.

Marissa Corey snatched a pillow, hugged it to her chest, and dropped her head, weeping and letting out sad little burp-like noises. Her younger sister sat pressed against her, erect and blank-eyed, hands on her knees. Since learning of their shared tragedy, both girls had undergone a strange, contradictory transformation: rendered younger, almost child-like by helplessness, but aged decades around the eyes by the ultimate loss of trust.

Milo said, "Girls, we're so, so sorry."

Ashley slung her arm around her sister's shoulders. Marissa rested her head on Ashley's bosom. Two years older but more dependent? Maybe that was the reason her sister dormed out but she lived at home.

Ashley said, "Oh my God, Daddy!" As if she hadn't just mentioned him. "Does he know?"

"We just informed him."

The girls looked at each other. Ashley said, "He didn't call us."

Milo said, "He's pretty broken up, girls. We offered to talk to you first and as soon as we're through, he'll be over."

"He's our dad," said Marissa. "He should be here."

"He will," said Ashley. "Poor Daddy." She sighed, cried a bit. "It'll be the first time since the divorce."

Milo said, "That he's here?"

"Uh-huh."

Marissa said, "Mommy probably wouldn't have minded, they got along. But Daddy said it was best that he get his own life in gear."

Milo said, "At the condo."

"Uh-huh."

"You guys spend much time there?"

"Not really," said Ashley. "Sometimes."

Marissa said, "I need to throw up," struggled to her feet and ran across the room. Ashley turned to Milo: "What now?"

"Our only goal is to find out who hurt your mom. That sometimes means questions that can seem out of place, Ashley. So if we ask anything that—"

"Like what?"

"Well, for starts, something you said a few minutes ago. That it wasn't your dad. I'm curious why you said that."

"Why I said it was 'cause it wasn't Dad even though you might think it was."

"Why would we think that?"

"Because that's what cops always think, right? They assume it's the husband, I see it all the time on the murder shows."

"You watch a lot of murder sho—"

"Dad watches 'em and when I'm over, I do, too."

"So you wanted to make sure we didn't assume—"

"Admit it, you focused on him," said Ashley, louder. "So I cleared it up, okay? They were divorced but still friends—they worked together, no problems, not a single one."

"Okay," said Milo.

Ashley pointed a red-nailed finger. "Even if I believed Dad could do something like that and I don't, I know he didn't because he wasn't there when you said it happened, he was home."

Early on, she'd asked about the time frame. Not as certain of her father's innocence as she wanted us to believe?

I said, "You know he was home because—"

"I called him this morning and he was there and then he had to take another call from overseas business so he said to email him and I did. And he was right there and he answered me back. Twice."

We'd seen the email headings, so all true. But irrelevant if a contract killer had been used.

Milo said, "Thanks for clearing that up, Ashley. And let me empha-size, we don't have any suspects at this time, including your dad."

"I threw up," said Marissa Corey, reappearing around the corner. She sat back down, swiping her lips with a tissue and placing a hand on a flat stomach. "Everything just hurled."

Ashley said, "You okay?"

Marissa stuck out her tongue and grimaced. "Tastes like crap. Yech."

Ashley said, "I was just telling them that Daddy and Mommy got along well."

"Uh-huh." Marissa closed her eyes, threw her head back against the roll of the sofa-top.

Milo said, "I know this is a terrible time but if either of you has any idea who *would* want to hurt your mom—"

"No one," said Ashley. "Some criminal probably wanted to rob her."

Marissa said, "She was wearing total bling. I saw her when I was eating breakfast this morning."

Ashley said, "Mommy was the queen of blingdom, she loved her bling. That's why she went out, to make sure her jewelry was given to us fairly. She told us. We felt weird about it but when Mommy had an idea . . ."

"Fifty–fifty, girls," said Marissa, shifting to a British accent.

Ashley said, "Mommy was all about being fair, always."

"Robbery would be a good motive," said Milo. "Unfortunately, all of your mother's jewelry was in place. So were her cash and credit cards."

Both girls gaped.

Ashley said, "So what? Some ghetto-scum tried to rob her, pan-icked and . . ." She shook her head. More tears.

Marissa said, "I think I'm going to hurl again." But she sat there.

Milo said, "You're making good points and we'll certainly look into them. Is there anything else we should consider?"

"Why would we know?" said Ashley.

"You were close to her."

"So what, if it was about her bling?"

"True, but let's consider alternatives. Was your mom dating any-one?"

Both girls shook their heads.

"No one?"

Ashley said, "The business kept her busy, she was always travel-ing."

"So no steady boyfriend."

"Uh-uh."

"Did she ever speak of anyone hassling her?"

"Like a stalker?" said Ashley. "No."

"What about a problem with someone related to business?"

Blank looks. Then Marissa shot a glance at her sister. Whatever message she was trying to convey didn't get through. Ashley continued to look glazed. She slumped low and knuckled her eyes.

I said, "Something came to mind, Marissa?"

"No," she said. In a soft voice, to Ashley: "Not even Phyllis, right?"

Ashley stared at her. "Phyllis? That's crazy."

The obvious next step was to ask who Phyllis was. Milo said, "Tell us about the hassle with Laura."

"Stupid bitch Laura," said Marissa. "We're all going to the city, House of Blues, Chainsaw Waltz is playing, Laura's like 'I'll drive.' She's a sucky driver, we should've known, but she had her father's car finally and wanted to show it off."

I said, "Nice wheels?"

"Bentley Speed? You *think*?"

Ashley said, "She hit a pole in her Audi the week before so it was in the shop and her dad finally let her use the Bentley. She's like, 'C'mon, they'll valet us in front, we'll get vipped all night, maybe get into those hidden private rooms they have there.' So we're like, 'okay.' Then in-stead of getting onto the 101 she takes some side streets because she wants to show off without highway patrol up her butt. So now she's up to ninety and we're like, 'Stop, Bitch, this is stupid.' And then a sheriff blue-lights her and we all have to do the Dewey test."

"The Dewey test?" said Milo.

"Dewey," said Marissa. "D-U-I? Walking like straight, touching our noses?"

Ashley said, "We passed but Laura didn't, we didn't know she had some beers before. So the sheriff fails her and then he says I'm gonna look inside the car and Laura's like 'Fine,' doesn't even ask for a warrant. Then he searches and finds a Baggie of weed in the glove compartment and Laura claims it's her dad's. Which could be possible, he's like a music executive, got a ponytail. Then another sheriff car comes and we all get taken to the station and we call Mommy but she's not answering her phone and Laura's dad finally answers and he comes over and gets totally pissed when he finds out Laura tried to rat him out, tells the cops feel free to teach my daughter a lesson."

"Cold," said Marissa. "Usually, he's mellow. Like friend-type dad."

I said, "Doesn't sound as if you guys had anything to worry about."

"That's what we figured," said Ashley. "But they held us and said we'd still have to go to court. Finally we reached Mommy and she called Fellinger and he got us out of there and fixed it so we don't have to go to court. But Laura still does, only her dad finally mellowed out and hired a lawyer who keeps postponing it. That's what we figured you guys were here for, like to convince us to rat Laura out."

She sucked in air. Hung her head. "Now I wish that *was* the reason."

The girls gripped each other again, rocked and scrunched their eyes shut and went silent.   ⱴ

Milo got on his cell. "Mr. Corey? Lieutenant Sturgis. Your daughters need you. Good, I'll tell them."

Ashley opened her eyes. Marissa did the same seconds later.

"Your dad's on his way."

"Okay," said Ashley. Her voice had gone flat. Her eyes were dull.

I said, "So you dorm at the U., and Marissa, you live here?"

"Um, not really," said Marissa.

"We share an apartment," said Ashley, blushing behind her ears.

"Are you in school?"

Hesitation. Slow head shake. "I dropped out. Could've studied but it was a total waste. I want to do business like my parents."

"Import–export?"

"No, by myself, maybe in fashion." She twisted a foot-long strand of blond hair. "I'm figuring it out."

"Me, too," said Marissa.

"So you guys are here today because—"

"Sydney and Jasper need us. We come like three, four times a week to groom and feed them and do a little exercise. Otherwise their muscles go flabby and they get unhealthy."

"And the other days?"

"Mom does it . . . oh, God!"

Marissa said, "What's going to happen to Sydney and Jasper?"

I walked to a cavernous kitchen, found ice water in one of two fridges, and poured glasses for the girls. They began by sipping, ended up slurping.

Milo said, "Thanks for your time, girls. Anything else you want to tell us?"

Fluttering lids. Dual drowsy head shakes.

"We're happy to stay until your dad gets here."

Dual "Uh-uhs."

"You're sure?"

Ashley said, "We really want to be by ourselves."

Marissa nodded.

Milo said, "I understand," and we stood. "Take care of yourselves, girls—oh, by the way, who's Phyllis?"

Ashley said, "Phyllis Tranh. She was Mommy's friend and then Daddy dated her."

"He dated her after the divorce."

"Of course, after," said Marissa. "Daddy's not a cheater."

"But not for long," said Ashley. "Maybe it got awkward."

"Phyllis Tranh," said Milo. "That's a Vietnamese name."

"Yeah, she is. Mommy knows her from business, Phyllis retails."

Marissa said, "Her and Mommy used to get their nails done together. When Mommy went to Beverly Hills."

"All the nail places in Beverly Hills are Vietnamese," said Ashley.

"Everywhere," said Marissa.

"Phyllis like goes in and talks to them in their language and she and Mommy get vipped."

Milo said, "Did that change after Phyllis started dating your dad?"

"I don't know," said Ashley. "No one ever said."

"I don't know either," said Marissa. "What people do is their own business, anyway."

CHAPTER

6

As we exited the house, one of the horses neighed and the other stared.

Milo said, "My kingdom for a talking steed—no Mr. Ed comments, please. He was a dilettante."

He began working his phone as we returned to the Seville.

Phyllis Tranh was chief financial officer of Diamond Products and Sundries. The CEO was Albert L. Tranh. Headquartered on Santee Street, east of downtown, the company sold goods on the web as well as in retail stores and served as a jobber for importers and wholesalers. The website could be accessed in English, Spanish, Chinese, Thai, and Vietnamese.

Milo whistled. "They're into everything from aquarium supplies to yeast. Including religious supplies for Catholics, Protestants, and Buddhists. Like you said, a woman with that background might serve as a nifty replacement for Ursula." He loosened his tie. "Fooling with your friend's spouse, same old story. Okay, let's see where this entrepreneurial lady lives. Meanwhile, my head's killing me, try to find a place for coffee before we get back on the freeway."

◆

I drove out of Rancho Lobos Estates the way I'd come in. The guard-house was unoccupied but the gate's exit function was activated by pressure.

As I hooked back onto Lobo Canyon, Milo kept searching for data on Phyllis Tranh.

"Here we go, North Maple Drive in Beverly Hills. Lives with Al-bert Tranh." He turned to me. "She's married, it opens up a whole new chapter . . . looks like neither of them has committed a criminal viola-tion. Pity. Onward to DMV—shit, never looked up Richard's wheels."

That info egested quickly: Corey drove a two-year-old black Range Rover, Phyllis Tranh a three-year-old gray Maserati, Albert Tranh a seven-year-old Lincoln Town Car.

Milo reached Moe Reed and asked him to be out on the lookout for all three vehicles on the security tape.

Reed said, "Nice to have diversity, L.T. Been looking at a bunch of German engineering for the last hour. You'd think the whole world's BMW and Mercedes and Audi."

"Nothing iffy, so far?"

"Not yet. A couple of commercial delivery drivers who arrived early on did come up with records. But nothing close to homicide."

"How far from homicide?"

"One guy did a short stint for forgery six years ago, the other had a narcotics conviction."

"Look into both of them, Moses. Unless something really juicy pops up."

"Ms. Maserati or Mr. Range Rover," said Reed.

"A boy can dream," said Milo.

In a strip mall on Kanan Road just south of the 101 I spotted promising signage over a storefront: *Tyrolean Gourmet: Baked Delicacies and Gourmet Coffee.* Inside were sweet aromas and immaculate floors, a long take-out counter filled with temptation.

Only two ice cream tables for eating in. But for a woman in her six-ties behind the counter, the place was empty.

Instant smile. "Vut ken I do for you, Surzz?"

Milo studied the glass case, selected a headache remedy in the form of a raspberry torte the size of a minor Alp as well as a similarly scaled slab of carrot cake.

The woman said, "Und you, Surr?"

The cake looked good so I ordered my own. We sat down with cof-fee and calories. He looked at my plate and chuckled.

"What?"

"Adonis actually ingests? Finally, I'm a bad influence?"

"You're always a bad influence. I just happen to be hungry."

He finished both of his pastries, returned to the counter, said some-thing that made the woman giggle, and returned with a cream-filled something. A single bite obliterated a third of it. He wiped his mouth. "Real cream, not that aerosol crap. Try some?"

I was halfway through my cake. Denser than it looked. "I'm okay."

"Bah humbug." He drank, ate, exhaled in contentment, repeated the sequence a few times.

Finally, he paused for a longer breath. "Richard made Ursula out to be Lana Libido but the girls don't know of anyone she's dating. There was also no sign they suspected anything about her and Fellinger. So who knows if that ever happened."

I said, "The girls didn't live with Ursula and most parents don't discuss their sex lives with their kids."

"They also don't discuss it with spouses, current or ex. So I'm won-dering if Richard *is* a paranoid whack-job or just a devious liar trying to distract us away from himself. Either way, he remains at the top of the chart. And now he's got a co-tenant. Phyllis Tranh's got to be the girl-friend he told us about."

"I'd take that bet. What I found interesting was Ashley's comment about it not being Daddy."

"The daughter doth protest too much?"

"She blurted it right after finding out. Sometimes those are the truest statements. Then there was Marissa's reaction when you asked about business disputes. 'Not even Phyllis, right?' "

"Richard and New Love Interest. Down deep the girls are bothered by the relationship but they can't deal with it so they say the opposite. You guys have a name for that, right?"

"Reaction formation."

"Guess it's kind of like political correctness," he said. "You know how it is, some simp talking-head goes on too long about racism, sexism, homophobia, I start to look for KKK robes under the bed. Anyway, Ms. Tranh bears looking into and B.H. isn't too far out of the way. You have time for a spontaneous drop-in on Maple Drive?"

"Sure."

He fetched himself a refill of coffee, removed his jacket, and fanned himself with one hand. "What about the daughters?"

"What about them?"

"They give off any iffy vibe?"

I said, "Not to me. What, shades of the Menendez brothers?"

"At this point I need to consider everything. Lyle and Erik were spoiled slackers looking to cash in, why not a couple of spoiled rich girls in line for big bucks? They did know exactly where their mother would be this morning."

"The Menendez brothers shotgunned their parents themselves and left tons of evidence. I don't see these girls being smart enough to find a reliable contract killer."

"I'm sure you're right." A beat. "Remember Katherine Hennepin? All my assumptions coming to squat? It does wonders for a boy's self-esteem."

"Why don't you call Fellinger, see if you can learn where Ursula's money is going to."

He punched the preset he'd loaded for the lawyer's office, caught the woman behind the counter edging closer, and took his phone outside the bakery. When he finished talking he motioned for me to join him. I paid for the food and we returned to the car.

"How much?" he said, reaching into his pocket.

"On me."

"No way."

"Fellinger give up anything about Ursula's will?"

"Off the record, the estate's divided four ways: Thirty-five percent goes to Richard because that was the amount Fellinger and Cohen finally negotiated after three years of bickering. Another twenty-five percent goes to a list of charities Ursula stipulated and the remaining forty is divided equally between Ashley and Marissa. But it's in trust, they don't get their hands on it for years."

"Who's the trustee?"

"Not Richard, a lawyer in Fellinger's firm."

"Fellinger recused himself from that function?"

"The other guy's a trust and inheritance specialist, Fellinger said he wanted it done right."

I said, "How much delay of gratification are we talking about?"

"The girls will have their basic needs taken care of from the get-go but no access to big bucks until they turn thirty. When they're thirty-five, the trust terminates and they get everything."

"Do the girls know the details?"

"As far as Fellinger knows, they don't. They were described to him by both Richard and Ursula as not interested in the world of finance."

"So Richard gets the single biggest chunk."

"Nice for him," said Milo. "Let's see what his ex-girlfriend has to say about it. Maybe her husband, too."

Long day since I'd seen Ursula Corey's corpse in the parking garage. Darkness had settled by the time I drove into Beverly Hills.

The Tranh residence on the 600 block of North Maple Drive was an ungated, two-story, salmon stucco Mediterranean with a clipped lawn and a modest bed of palms and begonias. The neighborhood was mansions of varying vintage. Compared with its neighbors, this house was understated.

An elderly Asian man answered the bell ring. Barely above five feet, he wore a spotless white shirt, cream linen slacks, and blue velvet slippers with lions embroidered at the toes. One thin-boned hand held a rolled-up copy of *Forbes.*

"Yes, please?" Soft voice, oddly boyish.

"Lieutenant Sturgis, Los Angeles police."

The man's eyelids quivered. "Did something happen at the store?"

"No, sir. We're looking for Phyllis Tranh."

"That's my daughter. She's out of the country. May I ask what's going on?"

"Could we come in, Mr. . . ."

"Albert Tranh. May I see that badge again, please—yes, of course, come in."

A thirty-by-twenty living room was furnished completely in American Colonial, much of it actually from the period. Albert Tranh rang a small pewter bell with a gold handle and a blue-uniformed maid appeared.

"My coffee please, Irma. And for you gentlemen . . . ?"

"Nothing, thanks," said Milo.

"Bring some sweets, Irma," said Albert Tranh. His English was barely accented. Precise elocution said he'd worked hard to achieve that.

As the maid left, Albert Tranh pointed to a silk brocade sofa the color of bruised plums and waited for us to take our places before settling in a yellow silk Chippendale side chair. Dominating the room was the single break in the Colonial motif: a lithograph above the mantel, Jasper Johns flag.

The rest of the wall art consisted of framed samplers, landscapes portraying bygone Hudson River edens, and stiff-looking portraits of puritanically garbed people with severe faces. Deputy D.A. John Nguyen had once told me that his family and their community of Vietnamese emigrants loved America enough to make a DAR lady blush.

Milo informed Albert Tranh of Ursula Corey's murder. The old man's free hand wafted like a dry leaf before settling on his chest. The copy of *Forbes* bent as fragile-looking fingers squeezed. "That's horrible. What happened?"

"You knew Ms. Corey well?"

"Oh, yes, very, we did business together. A lot of business. You can't tell me what happened?"

"She was shot to death, sir."

"Good grief. Where?"

"Century City."

"Century City? In the mall?"

"In a parking lot."

"A parking lot," said Tranh. "A robbery? A carjacking?"

"Doesn't appear to be either, sir."

"Yes, of course," said Albert Tranh. "Why would you be here if it was a robbery?" He frowned. "May I ask why Phyllis is relevant?"

"Ursula's ex-husband told us about her friendship with Ursula."

"Richard said that," said Tranh. "Really."

"You find that surprising."

"Did Richard also inform you he and Phyllis had a relationship?"

"A romantic relationship?" said Milo, evading seamlessly.

"I wouldn't go that far, Lieutenant. Richard and Phyllis dated briefly. Nothing underhanded, this was well after Richard and Ursula's divorce. Nevertheless, I didn't approve, mixing business with personal. But Phyllis is a strong-willed girl. Would you excuse me one second?"

He was back in five seconds, carrying a framed photo that he handed to Milo. His "girl" was a beautiful woman in her forties, with upswept ebony hair, wide eyes ripe with amusement, and a pointy dimpled chin.

"My only child." Tranh frowned. "She is married, but only technically. Her husband has been living in Cambodia for seventeen years and has at least two other wives that are confirmed, quite possibly more."

"Sounds like a peach."

"Norbert Lam is a lowlife."

I said, "Phyllis has only been married once?"

"Yes. Big wedding." Albert Tranh's expression said a repeat of the experience would be unwelcome. "Ursula murdered, this is unbelievable. So you're here to learn more about her through Phyllis?"

"Why did Phyllis and Richard stop dating?"

"That." Tranh sighed. "Perhaps I'll regret mentioning it in the first place."

"We appreciate anything you can offer, Mr. Tranh."

"Hmm . . . why did they stop? From the little Phyllis told me, she decided that Richard held on to feelings for Ursula and that caused her to—I believe the expression is, she bailed?"

Milo smiled. "Yes, sir."

"I taught English and American history in Saigon, spent time as a graduate student at the University of Illinois in Urbana. The key, obviously, is to learn idioms. But keeping up is difficult."

I said, "Could you tell us about your business relationship with Ursula?"

"With Ursula and Richard. They continued working together even after their divorce. Are you familiar with their company?"

"Urrick, Ltd."

"We are among their customers."

"What do you buy?"

"There's no simple answer for that," said Tranh. "We sell deeply discounted merchandise, mostly domestic overstock and budget imports from Asia. It's a fluctuating inventory, based on educated guesses about customer demand."

Irma the maid brought a silver tray holding a coffeepot, bone china cups, and a plate of wafer cookies. She poured for Tranh first, offered us the opportunity to change our minds.

I said, "No thanks."

Milo said, "Just half a cup."

Hard to imagine his digestive system had any room to spare, but maybe taking two cookies was exhibiting good manners in service of rapport and I was the rube. I watched him chew energetically and reach for a third cookie.

When Albert Tranh placed his cup on a coaster, I said, "That type of purchasing sounds risky."

"Risky but exciting, we're always having to figure things out," said Tranh. "And we've had our disasters." He smiled. "Would you by any chance be interested in ten thousand, five hundred and thirty-six tiny stuffed red crocodiles that disintegrate when water touches them and end up smelling like week-old pot roast?"

Milo said, "Hmm, let me talk to my people about that."

Tranh's smile widened then dropped off his face. "The key is to win many more bets than we lose and for the most part we've been able to do that. And I must say Ursula and Richard have helped."

"How so, sir?"

"Ursula has a terrific nose for product. Years ago, she and Phyllis traveled together on buying trips. The marketplaces in most Asian capitals are vast, I'm talking about thousands of stalls covering miles. Phyllis said Ursula's energy outstripped hers and that she noticed things Phyllis walked right past. So in a sense, Ursula became more than just a wholesaler, she was almost an unpaid purchasing agent for us."

"You don't do your own buying because—"

"We're retailers and we stick with what we know."

"What about Richard? How has he helped you?"

Brief pause. "Richard is honest and efficient, delivers what he promises in good condition and on time. With him you get none of the attitude we experience with other wholesalers because we're not Kmart." He sat forward. "If not a robber, what?"

"We don't know, sir," said Milo. "Is there anything you'd like to say about their personalities?"

"Ursula was lovely," said Tranh. "A charming, refined, lovely person."

"And Richard?"

"You're asking about him because . . ."

"Because when we begin an investigation we ask lots of questions, Mr. Tranh, and hope some of them bear fruit. Kind of like you, sir, when you invest in merchandise."

"Fair enough, Lieutenant. What can I say about Richard . . . he's always been honest and dependable but he is not . . . engaging."

"More of a loner?"

"How shall I put this," said Albert Tranh. "Hmm . . . all right: He'll make conversation but one can't help feel he's not enjoying it. I suppose he just wasn't blessed with a huge dose of gregariousness."

"Ursula was," I said.

"Ursula." He sighed. "Ursula had natural warmth. It served her well in Vietnam, we're a friendly bunch." His voice caught on the last two words. "Phyllis will be so sad—oh, no, the daughters, Ursula has two, do they know?"

"Yes, sir."

"How are they doing?"

"As well as can be expected, Mr. Tranh. Do you know the girls personally?"

"I've met them once," said Tranh. "Family barbecue, before the divorce. Nice children. Mostly they were riding their horses."

Milo said, "How long has your daughter been out of the country?"

"Six weeks."

"When's she due to return?"

"Not sure—if you'd like, I could try to reach her now."

"That would be great, sir."

Shooting a cuff, Tranh bared a gold Rolex, checked the date.

"Today I believe she's still in Bangkok, with the time difference it would be . . . she's probably up."

He rang his little bell, Irma appeared and hurried to fetch him a cordless land-model. "Phil? It's Pops. I'm afraid I have terrible news for you . . . no, no, I'm fine . . . unfortunately, Ursula has been murdered."

Milo and I sat there as Tranh did a lot of listening interspersed with brief words of comfort. After a long interlude of the former, he said, "All right, dear, please draw yourself together so I can give you to a detective."

Milo took the phone. Did a lot of listening and not much else.

When he was through, he handed it back to Tranh, who said, "All right, darling, I'm so sorry—yes, do that, you need your rest. Bye."

Albert Tranh said, "She says she wants to go back to sleep but I'm pretty sure she'll be calling me soon. For parenting."

Too late to retrieve Milo's car from the lot in Century City so I headed for the station.

He said, "In answer to your yet-unasked question about Phyllis, mostly she cried. I'm talking geyser."

"Over the top?"

He shrugged. "Sounded real to me but without nonverbal cues, who knows? She also volunteered the fact that she'd dated Richard briefly and that Ursula had been 'unbelievably gracious' about it but that she'd broken up with Richard because her friendship with Ursula was more important than 'any guy.' So unless I've wandered into the Actors Workshop, things are not looking up in the romantic rival department."

"Maybe it was over as far as Phyllis is concerned," I said. "But what if Richard blamed Ursula for the breakup? Not only does Ursula leave him, she gets her friend to do the same."

He thought about that. "Good point. So back to Mr. Charmless. You like him seriously, huh?"

"He's the best you've got."

"That's not what I asked."

"I like him plenty," I said. "The financial motive alone would keep me on him. What's planned for tomorrow?"

"Heart-stopping drama, amigo, as I honor Richard's permission to crawl through his phone records and his finances—but I'll still need subpoenas and a victim's warrant on Ursula's house to look for date-books or computer logs of her social life. Thanks for all your time, I'll see if I can put in a reimbursement request that actually gets you paid something."

Not-so-subtle way of easing me off the case because when a woman gets executed the husband's always the initial suspect, usually for good reason.

Allowing himself to start believing this one would turn out *not* to be different?

I had no problem with that.

CHAPTER

7

Ten days later, Milo phoned. "What's the opposite of a progress report, a regress report?"

"No luck on Ursula."

"The security tapes from the building zeroed out and so did Richard's financial records. I brought in a D.A.'s investigator with forensic accounting training. No suspicious payments to anyone. Pawing through Ursula's house turned up a couple of vibrators in her undies drawer and a date-book. She was a popular bachelorette, dated twenty-three swains since the divorce, listed their names and numbers. A few she found on an online dating service for attractive, affluent middle-aged singles. Most she met at upscale cocktail lounges or restaurants."

"Your basic casual pickup."

"Just add Martini. I talked to every one of them and they back up Richard's take on her as a lusty gal. But a classy one—several guys used the word. The only objection was she cut everyone off after three dates but did it diplomatically. Nothing personal, she needed to travel for a long time. Still, no one had a bad word to say about her, Alex."

I said, "Gracious or not, injured male pride's a great motive."

"Hell, yeah, wars have been started over it. Too bad every single one of these jokers has been ruled out with solid alibis."

"Twenty-three solid alibis?"

"Not as unlikely as it sounds because most of them are from out of town and can prove being in another city at the time of the shooting."

"She picked up travelers."

"The picture I got was she allowed *herself* to be picked up," he said. "Of the six locals she met online, three were also traveling. The last three work alone—screenwriter, freelance financial advisor, sculptor—but they, too, had eyewitnesses placing them at home."

I said, "She list any dates during her own Asian travels?"

"Nope."

"Maybe she cut off the wrong guy overseas."

"And he flew halfway around the world to express his displeasure? That would be nifty, lad, but during her travel periods, the date-book's crammed with business appointments. I'm talking dawn-to-dusk, visiting marketplaces, shipping agents, manufacturers, even farmers for stuff like bamboo. There really doesn't seem to be any allowance for partying and that was backed up by Phyllis Tranh who I talked to again, yesterday at her hotel in Hong Kong. She never observed Ursula do anything *but* business on business trips, we're talking one focused woman."

"Twenty-three men," I said. "Ashley and Marissa claimed not to know about any of them."

"I had a couple more sit-downs with Ashley and Marissa and their not knowing doesn't surprise me. Like that, they live in their own pad, mostly come by to play with their horses. Ursula would sometimes be there, working in her home office, but more often she wasn't."

"Do the girls work?"

"Apart from on their tans? Negative. Yeah, they're a couple of indulged rich kids but that's not a crime yet."

"Any boyfriends in the picture?"

"Nope, just a group from high school they still hang out with. The closest thing to criminal is that girl, Laura Smith, the one who played Le Mans with Daddy's Bentley and has had two weed busts over the last three years. Daddy is Imago Smith, this big-time hip-hop producer, and he's got a rep as a heavy partier so I suppose she comes by it honestly."

"How're the girls doing?"

"They still look seriously stressed. Ashley did mention that she's considering therapy. I fielded a call from the old lawyer, Cohen, wanting to know when I planned to release Ursula's house from the warrant. Apparently, Richard's thinking of selling it and taking his inheritance from the proceeds rather than cash in any of Ursula's stocks and bonds. I had no good reason to keep it going, so I freed it today. And that's it, boys and girls, unless you can come up with something to nurture hope."

I said, "The only thing I can think of is a man Ursula dated but didn't list in her book. Maybe because it *didn't* go well. Or someone managed to squeeze into her busy Asian schedule and long distance didn't protect her."

"Dark secrets of the Orient?" he said. "Hey, I know, I'll ask the chief to pay for a trip over there, will even settle for business class. On the other hand, to keep things a bit more realistic, I could serve as a model on *Project Runway.* Meanwhile, I surrender."

Two cold cases in a row. I couldn't recall that ever happening before, had no idea how he'd handle it.

Two days later, I was having lunch with Robin out in our backyard, sitting near the pond, eating sandwiches I'd slapped together after finishing a couple of psych reports. Our French bulldog Blanche positioned herself at our feet, panting and burping, trapdoor mouth ajar, waiting for fallen manna.

Robin had been working overtime and I figured drawing her out of the studio was a good deed. At first, she declined, citing a deadline. A quarter hour later she agreed but remained preoccupied. Then I fed the koi and she watched them burble and slurp and that seemed to draw her into the present.

She picked up a sandwich. "Roast beef. You read my mind, darling."

"Really?"

"No, but had I been thinking about food, roast beef might've come up eventually."

The phone in my pocket rang.

"Aren't you going to get that?"

"Not right now."

She shrugged and kissed my cheek.

Ninety seconds later, more chirping from my jeans.

Robin said, "You might as well."

I checked the window. Someone calling on my private line, not the business extension my service would pick up. Unfamiliar number. I let it go to voice mail. Seconds later, it rang again.

Robin laughed. I picked up. "Dr. Delaware."

Moe Reed said, "We kind of need you, Doc. Over at the Corey house."

"Which one?"

"Pardon?"

"His or hers?"

"Oh. Hers. L.T. wants to know if you can come over A-sap."

"Any reason he didn't call himself, Moe?"

Reed said, "Hold on, let me move away from the scene."

"Another murder?"

"No, this is . . . maybe even weirder. Why didn't he call himself, Doc? Because to tell the truth, Doc, he's kind of . . . I don't know, I guess stunned is the word? Never really seen him like this."

He explained why.

I said, "Be over as soon as I can."

Robin began wrapping up the sandwiches. "Drive carefully."

"You never say that."

"That's because I assume you will." She kissed me again. "But now, my darling, you're looking a little . . . accelerated."

I told her why.

She said, "That's crazy. Then again, who better to handle crazy than you?"

8

This time, the gatehouse at Rancho Lobo Estates was staffed by a young man who looked nervous. I announced myself. He let me in between "Alex" and "Delaware."

The four-slot parking area on the north side of Ursula Corey's house was filled, overflow vehicles parked on the side of the road. The quartet that had beaten me onto the property were Milo's Impala, two other unmarkeds, and a red BMW 3. I left the Seville behind a white Infiniti sedan, a bronze Jaguar S-type with customized plates reading *RE MIK,* and a white van bearing the seal of the crime lab. The cars were unoccupied. Two techs sat in the van listening to something on earphones.

The horses were gone but the smell of horseshit lingered. The house's front door had been propped open and Detective I Sean Binchy stood in the octagonal entry, wearing his usual dark suit, deep-blue shirt, black tie, and Doc Martens. His red hair was spiked, his long, big-jawed face smooth and freckled and glowing.

"Doc!" he said, as if my arrival made his day.

Years ago Sean had begun a metamorphosis that took him from

surfer to punk-ska bassist to born-again crime solver. Maybe it's faith that keeps him cheerful, maybe he's just wired that way, but nothing bores him, nothing disappoints him, and he's got the attention span of a severe obsessive-compulsive without the anxiety and the troublesome habits.

Cloning his neural fluid could make someone rich.

He gripped my hand and said, "You're going to be interested, Doc, it's really *psychological.*"

"Can't wait, Sean." Walking past him, I encountered Detective I Moses Reed at the mouth of the great room. Reed had probably played cop in the crib. His half brother had once been an LAPD ace and his father's life distilled down to military service, Central Division patrol, premature death.

He said, "Doc," and thumbed me forward.

Milo was sitting on the big leather couch. No sign of Ashley Corey but Marissa sat next to him, looking like the victim of a natural disaster.

Perched on chairs to the right were a man and a woman. He was forty or so, dark-haired with a perfectly triangular soul patch below a pouting lower lip, wore a gray sharkskin suit and green crocodile loafers, no socks. She was midthirties, plump and pretty in a brown silk top over black leggings. She glanced at me, returned her attention to Milo.

I wondered how he'd introduce me. He didn't, just said, "Okay," and stood.

Soul Patch said, "We're done?"

Milo said, "Not quite."

Soul looked at his watch.

Milo said, "I'll be quick, Mr. Ballou."

Mr. Ballou's lower lip didn't take the news well but the rest of him sat there.

Milo led me into the giant kitchen where I'd fetched water for the Corey sisters. This time I took in details.

What had to be a thousand square feet, one of those designer "caterer-ready" showpieces rarely used for anything beyond microwaving.

Milo kept going, past the dual Traulsen fridges, the nine-burner Wolf range, the quartet of sinks, a host of warming drawers, convection ovens, commercial-sized dishwashers, equipment I couldn't identify. Everything was brushed steel and black wood and white marble.

The room echoed as Milo ended up at the far end, where the space tapered to an eat-in breakfast area. Rusticized table and chairs centered an octagonal area that was mostly windows, offering an eyeful of lawn, well-placed shrubbery, and mountainside.

Pretty, but the relevant view was interior.

The table could accommodate eight but was set for two. The menu du jour was a pair of tossed salads, now wilted, wineglasses half poured with something the color of straw, a crystal pitcher of water, ocher-colored plates arranged precisely.

Boneless grilled chicken breasts, blanched fennel, cakes of little round things that were probably lentils. On smaller plates, some sort of dried fruit concoction was molded like sand in a child's beach bucket.

On a nearby counter stood a wicker basket of grapes, peaches, and plums.

I said, "Bon appétit."

Milo said, "Goddammit, I'm never gonna be hungry again."

That was as likely as the Messiah detouring to the craps tables in Reno.

I said, "See what you mean."

We returned to the great room. Milo said, "Please repeat what you told me, Mr. Ballou."

Ballou, warming to his new audience of one, smiled and gave a finger-wave. "Mick Ballou, West Valley Executive Properties. I've got the exclusive listing on this wonderful estate. It looked great from the outset but obviously we wanted to explore a bit of staging. To make it more polished but lived-in, you know?"

Marissa Corey made a choking sound and began dabbing her eyes furiously.

Mick Ballou, puzzled by her reaction, stared for a moment, then resumed. "As I was saying . . . this morning . . . around ten, I arrived with Candy to set up a plan."

The woman in the brown silk top said, "Candace LaGuardia, Bijou Staging." Low volume, low enthusiasm.

Ballou said, "Anyway . . . Candy brought a *van*ful of items but first we had a look. And lo and behold, someone had begun staging the breakfast room. Or so we thought. That made us wonder if our wires had somehow gotten crossed so we called the client but he was out. So we called our secondary number and that turned out to be Marissa here."

Marissa said, "Daddy didn't tell me he'd given them my number. I didn't know what the frick they were talking about."

Ballou winced. "Anyway . . . Marissa, here, wanted to come down to see exactly what was going on. That's when she saw what we saw and got pretty upset." To Marissa: "I'm sorry but I had no way of knowing."

Marissa looked at me. "I freaked because I was here yesterday afternoon to make sure Sydney and Jasper were okay and none of that frickin' shit was here."

I said, "What time was that?"

"Like two to like six," she said. "It made me thirsty so I went inside to get some juice so I was definitely in the kitchen and *that* frickin' shit wasn't."

I said, "Someone got in after six."

Marissa smirked. "You *think*?"

"Who has a key?"

"Me, Ashley, and him." Pointing to Ballou.

Ballou said, "Your father, as well, seeing as he's the client."

"Whatever."

Candace LaGuardia said, "I don't have a key, this is the first time I've been here."

Marissa said, "I called Ashley and Daddy, both of them thought it was insane. Cooking a meal and leaving it frickin' here? What the frick is that about? It's like . . . perverted. Breaking in and saying this is *my* place."

Out of the mouths of babes.

"Then," said Marissa, "because it was frickin' weird, I called him." Her eyes drifted to Milo's. Everyone else's eyes tagged along.

Mick Ballou said, "After you said not to touch anything, Lieutenant, obviously everything ground to a halt." Another look at his watch.

Candace LaGuardia said, "They did a pretty good job décor-wise. Except for the food, you never do that. Food goes bad fast."

9

I pretended not to probe for nonverbal tells from Ballou, LaGuardia, or Marissa Corey. All three looked stunned. I nodded at Milo and he said, "Appreciate your patience, we'll take it from here." We accompanied Ballou and LaGuardia out of the house, stayed with him at the bronze Jaguar, and let her approach the white Infiniti. Marissa Corey had already raced far ahead of them and was backing the red BMW fast enough to set off a dust storm. Fishtailing, she straightened and sped off toward the gatehouse, tires squealing.

Ballou said, "Whoa, Speed-Racer. So can we go ahead with the staging, Lieutenant?"

"Not yet, sir."

"When?"

Milo motioned to the crime scene van. The two techs got out, retrieved cases from the rear, and walked toward us.

Ballou said, "Whoa. CSI?"

"Just like on TV," said Milo.

"You think something bad actually happened here? I mean there was nothing but food. Maybe it's just a kid pranking."

"Maybe but we need to check it out."

Mick Ballou said, "Can you at least give me an estimate of when?"

The techs reached us, a couple of men in their twenties. Milo said, "Breakfast area at the end of the kitchen. I'll be in soon, tell you what to do."

Ballou said, "Can you give me an approximate—"

"No, sir."

"Candy's got a tight schedule."

"I'll keep that in mind."

"In a fluctuating market, timing's everything, Lieutenant."

"Have a nice day, sir." Milo opened the Jaguar's driver's door.

Mick Ballou said, "Shit, I thought this would be an easy one."

As he drove off, Milo said, "Join the club, moron."

As we returned to the house, Binchy and Reed emerged and Milo told them they could go. In the breakfast room, he instructed the techs to check out every inch of the space, then move on to the entire kitchen. One man was six four and thin, the other a head shorter and even skinnier. Both wore stubble goatees and eyeglasses.

"Humongous place," said Tall. "Give me a poor victim in a one-room shithole any day."

"No victim I see," said Short. "We're checking out food, dude."

Tall looked past him. "Vast, we could be here all day."

Milo said, "If you get hungry, I'll call out for dinner."

Short said, "Ironic. Ha. I vote for Mexican."

Tall said, "I vote for finishing before dinner."

Milo and I returned outside. He leaned against the empty corral, rubbed his face, stared at the pretty sky.

"You know and I know," he said. "Ain't we the lucky ones?"

A beat.

I said, "Hennepin redux?"

He cursed. "How the hell can it be, Alex? Someone's out to plague me?"

Suddenly he loped toward his car, slapped the trunk hard enough to redden his palm, returned looking ready to commit an atrocity.

"First salmon, now goddamn boneless chicken breast?"

I said, "The kind of meals a man might see as girlie."

"Meaning?"

"Low fat, plenty of fiber, moderate portions." I wasn't sure if I was kidding. Milo didn't see any humor in it.

"C'mon, Alex, what the *hell*? Someone with a thing for *me*? Poor Ursula was nothing but a *pawn*? I mean how would they know?"

I thought of his favorite bumper sticker: *Even paranoids have enemies.* "Maybe Hennepin and Corey are somehow connected."

"An accountant and a tycooness?"

"Tycoonesses need accountants. Who was Ursula's?"

His smile was instantaneous, feral, frightening. "You probably think that question will stymie me but *as* a matter of fact, I've got the answer at my fingertips because I combed through her and Richard's finances for a solid goddamn week and it's not the Hennepin's bosses—the Grosses. No sir, Urrick's taxes are handled by a hoohah firm in the same building as Fellinger."

"Really," I said.

"What?"

"I'm grasping but maybe the building's the link," I said. "What if Hennepin had reason to be there—running an errand for the Grosses—and she got sniffed out by the same predator who went after Ursula?"

"So everything I've worked on Ursula—the money motive, Richard, some unhappy boyfriend—was a total waste of time and there's some random psychopath stationed on Avenue of the Stars looking for random prey?"

It's never random. I said nothing.

"Great, that's fantastic, beautiful. Phantom of the office building?

Even if I thought it made sense, why would he strangle and overkill-butcher one victim, wait four-plus months, and do another one execution-style?"

I said, "Well—"

"You're gonna tell me it's the signature, not the M.O., right?"

I smiled.

He said, "So what's this guy signing his name to? The joys of cuisine?"

"Marissa may have stumbled upon it a few minutes ago. Pride of ownership."

"He cooks a meal so he owns his victims? Why that, specifically? His mommy starved him in the crib? Insufficient breast-feeding?"

He strode away a second time, walked out to the middle of the road, and stood there, arms folded across his barrel chest. As if challenging a car to appear.

None did. Not a sound other than bird peeps. Beautiful place. Ursula Corey had left it, expecting a lovely day sweetened by altruism toward her children, only to die on oily asphalt.

When Milo returned, I said, "It wouldn't need to be someone who's at the building regularly. People come in and out. Occasional would be enough. That could explain four months between victims."

"Reed studied those tapes. No one iffy entered or exited the morning Ursula was killed."

"Define iffy."

"In the case of a motorist, a tag that traces to a criminal record. In the case of a pedestrian, lurking, loitering, acting generally creepy or spooky, any sort of purposeless behavior."

I said nothing.

He said, "Okay, it was a waste of time. Any better suggestions, genius?—aw, sorry, you're the last person I should go off on. It's just that this is nuts. The last thing I expected."

"Same here."

"God, I hope it's *not* the building. Even compiling a list of employees and staffers would be impossible, people come and go."

He turned toward the house. "Meanwhile, I've got a freaky food diorama in there. Boneless *chicken* . . . and guess where there also *isn't* a camera?"

"The house."

"The house for sure, but more to the point, the entrance to the goddamn development. Why they even bother with a gate is beyond me, the people they hire have no experience and anyone can walk through, which is obviously what happened. Probably after dark. Asshole with a picnic basket, he could just carry it in. On foot."

I said, "He'd need to get into the house. Was the alarm set?"

"Marissa doesn't remember, which probably means it wasn't. And no signs of break-in, so for all we know, a door was left unlocked. Safe neighborhood and all that."

"For someone to be aware of lax security, he'd have to be familiar with the area and/or the property. There's a guard out there, now. When did he come on duty?"

"Eight a.m., and no one was in the booth between eight p.m. and then. Logical, huh? I had Sean and Moe canvass the neighbors about intruders, unusual vehicles, anyone walking on the road. Nada."

I said, "With properties set this far back and with darkness, you'd have to be looking to spot anyone. Any indication the food was cooked in the house?"

"Just like Hennepin, the place was left spotless, though he did use plates and cutlery from the house. So he either pre-prepared his munchies or cleaned up compulsively."

He swore under his breath. "I came, I saw, I catered."

I said, "Marissa said Richard didn't have a key but Ballou contradicted that. Be good to find out how Richard got hold of it."

"As a matter of fact, lad, I can supply that data, because after I got Marissa's call, I phoned Richard. His story is that when he decided to sell the house, he came over and retrieved one from a secret hiding place he and Ursula had, in case they ever got locked out." He pointed. "Over there, in the barn. But before you get too excited, Richard's been in San Diego for two days. And I didn't just take his word for it, I confirmed with the Manchester Grand Hyatt. His card-key record has him out of his room between seven thirty and ten p.m. last night but his bar and restaurant tabs confirm drinks paid for at eight thirty and dinner at nine fifty."

"Dinner with who?"

"Clients. I called the hotel restaurant and they back him up. Richard and several Asian gentlemen."

"Stay-at-home loner traveling on business," I said. "That's a switch."

"A hundred twenty miles to San Diego ain't Phnom Penh, but yeah, it's different and Corey talked about it, he needs to get out more and schmooze now that he doesn't have Ursula. I'm not saying I can't be fooled but, Alex, he did not sound overjoyed. More like overwhelmed. Out of his element."

"He have any opinion about what happened here?"

"He thought it was insane. Guess we can reach a consensus there."

We checked with the crime scene techs. Short said, "Nothing so far, Lieutenant. It's been wiped down super-carefully."

Milo said, "Any sign of cooking?"

Tall said, "Not for a long time. I had a place like this, I'd be dishing up barbecue every Sunday."

Short said, "You had a place like this, you'd have someone cook for you."

"Nope," said Tall. "Rich doesn't have to mean lazy."

"Who said that?"

"I just did."

"Great," said Short. "Here I was, thinking I'd learn something today."

◆

Back at the cars, I said, "I'd still try to find out if Kathy Hennepin was ever in that office building."

Fishing out his phone, he called the Grosses' accounting firm, got voice mail, hung up. "Too complicated to leave a message. Anything else?"

"Hennepin's chef boyfriend—Kleffer—was alibied solidly, but now we've got two dinner scenes."

"Darius the Elusive returns? Not ever talking to him was sloppy, huh? Maybe I'm slipping."

He grabbed my hand, shook it vigorously. "Thanks."

"For what?"

"I slip, I could fall. Sometimes you supply a net."

10

The following morning Milo called and asked if I'd take another look at the Hennepin murder book. I said, "Sure," and six minutes later, Sean Binchy was at the door delivering the blue folder.

The request, just a formality. I supposed that defined friendship.

I went to my office and read after Robin had gone to her studio, concentrating on linking Katherine Hennepin to Ursula Corey any way I could.

The only thing they seemed to share was death followed by creepy culinary displays. I gave the files another try. By the fourth go-round, I might as well have been reading Sanskrit.

When you hit a wall, take another route. I refocused by stepping away from the details.

Milo's initial reaction to the dinner scene at Ursula's was to take it personally. Understandable response to surprise and frustration. But what if he was at least partially right and the killings were a power play against authority?

Making fools of the cops by setting up crime scenes designed to misdirect, because detectives play the odds. We all do.

Spot an eighty-year-old woman hobbling your way down a dark city street and your blood pressure, pulse, and respiration are unlikely to spike.

Switch the scene to a husky young male swaggering toward you and your sympathetic nervous system jams into high gear.

Sure, it's profiling and sure, it's imperfect. Get close enough to that old woman and realize she's a guy in drag whipping out a gun and you've lost out to limited thinking. But for the most part, things *are* what they seem and we all bank on that.

Try living randomly and see how far it gets you.

When it comes to police work, professional judgments about a crime are often formed early, sometimes during the first moments of viewing a crime scene. That can lead to tunnel vision and rushes to judgment. But more often than not, seasoned detectives' expectations are met because patterns do exist and ignoring patterns is stupid and reckless.

A bright detective keeps a sliver of mind open. Milo's one of the brightest but his assumptions had just been churned to sludge.

He wouldn't be forgiving himself anytime soon, but I was coming to believe that he deserved a pass. Because the slaughter of Katherine Hennepin *was* a textbook example of an overkill slice-job by someone the victim knew well. And the assassination of Ursula Corey *did* bear the hallmarks of a for-hire hit prompted by money or passion or both.

A pair of textbook cases that had skidded way off the page. A couple of obvious prime suspects who'd alibied out.

Was blowing probability to bits the big thrill for the monster who'd choreographed, directed, and starred in all this violence?

Were the killings little more than stage shows? Dinner for two, the props?

But why *these* two women? The victims mattered. The victims always matter.

Full circle . . .

I brewed coffee, drank too much of it, walked around the house and out to the garden and back, developing a killer headache that proved oddly reassuring.

Dinner for two. Pleased at his first tableau and repeating it? Because something about setting up a cozy culinary scene made his penis hard and flooded his shallow mind with pulsating memories?

Or did it all reduce to an ad for himself? Just another *look-at-me* vanity production.

Murder as bragging.

If so, how many other women would be sacrificed to a metastatic ego?

Were we dealing with someone who'd never matured properly due to abuse or neglect? Or one of those mutants who defy explanation?

If I was right about his wanting to humiliate law enforcement, he'd probably had run-ins with the cops and come out on the losing end.

An underachiever who'd overestimated his own intelligence, convinced himself his failures were someone else's fault.

Yet, for all that, a man sufficiently clever/smooth/innocuous to worm his way into Katherine Hennepin's apartment.

To stalk Ursula Corey in a basement parking lot without her suspecting anything until it was too late.

Shooting her in the face fit an ego run amok.

Look at me look at me look at me.

No shortage of attention whores in L.A. Showbiz and haute couture and politics wouldn't exist without them. But presidents and movie stars and supermodels get to flaunt themselves publicly. Our boy wasn't able to.

Or he'd tried and failed.

So he'd retracted like a venomous mollusk, concealed by a shell of anonymity?

A guy you wouldn't worry about if you saw him walking toward you.

If you noticed him at all.

Profound, Delaware. You are hereby christened the Grand Duke of Generic Psychological Guesswork.

After photocopying Katherine Hennepin's enlarged DMV photo, I showered, but didn't shave, put on a T-shirt, jeans, and sneakers, and drove to Century City.

Leaving the Seville in the pay lot of the office building directly across the street, I climbed the broad steps leading to the structure where Ursula Corey had died.

Rather than enter the lobby, I stood around, slightly left of center, studying the foot traffic in and out.

No spew of humanity, just a thin but steady parade of people looking purposeful.

I did my best to look aimless, figured clothes that didn't fit in would help. No one noticed or cared. The flow parted around me and resumed; I might as well have been a traffic cone.

Invisible man. Was that the way *he* felt all the time?

Maybe a smidge of odd behavior would help. I lowered my head, bobbed up and down, pretended to study at the ground, a loner caught up in a private world.

When that failed to raise a reaction, I looked up and altered my facial expression: sneering at the universe.

That caught the eye of a few people and made them frown and widen the berth they gave me. But no slowing of pace. Now I was a traffic cone soiled by dog shit.

Finally, a pair of young brunettes in short skirts muttered something that sounded cruel as they stilettoed past.

Then: more invisibility.

I supposed it made sense. Kids are taught not to stare and people are repelled by abnormality.

But maybe it was more than that. Because despite all the so-called social networks and the transitory clans they breed (the yoga community, the yogurt community, the Yogi Berra community), ultimately, we all drive solo. And that can lead to self-absorption.

More so in California where nice weather and cinematic promises of happy endings can erode any but the most passionate or paranoid person's sense of threat.

I'd just proven to myself how tough it was to get anyone to pay attention. Had that helped the killer take Ursula Corey?

Decked out in bling, she'd marched happily to her Jaguar, secure in the knowledge that she was rich and charismatic and sexy and therefore owned the world. Gladdened further by what she'd just accomplished: willing a whole bunch of shiny stuff to her daughters, how delighted they were when she told them, maybe the three of them would go out to dinner tonight to celebrate, something spontaneous, she'd pop it on them when she got back to Calabasas.

The last thing on her mind . . .

Easy pickings.

Satisfied there was nothing more to be learned here, I'd turned to leave when a fingertip poked my shoulder hard enough to hurt.

"Can I help you, pal?"

Rotating, I faced Alfred Bayless, wearing the same black blazer, gray pants, and white turtleneck and taking up a whole bunch of my personal space. Up close, the building's security chief smelled of Aqua Velva and ire. His nostrils flared. His pupils were dilated. Then he recognized me.

"Oh. Sorry, Doc. Noticed you hanging around but couldn't see who you were from a distance. What's going on?"

"I was doing some observation."

"Of what?"

"How people react to an outlier. You're the first person to pay me serious notice."

He frowned. "What, you're testing the system? Well, guess what, I saw you right away on the monitor, figured I'd watch you a bit, make sure you were actually a loony or a bum and not some rich dude in cheap clothes waiting for a big-shot lawyer, this is L.A., right? I mean no offense about the clothes."

"It had nothing to do with your system," I said. "I wanted to see—"

"Because maybe the fool who shot that lady hung out here? I could've saved you some time, Doctor. People don't see a damn thing. They're sheep." He smiled coldly. "So nothing's come up, huh?"

"Not yet."

"Sturgis must be growing an ulcer."

A trio of well-fed men in hand-stitched suits left the building. One of them, a silver-haired man in all black, eyed Bayless. Bayless had already spotted him.

Hard looks and curt salutes all around.

Bayless's mouth turned down as he watched them pass from view.

I said, "Looks like you're the exception."

"What do you mean?"

"You just got noticed."

"That's 'cause I'm so handsome," said Bayless. "No—off the record? Those guys are top brass. The one in the black silk Brioni manages big projects for the folks who own the building. The others work for him, they all flew in this morning for a security meeting."

"Big-time fun."

"Oh, yeah."

"Any progress?"

"In terms of getting some actual security?" Bayless laughed. "The plan is they go back to the über-boss and he consults personally with God and then there's a meeting about having a meeting and then it's shelved and reopened and maybe another set of meetings and who knows, Doctor, anything's possible . . . so nothing at all on Ms. Corey?"

"Wish there was."

"Well," he said, "tell Sturgis I haven't forgotten him. They may not be giving me cameras but I did manage to squeeze a couple of new hires out of them. Minimum-wage kids, no experience, but I have them patrolling the parking tiers."

"I'll relay the message."

Bayless ran a finger under the hem of his turtleneck. "I keep thinking about that poor woman. Ran the tapes a bunch of times myself. Level with me, Doc: Did you come here because you think we're high risk for a repeat?"

"No, just trying to figure out the bad guy's approach." I pulled out Katherine Hennepin's photo. "Ever see her here?"

He studied the image. "Nope. Who is she?"

"Another victim. She got killed somewhere else."

Bayless's eyes widened. "Same offender?"

"Could be."

"You think she was here?"

"Nothing links her to here," I said. "I'm trying to eliminate the possibility."

"No links at all?"

"Zero."

"You're a careful guy, Doctor, I heard that about Sturgis, too. Mr. Compulsive, figures he'd have someone like you doing psych work."

I smiled.

He gave the photo another look. Longer. No stranger to meticulousness, himself.

"Nope, never saw her. That's all I need, huh? Maniac lurking in the ductwork. Like a case back in New York, 'round forty years ago, when I was a kid. Lady violinist got raped and murdered in the Metropolitan Opera. Right in the building, place was a maze. My dad worked a shoeshine stand in Lincoln Center, he was always talking about it until they solved it. Perp was a stagehand, met her in the elevator."

He wiped sweat from his forehead. "Scared the hell out of me, Doc. I grew up in Harlem, dope shootings was one thing but sick stuff where the rich folk went? There was nothing to *aspire* to? That's when I decided to be law enforcement. Take some control of the situation."

He smiled. "I'm gabbing, need to get back to work."

I said, "Okay with you if I go inside for a sec?"

The smile disintegrated. "Free country, can't stop you, but what for?"

"Just to get a feel."

"I'm getting an *off* feeling, Doc. One moment you're telling me it's unlikely to have anything to do with the building. Now you're saying you need a feel."

"Frustration does that," I said.

"Does what?"

"Leads me to take the extra step."

Bayless rocked on his feet. His hands were huge, gnarled, curled into fists. "I guess I can relate to that, but do me a favor and don't make a big deal out of it, okay? They might be sheep but eventually someone's going to report a problem and problems have a way of finding their way to me."

11

I entered the lobby right after Bayless, hung back as he stepped into the lunchtime throng. Making sure he was nowhere in sight, I headed for the directory, used my phone to photograph the names of tenants sharing the seventh floor with Grant Fellinger's law firm.

Not much to shoot; another group of lawyers and a financial management company.

For all the people leaving for a midday meal, the line at the ground-floor snack bar was thin. I waited until no one was in line, went over and bought coffee, only yards from Bayless's office. Overpaying by two bucks, I said, "Keep the change," and showed Katherine Hennepin's picture to the pimply kid working the counter.

A guy in a T-shirt and jeans flashing a photo deserved an explanation but the kid just looked and said, "Nope. She a shoplifter?"

"Get a lot of them?"

The kid smiled slyly. "Like you don't know. Being a narc?"

"Me?" I said, grinning.

He grinned back. "Gonna bust someone?"

"Given the opportunity. So you don't know her?"

"Nope."

"Been having shoplifter problems?"

"You kidding? Turn your back and half the sugar packets are gone. Turn again and there's no ketchup." He huffed. "Rich people are cheap." Third look at Hennepin. "Yeah, she's definitely sketchy."

I returned to the center of the lobby swarm, mingling aimlessly as people eddied around me.

Something Bayless had said stuck with me. The murder at the opera.

Met her in the elevator.

No cameras in these elevators. What better place to hunt unobtrusively?

I got closer to the bank of lifts, watched doors open and close, disgorging hungry-looking folk. Some had their cigarette packs out in anticipation. The sound level rose. Or maybe that was just the noise in my head.

Nothing more to do here and no sense annoying Bayless. I made my way toward the exit.

Got that itchy feeling on the back of my neck.

Someone watching me? More likely, too much coffee and failure.

I half turned anyway. Saw nothing. Then I did.

A sudden shift as a man moved into the crowd quickly.

Not quick enough to avoid identification: Grant Fellinger trying to wedge his stocky frame into the throng. Hustling toward the elevators.

Had he been watching me? Even if he had, the explanation could be simple: recognizing me but not in the mood to deal with police business.

I resumed my exit, allowed myself a brief half turn.

Fellinger had turned also. Tight-faced. Fear? Anger? Both?

For a second, we locked eyes. Then he swiveled fast and showed me his back.

Not a phantom? A man who worked here, had good reason to be here?

A professional man who'd had a professional relationship with Ursula Corey? Far beyond professional if Richard Corey could be believed.

Who better to put a woman at ease as she walked to her car than her own lawyer? The man she'd come to see in the first place.

What bigger surprise than to see that man aiming a gun at her face?

No one—not the pretty receptionist in the black dress nor Fellinger's assistant—had mentioned Fellinger leaving the office with Ursula the morning of her murder. But bosses didn't check in or out and if the young woman had stepped away from her desk, who'd have known?

Sheep. Uncharitable appraisal of humanity but as I'd just seen, accurate.

I left the building, was talking on my phone by the time I got across the street.

Earl Cohen, Esq., had agreed to meet me in his office if I got there soon but when I arrived, his secretary said, "Mr. C.'s having lunch. Café Europa, it's next door."

"Café" turned out to be hype for a niche with a three-foot take-out counter on the ground floor of an adjoining medical building. Two young women in nurse's uniforms waited for packaged salads. The single eat-in table in the corner was occupied by Earl Cohen.

In bright light, the old man was a wax apparition in bespoke tailoring. Lunch was monastic: unflavored yogurt, plastic spoon, glass of water.

I sat down. Cohen waited for the nurses to leave before speaking. "What now, Dr. Delaware?"

"As I said the first time, Grant Fellinger spoke highly of you. First time I've heard that from an opposing attorney."

Cohen grinned. "Maybe I deserved the accolades."

"No doubt," I said. "But you weren't as enthusiastic about him."

"How uncharitable of me."

"Anything you can tell me about Fellinger would be helpful."

"You suspect him of having something to do with Ursula's death?" No trace of surprise.

"It's not at the level of suspicion but I find him interesting."

"Why?"

"For one thing, we've been told he was sleeping with his client."

Cohen smiled. "Which client, in particular?"

I smiled back. "It's like that, huh?"

"Well," said Cohen, "I've never heard of Grant going for men, but several female clients are reputed to have fallen under his charm. Such as it is."

"Legal lothario."

Cohen laughed. "Hard to understand, but so I've been told."

"This is common knowledge among your colleagues."

"Not common. The topic has come up a few times. Off the record and destined to remain that way. Including this conversation, Doctor. I'm too old for complications."

"Has anyone ever filed a harassment complaint against him?"

"Not that I've heard," said Cohen. He spooned yogurt. "Maybe he's a command performer, leaves the gals happy and sassy."

"What exactly have you heard?"

"Exactly? At my age, precision is out of the question. Approximately? Seeing as poor Ursula's dead? Anything's possible," said Cohen. "As long as it remains off the record."

He deposited yogurt on the tip of his spoon, treated himself to half a calorie. "Off the record means you keep it to yourself."

I shook my head. "Off the record means your name doesn't enter any official files. But anything relevant will be passed along to Lieutenant Sturgis."

"Well," said Cohen, "I appreciate your honesty, don't encounter it often in my line of work."

He fingered his tie. "You say you don't suspect Fellinger but you want to pry into his personal life."

"If it has to do with Ursula Corey."

He put down his spoon. "I don't know why I agreed to see you. I'm getting the distinct impression you're a young man who thrives on complications."

"Just the opposite, Mr. Cohen. My goal is always to simplify."

He studied me. "If you were a woman, I'd call you a yenta."

"Busybody's fine," I said. "And it's gender-neutral."

Cohen laughed loud enough to draw attention from the counterman. He finished with a wheeze, stroked the section of his neck that had been hollowed out. "For a psychologist, you're direct. Aren't you people all about nuance?"

"What I hear you saying is that your feelings could be explained by emotional factors but on the other hand . . ."

He laughed again. "Wise guy. Listen, I'm a geezer who's had two types of cancer and what the heck, what can anyone do to me? So here's the dirt: one day I noticed Grant's pudgy paw finding its way to Ursula's shapely buttocks when he thought no one was looking."

"Where did this happen?"

"In the elevator of his building. We were all riding down—Richard, Ursula, Grant, and myself—having finished a conference."

"Fellinger groped her with Richard right there."

"I imagine that was part of the thrill."

"How'd she react?"

"Tiny little smile."

"The meeting was in Fellinger's office, but he left too."

"He was *accompanying* Ursula," said Cohen. "Going the extra mile, a gal*lant*."

"But the real reason was sticking it to the ex. For both of them."

"That was my interpretation." He lifted a quivering hand, curled knobby fingers. "Not just a tap, he was squeezing her repetitively."

"And she was enjoying it."

"She smiled throughout the process," said Cohen. "The inescapable conclusion was a long-standing private joke. I realized Richard hadn't been blowing smoke when he claimed Fellinger was having his way with her all through the process."

Richard had claimed the same about Cohen. I said, "Thanks for the information. Anything else?"

"It offended me," said Cohen. "Not the sex part but the fact that Fellinger would breach professional ethics so baldly. I'm old-school, Dr. Delaware. Work is work, play is play."

"Did Richard ever tell you Ursula had cheated on him while they were married?"

"No, that was the point."

"The point of what?"

"I can't speak to their lives prior to the divorce but any sexual adventurousness on Ursula's part that he cited occurred only after the divorce. Therefore, I advised him to mind his own business."

"How'd he take that?"

"He said he understood intellectually but it made him sad. Ursula doing that to herself."

"Worrying about her welfare," I said. "A caring ex-husband."

Cohen took a dainty sip of water and got up shakily. "No more, Dr. Delaware."

I said, "Let me just clarify: Richard implied Ursula was somehow hurting herself by sleeping around."

Cohen pointed to the ceiling. "Time flies. I'm headed upstairs to see one of my doctors who will be of no use to me."

I phoned Milo.

He said, "Probably no big deal, but Darius Kleffer's back in L.A. No local address or car reg but he's been working at an Italian place called Beppo Bippo for around a month. Got that bit of wisdom by surfing the food blogs."

"He's that well known?"

"No, he posted the news himself on a site called *Big-Eyes Gourmandize*. I phoned the place, it's Kleffer's day off. Manager said he'd give Kleffer the message. If he doesn't, I'll go over there. What's up?"

"Got a suggestion for you."

"What?"

I told him.

He said, "Meet me in front of the station. Maybe we'll grab a snack."

12

The Seville had barely come to a stop when he flung the door open and hurled himself in. He landed hard. A truckload of flour sacks hitting the pier.

"Fellinger," he said. "He gave you that bad of a feeling?"

"I can't help thinking my being there upset him. And guess what, he's got a thing for elevators."

I repeated Cohen's account.

He said, "That couldn't be one lawyer getting back at another?"

"I had to pry it out of Cohen and he didn't enjoy telling the story."

"Escorting her," he said. "Then he decides to shoot her in the face? Why?"

"Maybe she knew something that threatened him," I said. "Or he's just that kind of guy. If he did Katherine Hennepin, he's definitely that kind of guy."

"Your basic homicidal psychopath with a good day job."

"Unfortunately not so basic," I said. "He's an intelligent man. Far from a hunk, in fact he's a conspicuously homely man. But despite that, he was able to charm a beautiful woman like Ursula into bed. Had the arrogance and confidence to play grab-ass with her ex standing a few feet away and know she'd go along with it and enjoy it. Someone like Katherine—shy, beneath him socioeconomically—would've been a snap. But conquest isn't enough. He needs to be the one who breaks off the relationship. Permanently. To put his brand on it by arranging dinner for two because that's his way of thumbing his nose at romance. At women, in general."

"I look like a troll but I rule."

"Looks aren't destiny, Big Guy, but they can be a factor growing up. Even toddlers rate their peers on attractiveness. All other things equal, cuter kids get treated better by children and adults."

"Tell me about it."

"Such self-pity," I said. "Rick showed me your high school yearbook. More all-American than troll."

"That was good lighting," he said. "He showed you the damn yearbook? Why? When?"

"One night when Robin and I were over for dinner. You were griping about something, big surprise, and when you went to the bathroom, Rick said you always claimed to be a big outcast and he used to believe you until he found the book. Varsity football and wrestling, ROTC, couple of honor societies. He had the page tabbed with a Post-it."

"He's always trying to convince me life rises above the dank bog of Irish doom." He snorted. "So that's Fellinger's defense? He was a poor little ape-boy? Sounds like the pop-psych stuff you hate."

"Not a defense, just trying to understand him."

"Because he avoided you in the lobby."

"No one else noticed me," I said, recounting the experience. "But he did and while I can't prove it, I think he made sure to avoid me. I know it's not much but what else do you have? The elevator grope combined sexuality, cruelty, and manipulation. Which is exactly the kind of person we're looking for. Cohen also felt it looked like a game that Fellinger and Ursula had played before. That shifted my perspective. I'd imagined the killer as an underachiever. Someone who viewed himself as brilliant but fell well short of success. Fellinger's an out-wardly successful man but feelings of inadequacy can come from all sorts of places."

"He's got dough and prestige, snags babes like Ursula. So what, he's working through his childhood? Even if, how does Hennepin fig-ure in, seeing as there's nothing connecting her to Fellinger?"

"If she visited Fellinger's building, she figures in nicely. I photoed down his co-tenants on the seventh floor. If we can tie her to any of them, it's a big step."

I showed him the snaps.

"You've been a busy lad."

"Anything for a friend."

He breathed in deeply. "Ape-Man Meets the Accountant. Speaking of which." He phoned Katherine Hennepin's bosses. They were in, agreed to meet. Again.

RM-Accu Accounting operated out of a storefront on Woodman just south of Magnolia. Their strip-mall neighbors were four ethnic restau-rants: Mexican, Thai, Israeli, Lebanese. Each one seemed to be thriv-ing, with lines forming outside entrances.

What if food really was love and world peace could be a reality?

The firm was a fifteen-by-fifteen room set up with three desks and half a dozen file cabinets. Interior design consisted of flyers spelling out IRS small-print regulations; surrealism for the twenty-first century.

Ralph Gross boomed, "What, you expected Ernst and Young?"

It sounded like something he said all the time. Milo's weak smile confirmed that.

Ralph was in his eighties, tall and thickset with a hound-dog mien. Maureen looked to be slightly younger with a pie-face and rosy cheeks.

She said, "Lieutenant, nice to see you again. You brought a hand-some friend."

Milo said, "This is Alex Delaware."

"You're lieutenant but he's first-name basis?" said Ralph. "We talking a civilian? Something you don't want to tell us?"

Clever man attuned to details; this might turn out to be useful.

Milo laughed. "Sorry, it's Dr. Delaware. He's our consulting psychologist."

"Yours, as in he works *for* you? Or he's a Hessian—a freelance."

"Freelance."

"Really," said Ralph Gross. To me: "That must be interesting, Dr. Hessian."

Maureen said, "A psychologist! I knew it! You think we're nuts!"

Milo said, "Hardly, ma'am. I'd like to talk to you again about Katherine."

"Kathy was killed by a nut?"

"We're exploring all possibilities."

"Love how you avoid a direct answer," said Ralph. "You could work for the government."

Maureen said, "He already does."

Ralph said, "I meant the geniuses in Washington . . . but yeah, you are a civil servant. I hear you people get great pensions. Part of the reason the state's going broke but heck, don't feel guilty."

Milo said, "Thank you, sir."

"Hope you're investing it wisely."

"Doing my best."

"If you have any pension questions—simple ones—call and I'll shoot you a freebie, Lieutenant. Show of appreciation, and all that. You may not have solved the case but at least you take the job seriously."

Maureen said, "We were certain it was that maniac chef but you insisted no."

"He was definitely in New York, ma'am."

"Too bad. What a nut." To me: "You should've seen him in action. Crazy."

"Nasty temper," said Ralph. "He barged in here twice, trying to bully Katherine. Demanding she talk with him. The first time, he left quietly. The second time I had to get in his face, as the kids say." He rolled up his sleeve, revealing a hairless but bulky forearm. *Semper Fi USMC* tattoo.

Maureen said, "I thought they'd come to blows. That wasn't smart, Ralph."

"He got the hell out of here, didn't he? Okay, so what do you want to know, now, Lieutenant? And Dr. Psychologist."

Milo said, "Could you describe Katherine's job for us?"

"Her job?" said Ralph. "She was a bookkeeper. She kept books."

"For any particular client?"

"For anyone we told her. We do the returns but she collated and filed the data. To some it might sound boring but Kathy was very happy here. She was a good employee."

Milo read off the address of the building on Century Park East. "Do any of your clients have offices there?"

"Century City?" said Maureen. "We do mostly individual accounts. A few small businesses but nothing fancy-shmancy."

"That crap is too rich for our blood," said Ralph. "Like sugar diabetes; you indulge but you pay. We had enough of the Big Four, met at Ernst, left that world forty years ago. Why're you asking about Century City?"

Milo avoided an answer. "Did Katherine run errands for you?"

"What, like gofering?" said Ralph. "No, her value was sitting right there." He pointed to the left-most desk. "Excellent employee, we've replaced her with a girl who comes in part-time. Good enough but Kathy was better."

Milo said, "So she never left the office."

Maureen said, "Never? That I wouldn't say. Occasionally she'd go out for us. Infrequently."

Milo said, "For what?"

"Picking up lunch next door at Thai Temple, they get an A from the health department. Sometimes we're in the mood for Mexican but we don't like Don Pepe since they got a C, so she'd drive to La Fiesta Buffet on Fulton."

Ralph said, "Mo, they don't care about our eating habits. Once in a blue moon, we'd ask her to deliver papers to a client."

"Nothing in Century City."

Maureen said, "I don't think so . . ."

Ralph barked, "What, Mo?"

"Remember that lawsuit, honey?"

"Be specific, Mo."

"That landlord, the Iranian—Hooranian, Hoorapian?"

"Frivolous," said Ralph.

"Sure was," said Maureen, "but weren't the other side's attorneys in Century City?"

"Heartless developers," said Ralph. "Who remembers?"

Milo said, "What was the lawsuit about?"

Maureen said, "Clients of ours, the Hoor—no Har—the Hargarians, that's it, the Hargarians, a nice couple, they owned a couple apartment buildings in North Hollywood, some developer bought up the rest of the block, tried to force them to sell by going to the city claiming they were neglecting the property, causing a public nuisance."

"Frivolous," Ralph repeated. "And nasty."

I said, "What was the outcome?"

"What do you think? The bastards made life miserable for the Hargarians and they sold."

Maureen said, "I think the other side's lawyers *were* in Century City. Or maybe it was the developers. Ralph and I only got involved at the end, when they were negotiating the terms of the sale, the other side wanted a look at tax records to verify rental income."

"Katherine Hennepin delivered the records?"

"I'm not saying that, Lieutenant, I'm only saying it's possible."

Ralph Gross said, "I didn't deliver them and you didn't."

"True," said Maureen.

"Who does that leave, Mo?"

Maureen said, "Hold on," and began tapping computer keys. "Hmm, nothing on Hargarian . . . no listing for Hargarian."

Ralph said, "You probably got the name wrong."

Maureen silenced him with an outstretched palm. Tap tap tap. "Here it is, three months ago . . . *Shagrarian* . . . ah, yes, three hours' billing for Katherine's services—ah, I remember, she was so sweet, she volunteered but I insisted on including it on her hours worked."

She beamed. "Maybe I could be a detective, Lieutenant."

"Apply and I'll give you a recommendation," said Milo.

Ralph said, "Why the dickens is this building so important?"

Maureen said, "Obviously dark deeds are going on there."

They both looked at Milo.

Milo said, "Let's leave it at that."

"Oh c'mon," said Ralph.

"It's probably nothing sir, just being careful."

"Ha. You'll probably never want to retire, the job being so juicy and all."

"Good for him, retirement is death," said Maureen.

"More like death is a *form* of retirement," said Ralph. "Still, that pension's something to think about." Squinting at Milo. "At your age."

Milo said, "Who specifically did Kathy deliver the papers to?"

Maureen tapped some more. "Says here Dublin Development." She copied down the name and handed it to Milo.

"Thanks so much, Mrs. Gross."

"You bet, Lieutenant."

Ralph said, "Thank us by solving the case. And think about this: The Shagrarians retired. She worked for Warner Brothers, had a good pension."

Dublin Development occupied a quarter of the ninth floor of Grant Fellinger's building.

I said, "She rides down after delivering the papers, it stops at seven,

Fellinger gets on, works his charm. Be good to know if any other women in the building had the same experience."

"If they did, it didn't end the same way. One of the first things I looked into when I worked Hennepin was to check for any other nasty cases with a food connection. Lots of domestic violence goes down in the kitchen—heat, knives, not enough salt in the stew. Mostly assaults, but I found a few homicides. Including an idiot who shotgunned his wife because she cooked liver for dinner and while he used to like it, he'd changed his mind. But nothing unsolved and nothing remotely similar."

"Maybe dinner for two was a later development."

"And?"

"And the crucial link is still the building. Women who worked there or visited."

He stared at the paper with Dublin's address. Phoned Binchy and said, "This will not be a fun job, kid, but if anyone's up for it you are." He outlined the parameters. "You can start with the computer but don't stop there because we're not talking actual crime scenes, it's not likely to make it into the computer. You need to talk personally to the Hom lieutenants at every division and see if they remember anything related to the damn place or can send you to someone who does. A work address, visiting someone who's got an office . . . what's that? . . . I'm glad, Sean. Everyone has their own definition of fun."

As we crossed Mulholland and began the descent to the city, he said, "I know I've been a bear, but thanks for the help. It's getting weirder but at least it's getting somewhere."

"What's next?"

"You enjoy life and I take a crash course on the life and times of Grant Fellinger."

His phone played Grieg. "Sturgis . . . oh, hi . . . thanks . . . sure . . . yeah . . . be there right now."

I said, "Change of plans?"

"That was Darius Kleffer, the maniac chef. Sounded kind of quiet, actually. Happy to meet, anything to help."

"Where and when?"

"His place of employment. Hungry?"

"You mentioned a snack."

"That was then, this is now. It's gone way beyond snack. Agree?"

"Sure."

"Yeah, right," he said. "Iron-clad self-control. Don't worry about it, we all have our failings."

13

The latest big thing restaurants in L.A. cluster like spores on Third Street, Beverly Boulevard, and Melrose. Beppo Bippo was converted from a former Chinese laundry on Beverly just west of La Brea. I knew the history because back when I'd worked at Western Pediatric Medical Center, I'd drop off or pick up fluff and fold.

Milo said, "Beppo, the comic book monkey."

"Don't know that one."

"Oh, yeah, real cute. Mr. Fellinger could've picked up beauty tips from him." A beat. "It's also a poem by Byron."

I whistled. "No kidding."

He said, "Hey, the master's degree's pretty much useless except for crosswords and I hate crosswords."

"American lit leads you to Byron?"

"Okay, you found me out, once upon a time I read all kinds of books—pull over there in the yellow, I'll put my card on the window. You get ticketed, I'll tell them we both have advanced degrees."

◆

Back in laundry days, Mr. and Mrs. Chang had dressed up the dismal space with travel posters and photos of celebrities. Whoever had occupied it since hadn't done much to remedy crumbling brick walls, cracked cement floors, clumsily taped AC ducting snaking across raw wood ceilings.

Why bother in the age of lowered expectations?

A trio of black-garbed chefs worked frantically in an open kitchen to the rear. Tables and chairs looked to be castoffs from an inner-city school. It was midafternoon, an off period between lunch and dinner, but every seat was occupied by people working at edgy with varying degrees of success.

Drinking, feasting, and chattering competed with the passionate kissing of air and occasionally flesh. All those hard surfaces created a sea of noise as Milo and I made our way through narrow aisles created by sardine-pack ambience. Plates were small, portions Haute Scrooge. What looked like a mix of Italian and Japanese. Maybe some French thrown in.

Milo muttered something.

I said, "What?" and he cupped his hand over my ear and raised his voice. "Crudo meets sushi."

"Meets Godzilla," I said.

He laughed. Then we got closer to the kitchen and he turned serious.

A black-clad female server stood opposite each of the three chefs. None of the women was tall and it was easy to peer over them.

The chefs were men. One was hefty with a rabbinic beard tucked into a snood-like net and long hair balled up and crammed into a greasy black Stetson. The other two were thin guys with sunken cheeks sporting Mohawks. Blue spikes in the center position, black to the right.

Darius Kleffer's DMV shot matched Black. But Blue could've passed.

Kleffer spotted us, held up a delaying palm and kept working. Chop chop dice dice; a plate was shoved at one of the waitresses, who danced off to serve. Curly bit of shrimp spooning with a tiny crescent of foie gras. The pâté's illegal to manufacture in California but you can still import it, goose and ducks be damned.

Wiping his hands on a towel, Kleffer stepped from behind the counter, already smoking an unfiltered cigarette.

He said, "Outside, okay? We got no open tables."

We followed him through the restaurant. A few diners tried to catch his eye, students seeking the teacher's approval. Kleffer ignored them, head pushed forward like a battering ram. He caught ash in his palm and managed to carry most of it outside. By the time we reached the sidewalk, two-thirds of his smoke had been sucked down and he chain-lit another before pinching out the glowing end with bare fingers. Brief sizzle of simmering skin; it didn't seem to bother him.

Ducking into a cut between the restaurant and a perennially going-out-of-business Italian furniture store, he leaned against a grubby wall. "I litter, okay?" Ash and the dead butt sailed to the ground.

"Okay," he repeated. He had a soft voice designed for apology, bloodshot brown eyes, a face blanketed with two days' of spotty gray beard and some sort of accent, probably Northern European. His left arm was ink from knuckles to above his biceps. The right one was clear. Plenty of pinholes in both ears, but no jewelry in evidence.

Milo said, "Thanks for meeting with us on short notice."

Darius Kleffer said, "Sure. Sorry I didn't answer the first time." Downward glance.

"You were in New York."

"I still could've answered your calls." Head shake, twitch of jaw. "It was too hard. Sorry."

"Talking about Katherine."

"Yeah." His cheek twitched.

"Ready to talk about her now?"

"I guess."

"As I told you, we haven't solved it. So anything you know that could help us would be appreciated."

"I wish," said Kleffer. "Sorry for not answering the first time. Really."

"No need to apologize, Mr. Kleffer."

"I know, I know—I guess I want to show you I'm no asshole. Even if you heard things about me."

"From who?"

"Anyone who sees me when I'm drinking. When I drink, I'm a total asshole. When I don't drink I think I'm a pretty much okay guy."

Looking to us for validation.

Milo said, "Do you drink often?"

"Most of my life," said Kleffer. "When I was with Kathy, I stayed clean and sober. Then I moved to New York and got back into it heavy. It's the lifestyle, but no excuses. I made a big mess of myself a bunch of times."

Milo looked at me.

I said, "What would you like us to know about Katherine?"

Kleffer reached for another cigarette. "To know? She was a great girl. A nice girl. Shy but very sweet."

"How'd the two of you meet?"

Kleffer lit up. "Why would she go for a freak like me? You tell me, I never really figured it out but I didn't complain about it." Deep drag. Wet eyes. "You need to know this: I loved her."

Milo said, "We need to know because . . ."

"I don't know why I said that. I guess . . . I don't know what I'm saying, guys, okay?" He looked to the side. "This is embarrassing, man. I told myself don't wimp out in front of the cops, but . . ." He patted his chest. "The feelings, you know? I been pushing them aside. Now that I'm clean and sober again, they punch me hard."

I gave him time to smoke. "So where'd you and Kathy meet?"

He smiled. "Oh, yeah, that question. At a restaurant. Funny, no?"

"You were working?"

"No," said Kleffer. "I was eating. Thai food, there was a little strip-mall place near where she worked. I was in the Valley to pick up provisions and saw it and said what the hell."

"Slumming," said Milo.

"No, no, freaks who cook fancy for other people like to eat simple. Go into any Michelin star place after closing and check out what everyone's eating. Bread, soup, a burger."

I said, "Getting away from complexity."

"Yes, yes, exactly. So that's where I met Katherine. I was eating pad Thai and she was eating something with green curry and too much lemongrass, I could smell it from my table. Our tables were close, she was pretty—not in the hottie way, like . . . what I used to see in village girls in Germany. Natural, you know? I didn't look so freaky, had a skinned head, but none of this Mo-Joke." Ruffling the black spikes. "I should cut this shit off . . . anyway, I started talking to her, asked for her number and she surprised me by giving it. But the rest is not history."

Milo said, "Why not?"

"I called her the next day, she said no thank you. She didn't want to be rude but she had second thoughts, we didn't have enough in common. I was bummed but I admired her for being brave."

"Brave how?"

"I mean she could've just not answered the phone, right? Couple times, you give up. I was surprised she gave me the number in the first place. I am not every mother's dream."

Milo said, "So what happened?"

"I kept trying," said Kleffer. "Not crazy stalking—I waited a week, then another. Why? I can't tell you exactly, but something about her. She was different from the freaky chicks I meet at work. Old-fashioned, you know? Maybe it reminded me of my family, I don't know. Solid people, my grandparents have a farm . . . I don't know, who ever knows why you do things?"

I said, "So you kept calling."

"And each time Kathy answered and we talked and that encouraged me to keep trying, maybe be more of a normal guy." Kleffer laughed. "I grew out what hair I have, kind of a straight-dude look, you know? I figured if I ever got to see her again I'd wear long sleeves." Rubbing his inked arm. "I don't know why I did all this shit to myself in the first place."

I said, "How many calls did it take before she said yes?"

"Four. I took her to a chamber music concert, then to a straight-guy steak house, nothing radical. We had fun talking, there was rapport, you know? I dropped her off and was okay with a cheek kiss. Eventually, it got more . . . we got involved."

"Until . . ."

"Until Kathy broke it off. Why? Can't tell you that, either." Kleffer smoked, coughed, looked at the cigarette and shook his head and murmured, "Killing myself . . . after she dumped me, I went back to drinking, to being my asshole shithead self. I even went to her work to try to convince her to come back, she works for old people, I thought they'd have heart attacks but thank God they didn't. Thank God Kathy didn't file a complaint for stalking. I already had a couple of problems—losing my temper in bars. But you probably know that."

Milo said, "How many times did you go to her office?"

"Just twice—I know, that's two more times than right. I kept calling her, wanting to know why." His eyes grew moist.

I said, "Did you ever get an answer?"

"She never came out and said it but there was another guy, had to be."

"Why?"

"She started acting different. No time to hang out, too busy. She wasn't nasty about it, just . . . when I was with her, she wasn't really there. Like she was seeing me different. And when I asked her if there was someone else, she never said yes or no, just changed the subject."

"Did you try to find out who he was?"

"We have to get into that?"

I smiled.

"Okay, okay," said Kleffer. "Did I drive by her place a few times? Yeah, yeah, sure. I was drinking, there was like a big hole, you know? In my heart, guys, in my brain. Then I heard about a TV pilot, being on a team with Mr. Luong, he's a fucking genius. So I fly to New York, apply cold, get the gig and work a million hours and forget about women, including Kathy."

He looked at Milo. "Then one night I get home late, listened to my messages, there's that one from you. Homicide cop? Kathy? I just fell apart, man. When I started with Mr. Luong, I went clean and sober. I listen to your message, I'm right back on the Jack." Insipid smile. "Good American booze. Patriotic, no? I knew it was getting totally out of control. Maintaining my knife skills and sucking the bottle. I tried to stop suddenly, ended up in the E.R. at Bellevue with a detox reaction, they said I could've died. I said fuck the rent and got evicted, slept on couches, finally got this gig and came back."

"Everything going okay?"

"You mean drinking?" Kleffer crossed his fingers. "So you don't know who killed my Kathy?"

Milo said, "Not yet."

"Not yet," said Kleffer. "American optimism. You guys believe in the future, that's why Americans invent all the good stuff."

"Is there anyone who might want to hurt Kathy?"

"No one. She was a nice girl." Kleffer bent a knee and scuffed the wall with one clog. "Obviously, someone didn't agree with that, but who? I can't tell you."

"Did you introduce her to any of your friends?"

"What, you think some freak killed her?"

"We're looking into every possibility."

Kleffer grimaced. "Okay, sure, but no, we didn't socialize with anyone from my work. I wanted to keep her away from freaks, didn't want to share her with anyone. She calmed me down, I liked being alone with her."

I said, "The man you figured she was dating. Any ideas about him?"

"Ideas?" said Kleffer. "Yeah. He outclassed me." Barking laugh. "Not too hard, right? I figured it was money, prestige, a nice car, all the stuff women like."

"Did she say something about that?"

"No; she never admitted seeing anyone but I figured. Because I *didn't* have all the good stuff and she dumped me."

"How'd she do it?"

Kleffer grimaced. "She called me and said I'd been a great friend, she'd enjoyed our time together but she needed for it to end."

"She used the word 'need'?"

Kleffer thought. "I'm pretty sure that's how she put it. I see what you're saying, the asshole pressured her. She also said she wanted stability in her life and I told her I could provide stability. Kathy didn't argue, she just kept quiet and that was even worse."

"Dismissing the idea."

"Knowing the idea was bullshit but too polite to say so," said Kleffer. "It kind of drove home how she outclassed me."

I said, "Stability."

"Chicks want that."

Milo said, "Most people want that."

"Yeah, sure. Maybe even I want it, who knows?" Kleffer looked at the ground. "Can I ask what exactly happened to her?"

"We're keeping the details confidential right now."

"Oh. Yeah, sure. I just hope she didn't suffer a lot."

I said, "Would Kathy let a stranger into her apartment?"

Kleffer straightened his leg. "She let him in?"

"That surprises you."

"I was thinking some scumbag broke in to steal something and got crazy."

"Why's that?" said Milo.

"Because that's what happens mostly, right?"

Neither of us replied.

Kleffer said, "It didn't happen that way?"

Milo said, "There was no sign of forced entry."

Kleffer pressed his back to the wall and began sliding down. Lowering himself several inches, he lost balance and forced himself upright. "She let some asshole in? Oh God, I used to tell her be more careful."

"She was careless?"

"Not like crazy reckless, more like, don't go shopping by yourself at night. You need stuff, tell me and I'll pick it up for you. I also said get an alarm, you're a chick living alone. She said thanks for caring, I'm fine. You're telling me she let someone in. Fuck! The new guy? Maybe I should've found out who the hell he was."

Milo said, "At this point, I wouldn't jump to conclusions, sir."

"She let him the fuck in," said Kleffer. He punched stucco. Bloody speckles rose on his knuckles, dark dew. He wiped his hand on his apron. Fresh red human stain mixed with the blood of other species. "*Stupid* girl."

14

Darius Kleffer returned to work, plodding slowly and smoking and rubbing his hand.

Milo and I lingered in the alley. He said, "Any thoughts besides he's a litterbug?"

"We know he didn't kill Kathy Hennepin himself and I don't see him hiring out. Plus, he's not someone Ursula would likely be attracted to."

"So total waste of time."

I said, "Maybe not. His suspicions about another man could dovetail with Fellinger getting together with Kathy."

"Someone to provide stability."

"A Century City lawyer would fit the bill."

"You don't see that as Kleffer's low self-esteem? When he drinks he gets low."

"It's possible," I said. "But Kleffer's reasoning makes sense. Right from the start he and Kathy made an odd couple. She resisted him, finally gave in but eventually she went back to being a conventional woman with conventional tastes. Maybe because an older lawyer flirted with her in the elevator of a high-rent office building. Someone self-confident and worldly and smooth around the edges, talk about the anti-Kleffer."

His turn to kick the wall. "And hell, maybe he even cooks."

"Catering to her every need."

"It's still a long way from evidence," he said. "But like you said, what else do I have? Let's learn more about the monkey-man."

Back at the station, we detoured for toxic coffee in the big detective room and headed for Milo's closet-sized, solitary-confinement office. While he logged onto his email, I pushed the spare chair into a corner and checked my messages. Robin saying hi, no need to call. I stepped out into the hall, anyway, and took a vacation from ugly. Hearing about her day, divulging as little of mine as possible, planning dinner at home, the two of us grilling hanger steaks.

"Wine?" she said. "Or we stay clearheaded?"

"No payoff in clear," I said.

"Because no progress?"

"Something like that."

"No sense getting into it?"

"I'll tell you over wine."

Reentering the windowless cell, I found Milo working his desktop with the grim concentration of a truant kid video-zapping alien spacecraft.

His targets: the criminal files, local and NCIC.

Nothing on Grant Fellinger.

DMV gave up three moving traffic violations in as many years, two near Fellinger's office, one less than a mile west on Santa Monica Boulevard near Westwood. Two vehicles, a BMW 6 series and a vintage Dodge Challenger. Same offense each time: incomplete stop.

Milo said, "Man in a hurry. That mean something psychologically?"

"If I could answer that with a straight face I'd have a talk show."

"Dr. Alex," he said. "Dispensing folksy wisdom and tough love in between commercials for reverse mortgages . . . onward, here are his real estate records . . . he's got a house in the Palisades . . . not real close to Hennepin's apartment but not that far, either, he gets the urge, easy enough to booty-call and drop over."

"Booty-calls would've meant phone calls between Kathy and him."

His mouth worked. He checked the Hennepin murder book, just in case. Slammed it shut. "Zilch. So what, he just drops in, joy of spontaneity and all that? She's impressed by him, rich confident guy, making her feel *stable*. Which to her also means safe, she leaves the door unlocked for him."

"So he can tote in the evening's refreshments."

"With all that, you'd expect someone to notice, Alex. But like I said, the only guy anyone ever saw go in and out was Kleffer."

I said, "Kleffer's hard to miss. A middle-aged guy arriving after dark wouldn't be. Or for most of their trysts they used Fellinger's place, not Kathy's. Any record of a second home?"

"Little fun pad for ol' Grant? I like it." He typed.

His enthusiasm was short-lived. No other real estate listings in L.A., Ventura, Orange, or San Bernardino counties under Fellinger's name, his family trust, or his law firm. He turned away from the screen.

"Doesn't rule out rentals, but no way to uncover that. Or maybe ol' Grant likes hotels. Where would you start? Four-star or easy-sleazy? Either way, unless he used his own name, forget it."

I said, "If he over-plied his charm at work, perhaps a female employee complained about him."

He logged onto the criminal court docket, found nothing and tried the civil suit roster. Sitting back heavily enough to make his chair wheeze, he pointed at the screen.

No one had complained about Grant Fellinger but just under a month ago, he'd filed harassment charges against a woman named Deirdre Mae Brand. No further details.

Milo looked Brand up. No driver's license, no address. "He goes after a phantom?"

"If we're right about Fellinger, his thing is controlling women. The fact that this woman threatened him enough for him to sue, could mean she managed to intimidate him."

"Scary lady?"

"Scary enough. See if anyone else has ever filed on her and if that doesn't work, check for a criminal history."

Deirdre Mae Brand, age forty-nine, had an extensive multistate record for vagrancy, theft, larceny, and drug possession. The chronology of her arrests was as good as a road map: westward trajectory through Illinois, Missouri, New Mexico, Nevada.

Nothing violent, but people do things they never get caught for.

One way or the other, Fellinger and Brand had developed an explosive chemistry.

My bet was their clash had occurred at or close to Fellinger's office building, because Deirdre Brand's most recent arrest had been for attempted shoplifting at a nearby boutique in Century City. Two months before Fellinger lodged his complaint.

Milo searched for records on the lawsuit, found no trial date assigned, no settlement.

"He's a lawyer and he just folds his tent?"

"The complaint could've been enough to scare her off," I said. "Scroll back to Brand's arrest record."

That revealed a pattern: Brand had always been released with no charges or after spending a night or two in local jails. Not a single day in prison.

Milo said, "She's got charm of her own?"

"Or she has reason to be pitied."

"Such as?"

"Mental illness."

Pulling up Deirdre Brand's mug shots created a sad photo-tour.

At nineteen she'd been a fresh-faced towhead busted for marijuana. But even back then, she'd worn a numbed expression emphasized by flat, hostile eyes, with none of the fear you'd expect at a first arrest. Meaning she'd had previous run-ins with the law that never got to the point of arrest.

Or her affect was blunted by psychiatric disease.

By twenty-five, she'd aged freakishly fast, shedding enough teeth to collapse her face. In the final photo, thirty years into her criminal career and not yet fifty, she was withered and drawn with a misshapen hatchet face, bony where it wasn't bloated and topped by a bird's-nest of wild white hair. A roseate glow seemed to incandesce her skin, the gloss that comes from years of living on the streets.

A different variety of flatness in her eyes now: a locked-ward vacancy I'd seen so many times.

Forty-nine; I'd have pegged her at seventy.

Milo said, "No address 'cause she's homeless. She looks pathetic, Alex. This is who scared Fellinger?"

"Maybe I was wrong and she just became a nuisance he couldn't get rid of."

"We're trying to make Fellinger a psychopath killer. Why wouldn't he fix his problem the old-fashioned way?"

"Who says he didn't?"

"Oh, Jesus."

He began the tortuous search for the paperwork on Fellinger's complaint. A challenge because cases that don't go to trial are non-events that can get discarded or filed in obscure places or simply lost. Finally, he received a verbal summary from a law student intern at the city attorney's office.

He hung up. "You're right, it happened at the shopping mall west of Fellinger's building. He was lunching there and Ms. Brand was a frequent panhandler and chronic pain in the ass. The loitering laws have pretty much been destroyed by court decisions so unless she got physically aggressive there wasn't much mall security could do. Her problem with Fellinger occurred after she'd cadged change out of other people but not him. Words were exchanged and he claims she tried to hit him, though no one else verifies that. He made a citizen's arrest, put her down on the ground to do it, and confined her until the real cops showed up. D.A. refused to file criminally so Fellinger went the civil route, claiming Brand had exhibited 'conspicuous socially hazardous behavior.' That mean something to you?"

"She bothered him."

"Ha. Brand spent forty-eight hours in County psychiatric and was released. She never showed up for preliminary hearings and Fellinger eventually dropped his complaint."

"She irks him enough for a citizen's arrest, then he develops a soft heart?"

"I don't like the smell of it, either."

Deirdre Brand's name was nowhere to be found in any division's victim roster nor at the crypt on South Mission Road.

Milo said, "Woman like that would be the perfect throwaway, she could be anywhere."

I said, "Unless he reverted to type and left her out in the open to brag."

"Along with dinner for two?"

"Maybe fastfood," I said. "Social ranking and all that."

15

B y the time I was ready to leave Milo's office, he'd set his priorities.

No sense searching for a mentally ill homeless woman who could be anywhere. And though he still wasn't convinced Grant Fellinger was his killer, the lawyer would be the focus of a three-man surveillance carried out by himself, Binchy, and Reed.

"Kiss the woman, pet the pooch, enjoy the steaks." He turned toward his monitor.

I said, "How about a copy of Deirdre Brand's last mug shot?"

"You planning to look for her yourself?"

"If time permits."

"How?"

"Don't know yet."

"Your educational level, you could be spending time more profitably." But he pressed the *Print* button.

That night, in my office, I organized my own priorities. During holidays and sometimes at random times, Robin and I deliver food and clothing to homeless people too independent or paranoid to enter shelters and soup kitchens, so I knew some of the places where the forgotten congregate.

Communicating with psychotic people can be tortured, and for all its affluence, the Westside of L.A. has too many fetid hideouts to canvass in a week. But I figured I'd start with a few freeway underpasses, see where that led.

The following morning, just as I was about to let Robin know I was leaving, I thought of something: Milo had searched the coroner's records for a file under Deirdre Brand's name. But people like her didn't carry I.D.

If her corpse had come into the crypt unidentified, a check of the fingerprint database could've pulled up a match to her arrest records. But when the bodies pile up, steps can be overlooked.

I phoned a friendly face at the coroner's, an investigator named Gloria Mendez. She said, "Hi, Alex, I'm out in the field. Literally, vacant lot in East L.A., billowing weeds, looks like Kansas in *The Wizard of Oz*."

"Gang shooting?"

"Good guess. Fifteen-year-old nails a sixteen-year-old because the other kid had the nerve to live two blocks south. What's up?"

I told her.

She said, "No, we always run prints. With a criminal record, we'd know who she is."

"Okay, thanks."

"On the other hand, I don't want to give you false hope but sometimes even when matches do come up they don't make it into the files immediately, all the backlog. The person to call is Martha Shisick. I don't have her extension offhand but she's always at her desk."

"Thanks for the tip. How do you spell Shisick?"

"Not sure, she's got lots of consonants. But if you log onto our site then onto Records, she'll be listed. If you catch her in a mood, use my name."

◆

Senior Data Processor Martha P. Szcyszcyk listened to my request without interruption then answered guardedly. "Gloria said to use her name to butter me up, huh?"

"She did."

"Let me get this straight: You're a civilian psychologist, not part of Behavioral Sciences."

I began to explain my relationship with Milo.

"Sounds complicated," she said. "I know who Sturgis is. If I call him, he'll verify you?"

"Absolutely."

"Hold on . . . okay, here you are. He logged you in last year as an authorized recipient of data."

"Great."

"Doesn't look as if you tried to access anything—oops, my bad, access was limited to a single case, unfortunately you're expired, Doctor."

Interesting way to put it, given her job. I said, "If you would call him—"

"Hey," said Szcyszcyk, "he liked you once, he probably still does, and you're not exactly asking for state secrets. Give me a name and some stats on this vic."

I rattled off basics on Deirdre Brand. "She's forty-nine but looks much older so she may be described as elderly."

"Most of them do," she said. "When do you figure she came in?"

"Within the past month or two."

"That's a big range but seeing as she's Caucasian, it narrows it down."

She put me on hold. One salsa version of "Hey Jude" later, she was back on. "No one by that name but I've got two possible Jane Does for you. One has no teeth at all, one has a few."

"Where were they found?"

"City of Industry and Santa Monica."

"Where in Santa Monica?"

"Questions, questions, questions . . . Douglas Park on Wilshire. Died at night, morning cleanup crew found her."

The beach city bordered West L.A. Division but was outside of Milo's jurisdiction. I said, "Cause of death?"

"Blunt force trauma to the head, manner is listed as undetermined."

"Blunt force but not a homicide?"

"Undetermined," she repeated. "Can't tell you why."

"Was there food at the scene?"

"Pardon?"

"Any sign she was eating a meal?"

"That wouldn't be in here, Doctor. Do you have a last known address for your Ms. Brand? I could plug it in and try to cross-reference."

"None, longtime homeless," I said. "She does have a record so when you ran AFIS, I'd expect—"

"She's on AFIS? So why are we even bothering?" said Szcyszcyk.

"I've heard sometimes it takes a while for I.D.'s to be logged."

"Have you? Yeah, well, I wish that wasn't true but . . . uh-oh, hold the hearse. Says here we tried to print the body but couldn't 'cause her fingertips were eroded."

"From what?"

"Doesn't say. But it happens more often than you'd think. My mother, she's in her eighties, likes to travel, tried to get one of those Global Entry Passes, make her life easier at passport control. They kept trying to pull up usable prints, couldn't, so when she flies in, she still has to report in person. You see it more in older people, stuff wears out. Also in folks who've lived hard, been exposed to the elements, like your vic. Musicians, too—guitarists, they can really alter their fingers. It's worse with computer scans, when you ink up manually you have better luck, but obviously that didn't help with Ms. Santa Monica. Now that I've got her name I can go backward, start with her prints on file and see if the computer will accept fewer points of agreement. That happens, I'll phone you—better yet, I'll tell Sturgis. Bye, Doctor."

"One more question. Who at Santa Monica PD picked up the case?"

"Says here Detective A. Barrios."

"Do you have a number?"

She read it off.

"Thanks."

"Hey, it's in my best interest," said Szcyszcyk. "I hate sending Does to the crematorium, anytime we clear one, it's a good thing."

Detective Augustin Barrios had a deep, mellow voice and the speech cadence of a man resistant to excitement.

I began by running through my credentials just as I'd just done with Martha Szcyzcyk. Barrios said, "That's great, working with a psychologist. What can I do for you, Doctor?"

"You recently picked up a case in Douglas Park. I might know your victim's I.D."

"Really," he said. "Tell me."

When I was finished he said, "Okay, I'm pulling Ms. Brand up . . . have a mug shot from when she was younger . . . I guess it's possible."

"She's got a collection of mug shots, try the latest."

"Oka-ay . . . yes, that's her. Thanks, Doctor."

"The crypt told me COD was undetermined. May I ask why?"

Barrios said, "Guess I'd better be conferring with Lieutenant Sturgis. Appreciate the tip, Doctor."

An hour later, Milo phoned on his mobile. "Just heard from a Santa Monica D who's all hinky about you."

"Were you able to set his mind at ease?"

"Best I could." He laughed. "Yeah, he's okay, but not too pleased Brand could end up a homicide. He'd put the file away as undetermined."

"So they said at the crypt. Barrios wouldn't tell me why."

"Blood on a nearby park bench fit with a bad fall. So did Deirdre having a BAL over three times the legal limit and no evidence of a struggle."

I told him about Brand's eroded fingerprints.

He said, "Sure, I've seen that. Had a vic years ago, longtime fabric dyer, too many caustics, no more whorls and swirls. Fortunately we didn't need to I.D. *him,* his wife stabbed him in the backyard." He sighed. "So now I've got to consider Ms. Brand as a new member of a really bad club."

"You're not buying into a bad fall."

"Normally, I might, but like you always say, context."

"Did you ask Barrios if a meal was left—"

"Just about to tell you. Exactly the cuisine you predicted, given poor Deirdre's station in life."

"Fast food."

"Burger, fries, small chocolate shake from Mickey D. Arranged neatly on the bench that was used to brain her."

"Any of it eaten?"

"Not a crumb."

"Barrios didn't think that was strange?"

"Barrios wasn't looking for strange. Also, there was an empty forty and a half-empty Night Train Express nearby. Barrios figured she blitzed herself dizzy, tumbled and smashed her head against the bench before she could go for the protein."

I said, "Wining and dining her in the style to which she's become accustomed."

"Bastard. But why kill her when he'd already taken the time to sue her?"

"Maybe he lost patience. Or the suit was a way to intimidate her into hiding. He follows, goes after her. Thrill of the hunt."

"He shows up at the park, she's not going to panic?"

"With that level of intoxication, a sneak attack doesn't sound too challenging. When do you start surveillance?"

"Past tense. Fellinger left his office twenty minutes ago and I am presently following in a professionally unobtrusive manner. As in sitting in traffic on Santa Monica Boulevard."

"Good luck."

"Good luck for me could mean bad luck for another woman, as in I spot him with another potential victim and can't do anything unless he acts out in front of me."

"At least you'll be there."

"Armed and dangerous."

I hit three freeway underpasses, showing Deirdre Brand's photo to any homeless person willing to acknowledge my presence. The financial outlay totaled a couple hundred bucks.

No one recognized her so I drove to Douglas Park on Wilshire and Twenty-Fifth Street. Pretty place, jeweled with ponds and play areas and smooth-skinned, happy-looking people. I strolled until I spotted an outlier: a grizzled, emaciated man sitting under a magnificent date palm.

I sat down next to him and he ignored me until I slipped a twenty into a filthy hand. Flashing pale toothless gums that said his liver didn't have much longer, he licked his lips, already tasting the fortified wine he'd buy with the money. Trying to lift himself up with shaky arms, he failed several attempts and gave up.

I positioned the mugshot in front of him.

Nothing.

"You don't know her?"

"That's DeeDee," he said, as if the fact was self-evident.

"She hangs out here?"

"She fell down and kilt herself." Pointing to a bench in the distance.

"She fall a lot?"

He thought. "There's a first time for everything." His laughter was wet and constricted. Drowning in his own wit.

"Who'd she hang out with?"

"No one unless she wanted money, then she could get friendly."

Yards away, pretty women watched and conversed as their children explored the edges of a pond. A young couple snapped selfies on their phones and laughed.

I said, "Did DeeDee get friendly with anyone in particular?"

"Naw, you don't do that."

"Don't do what?"

"Bother the citizens, they get scairt. You got another twenty?"

I handed him a ten. He said, "Hey, just keep it comin'."

I didn't answer.

"You rich for a cop."

"Salary's okay, pension's better."

"Haw?" He squinted as if faced with a tough math problem, made several more attempts to rise, succeeded the third time.

I stuck with him as he hobbled toward Wilshire. He smelled like the bottom of a clothes hamper seasoned with overcooked fish.

I gave him a five. "So DeeDee didn't panhandle here—"

"Century City. Where the suits are."

"She have any problems with the suits?"

"She didn't tell me."

"Did she have hassles with anyone?"

He stopped, swayed, looked up at the sky. "DeeDee was . . . she kept to herself. Real omnistical-socialistic, you know?"

"Omni—"

His look said I was mentally slow. "Means no friends, you just do your thing." He squinted. "Someone said that."

Returning to the park, I checked the bench he'd pointed to. Plenty of pigeonshit but time had erased any trace of blood.

Why was I bothering? What difference would finding an old stain make?

Because that's what compulsives do to allay anxiety. Even with no destination, the motor keeps running.

Someone had probably said that, too.

CHAPTER

16

By eleven p.m., Robin and I were in our pajamas watching a movie on the couch, something forgettable and pretentious based on a book no one had read.

Ninety-four minutes of meaningful looks and pointless long shots accomplished what we'd hoped: readying us for sleep.

Each of us was wired and needed the help. Robin, because an aging rock star with *über*-money and *unter*-intelligence was pressuring her to take on a massive job—fashioning dead-on copies of iconic instruments, down to scars, dents, and scratches.

"I keep telling him every company does relics. As if Charlie Christian's 150 and Bo Diddley's Gretsch need improvement. Not to mention the other twenty-seven he wants."

"How long you figure it would take?"

"To do it right? Years. That's without factoring in Uno's ADD."

"It'll raise your tax bracket."

"And alienate me from all my other clients and turn me into his high-paid serf. I've told him no twice. He insists he needs me."

"I can understand that."

"There may be some of that, too," she said.

"I can always break his fingers."

She laughed. "I need to get out of this without having him bad-mouth me all over the industry."

"He gets nasty, I'll break his fingers *and* his toes."

"Not much of a challenge, darling, seeing as meth and tobacco and whatever have weakened his constitution. But those apes who follow him around are another story."

I gorilla-beat my chest. Robin put her head on it and we watched for a few more minutes. An actress stared at an actor. He pretended to be contemplating something weighty. Ponderous music played, stopped, resumed. The camera swung to a steeple top. Then to an empty room. Then to a hand.

Ah, art.

Not that anything could've captured my interest. I'd been obsess-ing on three murdered women and the fact that others were likely to follow. I knew Milo was out there, somewhere, watching Grant Fel-linger. Long, dreary process, no guarantee of results . . . the camera swung to a screen-filling blue eye, unblinking. Maybe this was the scene the critics had found "compelling."

My cell beeped. As I read the number, Robin used the call as an excuse to turn off the TV. "Time to brush my teeth. Then I'm emailing Uno, tell him no in capital letters."

"Bravo."

I clicked in. "That was quick, Big Guy. You learned something."

Milo said, "Hope you're not too comfortable. Even if you are, you'll want to get the hell over here."

He rattled off an address in Mar Vista.

I said, "New catering?"

"Oh, boy. This one won't help your appetite."

The residence had once been the garage of a moderate-sized mock-Tudor on Grand View. Mar Vista's name promises ocean views. Many of its streets don't deliver but Grand View does. It was too dark to make out much of the Pacific, now, but I did spot a triangle of gloss beneath a tiara of city lights.

Taking a second for a moment of beauty before it started.

The victim was a twenty-four-year-old woman named Francesca DiMargio who worked at a bookstore in Silverlake.

Milo learned little else from her landlords, a retired couple named Eileen and Jack Forbisher who spent a lot of time "cruising." Meaning ships, not low-riders.

They'd returned a few hours ago from a three-week voyage embarking from Puerto Vallarta, crossing the Panama Canal, and ending up back at Long Beach. Everything seemed in order until Jack Forbisher toted an armful of junk mail to the trash cans at the rear of the property.

"I get closer to the back house and what a stink," he said. "Even with my allergies, you never forget that smell."

"Where've you smelled it before?" said Milo.

"We were in India last year, they have places where dead bodies are left out in the open." Forbisher glanced through a rear window of his family room. What he called a back house was a converted garage, now blocked by a tarp on a vertical frame and yellow tape turned bright by a standing LED lamp. "I knew right away something had died but I thought it was a possum or a raccoon or a dog."

Eileen Forbisher, finally able to steady her voice, said, "This is disgusting, terrible, disgusting. Frankie was supposed to be watching the house for us."

As if the dead woman had failed to live up to expectation.

Her husband said, "Obviously, she couldn't even watch for herself."

"Jack! How can you be so matter-of-fact?"

He shrugged.

His wife said, "Yecch, I can still smell it and I haven't even been out there."

"I wouldn't let her," said Jack Forbisher, sniffing. "You really think you smell it in here?"

Eileen said, "Putrid."

My nose picked up nothing.

Milo said, "So then what happened, sir?"

"I poked around near the garbage and there wasn't any dead critter and as I got closer to the back house the smell got worse. I'm still figuring nothing terrible, maybe she left and a critter got inside. Her lights were out and her door was locked so I let myself in with my key and saw what I saw." His nose wrinkled. "I got the hell out and called 911, end of story. When can we clean up?"

"Jack," said Eileen, "she was a person."

"Not anymore." He canted his head out of his wife's view and favored us with a *see-what-I-go-through?* eye roll. "Anyway, I got the hell right out, don't worry, didn't mess up your CSI."

Milo said, "Appreciate it, sir. What kind of person was Frankie?"

Eileen said, "Quiet. Different from us, but no problem."

"Different, how?"

"The tattoos, the rings and studs, paper clips, whatever."

Jack said, "Without all that crap, she'd probably be a nice-looking girl. But no personality, you'd say hi, she'd pretend not to hear you."

"Shy," said Eileen. "Really shy. She had trouble making eye contact."

Jack said, "She applied to rent, I said to myself nutcase hippie, forget about it. But once you get her to talk you can see she's basically a quiet girl, no ax to grind. I'm a good judge of character, worked in L.A. Unified for thirty years."

I said, "Teacher?"

"Maintenance coordinator, I ran all the electrical and plumbing for the northwest sector. That means dealing with people, I can tell who's going to be a problem and who isn't."

"Frankie wasn't a problem."

"Quiet as a mouse," he said. "Afraid of her own shadow, one of those nerds."

"She was *so* quiet," said Eileen. "You wouldn't know she was there."

Milo said, "Did she have a boyfriend?"

"Never. We never saw any visitors, period."

Jack said, "The only thing was once in a while she'd come home late. Real late, like early morning. I could hear footsteps."

"More than one set?"

"Nah, just her. I can look out from our bedroom, sometimes I'd look and see her. You think some kind of boyfriend did it?"

Milo said, "It's too early to think anything."

"I sure as hell hope that's not it. Some lunatic knowing where we live." He puffed out his chest. "I own firearms but I'd prefer not to have to use them."

Eileen said, "You just keep them in the safe, I hate those things."

Jack said, "Frankie had a gun, she might still be alive."

Eileen turned to Milo. "Are we in danger, Lieutenant? Please tell him not to play Rambo."

"This kind of crime is generally directed against a specific victim."

"See, Jack?"

"He has his opinion, I have mine."

Milo said, "What else can you tell us about Frankie?"

Eileen said, "She was always timely with her rent."

"How much did she pay."

"Thousand a month," said Jack. "And lucky to get it."

"How long has she been your tenant?"

"Nine months."

Eileen said, "And we probably spoke fifty words in all that time."

I said, "Not a single visitor?"

"Not that we saw but nowadays we're always traveling, so I can't say never."

"Did she have a lease?"

"Nope, month-to-month," said Jack. "Leases are useless. If some-one's shifty, try recovering a dime, and if they're honest you don't need a lease. Month-to-month is smart, they give problems, you give 'em the gate. You think this had something to do with her lifestyle?"

"What lifestyle is that, Mr. Forbisher?"

"The holes she put in herself. That crazy stuff she collected."

"That's prejudice," said Eileen.

"I don't think prejudice is her problem now," said Jack.

Eileen said, "May I ask when you'll be finished?"

Milo said, "Soon as we can."

"And you'll be cleaning the back house, I assume."

Milo crossed his legs. "Strictly speaking, ma'am, we don't clean up crime scenes."

"What?" she said. "You expect me to get down on my hands and knees and scour all that . . . that horror?"

"There are services that specialize, Mrs. Forbisher. I can give you their—"

"All the taxes we pay and we have to pay more? That's outrageous, Lieutenant!"

Jack said, "All for the better, Eileen. Something like this, you'd sure as hell want a specialist, not some cop pretending to be one." To Milo: "Give me at least two outfits, I always comparison-shop."

Milo passed along cards from three cleaning services.

Forbisher entered the information in an address book, writing in laboriously precise block lettering.

Eileen stood. "I can't take the stench, need a bath. If you need any-thing else, Mr. Sharpshooter will tell you."

Without his wife present, Jack Forbisher seemed more eager to help. Had more to offer than we'd expected.

The bookstore where Francesca DiMargio worked was called Even Odd.

Her parents lived close by in West L.A. "Never met 'em but you could say we've done business because usually the rent came from them."

Milo said, "How much is usual?"

Forbisher thumbed his address book. "Six out of nine months. Also the damage deposit. They're not going to be seeing any of *that* again."

Milo said, "Their address, please."

Forbisher read it off. "So tell me, which of the three cleaners is best?"

"They're all good, sir."

"There's always one who stands out."

"Try Bio-Vac."

"Hope they're the most reasonable," said Forbisher. "I don't think I should have to pay a dime but no sense fighting City Hall." Brief glance at the diamond window. "I don't even want to know what they're doing back there. My wife needs to get back to normal or *my* life will be a living hell."

Milo lit up a panatela, blew out enough smoke to envelop his head for several seconds, rematerialized and led me into the backyard. Wafts of cheap tobacco didn't help. Neither did being outdoors. The stench was overpowering, a stomach-churning, brain-searing reek that saturated the ten yards separating the main house from the structure that still looked like a garage.

Jack Forbisher was right about one thing: Once you smelled decomp you never forgot it. Despite a steady breeze from the west, my eyes began to water. Milo dragged hard on his cigar. He turned and I spotted sheen around his nostrils. Lining his nasal passages with Vapo-Rub. He offered me the tube. I used it and it helped, but not much.

A thousand bucks a month had gotten Francesca DiMargio a hundred fifty square feet of what real estate agents call "open plan." The space was now filled with techs wearing white hazmat suits and gas masks. Most worked steadily. One figure stood to the side, doing nothing. He waved.

Milo said, "Sean. He caught the call."

Binchy's arms dangled at his side. Relaxed, nothing bothers him.

Plenty to get bothered about, here.

The thing that had once been Francesca DiMargio was a brown/black/green/maroon putrid mass dissolving onto the polished cement floor at the mouth of a one-step kitchenette. Tooth and bone flashed white beneath sloughing skin. Metallic glints, at least seven that I counted, indicated the body piercings. Hard to say where they'd been located originally because so much skin had collapsed and oozed.

Four festering limbs had been positioned in a way that evoked Kathy Hennepin. So did the use of a bedsheet to completely cover the body. What remained of the linen had been pushed aside so that the photographer could snap and pop.

Near the corpse was a makeshift table fashioned from a giant electrical spool laid on its side, the kind used to feed wire for massive projects. Atop the raw wood surface was more decaying matter.

On dishes.

Welcome to dinner.

Impossible to say what this last meal had consisted of. The crockery bearing it was white just like Frankie DiMargio's teeth and bones where they weren't streaked with oozing, clotted matter. The same went for silvery utensils and red glass goblets.

A bottle of wine on the counter was obtrusively clean.

Milo read the label. "Prosecco. Cheap."

The techs never let up but all of them kept their distance from the body when possible.

Milo motioned to the nearest tech. His suit and mask evoked a *Star Wars* stormtrooper.

Resonant rasp: "Yes, Lieutenant?"

"Any idea what the food is, yet?"

"I think I spotted some kind of fish—white, flaky. Or maybe it's chicken. Maybe also peas, at least some kind of little round green thingies. I mean I hope they're peas but I'm not committing 'cause what I thought was rice turned out to be dead maggots."

"Think of that," said Milo. "Cuisine strong enough to kill a maggot."

"You know how it is, sir. Sometimes the little buggers get overenthusiastic and sink in too deep and can't wiggle out. The lucky ones become flies."

"Survival of the fittest maggot," said Milo. "The essence of police work."

Asthmatic laughter through the mask's activated carbon filter. "Anything else, Lieutenant?"

"A time of death guess would help. I won't hold you to it."

"It would have to be a long time for this level of decomp, Lieutenant. For sure, days, maybe a week. Or even weeks, temperature's not too high, the rate could've been slow. But I'm really not the guy to ask, you'll have to find out from the coroner."

"How about cause?"

"This much mess?"

"No obvious wounds."

Trooper's white chest heaved. "The way it looks, she's one *big* wound."

"Don't suppose you noticed a computer."

"Not so far. And there's no closet space plus we checked the drawers, so I'd say no."

"How about a diary detailing who the bad guy is, including physical description, address, telephone number, and political preferences?"

More rasp. "Something else I'm surprised hasn't shown up, Lieutenant: No cell phone. Although maybe we'll find it, with all the crap she collected, you never know."

"The crap" was far too much thrift-shop and dozens of taxidermy specimens. Snakes baring fangs coiled around branches. Glass-eyed heads of wolves and foxes, sheep and cows, skunks and badgers stared at one another relentlessly. Gleaming jars on makeshift shelves held what looked to be fetal creatures in suspension. Added to all that were random animal parts, including an elephant's foot serving as a repository for black silk flowers.

Much of the preservation appeared past its prime, pelts flea-bitten and mangy, specimens closest to the body flecked with gore. The smell got the better of me and I ran out, retraced through the yard, sidled along two cars parked side by side in the driveway. The Forbishers' bronze Cadillac CTS and a battered black Kia that had been Frankie DiMargio's daily ride.

Even back at the curb, my nostrils remained saturated. I was twenty feet up the block and chewing my fourth breath mint when Milo joined me.

"You probably didn't need that."

"Glad I saw it."

"Why?"

"Seeing the way she lived."

"Meaning?"

"People with unusual interests often find others who share their tastes. Frankie sounds like a loner but there were times she came home late, so some sort of socializing was going on. Maybe you'll find a tight little social group that can enlighten you."

"Fellow formaldehyde freaks? Can't wait." He lit up another cigar. "All that dead stuff she collected. To me it's like trivializing what I see every day."

I said, "Obviously, death holds no fascination for you. Same for kids growing up on farms, or in places like India where bodies are displayed openly. But our culture hides it and that can make it even more terrifying. For some people, manipulating specimens helps by simulating control."

He smoked. "Manipulation sounds like our bad boy. You see a suit like Fellinger hooking up with someone like Frankie?"

"Affairs of the heart, there's no telling."

"Seriously, Alex."

"I mean it. One thing Frankie had in common with Kathy Hennepin is shyness. Someone—even a suit—who could make her feel comfortable might have an advantage."

He took a few steps, reversed, returned. "The food, the whole staging thing. Seeing those specimens in there got me thinking. That's what taxidermists do, right? Arrange bodies, create tableaus. What if Fellinger—or whoever—met Frankie through her hobby and decided she'd be *his* specimen?"

"Whoever? You've got new doubts about Fellinger?"

"Time to think gave me doubts. Nothing happened during surveillance and let's face it, I've got nothing on him but theory."

He dropped what was left of the cigar, ground it out with his shoe. "Another family to talk to, fun-time—let me ask you, amigo, what that tech said, everything tastes like chicken. You think chickens say everything tastes like corn?"

17

By one thirty a.m., nothing new had emerged from Frankie DiMargio's crime scene.

Milo said, "I'll notify her parents tomorrow, give 'em a few more hours before their world changes."

I said, "When?"

"I'm thinking nine, ten. You free?"

"Give me an hour to get ready."

"Putting on your game face? Mine never seems to fit."

He didn't get in contact until just after one p.m., thick-voiced and wrung-out. Rather than sleep, he'd returned to watching Grant Fellinger's house. Fellinger's Challenger and the BMW probably driven by his wife remained in place until seven fifty-eight a.m. when Fellinger left his house and drove the Dodge back to his office in Century City.

Moe Reed took over the watch, allowing Milo a brief stop at home in West Hollywood, where he showered, gobbled half a cold pizza and a generous square of cold baked ziti, while reading the paper. Sitting across from Dr. Rick Silverman, who breakfasted on fruit and Rice Krispies. While reading the paper.

"*Wall Street Journal* for him, *Times* for me. Neither of us are great in the morning, this morning we're grumpy as hell. Finally, he got paged from the E.R. and I'm about to leave when I see I need to change my shirt, got tomato sauce on it, and that pissed me off more than anything. You think it's a subconscious blood thing? I chose Italian out of big-time empathy?"

I said, "You've always liked pizza."

"There you go again. Doing your reality thing."

William and Clara DiMargio lived in an olive-green, one-story bungalow south of Pico and east of Overland. I waited ten minutes before Milo pulled up. He wore a gray suit that matched the sky, a chartreuse shirt, a tie the color of mud, the faithful desert boots, resoled for the umpteenth time. His hair was slicked and he'd shaved haphazardly, creating a grid of nicks at his jawline. His eyes were bloodshot, his head stooped.

Three-hundred-plus homicides. Here we go again.

A woman answered the door. Sixties, five three, black hair cut short, pretty face, small body swallowed up by a quilted blue housecoat.

She said, "Yes?"

"Mrs. DiMargio?"

"That's me, what is this?"

Milo flashed his badge. Not the card; the card says *Homicide.* "Is Mr. DiMargio here?"

"Why?"

"It's about your daughter Francesca. If we could come in, ma'am?"

Clara DiMargio said, "Can I see that badge again?" But she stepped back, gripping the doorframe for support.

A man's voice said, "Clara?" just before its owner appeared. William DiMargio wasn't much taller than his wife. Older than her or just aging faster, with frizzy white hair, eyelids surrendering to gravity, rough, weathered skin. An indifferently trimmed mustache spiked in all directions.

"The police, Bill."

"What's going on?" Bill DiMargio demanded. But he, too, made way for us.

As always, Milo did his best. As always, it didn't seem to matter.

Clara DiMargio wailed and shook. Her husband held her at arm's length as if he wanted to throw her away. Jut-jawed, eyes full of rage, spittle collecting at the corners of his lips as he mouth-breathed.

I went to the kitchen and fetched water and a box of tissues, placed everything on the coffee table in front of the couple. The table was shaped like a lyre, pecan wood with tiny black freckles, resting on gilded griffon legs. A basket of wax fruit, a bronze nutcracker shaped like a crocodile, and a collection of framed photos crowded the surface.

Most of the pictures were of conventional-looking people in their thirties—two couples, each with a pair of small children. In one picture, Clara and Bill stood among them. No one with tats and pierces.

A single shot off to the left portrayed a cute young teenage girl who resembled Francesca Lynn DiMargio's DMV photo if you factored out the blue-and-scarlet buzz cut, the snaky black neck tattoos, studs, hooks, and barbells inserted into eyebrows, nose, lips, and the tender space between lower lip and chin.

Pierces everywhere *but* her ears. A shy girl shouting defiance with negative space?

I studied the expression on her pre-modification face. Forced smile. Tense, preoccupied. Posing but still caught off guard.

Clara DiMargio grew silent. Her husband removed his arm from her shoulder and scooted a few inches away.

Milo said, "We're so sorry for your loss, but if you could talk to us it might help find out what happened."

Bill said, "What happened is probably she lived like a freak and it got her."

His wife cried out, "Oh!" and used both hands to grab her own cheeks.

"Like it matters now? Like she's gonna get upset?"

Clara howled. He set his mouth tighter and his mustache bristled.

Milo said, "We're open to any information you want to give."

Bill said, "She lived her own life, shut us out."

"Oh, God," his wife whimpered.

He shifted farther away. "Like that place she supposedly worked. Like it was a real job and we were supposed to be thrilled."

"Even Odd. You've been there?" said Milo.

"Why would I? Being in a bookstore in a bad neighborhood at night is a job? Who buys books at night?"

Clara dried her tears. "Frankie said people came in."

"She told you that?"

"Yes, she did."

"Hmmph. Well, she never told me nothing." To us: "In the slums they're all of a sudden big readers?"

Clara said, "Silverlake is not the slums."

"Right, it's Beverly Hills. Look. These guys are here for information, I'm giving them information. You want to tell me hanging out with losers couldn't a had something to do with it? Gimme a break, Clara."

He shot up, walked into the kitchen, shaking a fist.

Clara said, "He's upset."

Milo and I sat there. Moments later, Bill DiMargio was back, empty-handed. As if spotting the water for the first time, he poured himself a glass and slurped noisily.

I said, "Did Frankie have problems with nighttime customers?"

"No," said Clara. "Not that she said."

Bill said, "Just 'cause she didn't say doesn't mean nothing. She never said nothing."

"Oh, please, Bill."

"Be honest. If she had a problem, would she a told us?"

Silence.

Clara said, "Frankie was a good girl. She needed her freedom, is all."

"Which we gave her. We gave all three kids freedom but the others respected it." Bill DiMargio's face crumpled. He swung his head toward us, drifted from Milo to me, settled on me. Tears oozed down his weathered skin. "Lord Jesus, what happened to my *baby*?"

Milo said, "Someone murdered her in her home."

"How? What'd they do to her?"

"We don't have details yet."

"You were there. You don't know?"

Milo said, "The autopsy will clear that up."

"I don't understand," said DiMargio. "You can't just look at—what they poisoned her, you can't tell from the outside? Some crazy drug?"

Clara said, "I don't want to hear this." Her turn to escape. She walked down the hallway at the far side of the living room and turned right.

The sound of retching. A toilet flushed.

Bill DiMargio said, "That's what happened? They poisoned her with some crazy dope?"

Milo rubbed his face. "I'm afraid the body was there for a while, sir, and that makes it hard to—"

"Ohhh!" DiMargio cupped both hands over his face.

Clara returned, wiping her mouth, several shades paler.

Her husband said, "Don't ask them any questions, you won't like the answers."

Both of them finished their water. I got more, took time to check out the photos on the fridge door.

Again, everyone but Frankie.

When I got back, Milo was saying, ". . . terrible to go through this.

But we never know what's going to solve a case, so whatever you can tell us—like who Frankie's friends were—"

"She had no friends," said Bill.

"We don't know that," said Clara.

"We don't? Name one."

Silence.

When Clara started crying again, Bill left for the second time, came back toting a framed photo larger than the ones on the table and thrust it at us.

Formal portrait of Frankie DiMargio around fourteen, wearing a white dress, her hair long, brown, luxuriant. Clear skin, clear eyes. The only metal in her face, orthodontic.

The same tentative, beleaguered smile.

"She was a good-looking girl," said Bill. "Until she started to mess with herself. Got her first tattoo at fifteen. But we never knew. On her back, down at the bottom, she hid it from us for a year, if I'd a found out who gave it to her, he'd be sorry. But she wouldn't say even after I grounded and re-grounded her, took away her CDs. She was always difficult. Contrary. Wouldn't go to parties she got invited to. Wouldn't answer when you talked to her, like you weren't there."

"Bill," pleaded Clara.

DiMargio's mouth tightened. "I'm *trying* to be helpful. So they can *solve* this damn thing."

His wife stared at him. Stood and left for the third time, bustling straight up to the end of the hall. A door closed hard.

Bill DiMargio said, "Now she'll sleep all day, that's what she does, she sleeps it away. As usual, it's my fault—you wanna hear about Frankie? I'll tell you. Her problem was she always had to be different. I know, I know, that's normal, everyone has to do their own thing. Plus she's shy, afraid of people, life is hard, I get it, she needs to *express* herself. But let me tell you, shy doesn't have to be a problem, lotsa people are shy, right? And they don't get into trouble."

Footsteps sounded. Bill DiMargio folded his arms across his chest.

Clara returned, dressed in a black blouse and slacks, black sneakers. Sidling close to her husband, she slipped her hand into his.

He said, "You okay, hon?"

She sighed and turned to us. "May I tell you about our little Francesca? She was so, so, so *shy.* Just born that way."

Bill DiMargio said, "Finally, something we can agree on."

The history was one I'd heard hundreds of times. Quiet, somewhat withdrawn child, previously well behaved, finds a social niche among a loose band of fellow outcasts in junior high and everything changes: dress, taste in music, school performance, adventures with drugs.

"But nothing addictive," said Clara DiMargio.

Her husband humphed. She withdrew her hand. "I'm not saying she was blameless. There was some drinking, some marijuana. But nothing serious and until then she'd never done anything even naughty. Just the opposite, she was our little Goody Two-shoes, refused to even taste mulled wine at Christmas."

Bill DiMargio said, "If only that had lasted."

"She did *not* have a drug problem," said Clara.

"You say so."

"I do. You know I'm right, Bill."

"Probably," he conceded. "Though there were times she looked like it was more than just wine and reefers."

"Say what you want," said his wife between clenched jaws. "She was *never* addicted to anything. Everyone told us that."

I said, "Everyone meaning—"

"School counselors," she said. "She tested with learning problems but never once, not ever, was there even the slightest suspicion of addiction to anything." Glaring at her husband.

He muttered, "Must be true, they're the experts."

Clara said, "Which isn't to say whatever she was doing was acceptable. Frankie's grades suffered. She was never the greatest student but up until eighth grade she'd managed to pass everything. After the change, she began failing."

"Once it started, banzai," said Bill. Forming a wing with one hand, he dive-bombed sharply.

Clara said, "We had her tested several times, she's at least average, above average in some things. Like creative thinking, she was definitely creative. School was even harder for her because her sister and her brother had found it easy. Classes and the social things."

Bill said, "That's for sure, Tracy could party in her sleep."

"Tracy's our older daughter," said Clara. "She's extremely social. Works as a party planner."

"Bill Junior's an accountant," said her husband. "Smart as a whip."

"Do they live in L.A.?" I said.

Clara said, "Tracy lives outside of Chicago, Bill Junior's firm is in Phoenix."

"Raking in the big bucks," said Bill. "He was the easiest one to raise."

"Thank God *everyone's* doing well," said Clara. "Including Frankie, she really had pulled things together." The unspoken word: *finally*.

I said, "When's the last time you saw Frankie?"

Long silence.

Bill said, "We really didn't see her. Not since . . . maybe four months. She came by to get some cash."

"Cash for . . ."

"Living. That's on top of we're already paying her rent."

Clara said, "Not all of it."

"Most of it," he said. "Never even saw the place. She didn't want us to."

Clara said, "I saw it."

"Once. Before she moved in. It's not like we pay the rent and get to be entertained the way Tracy and Bill entertain us when we visit."

"Everyone's different. Frankie needed to live her own life."

Bill grunted.

"She was painfully shy," Clara persisted. "Social things were so hard for her."

I said, "Did she have any friends after high school?"

"I'm sure."

"Any idea who they are?"

"People at work, I'd imagine."

"Losers," said Bill. "Nutcases. You want who did this, look there. A loony or some ghetto lowlife."

I said, "Did she report any problems at work? With anyone?"

"Never," said Clara.

"Like she'd tell us?" said Bill.

Clara sprang up and ran out. This time she didn't return.

We sat there with Bill but something in the air had changed and every subsequent question evoked a slow, weary shake of his head. As we turned to leave, he remained seated.

Milo said, "Thank you, Mr. DiMargio."

"For what? All I did was fucking *cry*. And now *she's* pissed off."

18

Bill DeMargio didn't look at us as we left his house.

Outside, Milo said, "Poor people. Not exactly a model family, huh?"

I said, "Does that exist?"

"Good point. You see or hear anything relevant?"

I said, "I heard confirmation of my guess last night. Frankie's shyness could've led her to trust the wrong person."

"Doesn't shyness usually make you suspicious? My mother always talked about her middle sister, my aunt Edna, being afraid of her own shadow as a kid. When I knew her, she was a scary crone who rarely left her house, hated the Masons and the Baptists and kept a shotgun propped by her bed."

"That sounds like more than shyness."

"Probably. You don't want to know about most of my relatives." He laughed. "Model families."

We got in the car. I said, "Shyness isn't a single trait, anyway. There are people who just enjoy solitary pursuits. Without them, there'd be precious little music, art, or literature, not to mention higher math.

Others withdraw because they're anxious about being judged. Some of that's probably hardwired at birth—babies who startle easily are more prone to be introverts. But that doesn't imply pathology, just human variety. Plenty of introverts are perfectly happy to be that way. But in Frankie's case, it sounds more problematic. Poor social skills and trouble reading people can create a confusing world. When your head's filled with static, you can lose your balance. A predator able to overcome her resistance would score an easy target."

"He'd have a good victim, too," he said. "No problem leaving behind physical evidence."

"The time it took to find the body."

He nodded. "Parents live minutes away but she shut them out and ends up lying there, undiscovered for at least a week. Pathetic."

"She was the family outcast," I said. "Her sibs are more conventional and outwardly successful. The fridge is plastered with a lot of photos. Everyone *but* Frankie."

He looked at me. "That's why you got the water?"

"No, I got it because they needed it. Seeing the fridge was an added benefit."

"Reward of virtue . . . you really see Frankie succumbing to someone like Fellinger?"

"Would you imagine Kathy Hennepin dating Kleffer? There's no way to know which key fits which lock until you try a bunch out. I'm sure Fellinger gets out of his suit once in a while."

"What, he comes into the bookstore wearing a concert T-shirt and jeans with calculated holes, buys something weird, and Frankie falls in love?"

"More like she sank slowly into love. He'd take his time, dropping in repeatedly, browsing, ignoring her. All the while, he's scoping her out until the time comes to begin worming his way into her life. Probably by claiming some sort of mutual interest."

"The Joy of Two-Headed Embryos."

"That would work. So might the fact that he's older—substituting for a father who disapproves of her."

"Yeah, Bill's no peach."

I pulled away from the curb. "Something else just occurred to me: her landlords and her parents."

His eyes widened. "They're alike."

"From what we've seen they are. Grumpy Dad, softer Mom, lots of obvious discord. Frankie managed to find lodgings that replicated her home life. Probably unconsciously. That tells me she had a giant hole in her soul."

"Big-time rebel when all she needed was a cuddle?"

"Pretending to reinvent herself but wanting the comfort of the familiar," I said. "Poor kid, life's been tough for her."

"And now it's ended. Her parents couldn't tell me much. Think it's worth talking to her brother and sister?"

"Definitely."

A mile later, he said: "Okay, Kathy and Frankie were shy and Deirdre Brand got on his nerves. But I don't see Ursula fitting in. Just the opposite, she sounds like a social superstar."

"But she met Fellinger during a particularly stressful period and grew dependent on him. The fact that she came back to him after the divorce settled—to tweak her will—says the dependency was durable. I agree, her murder stands out: She wasn't taken at home, there was no blitz-attack, and the dinner scene wasn't set up until later. But that could just be practicality on the part of a smart killer. And for all we know, despite sleeping with Fellinger, Ursula kept him at arm's length, never invited him into her home. So he took her on his own territory. But when you get down to it, she was hunted and bagged, just like the others."

"He handles her divorce and decides to kill her."

"Maybe she pulled away sexually and he doesn't take well to rejection."

"Bang, bon appétit," he said. "Moving up to a designer kitchen."

"But the message remains the same: I run the show."

"He took his time setting up Ursula's scene, careful to make sure no one would be home. He's able to delay gratification."

"I hate that in a criminal. Okay, time to drop in at the bookstore where Frankie worked. If Fellinger was a regular, someone's gotta know."

"I was figuring the same thing, Big Guy."

"Great minds," he said. "Or we're both rowing in circles."

He said he'd need his car later so I dropped him at the station and we continued separately. The address he gave me was on Sunset Boulevard east of Hollywood, the initial fringes of Silverlake. At this time of day, a forty-five-minute drive, minimum, which gave me plenty of time to think about what I *hadn't* told him.

A killer icing the cake by misleading the cops.

My thoughts about that had solidified because each of the murders had been ripe with misdirection.

Katherine Hennepin set up as a textbook crime of passion and lust committed by an intimate.

Ursula Corey set up as a textbook professional execution.

Deirdre Brand, the "obvious" victim of an unfortunate lifestyle.

And now, Frankie DiMargio, perhaps the most vulnerable of all of them. A victim who'd made textbook easy.

Unconventional woman left to decay in a room full of oddities, the obvious assumption, something related to a strange, possibly dark lifestyle.

Meaning the real reason was anything but?

Meaning the visit to the bookstore might very well dead-end.

My tendency to put a positive spin on life was a perpetual source of amusement to Milo.

There you go again, doing that optimistic thing.

I doubt he knows that it's learned behavior, not instinct. Growing up with a chronically depressed mother and a violent boozehound father, you figure out a survival strategy or you perish.

Friendship's a fine thing but in the end we all walk alone.

Milo's my best friend. No reason to disillusion him.

This time, he arrived first, unmarked parked in a loading zone but no sign of him.

Even Odd was a brick-faced storefront with a black-painted window. Carelessly applied orange paint rimmed the glass. Every day, Halloween.

I went in, found Milo talking to a heavyset woman around thirty wearing—big surprise—all black. Her butt-length hair was dyed to match, ironed straight in spots, looped and plaited in others. The skin of her arms and what I could see of her upper chest was more ink than clear space. A blue-dot tattoo centered her chin and her eyebrows were pierced by a row of what looked like ordinary office staples.

The crowning touch was a nose-ring hefty enough to restrain a bull: a circle of oxidized iron assaulting the cartilage of her lower septum and grazing the top of black-glossed lips. Sneezing couldn't be fun; I hoped she wasn't prone to hay fever.

The obvious metaphor was someone willing to be led around by the nose. Her body language said otherwise, reminding me why I'd grown allergic to quick assumptions.

The DeMargios had described the place as a bookstore but no books in sight. No taxidermy, either, just tables of CDs labeled as *Aunti-Q Sounds* and carousels crammed with vintage clothing. Emphasis on gauze, camouflage, and what looked to be fake leather.

Milo was saying, "We know Frankie DiMargio works here."

The woman had ignored my arrival, paid no mind as I stepped next to him. Staring directly into his eyes. Placid. Mute.

He said, "It's not a trick question, honestly. Does she work here or not?"

The woman said, "Maybe no trick, but it's a question." Deep voice, borderline masculine.

"Is that a problem?"

She smiled. Her outfit was a frayed lace top over a crepe A-line skirt. The skirt's waist was set high, emphasizing melon-breasts.

Milo said, "C'mon, yes or no. Please." Straining as he tagged on the nicety. Fighting to keep his voice even.

The woman cocked a hip and looked away.

Milo said, "This is important—"

"Yes, it is," said the woman. "She comes in but I wouldn't call it work." Rotating back toward us.

"Okay." Lowering his voice the way he does when he's really fighting anger. "Could you please clarify that?"

"I give her things to do because she said she wanted to help. It's not an official job."

"You're doing her a favor," he said. "Does she get paid?"

"Minimum wage."

"Okay," he said. "Thank you. When did you first meet her?"

"I didn't."

"What?"

The woman said, "Meeting is a formal rite, preceded by introduction. She just walked in and said, 'I could do things around here.' I'm essentially lazy so I said okay."

"You own the store."

"No."

"Who does?"

"Koichi."

"Koichi who?"

"Koichi Takahashi."

"Where can I find him or her?"

"You can find *him* in Tokyo."

"Absentee owner."

"Quite."

"How does that work?"

"Just fine."

"I mean—"

She smiled. "I'm funnin' with you, John Wayne. How does it work? He wanted a store to help his collection, has a rich father who bought the entire block."

"What does Mr. Takahashi collect?"

"Italian American vocalist CDs."

"Frank Sinatra."

"Obviously," she said. "Also Dean Martin, Perry Como, Lou Monte, Jerry Vale, Vic Damone."

"A guy sets up a store so he can snag the best stuff?"

Reaching beneath the counter, she brought out a magazine. Peacock blue Japanese characters blazed above a color photo of a young, long-haired man surrounded by walls of compact discs displayed faceout, like paintings. The man's hair was dyed turquoise. His smile spelled enchantment.

The woman groped a bit and showed us something else. CD, still sealed in factory plastic. Sinatra's face. *Nothing But the Best.*

The woman said, "I'm sending him this tomorrow. He's got fourteen hundred and thirty-seven other copies."

Milo said, "Quantity and quality."

"The road to happiness."

"Unfortunately, Frankie DiMargio's not happy. She's not anything unless you include dead."

The woman's smile flickered out. She braced herself on the counter. "You didn't say that."

Milo said, "Now I have. Let's start again."

Act II: Strange conversation.

"You hired Frankie DiMargio."

"I'm not trying to be a pain, but I can't really call it that."

"Hiring's a formal arrangement."

"She came and went as she pleased." A beat. "What happened to her?"

Milo said, "Someone ended her life and my job is to find out who."

"I hope you succeed." Sounding like she meant it. "Do you believe in capital punishment? I do. Why should we pay to keep them alive? Maybe you can catch him and torture and kill him so we don't have to waste taxpayer money."

Milo studied her.

She said, "I have my opinions."

"Let's get back to Frankie. How many hours a week did she spend here?"

"Ten, fifteen tops. I can't tell you anything about what she did because when she came, I left. She was my excuse to get out of here."

"Any predictability to her schedule?"

She gave that some thought. "She usually came in later. Four, five, six."

"When do you close?"

"When I feel like it."

"Did you leave her to close up?"

"It's not a big deal, the door self-locks, you just leave."

"So she was here by herself."

"Yes."

"Any idea where she was when she wasn't working?"

"Not a one."

"You two never hung out."

"I don't hang out," she said.

"With anyone?"

"With anyone."

"How about Frankie's friends? You ever see any?"

"No."

"Did she ever mention annoying customers? Someone who bothered her?"

"She never said anything. We never talked because the minute she showed up, I bailed."

Milo waited.

"I'm telling you the truth, Mr. Detective. I want you to catch him and torture him."

"Okay, thanks for your time. What's your name?"

"Bekka, two k's."

"Bekka what?"

"Bekka Mankell, two l's." She licked black lips, allowed her tongue to linger. The tip had been forked surgically. "May I ask you something?"

"Sure," said Milo.

"How was she—what was done to her?"

"We don't know yet."

"You don't have a body?"

"We have one but it had been lying there for a while."

"Oh." Black lips folded inward.

"That kind of thing," said Milo, "time of death is tough to determine. When's the last time you saw her?"

Bekka Mankell said, "Hmm . . . has to be a week."

"Her being gone didn't alarm you because it wasn't a real job."

"I don't even have a phone number for her."

"She didn't want to give it to you?"

"I didn't ask. I know it sounds strange to you but I was just doing her a favor. She was sad."

"Sad how?"

"Mousy, looked at the floor, never at you." Demonstrating her own skills by locking in again on Milo. "Mousy and afraid of mice. We get them all the time, they live in the walls. First time she heard them scurrying she turned white. I gave her chamomile tea."

Milo said, "She got used to it."

"I guess. She never said anything. Never talked much about anything."

"Shy girl."

"More than that. Afraid."

"Of what?"

"I guess life."

"Okay," said Milo. "Anything else you can tell me, Bekka with two k's?"

She continued to look into his eyes. Hers had grown dewy. Without shifting, she took his hand, kissed it. Five times, rapidly. A peck for each knuckle.

He stood there, too stunned to react.

She released him, gave a small bow. "That was for good luck. Evil pervades the world."

I said, "Have any customers bothered *you*?"

Continuing to engage Milo visually, she said, "We don't get much walk-in. Half the time, I keep the blinds drawn and the *Closed* sign on."

Milo said, "How do you make money?"

Bekka Mankell smiled. "We don't, for the most part. Just a bit of mail order—Frankie did some of that."

"Some of what?"

"After I verified payment and filled out the forms, she'd pack."

I said, "Do you ever deliver locally?"

"Once in a while if it's easy." Her eyes brightened. "Hey, Frankie did that, too."

"Delivered CDs."

"Not CDs, the only thing we deliver is clothes. And not often, most people want everything sent."

Milo said, "Any repeat deliveries?"

"Hmm," said Bekka Mankell. "There's a woman who came in once to browse, bought a whole bunch of pleather. After that she started calling up for more, asked if she could pay extra for personal delivery. We don't get that much of it but we sent her a couple of boxes."

"Pleather."

"It doesn't breathe," she said. "People use it to party. Like rubber

goods. I know she used it to party because she asked for bustiers, cor-
sets, and she wanted an unmarked box and had to accept it personally."

"From Frankie."

"Both times. Frankie said it was on her way home, anyway."

"Where does this woman live?"

"Not her house, she had it sent to her office."

"Where?"

"Century City."

"Avenue of the Stars?"

Nod. "You think she killed Frankie? Wow. Over the phone she was
mellow. Except when she talked about how to deliver it. She wanted it
brought down to the parking lot. That's part of the fun."

"Being naughty."

"Being sneaky. Do you want to know her name?"

"You bet, Bekka."

Another search behind the counter produced a small laptop. Tap
tap. "Flora Sullivan."

She read off the address.

No need for that.

We convened an hour later in Milo's office. He pounded his keyboard
without bothering to sit.

Flora Sullivan, Esq., was a partner in the Southern California
branch of a national law firm. Her specialty was real estate. Forty-five
years old and blameless in the eyes of the criminal justice system and
the state bar association.

A headshot on the company website showed a thin woman with a
notably long neck, a narrow mouth that probably looked pursed even
when it wasn't, and a small face under a cap of dark, curly hair. Square-
lensed eyeglasses framed slightly bulging eyes.

Overall: bookish and birdlike. Imagining her in a pleather bustier
brought up some strange pictures.

Milo scanned her brief bio. "Yale grad, Boalt law . . . look at the suite number. Eighth floor, one above Fellinger. The damn building, you were right."

I said, "With the exception of Deirdre Brand, he met all of them there. And Deirdre panhandled nearby."

"Those are the ones we know about. The bastard's middle-aged. What self-respecting serial starts that late?"

He phoned Binchy, watching the building from across the street. "Sorry, nothing, Loot. He went in at nine, hasn't left."

"What I'm calling about is your looking for similars at other divisions."

"Sorry, again," said Binchy. "At least at the ones I reached, but I'm still trying. At least we got the bullet."

Milo sat down. "What bullet, Sean?"

"The coroner found one in Ms. DiMargio's head. Twenty-five, same as Ms. Corey, Moe's hand-carrying it to the lab for comparison."

"Woulda been nice for him to let me know."

"Maybe he tried and couldn't get through, Loot. He's always been a good communicator."

"Loyalty," said Milo.

"Sure," said Binchy. "But it's true."

Milo checked his phone. Three unheard calls from Reed in quick succession.

"Somehow it got muted . . . okay, sorry, young Moses." He reached Reed. "Just heard."

"Small step, L.T., but at least a step. Her brain was pretty much liquefied, but they did locate the entry wound. Back of the skull, down low. I'm on my way to the lab but between us, L.T., I'm willing to bet it'll match Corey."

"I won't wager against you, kid."

"The bad news," said Reed, "so far there's no record of DiMargio having a phone, land or cell, plus no TV hookup or computer subscription, not even a paper appointment book but I'll keep looking. Plenty of other things, though: bear gallstones, schnauzer bladder stones, dinosaur poop, plus all that stuffed craziness. It's like she was cutting herself off from the real world and creating a weird one of her own. Though she did look after her diet. Those little green things on the plates, what we thought were peas, were really green lentils, they got puffed up by bacteria to look like peas. There was also some grain-type stuff they think might be quinoa and the white stuff isn't fish or meat, it's fake-o, soy-based."

"Vegetarian feast."

"Vegan, L.T. And the wine was organic. Healthy way to die."

CHAPTER

19

After hanging up on Reed, Milo paged through his pad. "Time for the respectable DiMargio offspring."

William Anthony DiMargio Jr. sounded weary, with little to say about his younger sister, other than she'd always "stayed to herself, there's five years between us." When Milo probed, he clarified, "Don't get me wrong, she wasn't unfriendly, just off in her own world. When she was a kid, she was *real* cute . . . who would *do* this?"

"That's what we're trying to find out, sir. If there's anything you can tell me—"

"Me? I haven't seen Frankie in years. Obviously some lunatic is involved, I remember L.A., nutcases everywhere."

"Vancouver's better."

"Hell, yeah," said Bill DiMargio Jr. "Cleaner, more civilized, and the weather's almost as good."

Sister Tracy's input was more of the same, wrapped in a softer package.

Frankie was "lovely but always private. I always thought she preferred animals to people. When she was little, she'd take in wounded birds, bugs, that kind of thing."

Milo scrawled something and showed it to me. *From that to dead ones?*

I nodded.

He said, "Did you know she was into taxidermy?"

Tracy Mayo said, "She was? No, I didn't. Back when we were kids, the zoo was one of her favorite places . . . it's been a while."

Milo said, "What can you tell me about her dating life?"

Tracy Mayo's phone sigh was audible from where I was sitting. "Lieutenant, there's eight years between Frankie and myself. By the time she was of dating age I was out of the house. Out of California."

"Chicago?"

"Evanston," she said. "I went to Northwestern, did media studies, thought I'd be an anchorwoman." Small laugh. "I'm sorry, I wish I could tell you more."

"So, no boyfriends."

"Not that I—wait a sec, there was *someone* she mentioned, but it was a while ago."

Milo sat up. "When?"

"Months ago. Let me think . . . the last time Frankie and I spoke on the phone . . . okay, it was right after my youngest son's birthday, which would be three months ago. Just a brief chat because Frankie didn't like talking over the phone. She sent Jaydon a little stuffed lion, so I called and had him thank her, then got on the phone, myself. Frankie sounded fine. Happier than usual, actually, I asked her what was new and she said she met a new friend."

"A man?"

"I assumed a man because, as I said, she sounded different. *Lighter* than usual. Then she backed away, like she always did, said she had to go and just hung up. You think there could be a connection? She met the wrong person?"

"We always look at close relationships, Ms. Mayo."

"So you don't know who he is."

"No, ma'am, but we'll look into it."

"Darn," said Tracy Mayo. "Maybe if I'd been nosier. But probably not, Frankie was never one to confide."

"New playmate three months ago," said Milo.

I said, "A month after Kathy Hennepin's death."

"Time to groom a new one . . . I need to think, let's score some home-brew."

We had another go at nasty coffee in the big detective room. The room was nearly full and a look around explained why: Someone had brought in lattes laced with cinnamon. Men and women sipped from cardboard cups as they worked. When Milo drank from his scalding mug of institutional sludge without pausing for breath, a single pair of hands applauded and others joined in.

He bowed and we headed back to his office. I heard someone say, "Didn't know shrinks were that tough."

He picked up his desk phone. It rang before he could use it.

Moe Reed said, "Good news, first: ballistics match between Corey and DiMargio. Now for the bad: DiMargio did have a cell phone account until three months ago, when she canceled it. But looks like the records have been deleted. What kind of person doesn't have a phone?"

"Someone disconnected, Moses."

"Guess so, I'd be lost without my cell—couple more things, L.T., might as well end on a positive. Coroner's willing to commit to an approximate time of death, based on dead maggots and tissue deterioration and assuming the room temperature didn't fluctuate wildly. Eight to fourteen days. No tox screens so far, because they're having trouble finding viable tissue, apparently decomp messes up the results. But apart from that unopened bottle of wine, there were no intoxicating substances in the residence."

"Any sales slips or labels on the weird stuff she collected?"

"A few," said Reed, "but they were old, like she bought the stuff used. A lot of the taxidermy came from Montana and the Dakotas, makes sense they're into hunting. Some of the phone numbers even had letter prefixes but I tried anyway. Nothing, sorry, L.T."

"Start compiling a list of thrift shops and flea markets near her residence and her work, say a half-mile radius for each. The amount she was hoarding, she had to be a regular customer somewhere. If no one admits to knowing her and you get a feeling, follow up with face-to-face. You need help, I'll scrounge up a couple of ambitious uniforms."

"Sure," said Reed, "but just to remind you, I do surveillance on Fellinger this evening."

"I'll take that, Moses. You look for oddity dealers."

"Will do. She's an interesting person, no? Keeping dead freaks for company."

"Unfortunately," said Milo, "she met a live one."

He checked in with Binchy.

"Nothing plus nothing, Loot. I trade surveillance with Moe soon."

"Moe's busy, I'm heading over there myself, Sean. Look for Dr. Delaware's spiffy Caddy."

"That's a nice car," said Binchy. "My grandfather had a Sedan de Ville."

This time Milo left his unmarked in the staff lot and we traveled together. As I drove, he called DMV, got a quick answer and wrote down the information.

Tag number of Flora Sullivan's white Porsche Cayman S.

I drove down the ramp leading into the building's sub lot. Milo said, "Keep going all the way to the bottom level and work your way up."

That led to a series of slow-mo revolutions that took me past the spot where Ursula Corey had been executed. He didn't ask me to slow and I kept going.

Despite a healthy number of high-end vehicles, the Porsche was easy to spot. Whiter than fresh notepaper, tricked out with smoke-gray windows, and chrome wheels sporting red brake calipers. A small spoiler sprouted from the rear end.

Ski Aspen sticker on the rear bumper. Milo pointed to a spot ten yards up, diagonal to the Porsche.

"Back in over there."

The slot was narrow, sandwiched between an Escalade and a Navigator. Neither driver had shown much respect for the painted lines. I slid in and cut the engine.

He said, "Nothing like a buddy with good spatial perception."

The spot was ideal for watching the Porsche. Close enough to make out movement and details, sufficiently distant not to raise suspicion. The only negative was the Seville, itself. In a row of newish chrome and paint, a thirty-year-old car stood out. I'd rolled back as far as I could, leaving the larger SUVs to serve as walls on wheels. Milo and I sat low. He began to nap.

Nothing happened for fifteen minutes. He was snoring lightly when that changed.

I nudged him. His instincts were finely tuned and even as he blinked into consciousness, he lowered himself farther.

Two people were approaching the Porsche. A tall, crane-like woman in a navy suit with gold buttons was instantly identifiable as Flora Sullivan. At her side, a shorter, stocky ape-like man wearing an open-necked white dress shirt and slacks.

No body contact between Sullivan and Grant Fellinger, but lots of smiling, animated conversation.

Milo said, "My, my."

I said, "Maybe he likes pleather, too."

We watched for several more minutes as attorneys Sullivan and Fellinger conferred. Then he opened the driver's door of the Porsche and she folded her long body inside.

Fellinger walked away, moving quickly, a spring in his step. He was out of view by the time Sullivan roared off.

Milo said, "What the hell was that?"

I said, "Who knows? But now it's confirmed: He does get out of his suit."

CHAPTER

20

Café Moghul serves competent, generic Indian food from a spot on Santa Monica Boulevard near Butler Avenue, a quick walk from the West L.A. station. Milo's been eating and working from there for years. Shortly after he discovered the place, he handled a few derelicts who wandered in from the street. The bespectacled woman who runs the place remains convinced he's a one-man security system and treats him like a deity.

The fare's decent enough but I've rarely seen the restaurant crowded. A mail-out offering temporary discounts on the already cut-rate lunch buffet ended up at the station, briefly attracting hordes of cops. That, too, was attributed to Milo despite his denials.

Nor was he blamed when the horde thinned.

"You are a modest man," the woman had assured him, heaping his plate with lobster claws absent from the buffet table.

At five fifteen, we were the sole patrons. The woman ushered us in, moving smoothly in a lime-green and lemon-yellow sari. I don't know her name and I'm pretty sure Milo doesn't either.

"Your table, Captain."

"Lieutenant."

"Soon it will be Captain," she said. "After that, Major."

As she scooted away, Milo muttered, "After that, six feet under."

He pulled out his cell phone. When she came back with chai and cumin-rich *papadum* and three kinds of chutney, he was well into his recent calls, deleting "toll-free bullshit" and "departmental bullshit" with grim satisfaction.

"What will you be having, Captain-Leftenant?"

"Anything's fine."

"Lamb?"

"Sure, great, thanks."

"Lamb and veal," she said. "The chicken looks good, also. The tandoori's nice and hot."

"Terrific."

"Seafood?"

"Really, don't go to any special trouble."

"For you, nothing is trouble."

When she was gone, I said, "I foresee a statue with your face on it over there, under the Delhi travel poster."

"Nah, too fat for a god."

"The happy Buddha?"

"Wrong religion."

"How about the elephant deity, Ganesha?"

"You're full of knowledge," he said. "Got any about what we just saw between Fellinger and Ms. Pleather?"

"I didn't pick up anything romantic or sexual but they seemed comfortable with each other."

"Coupla lawyers doing business?"

"Maybe that's all it was. On the other hand, they both have offices in the building, why confer in the parking lot? Maybe because Sullivan had used it before when she wanted to avoid notice."

"Getting her pleather fix."

"Clandestine drop-offs that drew Frankie DiMargio there. Same for Kathy Hennepin, who came to drop off documents. Both were tagged as prey and maybe Sullivan played a role in it."

"Couple of outwardly respectable types using the workplace as a hunting ground? What about Ursula?"

"Ursula didn't need to be lured, she walked right into it," I said. "Yes, outwardly, she was different, but something doomed her. I'm still betting on her breaking off the relationship with Fellinger."

"Prize pet tries to escape and gets put down," he said.

"Fellinger and Sullivan are both partners in high-level law firms, used to having authority. That fits being able to get Frankie to discontinue her cell phone account and withdraw totally. Frankie told her sister about a new person in her life. Soon after, she's off the grid."

"Change of slaves from Kathy to her. The novelty wore off?"

"Or Frankie ruined the game by asserting herself," I said.

"You hurt my feelings, I stop your breathing." He crunched a cracker to dust, brushed crumbs from his shirt. "Not only did Frankie drop her phone account; I spoke to her mother and she's been using cash for a while. No credit cards for two years because her parents thought she couldn't stay out of debt, found it cheaper to just give her money."

"So maybe her allowance got augmented by her 'new person.'"

"Same old story, pay to play."

The bespectacled woman carried over a platter piled high with animal protein and placed it in front of Milo ceremoniously.

When we were alone again, he shook his head. "Time for Ganesha to feast . . . not sure I have an appetite."

I said, "Don't disillusion me."

Midway through some marathon eating, he paused for breath. "No cameras in the damn tier. Fellinger and Sullivan would know that. You're right, it is a perfect place for a conference about something other than work because no one spotting them would think anything out of the ordinary. And two psychos would make it easier to subdue victims."

He grimaced. "Help setting the damn table, you wash, I dry."

"Or Sullivan's role was more subtle," I said. "You know what we usually see when there's a female involved."

"She's the lure. If she *is* involved. Because let's face it, kiddo, we're running all over the place because she had a brief schmooze with Fellinger."

"It's more than that. She definitely knew Frankie."

He put his fork down. "Poor kid delivers party-kinky duds, gets tagged and bagged—hell, a woman might be even better at spotting female vulnerability than a man, no?"

"She'd certainly be less threatening."

"Maybe it went down that way with Kathy, too. It wasn't Fellinger who snagged her in the elevator, it was his partnerette and now I've got both of them to keep an eye on."

His eyes hooded. "Or we're wrong about Sullivan in a real bad way."

I said, "He's grooming her as his next victim?"

"Why not? Suppose she did play a role introducing him to Frankie but had nothing to do with the bad stuff? Offing Ursula turned out to be a huge kick so he's decided to raise his standards—capturing higher-level prey. That's the moral dilemma, no? We spot Sullivan hanging out too long with Fellinger, do we warn her? If she really is his co-star, we've just blown the entire investigation."

He downed two glasses of water, conference-called Reed and Binchy and informed them of the new surveillance regimen.

First step: pull up Flora Sullivan's DMV so they'd know what she looked like and where she lived. Then get right on her at the same time Fellinger was being watched. But separately, both of them assigned to the building on Avenue of the Stars.

A scenario that would work well with half a dozen detectives. Reed and Binchy alternating with Milo meant long shifts, the risk that new cases would pull the young detectives off.

"At least," he told them, "you'll earn mucho overtime, kids, I'll make sure of it."

"Either way, L.T."

"You bet, Loot."

Milo hung up, grinning.

"What?" I said.

"It's so nice when the kids turn out well."

CHAPTER

21

For three days running, Flora Sullivan and Grant Fellinger arrived for work between eight thirty and ten a.m. Neither attorney was spotted leaving the building during the day; each was observed driving out of the parking lot between five thirty-four and six fifty-eight, p.m.

Night one: Ensconced in his Pacific Palisades house, Grant Fellinger never left. Flora Sullivan, on the other hand, paused only for a one-hour stopover at her Georgian mansion on June Street in Hancock Park before emerging wearing a black-spangled trouser outfit and jewelry that Binchy could see glinting clear across the street. Her hair was brushed out, curls slackened to waves. She carried a white purse not much larger than a cigarette pack.

Pausing to study her reflection in the driver's window of her white Cayman S, she did a kissy thing with her lips, arched her back, got in the cool little sports car, and revved up.

Property tax records had her residing in the big, blocky house for the past fifteen years with one Gary Sullivan. But no man accompanied her as she turned east on Sixth Street and headed toward downtown through Koreatown.

Destination: the Biltmore Hotel.

Aha! thought Binchy. Rich person's version of a no-tell motel. Maybe he'd luck out and that Fellinger would show up, too.

But Sullivan had nothing spicy in mind. Walking straight to the hotel's gilded grand ballroom, she attended a benefit dinner for Planned Parenthood.

Binchy, wearing a suit and tie, as he always did, managed to blend in with the eight-hundred-plus people during the cocktail hour.

When dinner was announced, he watched Flora Sullivan pick up her place-card and take her seat, introducing herself to her immediate neighbors, a pair of elderly, elegant women.

"Two drinks," he reported the following morning. "Picked at her food, that's probably how she stays skinny."

"No boyfriend in sight," said Milo.

"Nope. She drove back home alone."

"Sounds like a fun evening, Sean."

"Didn't mind, Loot. I'm in the groove."

Night two, Reed on Flora Sullivan, Milo on Grant Fellinger.

Sullivan's turn to hunker down at home, appearing only to greet a *Real Food Daily* deliveryman, whom she tipped generously enough to evoke a smile.

"That's a vegan place," said Moe Reed. "Just like the stuff in Frankie DiMargio's place."

"Common ground based on no-cruelty?" said Milo. "I'm in danger of irony overdose."

He hung up and continued watching nothing happen at Fellinger's midsized contemporary abode. At nine fifty p.m., a woman stepped out, followed by the attorney. Milo recognized her as the aging brunette he'd seen in Fellinger's office photos. No signs of the two boys in the portraits and no cars other than the BMW and the Challenger. By now the kids would be in college, let's hear it for empty nest.

The woman Milo knew from real estate records to be one half of the Grant and Bonnie Jo Fellinger Family Trust dyed her hair blond.

One of those attempts at holding onto hubby as time did its thing?

He watched Bonnie Jo pocket a ring of house-keys and slip her arm through her husband's. The two of them walked up the block, heading north. Passing right by the Porsche 928 parked across the street.

The car was Rick's Sunday drive but he was always good about sharing it. Appreciating Milo's contention, tonight, that something "classy" would blend in on an affluent street.

Milo watched the couple stroll off and fade into the darkness. A few minutes later, the Fellingers were back in view, strolling languidly.

Bypassing their house, they continued south. Without breaking stride, Grant Fellinger planted a kiss on his wife's cheek. She pecked him back.

The two of them, marital bliss personified. Like one of those ads for cruise ships, middle age filled with romance, what a hoot.

They sure looked comfortable with each other. When they returned a second time, Fellinger's hand was draped over his wife's shoulders, and her arm looped around his thick waist.

Exhibiting the ease you saw in contented couples.

Milo supposed he and Rick could fit that description, all those years together, fewer arguments, almost no drama.

Huge accomplishment, given the stress of both their jobs.

Given the fact that both of them were prone to crankiness.

Also the fact that they were men raised during a certain era; gay or not, emotional expression had never been a big factor in their household.

So no arm-looping for the two of them, even in West Hollywood where PDAs were business as usual.

Times had changed. Intellectually, Milo was fine with that. But sometimes when he saw young guys in Boystown hugging and kissing and doing whatever the hell they pleased, it could jolt him and make him feel ancient.

Rick never said anything but it was definitely the same for him. Squinting the way he did, the compulsively barbered mustache rising and falling as his jaw flexed.

Hell, they *were* getting old. Just sitting around like this was freezing up his joints, let's not even talk about the urinary system.

The lovebirds returned to their house, Bonnie Jo laughing at something Grant said, laughing again as Grant patted her more-than-ample ass.

All that happy-hearth hoohah hadn't prevented the bastard from screwing Ursula Corey and Lord knew how many other women.

Helluvan actor.

Was he concealing a lot worse than adultery?

Bonnie Jo's laughter lingered in Milo's head.

She loves the guy.

This one would not be easy.

Night three, as Moe Reed follows at a safe distance, Flora Sullivan drives home to Hancock Park, stays inside her mansion for an hour and fifty-two minutes before emerging, pushing a man in a wheelchair. Guy around her age, gray-haired, handsome, and broad-shouldered, the contrast even more marked when his upper body is measured against his withered legs.

Sullivan steps in front of the chair. The man smiles as she straightens his collar. She propels the chair curbside. Parked cars are thin on June Street tonight, and Reed worries his three-year-old Mustang, borrowed from the Narcotics impound stable, will be spotted, sitting obliquely north.

But Sullivan and the man in the chair have eyes only for each other. They talk. She adjusts his clothing a few more times. He takes hold of her hand and brings it to his lips, briefly.

Sullivan kisses the top of his head and, standing behind him, bites her lip and stares off into the distance. That brief gnaw, out of her companion's view, the only hint life isn't absolutely peachy.

Her white Porsche is the only vehicle any of the detectives has seen at the mansion, no way it will accommodate the man and the chair so Reed isn't surprised by the silent arrival of a huge black hybrid van bearing livery plates and the discreetly gold-stenciled name of one of the city's larger limo services above the rear left bumper. A black-suited driver gets out. His instant smile and enthusiastic wave imply familiarity. So do the return waves from Flora Sullivan and the man in the chair.

The driver slides open the van's rear passenger door. An electric platform eases forward and lowers to sidewalk level. Taking the chair from Flora Sullivan, the driver wheels the man up the ramp and inside. As the door slides shut, Flora Sullivan walks into the quiet street, around to the driver's side, gets in before the driver can assist her.

The van drives away, slowly, smoothly.

Reed waits a while before picking up the van's taillights two blocks later. He follows the oversized vehicle onto Beverly Boulevard, hangs back as the van pulls into the valet lot of an extremely expensive Japanese restaurant just east of La Cienega.

Extremely because last year Reed took Liz there for her birthday and the bill was a shock, though he figured he'd hid that pretty well because the rest of the evening had gone great . . .

No problem for people who live in Hancock Park and can afford a chauffeur.

The van pulls up in front of the restaurant. The driver gets the man in the chair out. Flora Sullivan takes over. Someone who looks like a maître d' holds the door open.

Sullivan and her companion—a man who fits the stats provided for her husband, Gary, minus the disability—remain inside for nearly two hours. Halfway through, Sullivan comes out and brings the driver what looks to be a plate of sushi.

Fifteen minutes after arriving back at the mansion on June Street, lights out.

Two apparently happy couples. Milo and I and everyone else are beginning to doubt our hypotheses.

Day four of the surveillance, Milo's back watching the building on Avenue of the Stars and this time, Grant Fellinger leaves earlier than before, at just before five p.m. Not in the BMW, not in the Challenger. He exits on foot, accompanied by an extremely pretty young Latina wearing a dark suit and pearls.

The receptionist who'd been there the day of Ursula Corey's murder.

Okay, here we go, finally.

Too bad, Bonnie Jo, you seem like a nice woman.

But that big aha! moment dies when two more people join the party, a pair of fortyish women, one blond, the other black with beautifully coiffed gray hair, both wearing well-tailored dark suits.

The party of four walks abreast, waits for the green light, and crosses the boulevard, heading straight for the building where Milo has developed a nice relationship with the parking attendants based on mutual respect and cash.

A dark residential block is one thing, Avenue of the Stars drunk on incandescence is another. And no 928 to give him respectability; today he's behind the wheel of an LTD that might as well bear signage proclaiming *Unmarked!*

He starts the car up and bails out of there, driving half a block before hazarding a backward look.

Fellinger and the three women are entering the structure across the street.

From one office building to another? What the hell?

Milo drives around the corner, parks at a neighboring office structure, and overtips the valet outrageously to buy himself time and space.

Making it to the building Fellinger's group has entered, he learns from a sign in the lobby that a restaurant named Gio occupies the top floor.

Said establishment isn't doing a riproaring business, at least not this early; even the long, ebony bar is mostly empty. Maybe the tenants—mostly entertainment firms—want to get the hell out of there after long days of dickering and swindling.

Or the food sucks.

Whatever the reason, Fellinger and the three women are easy to spot because no one blocks visual access to their corner table with a terrific city view.

Fellinger and the black woman are seated with their backs to the untended maître d's booth. The other two women face them.

No way any of them will notice Milo; he is standing outside the restaurant, peering through the holes created in a wall of glass pocked artistically.

A waiter brings drinks: two oversized Martini glasses of something coppery-red garnished with fruit salad for the pretty young receptionist and the black woman, what looks to be cola but could be rum and Coke for the blonde.

Fellinger raises an Old-Fashioned glass of something clear—vodka or gin. Clinks all around.

A different waiter brings bread. Fellinger waits until all three women have selected from the basket and either buttered or dipped in what is probably olive oil. Only then does he bite into his roll. What a gentleman.

Menus arrive. Fellinger orders from a wine list. Two bottles, white and red.

Everyone relaxed, happy, chatting without care.

Nice boss, taking the staff out after work.

This could *really* get complicated.

Or worse, he's *really, really* wrong.

◆

I finished reading the surveillance summaries, put them down.

Milo said, "Fascinating, huh?"

He was at my house, at eleven a.m., sprawled on the living room sofa looking thrashed and discouraged.

"I still think you're going about it the right way."

"If you were anything but a shrink, I might take comfort in that."

He ran his fingers through black strands, trailed down to white sideburns—what he calls his skunk sticks—and plucked idly. "I rechecked every phone company, maybe we missed something and Frankie still had an account. Nada."

I said, "What if he bought her a disposable and her world became his?"

"Personal hotline? What would stop her calling anyone else?"

"That's assuming she'd want to. But even if she did, he could always examine her log."

"You asked Reed to check shops that sell taxidermy and oddities. No luck?"

"He found a couple of places in Venice and Echo Park. Echo Park got me hopeful because it's not far from Even Odd. But no one had ever heard of Frankie. I followed up myself, tried out-of-town shops— San Francisco, New York, and Boston. Everyone told me I was wasting my time, the stuff can be picked up at flea markets, thrifts, online auctions, general antiques stores."

He stood. "I'm off to catch some beauty rest. Sorry for spreading all the good cheer."

"Apology uncalled for. You're the one sitting in a car all night!"

"Empathy," he said. "That always come natural to you?"

It had.

I said, "Anything can be learned."

22

D ay five. Near the end of Moe Reed's daytime surveillance shift, during the second of two quick sneaks into the parking garage, the young detective narrowly missed coming upon Grant Fellinger and Flora Sullivan.

He was leaving an area just a few yards from where Ursula Corey had been gunned down when inaudible snippets of conversation caused him to duck behind a Buick SUV.

Stocky man and stork-like woman walking together. Aimed again for Sullivan's white Cayman.

Taking a perpendicular route, Reed jogged around a corner, emerged due west of the Porsche, made sure Fellinger's and Sullivan's backs were turned, and hustled behind an SUV.

Different body language from the amiable chat Sean Binchy had witnessed. Reed called in.

"Wouldn't call it a fight but definitely tense. She said something and got in her car and backed out fast. He didn't wait around, just left."

"Who did most of the talking?"

"Definitely Fellinger," said Reed.

Milo said, "Lovers' quarrel?"

"Guess it's possible, L.T., but it seemed more business-like. Whatever they have going on could be falling apart, at some point we might be able to wedge them apart."

"Wouldn't that be peachy, Moses? You doubling on Fellinger tonight?"

"No, Sean takes over and you're on Sullivan," said Reed. "At least according to my schedule."

Milo checked his own book. "You're right, congrats on a night off. Got a hot date?"

"Sir, at this point any date's fine with us."

"I'm ruining your social life?" Milo laughed. "Sorry, go have fun."

"The job's fun, too," said Reed. "More so if I didn't need a bladder."

On day six, Milo phoned at three p.m.

"Someone finally misbehaved. Want to guess who?"

"Easy odds," I said. "Fellinger."

"Shit, you're no fun. Last night around eight Sean followed him and Mrs. F. to LAX. Ol' Grant schlepps her luggage, hugs and kisses her and escorts her into the terminal. Then he goes to dinner. Want to guess where?"

Rising excitement in his voice made those odds easy, too. I said, "Century City shopping mall."

Silence.

"I'm wrong?"

"*No. You. Are. Right.* If you've got that good of a Ouija board, why the hell can't you solve the case for me?"

"No big deduction. He got into it with Deirdre Brand there. I figured he might consider it part of his turf."

"Right . . . okay, whatever, he had pizza and beer at a touristy place but no obvious hunting of humans ensued. He just stuffed his face and emptied a mug then drove to the Norman Hotel on the Strip."

"Don't know it."

"Yeah, you do. Used to be a grungy tiki-motel-type dive called the Islander, now it's a hipster hub, painted white, upside-down signage."

"That one," I said. "Rock stars and actors who last a season."

"No paparazzi according to Sean so maybe even the C-list has moved on. Anyway, you wouldn't figure a place like that for a guy of Fellinger's age and looks, right? However, turns out there's another group that frequents the place."

"Working girls."

"They congregate at the bar wearing mini-dresses and trawling for clients. Our man Grant didn't take long to rent *two* lovelies. Light-blond and dirty-blond, per Sean, he said together their ages maybe added up to Fellinger's."

I said, "Did they seem to know Fellinger?"

"Not that Sean could tell. Brief chitchat, Fellinger pays for a room with cash, rides up to the fifth floor. The girls finish their Cosmos and do the same. Sean drinks root beer and gets all nervous about what's going on up there, figures he'll give it forty-five minutes then hazard a look. At forty-one, both girls are back in the lobby, leave the hotel and walk up Sunset. Fellinger appears fifteen minutes later, gets his Challenger from the valet, and drives west. Sean's choice is either talk to the girls or stick with the surveillance. He follows Fellinger home, nothing else happens all night. I know it's not profound but it confirms that Grant's a bald-faced phony. Moment his wife steps into the security line, he's thinking playmates."

"If he can fool his own wife that easily, Kathy and Frankie would be no challenge."

"And one more thing, Alex: Sean said both the working girls had tattoos. Maybe it means nothing, lots of people ink up nowadays. But it got me thinking about Frankie. Maybe *that's* what turns him on. That's when I realized I hadn't checked the other victims for skin work, so I went back and re-read the autopsy reports. Not a dot on Kathy, but Deirdre had some prison ink, no surprise. And guess what: Classy Ursula had a tiny inscription in blue above her left shoulder blade. Pathologist listed it as 'Chinese characters,' no translation. I got the coroner to email it to Jim Gee, he's a robbery D at Hollenbeck. He had no idea but emailed his mother and she said it was some sort of prayer for prosperity. Anyway, three of my victims have endured the needle. Am I making too big of a deal out of that?"

"It's worth considering. Going to try to find the working girls?"

"Sean's going back to the Norman tonight, see what he can learn. Meanwhile, my night on Sullivan defined stultifying, she was home all night. The guy in the chair's definitely her husband. Gary Sullivan, also an attorney, now retired. His name came up in our files but not as an offender, as a victim. Nine years ago a drunk driver rear-ended a row of cars at a red light near the Staples Center after a Lakers game. Sullivan got hit hard, his spine was shattered. Flora stuck with him; from what we've seen, she takes good care of him, is nothing but a dutiful wife. You still see her as worth watching?"

"Think pleather and a tense chat with Fellinger."

"Thought you were my friend."

I said, "Here's proof I am: spent a chunk of today calling antiques dealers and thrift shops. No one knew Frankie by name and her description didn't ring any bells."

"No one knew Frankie," he said. "Guess that was the point."

For the next two days, I visited thrift and antiques shops within a mile of Frankie DiMargio's garage-apartment in Mar Vista. That encompassed a slew of establishments in Culver City, mostly on Washington Boulevard's newly gentrified design strip. Frankie's photo sparked nothing from proprietors and clerks.

The same went for tattoo parlors I found in the neighborhood. When the owner of one shop asked what I did for a living and I said, "Psychologist," he said, "I can ink Freud's face on your ass."

"No thanks," I said.

He smirked. "Afraid of pain?"

"Too repressed."

None of the detectives was successful locating the prostitutes Grant Fellinger had picked up at the Norman. Not one to dither during his wife's absence, Fellinger repeated the pattern at two other Strip hotels, settling for one woman per night. Moe Reed managed to corner the hooker from the second night, a girl who looked like a high school sophomore and had obviously fake papers saying she was twenty-five. She yawned a lot and described Fellinger as "just a john, nothing crazy."

"Meaning?"

"Suck and fuck, what do you think? I'm not saying nothing more on advice of counselor."

Reed said, "Counselor, huh? Like in summer camp?"

The girl stuck out her tongue and kept her extended middle finger close to her thigh as she wiggled up the Strip.

On day eight, Fellinger picked up his wife at the airport and took her to dinner at the Hotel Bel Air.

As the couple dined on Wolfgang Puck creations, Flora Sullivan was having sex with a man in a Rolls-Royce.

The site of the tryst was a quiet stretch of Hudson Avenue, near the Wilshire Country Club, a short walk from Sullivan's manse on June Street.

Milo told me about it, sitting in the garden between Robin's studio and our house, tossing pellets to the koi. Telling his tale with utter lack of salaciousness and a whole lot of weariness.

A week-plus of brutally disrupted sleep and little to show for it but garden-variety infidelity.

"She leaves her house just before nine wearing a loose dress and sandals, circles her own block a couple of times, passes a neighbor walking a dog, makes chitchat, heads back, I'm ready to nod off. But she continues to Hudson and stops at a car parked under a big tree. Black Rolls-Royce Ghost, you can barely see it. Flora lets herself in and stays inside for nearly half an hour, gets out smoothing down her dress. As she's putting on lipstick a guy exits the driver's side and walks over to her. Around her age, only thing I could make out was a light-colored shirt and dark pants. The two of them get all huggy and kissy and gropey and then he gets back in the Rolls and drives away and she walks home. The Rolls tags trace to Leon Andrew Bonelli, San Marino. Big-time real estate development, his online bio puts him at Boalt law school the same time as Flora and her husband."

"Auld acquaintances aren't forgotten," I said. "Any sign of pleather?"

"Can't speak for her undies. Normally, I wouldn't begrudge a girl her fun. Hubby's incapacitated, she gets lonely, life's short. But the possibility Sullivan had something to do with Fellinger's game means I'm gonna blame her every chance I've got. Where's that scarlet letter, Nathaniel?"

I said, "Maybe the tense conversation Reed saw between her and Fellinger means their relationship is fraying because she upgraded to a richer, more powerful man."

"She's in a Rolls, Grant's paying for sex? Yeah, could be."

"If we're right about Fellinger, he doesn't take well to rejection."

He turned to me. "Flora put herself in the crosshairs? So I keep watching her . . . he wouldn't be stupid enough to shoot a second woman in the parking lot."

"Not unless he's disintegrating mentally."

"You see signs he is?"

"No, but if he starts taking crazy risks, you might have to warn her."

Fish burbled. I threw in pellets.

Milo took the bag and tossed a few more. "Flora as Ursula Redux. That damn parking lot bothers me, if the morons would install cameras, it could make all our lives easier."

I said, "Why not offer to provide the equipment if Al Bayless gets authorization?"

"The barter system."

"It worked for a helluva long time."

Bayless thought it was a great idea. Then he backtracked. "Got to clear it with the bosses and they take their time."

We were half a block from the building, sitting in the arena-sized lobby of a tourist hotel, ignoring ESPN on multiple screens and nursing soft drinks.

Milo said, "What's to clear, Al? You're scoring freebie hardware."

Bayless picked at the lapel of his uniform jacket. "You know how it is."

"Not really."

"C'mon," Bayless insisted. "Those guys live for rules, everything needs to go through channels."

"We're talking cameras installed unobtrusively that you get to keep, not a penny outta your budget."

"Yeah, that's another thing. Unobtrusive. You'd have to do it after hours, no way I could agree to disrupting business."

"We'd want to do it after hours."

"That costs," said Bayless. "Opening up the building."

Milo glared at him.

"Okay, okay, I'm just being honest. And where would the feed go?"

"To you and to us," said Milo. "Which is the definition of a high-end system, right? Anyone else you know feeds directly to the cops?"

"Yeah, but that's not going to be forever," said Bayless. "Your investigation ends, you cut off the feed."

"But we'll leave the damn equipment, Al. Talk about the ideal partnership between private and public sectors. One day you can run for mayor."

"Oh, great," said Bayless. "How about just shoot me, now— Look, I'm sorry for being a pain, I just can't promise more than I know I can."

"Do your best, Al. But quickly."

Bayless sipped his diet Sprite. "You seriously think it could happen again? Another shooting down there? 'Cause that would *not* be good."

"I can't rule it out."

"Why?"

"Better you don't know, Al. Trust me."

"Damn . . . when I say it has to be done after hours I mean like one, two a.m. I'd have to come in, too."

"Pacific Dining Car's open twenty-four hours. I'll buy you a big steak afterward."

Bayless cracked his knuckles. His shoulders bunched but his eyes were submissive. "You bribing me, huh?"

"Absolutely."

Bayless snorted. "I'm a slut, ready to bend over, and spread for prime rib?"

"I was thinking the big surf-and-turf combo, that potato they have the size of Idaho, sour cream, chives, salsa if you're into that. Also Martinis, wine, cognac with the dessert. My preference is the pecan pie. Goes well with cognac."

Bayless rolled his eyes. "I'm getting reflux just listening. Dining Car on Sixth Street or Santa Monica?"

"Take your pick."

"It's not a matter of food, Milo, but yeah, I'll try to get it nailed down A-sap."

"Appreciate it, Al. And do let me buy you dinner."

"Thanks but no thanks," said Bayless. "Stomach isn't what it used to be and the idea of cholesterol clogging my pipes terrifies me—tell you what, bring some herb tea, I'll supply the hot water."

"You're destroying me, Al."

"Wish I was the man I used to be," said Bayless. "Make it decaf chamomile, no mint, mint reminds me of toothpaste."

"Oh, Lord," said Milo. "My mood's dropping beyond Prozac territory."

"Hey," said Bayless, "we actually save someone's life, your mood'll be fine."

T he purchase:

1. Seven aluminum signs, @ $10.45 each, discount for quantity order: $65.84

    Yellow triangle within a white rectangle bearing a message:
        You're on Film! CCTV Cameras in 24 Hour Use

2. Ten Night Owl Security Cameras, @49.99 each, with discount: $449.91

    Subtotal: $515.75
    Ca. State Sales Tax @ 9.00%: $46.42
    Grand total: $562.17

Milo wrote a personal check.

I said, "The department wouldn't have to pay sales tax."

"I'll bring that up when I face Saint Peter."

Labor was free; Milo, Reed, Binchy, and I, all versed in the instructions and armed with tools from home.

Al Bayless and a computer cop named Hal Wiggins made sure the signal fed to Bayless's console upstairs as well as to Milo's home and work computers.

Bayless had made sure no cleaning crews would be on-site but despite that, when the installation was over and we rode up to his lobby-level office, we came face-to-face with a man and a woman toting cleaning supplies across the expanse of granite and marble.

"What the hell." Bayless barreled toward them.

Terrified, the woman dropped a plastic bottle of glass spray. The man just gaped.

Bayless said, "What the hell are you doing here?"

"Clean," said the man, heavily accented, barely audible.

"Without authorization?"

"We always," said the man.

"What do you mean you always?"

"Clean. Two time a week."

"Where?"

"A'vent, thir' floor."

"Advent Investments?" said Bayless.

"Yeah."

"They bring their own crew in?"

The man fished a key out of his pocket. Bayless snatched it. "This is for the delivery door out back. You do deliveries?"

No answer.

Bayless said, "No one goes in or out of the delivery door unless they're accepting deliveries."

Silence.

"Comprende?"

"A'vent give," said the man. He looked at the woman. She hadn't taken her eyes off the bottle of glass spray.

Bayless said, "Go pick that up before someone trips."

The woman scurried to comply.

Bayless said, "Give me your company's name."

The man fished out a business card.

Bayless said, "Advent owns its own cleaning business?"

"Yeah."

"You wait here while I check." To Milo: "Keep an eye on these two."

The woman began to cry. The man said, "S'okay s'okay."

Milo's smile did little to calm her. The rest of us hung back.

Bayless returned a few minutes later. "Okay, apparently there's an arrangement no one told me about. Good night, you two."

The couple stood there.

"Go," said Bayless. "But you're not going to be able to use the delivery door anymore, I don't care what someone told you. Comprende?"

"Sí."

"At least someone gets something."

The couple hustled toward the freight elevator at the rear of the lobby.

Milo said, "Who's Advent?"

"Subsidiary of the company that owns this place. They take up floors three and four." He pointed to the directory. "Bastards, you'd think they'd tell me. You probably think I'm an idiot."

"I think you work for idiots."

"Ain't that the truth—damn, this is worse than the damn department."

Milo clapped his back. "Don't be hasty in your judgment."

Bayless looked ready to spit. "Spare me optimists and people with tiny dogs."

"What's wrong with tiny dogs?"

"They're fine, it's the people. My second wife owned a hairless mutt could fit in her purse. Liked me better than her. Ugly thing but it had good taste."

CHAPTER

24

Helping install the cameras got me home just before five a.m. I was sleeping six hours later when the phone rang.

Milo said, "Late enough? I waited."

"You pulled an all-nighter?"

"I crashed at home until nine, then a call came in from Earl Cohen, Corey's lawyer. He wants to meet, wouldn't say why."

"Where and when?"

"An hour, mini-park at Doheny and Santa Monica."

"See you there."

"Hoped you'd say that."

The park was little more than a circle of grass centered by an old limestone fountain. A couple of homeless guys lolled, soaking up sun. A woman who looked like a personal trainer put her Labrador retriever through a workout.

No seating; Beverly Hills's idea of hospitality?

I settled on the rim of the fountain and Milo joined me moments later. Soon after that, like a character in a stage play, Earl Cohen appeared, walking eastward from the residential streets of the Beverly Hills Flats, with a slow, unsteady trudge.

Despite the sun, he wore a full-length black coat over dark slacks and sneakers. His white hair blew in the breeze. A couple of times he looked as if he'd fall. No cane; he used his arms for balance. When he finally reached us, he was breathing hard and sweating, the scooped-out section of his neck glossy and pallid as tapioca.

Milo and I stood. Cohen said, "Sit," and followed his own advice. The three of us perched awkwardly on the rim. Cohen's position forced us to twist to see him. He gathered his coat, sank into the garment.

Milo said, "What can I do for you, Mr. Cohen?"

Cohen watched as the woman with the Lab began running it around the circle. The dog panted but she was merciless. One of the homeless men looked up. Glint of glass as he took a swig of something.

"Exercise," said Cohen. "I used to think it helped. Maybe it did . . . they say I've lasted longer than I should. Now they're giving me months, not years. That's why I decided to get in touch with you."

He chewed his lip. "What I'm doing is clearly unethical. If I was planning to be alive for an appreciable period . . ."

One of the homeless men got up and began walking north on Doheny. Cohen watched his exit. "The cards we're dealt . . . all right, enough mawkishness. I'm not even sure this is relevant but if I didn't tell you I'd be unsettled."

Several more silent moments. Cohen laced his hands, let them drop. Deep breath. "Yesterday, I had an unsettling experience with Richard Corey."

He coughed hard enough to flush his face, brought out a handkerchief, swiped his lips, licked them. "Until now, Richard's attitude regarding Ursula's death has been what you'd expect." Turning to me. "Psychologically speaking."

I said, "Grief."

"How much he missed Ursula, how terrible it was for the girls. Yesterday, he phoned asking for an appointment and I assumed the reason was to continue our previous discussion: how best to keep the business going without Ursula's expertise. Richard felt he'd either have to learn Ursula's job, which he wasn't sure he could do, or hire some-one. I'd given him the name of an executive headhunter, but he hadn't followed through."

He coughed again, played with a coat button. "Yesterday was dif-ferent, not only wasn't he grieving, he was ebullient. Physically he was different, as well, had shaved off his beard, was sporting a suit from Battaglia on Rodeo, where I've always told him to go. But he's never listened to that, either. His sartorial tastes generally leave much to be desired."

"New man," I said.

"Quite," said Cohen. "I've always seen him as one of those *farbiss-iners,* the type who'd win the lottery and complain about a paper cut from the ticket."

Milo and I smiled.

Cohen said, "You want jokes, I've got plenty. Worked my way through college doing summer shtick at the Pioneer Country Club in the Catskills."

Another bout of coughing, followed by wheezing. "It starts in the prostate, you'd think you could at least breathe . . . the new Richard wasn't limited to changes in clothing and mood. He's barely sat down when he's going on about to *hell* with the business, to *hell* with the girls' trust funds, they're spoiled enough. I said, 'What happened, Richard?' He said, 'Nothing, I just finally got smart, I've got enough dough, don't need to be working for a couple of brats.' I say, 'Richard, I understand your frustration, but let's not forget what they went through, losing their mother. Maybe it's better to wait before making changes.' "

Cohen sat up straighter. "That's when he said—and there was fire in his eyes—he said, 'To hell with them *and* their mother, Earl. It's time for a change.' I was taken aback, but okay, the man's been through a lot, he's riding an emotional roller coaster, I see it all the time in people, anger at the victim. True, Doctor?"

I said, "Absolutely."

Cohen said, "Then all of a sudden, the anger's gone and something strange has taken its place. He's grinning ear-to-ear. Glee. Smugness. Repeats 'To hell with their mother.' Just in case I missed it the first time. Not even using her name, which he always did in the past. Now it's 'their mother.' To hell with their mother. He's distancing himself from Ursula as a person, smirking, chuckling. Letting me know he couldn't care less that she's dead. Worse, he's happy about it. I mean, the man is chuckling about the murder of someone he professed to love."

Milo said, "Weird."

"Oh, it was, Lieutenant. Then to top it off, he says, 'You know, Earl, sometimes things just work out great' and *winks* at me. Then he starts barking orders at me, I need to organize his papers, figure out the best way to dissolve the company, do it immediately. I say, you're sure about this? And he laughs and winks *again* and says, 'Happy endings, Earl, happy endings.' As if we're sharing his nasty secret and he thinks I'm not free to divulge it because he's my client."

Milo said, "You think he had something to do with Ursula's death."

"I don't know," said Cohen, "but it gnaws at me. How triumphant he was, as if he'd pulled something off. I've worked with enough clients to be a pretty good amateur psychologist myself, and I couldn't help think the real reason Richard asked for the appointment was to brag."

He shook his head. "If I'm wrong, so be it. If I'm right, to hell with him."

Milo said, "Appreciate your telling us—"

"What will you do about it, Lieutenant?"

"Here's the problem, sir. Richard was the first person we looked at but there's no possibility of his shooting Ursula. Obviously, people of means often hire out but Richard opened his financial records to us, as well as his phone logs, and no suspicious money transfers came up."

Cohen's smile was chilly. "You're serious."

"What, sir?"

"No recorded transfers? Big deal, Lieutenant. Richard keeps substantial cash on hand and in terms of his calls, what's to stop him using one of those disposable phones? Which I happen to know he does use, because I've seen them in his possession. Cheap little doodads. One time I asked him why he needed them when he had normal phones and he said for backup."

Milo and I looked at each other. A disposable had come up as a means of controlling Frankie DiMargio.

Milo said, "How much cash are we talking about?"

Cohen said, "That I can't tell you but it's not pennies. The way the business works, the importing is done on the up-and-up but once the goods reach here and Richard negotiates with buyers in Chinatown or wherever, it can switch to all-cash."

"Tax evasion."

"I'm not a tax lawyer."

"Who does Richard use?"

"No one," said Cohen. "He does his own taxes. Which tells you something about his personality, what businessman at his level takes that upon himself?"

I said, "Easier to hide cash."

Cohen shrugged. "Let me tell you something else: Even when Richard said nice things about Ursula, I always felt that down deep he hated her. Not disliked, *hated*. His mouth would be saying one thing but his eyes would be communicating something else."

"Any idea why?"

"Sex, Lieutenant. He was convinced she was sleeping with everyone from the pool boy to the postman. Would gripe to me then explain it away. They were divorced, she was free to do what she wished, she was a woman with needs. I can't back this up but my feeling was he had longtime performance issues. He told me about Ursula's sex life—what he believed was her sex life—the first time we met. I thought this is one that could get toxic but Grant and I pulled off a minor miracle. Maybe major because I didn't think much of Grant, still don't. But I'll give him one thing: He listened to his client and Ursula was always about making peace. So we managed to settle amicably."

"After three years."

"That, Lieutenant, is a blink of an eye, divorce-wise."

I said, "Amicable but now Corey's smirking."

"It doesn't sound like much but I know." Cohen patted the area over his heart. "Tomorrow, I formally retire from the practice of law and prepare myself for what lies ahead. I couldn't hope for peace of mind if I didn't tell you."

He staggered to his feet. Held out a wavering hand for balance, drew himself up. "Good day, gents."

Milo said, "Can I give you a ride, sir?"

"No, thanks, I don't live far." Smiling lopsidedly. "Walking's good for longevity."

25

Milo and I remained on the rim of the fountain. The personal trainer was jogging in place and the retriever was back to running in frantic circles. A new homeless man had wandered in, pushing a shopping cart full of brown things. He spotted us and the malice in his eyes was unmistakable.

Shaking a fist, he kept going.

It's impossible to know how many street people listen to the worst kind of voices. That made me think about Deirdre Brand. Aggressive panhandler, not unwilling to face off with a man in a suit. Good odds paranoia swirled among the ridges and sulci of her addled brain.

Would someone like that be bought off on the cheap, by a bottle of fortified wine?

In light of Cohen's account—of all our preconceptions crumbling—that logic began to melt.

Perhaps she'd been killed by a man she'd never met. Someone who knew about her from his lawyer and decided to take matters into his own hands.

Milo's voice broke into my thoughts. "—you call what just happened with ol' Earl? A paradigm shift? Think I should take him seriously?"

"He's a smart man," I said. "Knows Richard as well as anyone and he has no obvious motive to lie. And if Richard does keep serious cash on hand and uses a prepaid, his previous alibi's useless."

"Prepaid. What we figured Frankie might be using."

"Courtesy of her master. And if Cohen's right about Corey's sexual issues, it could explain Corey's looking for alternatives."

"Hiring out," he said. "Doesn't have to mean a hit man. Could be a girlfriend."

I stared at him. "Frankie was the shooter?"

"Master–slave setup, why not? Someone with Frankie's personality—isolated, reads people poorly—she'd be perfect, right? Like one of those cult members, follows the master straight to the grave. Grooming her as a button-girl would be a dandy reason to control her, Alex. It would also be a nifty motive for blowing *her* brains out when he was through with her."

I said, "If that's how it happened, Frankie being familiar with the building takes on a whole new meaning."

"You bet. The Corey girls told us Richard knew about Ursula's appointment. Making it easy enough for him to set it up. And what better way to express hatred than have your love slave do the dirty work and report all the bloody details?"

I ran the images through my head. Pictured how the DiMargios would react to the news. *Not only is your daughter dead . . .*

Milo said, "It fits even better when you consider that Frankie didn't have a normal job, no one to complain if she didn't show up."

He made a phone call. "Bekka? Milo Sturgis . . . Fine, you? . . . Listen, I know Frankie didn't keep to a regular schedule but would you know if she was at work on . . ."

He listened. Frowned. Hung up laughing. "She has no idea."

"Why the mirth?"

"She asked me out."

"You accept?"

"Very funny." We began walking out of the park. "I told her I was flattered but committed."

"What she say to that?"

"She hung up."

We walked out of the park. He said, "So maybe Svengali is Corey, not Fellinger, but the production's the same."

I said, "Problem is, Deirdre Brand had a problem with Fellinger, not Corey."

He stopped. "What's that, tough love?—damn, I'm getting ahead of myself, Deirdre *doesn't* fit."

"Maybe she does if she was barter material. As in Corey traded favors with Fellinger."

"Corey killed Deirdre in order to buddy up to Fellinger? What could Fellinger offer him, he was Ursula's lawyer—ah."

"Ah, indeed," I said. "We already know Fellinger cheats on his wife. Maybe he also betrays his clients. Leaking Ursula's finances, her intentions—anything to give Richard a heads-up during negotiations."

"In return for taking care of a crazy-woman problem? Fellinger would take that big of a risk? Also, Corey didn't like Fellinger, just the opposite, he lost no time telling us Fellinger was sleeping with Ursula."

"He also told us Ursula was likely sleeping with Cohen. And according to Cohen, everyone else on the globe. Maybe that was a diversion on Richard's part. Trying to look like an emotionally fragile guy rather than a calculating mastermind. I've been wondering for a while if misdirection is the psychological essence of the killings. If the real trademark is setting up textbook crime scenes that lead to dead ends and humiliate the cops. Corey watches true-crime shows, maybe he thinks of himself as an expert on police procedure."

"You've been wondering for a while but didn't think to mention it."

"I didn't see it as helpful. Now I do."

"Or," he said, "you didn't want to hurt Uncle Milo's feelings, seeing as I'm the cop getting humiliated—hey, are those your special kid gloves?"

"Nope, left them at home with the self-esteem lotion."

He laughed. "Okay, an immediate problem: the surveillance on Fellinger and Sullivan. All this time and the only thing to show is some extramarital hanky-panky, not with each other. With Corey on the radar, it's even harder to justify the manpower."

"If I had to choose one of them to keep watching, it would be Fellinger because Deirdre Brand still remains a big question mark and Sullivan's big sin is receiving packages from Frankie DiMargio. Now that we know she has a boyfriend, the odds of a personal relationship with Fellinger drop and the tense chat Reed witnessed doesn't really add up to an emotional breakup scene, more likely business as Moe thought. But now I'm going to add to your problems: Ashley and Marissa. If their father is behind four murders, the fact that he's no longer feeling warm and paternal toward them is worrisome. The first time we met the girls Ashley blurted, 'It wasn't Daddy.' She claimed she was reacting to all the true-crime shows she watched with him, but gut reactions can be revealing. If Corey's showed his hand and they're scared, they may be more willing to talk."

"Why do you think his attitude *has* changed suddenly?"

"Maybe it hasn't. Maybe he's resented them for a while and finally decided to stop faking—oh, boy."

"What?" he said.

"A lawyer in Fellinger's firm is the trustee of the girls' trust funds. Talk about a good reason for Richard to buddy up with Fellinger. One dead homeless woman in return for bleeding the funds. Why would Fellinger risk it? Because he'd receive a commission."

"Kickback and no crazy person yelling at him when he takes lunch, yeah that's a decent payoff. Now try to prove it."

"Why don't we start by talking to Ashley and Marissa, find out if they're aware of any change in their father. For example, has he already begun to tighten the purse strings?"

"Robbing his own kids," he said. "Maybe planning to do worse."

"Enough time has passed for him to figure he got away with multiple murders," I said. "If he's impotent and a longtime cuckold, all the more reason to build himself up. His mistake was bragging obliquely to Cohen and figuring Cohen wouldn't break confidentiality."

"Bad bet, Richie."

"Let's hope he makes a few more."

CHAPTER

26

Neither Corey daughter answered her cell phone.

Milo checked his notes. "Let's go."

The apartment the sisters shared was a straight shot up Laurel Canyon, a right on Ventura Boulevard, a left on Vineland. Close enough to their mother's Calabasas house for laundry drops, far enough to discourage casual parental drop-ins.

The building was four stories of white filling an entire block. Three entry doors, one propped open by a large wooden block. Moving men toted furniture to a van on the street.

The free-form pool centering the interior was big enough for exercising orcas. Bikinied women and men in swim trunks occupied ten percent of the seating. No one swam. The median age was midtwenties. Empty beer cans littered the fake lava-rock decking.

The Corey sisters lived on the third floor. One of two elevators was propped with a similar wooden block. The other failed to respond and we took the stairs.

Milo knocked on the door to 315. A male voice said, "Yeah," and the door cracked. The bare-chested young man who stared at Milo's badge said, "Uh."

Twenty or so, six feet tall, he had long, curly, blond-tipped brown hair, square shoulders, and a patchily whiskered face. Good-looking kid if you discounted the confusion dulling every facial feature. Still, he'd do fine modeling in the kind of clothing ad that emphasized mental vacancy.

Milo said, "Police, may we come in?" and opened the door. The boy stepped aside, scratching his thigh. He wore white boxer shorts patterned with little red devil heads, nothing else. The area around his crotch looked starchy. The room smelled of sour sex, stale food, and weed. The cheap carpeting that came with the apartment was supplemented by an ankle-deep layer of wadded clothes, paper plates clotted with congealed food, empty cans, bottles divided between soda pop and vodka. The glass bulb of a bong protruded from a Jack in the Box take-out bag.

Milo said, "Are Ashley and Marissa here?"

"Uh . . ."

"Is it a tough question?"

The kid's expression said he'd just been handed the physics SAT. Looking over his shoulder, he shouted, "Lo?"

From an unseen location at the rear of the apartment: "Wha?"

"Cops."

"Wha?"

The kid stamped his foot. Unappealingly effete gesture. "Cahps!"

The third "Wha?" was accompanied by the appearance of a short, curvy girl towel-drying a mass of shiny black hair. She wore a flesh-colored bikini top and hip-riding shorts the color of scrambled eggs. A diamond that looked real pierced a navel that would have made any obstetrician proud. As she made her way through the detritus, a collection of bracelets circling her left ankle jangled.

Gorgeous girl with flawless bronze skin, petulant lips, ocean-blue eyes.

"Who the hell are you?" she demanded.

Milo asked to see the Corey sisters.

"They're not here."

"And you're . . ."

"I'm not them."

Milo smiled. "You're Lo."

"Laura," the girl corrected.

Little Miss DUI, the incident in Daddy's Bentley.

Milo said, "Laura what?"

"Laura Hot."

The dull young man laughed. Milo's glare silenced him. He sat down in the garbage.

Milo said, "You're Ashley and Marissa's friend—"

Laura jutted an adorable chin and bobbed her head. "I just *seh-ed*. They're not *he-ere*." Her speech cadence was rhythmic. Her father was in the record industry.

Sample a few seconds of her attitude, hand it to a rap-thug, and you might have a hit.

She rotated a hand. "*La*-ter. *Buh-bye*."

Milo kept his smile on simmer. "Where are Ashley and Marissa, Laura?"

"That's for you to find out."

"There's no need for—"

"You *thi-ink*?" she said. "I don't have to talk to you. Cops messed me *uh*-up."

"Sorry to hear that, but if you could—"

"Cops li-ed, I had to do community service in Wah-atts." Turning to the boy in the trash, she said, "Totally *bo*gus."

He'd managed to grow even more glazed, didn't answer.

"Hey!" She went over and snapped her fingers in his face.

He said, "Yeah."

"Yeah, what?"

"Mega-boge."

Milo said, "Sorry you got hassled but this is about Ashley and Marissa's mom. You know what happened to her, right?"

Internal power-struggle as the girl tried to muster boredom. Most of her succeeded but her eyes failed.

Quick blinks, suddenly dilated pupils. Emotional interest in the topic. Finally: "Yeah, so?"

"So I know they'd want you to talk to us."

"Cops lie. You coulda ruined my frikkin' life."

"Mrs. Corey *lost* her life, Laura. So if you could just—"

"How do I know you're not shitting and this isn't . . . whatever."

"Hey," said the boy, lifting the glass bong out of the bag.

"Get out of here," she screamed. Facing Milo: "No frikkin' way, you can't come in without a *warrant*."

"Laura, I couldn't care less about—"

"No, no, I don't have to take it, I don't, it's my rights." Sucking in breath. "You need to *go*."

"Actually, I don't," said Milo, scuffing his way closer. "This is Marissa and Ashley's residence, you're here with no explanation, for all we know you're trespassing." To the boy: "What's your name and how'd you get here?"

"Uh."

"Uh may be your philosophy but it ain't your name. *Cooperate*."

"Jared. I met her."

"Jared what?"

"LoPrinzi."

"Who's her?"

"Her." Glance at Laura.

"When did you meet her?"

"Uh last night."

Milo turned to Laura. She said, "I'm not saying nothing."

Back to Jared: "Find your clothes and get out of here."

"Uh they're in back."

Milo prodded the boy toward the rear of the apartment, leaving me alone with Laura. I tried a therapeutic smile. She crossed her arms over her chest and whispered something unpleasant. I turned to scanning the junk on the floor. Interesting stuff began to pop up; another bong, little plastic Baggies specked with white. Stare long enough and mastodon bones would probably emerge.

Jared LoPrinzi returned with Milo trailing, wearing a Foo Fighters T-shirt, jeans, and motorcycle boots. After he was gone, Laura looked even smaller.

Milo said, "Enough messing around. Ms. Smith, I could take you in right now for questioning."

Fear passed over the girl's face. She fought it with indignation. "Bullshit, they asked me not to say."

"The girls?"

"Yeah."

"Why are you here?"

"They asked me that, too."

"Why?"

"To take care of the place."

Milo eyed the filth. "Ah."

"Okay?" she said. "Now you can go?"

"Where are Ashley and Marissa?"

"Gone."

"Where?"

"Ask them."

"I would if I could reach them."

"Why don't you just cuh-*all* them?" said Laura.

"They don't answer their phones."

She giggled. "So what's that te-ell you?"

Milo pulled out his handcuffs.

Laura said, "No, no way!" Her lips crimped and she held her arms close to her torso, an infant who'd woken up starving. "Imago Smith's my father, he's had twenty-three number ones."

"Bully for him. Turn around and fold your hands behind your head."

She hesitated. Milo took one wrist and cuffed it. Laura Smith said, "Okay! They're using *prepaids,* okay! Ditched their regular ones, even I don't know the numbers, *okay?*"

"Why'd they do that?"

"Ask 'em."

"Laura—"

"I don't know—stop, you're hurting me, I'm gonna sue you, I don't have it, I don't know nothing!"

"You're house-sitting but they didn't tell you where—"

"I had a number, okay? Then it didn't work anymore. Okay? They probably used that one up and got another. Okay?"

"Sounds like they're scared, Laura."

The girl looked down at her shackled wrist. Small bones; Milo hadn't ratcheted tight, she could've slipped out. She began crying. "Are you really going to arrest me? I can't stand jail!"

"Not if you cooperate."

"They told me not to *say*! Okay? I'm doing what they *asked.* Okay? *Okay!*"

Milo removed the cuff. "I'm not here to hassle you, Laura. How about we start over?"

"But I don't know nothing—"

"What are they scared of, Laura?"

The girl's head swiveled from side to side, finally settled on a kitchenette as gross as the floor. She said, "I can't, they made me promise."

"C'mon," said Milo, gently.

The shift in tone made her look at him.

"Laura—"

"Sydney and Jasper."

"Their horses."

As if knowledge of that fact lent Milo new status; Laura Smith smiled at him. "Yeah."

"What about Sydney and Jasper?"

"They were gone. Okay?"

"From the house—"

"Ashley and Riss show up to exercise them and they're gone, totally gone, everything's gone, all the furniture inside, Sydney and Jasper's tack and food, everything. They thought it was a robbery, because someone broke in just before, put weird food in the kitchen. So they called him and he laughed and said, 'Funny thing 'bout that.' And they're like freaked out, totally freaked out, they tell him again and he says the same thing. 'Funny about that.' Then he says something really terrible."

"We're talking their dad."

Sniff. Tears. Nod.

"What did he say that was terrible, Laura?"

"He said, 'People need glue' and then he hung up. That means he's turning Sydney and Jasper to glue! They're totally totally freaked out but when they try to talk to him, he just hangs up. And when they try to call him again, he doesn't answer."

"Angry at them," I said.

"He's like turned into a monster, like who *is* this? They *love* Sydney and Jasper. *Glue?*"

"That is cold," said Milo. "They had no idea he'd do something like that."

"Nothing!" said Laura Smith. "It's like they . . . like he's a zombie dad, who ate their real dad, is like inhabiting his brain and his body."

"They're scared of him," I said. "That's why they left and are using prepaids."

"He's the one taught them about that."

"Prepaids?"

"He always has 'em, like when he wants to call out but doesn't want anyone bothering him."

I said, "They're scared of more than the horses."

Silence.

"They need help, Laura. The only way they can get it is if we know the facts."

She looked away.

I said, "You have reason not to like the cops but the cops didn't turn Sydney and Jasper into glue and the cops aren't going to hurt Ashley and Marissa. So—"

"They think he coulda *did* it!"

"Did what?"

"It," said Laura. "Her. You know."

"Their mom."

Three nods. "They didn't think that before but maybe now."

"What changed their minds?"

"They like . . . wondered about it in the beginning because they used to hate each other—their mom and dad. But then they said no way, he's our dad. But then he turned into a zombie and took Sydney and Jasper and everything in the house and talked mean to them."

"So they split and let you stay here."

She shrugged. "My dad's mad at me. I cracked his car up again."

"When did Ashley and Marissa leave town, Laura?"

"Like two days ago."

"You have no idea where they went."

"They said they'd tell me when they got there but they didn't."

"They haven't tried to contact you."

"Uh-uh. No."

We waited.

She said, "No. Really." Serious. No more snotty bifurcation of words.

Milo said, "If you do find out, is there any chance you'd tell me?"

Fear and skepticism fought for control of her pretty face.

"Laura, we're here because we want to keep them safe."

No answer. He gave her his card. She mouthed *Homicide*. "They talked about Vegas, but I don't know. If they call me, I'll tell them."

I said, "Thanks. And one more thing: Have you considered that by staying here you could be putting yourself in danger?"

"Why?"

"If Mr. Corey is that weird—"

She turned pale. "Oh. I need to book. I'm outta here, Daddy will be cool, he always is."

Milo said, "Get your stuff, we'll see you out."

"I got nothing here, just a few clothes." Glancing at the copper bong.

"Where are you parked?"

"Down below."

"We'll walk you."

A beat. "Okay."

Her car was a new red baby Benz, scratched and dented, in need of washing.

Milo said, "You're sure everything's cool at home."

"Yeah, Immy's cool. Not like *him.*"

"Ashley and Marissa's dad."

"I always thought he was a freak."

"Why's that?"

"He's like no . . . feelings? You say something and it's like android-freak-o in the room."

"Was he ever mean to Ashley and Marissa before?"

"Uh-uh. He bought them whatever they wanted, only thing is he'd want them to watch TV with him. They said it was boring, they'd try to get out of it."

"They don't like TV."

"You think?" she said. "You stream on your phone. He's a freak, watching stupid murder shows, they're like ge-ross. But he gave them money and stuff when they wanted."

"No more," I said.

"He's a frickin' *freak,*" said Laura Smith. "Stealing their stuff? *Glue?* Telling them *no?*"

27

The red Mercedes drove off.

Milo said, "My prayers answered, bastard made a big mistake."

"What?"

"Getting between girls and their horses."

We returned to the sisters' apartment, where he searched for a lead on their whereabouts. Plenty of evidence for a penny-ante drug bust and more than enough for health department shutdown but they'd covered their tracks.

I drove back to the city and he called Moe Reed, pulling the young detective off nighttime watch on Flora Sullivan and assigning him to keep an eye on the Corey girls' building.

"They're unlikely to show up, but maybe. The main thing is be on the lookout for their father, he's who they're running from." He described the changes in Richard Corey's behavior.

Reed said, "Killing their horses? That's cold, what does Doc think of all this?"

Milo said, "Angry man buttoned up for a long time, the buttons are popping."

"Poetic," said Reed.

Milo grinned. "Doc can get that way."

"So the theory is all that buttoning made him tense, he took it out on other women besides Ursula?"

"Good summary, Moses. Where's Sean?"

"Same as me, L.T., watching the building. Why do you think Corey's freaking out now?"

"He probably thinks he's in the clear, can do whatever he wants."

"Well," said Reed, "we'll see about that."

Call number two was to Oxnard PD where after several false starts Milo connected with Homicide Detective Francisco Gonzales and asked for help with Richard Corey. Gonzales, jovial sounding and deep-voiced, was nearing the end of a thirty-hour haul, closing a multiple-victim, home-invasion gang shooting.

"Got my confessions, now I need to get toothpicks for my eyelids."

Milo said, "Congrats. Listen, if it's too much of a hassle, tell me who else I can talk to."

"Nah," said Gonzales. "My case was morons against morons, yours actually sounds interesting. Give me time to catch some Z's, then you can buy me dinner."

"When and where, Detective?"

"Frank. Give me your number, I'll call you."

Three and a half hours later, Milo and I were at a corner table in an Oxnard winery restaurant. High-end industrial park, the kind of businesses that required massive buildings and didn't advertise.

This building was prettier than its neighbors, stuccoed ocher and rust and set up with a self-guided tour. The tasting room out front was filled with happy-looking sippers. I knew the place, had been there years ago for a meet with the young widow of a bad man. But I hadn't suggested the place, Gonzales had.

He arrived moments after Milo and I had been seated, a pigeon-chested, large-bellied six-footer with slicked black hair and a gray Zapata mustache. He wore a white polo shirt, black slacks, white-soled black deck shoes. Heavy man but firmly packed; he moved quickly and smoothly, a tree-trunk prop in a school play wheeled across the stage.

Handshakes all around. Gonzales had a strong grip and clear eyes, the only sign of fatigue some imprecise shaving where his jowls met his neck.

Dipping bread in olive oil, he chewed and swallowed, wiped the mustache.

A waitress showed up with menus and a special smile for Gonzales. The order was quick and easy: three 16-ounce rib eyes, medium rare, salad in lieu of potatoes the nod to virtue. The waitress said, "Of course," as if everything had been preordained.

The salads arrived quickly, followed by gratis bowls of cured olives, fried squash blossoms, and salt-cod beignets. Frank Gonzales wasn't surprised.

Milo said, "You're a regular?"

"Regular as I can be. Mostly I have to eat crap on the go."

"Know what you mean," said Milo.

Gonzales's curious, hazel eyes glided toward me. "Psychologist. My daughter wants to be one."

Milo gave him the short version of my involvement with the department followed by a short-version summary of all the murders. Even abbreviated the account took a while. Gonzales possessed a detective's most important trait: good listener.

When Milo was finished, he said, "So this Corey character, you're figuring a John List–type thing? One of those tight-ass types who offs their entire family and reinvents himself?" Aiming the question at me.

I said, "There are elements of that but most family slaughterers do it in one bloody show."

"This guy's more calculated?"

"Or his motives were mixed and he decided recently to get his daughters."

"Mixed how?"

"His wife was done for money and because he hated her, it took a while for him to feel secure enough to aggress against the girls."

"And the other murders?"

Milo said, "DiMargio—the one with the tattoos and the body piercing—was possibly groomed as the wife's shooter, then bumped when she was no longer necessary. The accountant may have been the first grooming candidate but she refused."

"And the homeless gal just got on his nerves—the lawyer's nerves," said Gonzales. "That's a little complicated."

"Oh, yeah," said Milo. "But any way you look at it, he doesn't like women."

"If his wife really slept with anything that moved, that couldn't have helped," said Gonzales. "But maybe he's just paranoid."

"Love to find out, Frank."

"Wow . . . this is more than interesting—right up your alley, Doctor." To Milo: "So what do you need from me?"

Milo said, "Don't know your manpower situation, but I could use as much of a watch on Corey's condo as possible. We drove by just before coming here. No car there, but he could be garaging it."

"Mandalay Bay," said Gonzales. "Access on both sides?"

"No, just on the street. Unless you consider a two-story deck access."

"Maybe if he's Tarzan. Yeah, I know the area. There's a little promenade paralleling the harbor. You check if he's got a boat?"

"There wasn't one in his slip when we met him."

"Easy enough to find out. In terms of our manpower situation, it's what the bosses say it is on any given day. I'll do my best to scare you up a couple of watchers but you might have to settle for kids, I'm talking real green. Rookies trying to score brownie points."

"Beggars-choosers, Frank."

"That's what my wife tells me."

Two hours later, well into evening, I pulled into the staff lot at the West L.A. station. As Milo unbuckled his seat belt, his phone played a Chopin étude.

Frank Gonzales's voice on speaker, basso, mellow, steady. "Back at you, Milo. Snagged myself a sweet deal that'll play to your benefit. Officially I'm on the job but I get to take *my* boat out and watch Corey's place from the water, department's even supplying binoculars. And no rules against fishing, in fact my captain agrees a couple of rods in the water will provide excellent cover."

"How'd you pull that off?"

"Put away a whole bunch of bad guys," said Gonzales. "Or maybe it's my minty-fresh breath. Anyway, if Corey does take a walk on the promenade, I can keep an eye on him for a good quarter mile in either direction. Same if he sails away because, yeah, he does have a registered craft, nothing fancy, twenty-foot cruiser."

Milo said, "Maybe it was out for maintenance the day we were there. As in he's preparing to take a little trip."

"Maybe, but the papers say he keeps it in Ventura," said Gonzales. "One good thing, he's not going to get far in that thing, though he could set out on a fake pleasure cruise, dock in Santa Barbara or farther in San Simeon, or go the other way and bail in Long Beach."

"Why keep the boat in Ventura when he's got a slip right behind the condo?"

"Still trying to find out. Meanwhile, I've got a two-person team rotating on him, just what I said, couple of clueless young 'uns willing to sell their own mothers for the privilege of having their butts fall asleep."

Milo said, "Eight-hour shifts?"

"Twelve," said Gonzales. "Poor little suckers. Then again, I never met their mothers."

Tracing the Corey girls' escape turned out to be simple. Milo cold-called Visa, MasterCard, Amex, and Discovery, struck gold with Visa, struck platinum with an astonishingly cooperative supervisor named Brenda. His assurance that it was a "life-or-death matter" might've cut through the red tape, but he hung up beating his chest and proclaiming, "The charm has been *reactivated*! Rico Suave is *back*!"

Like the old song says, little things mean a lot.

Each sister had her own card but the account numbers were sequential. Ashley's had been used to buy a tankful of gas just east of Palm Springs. The rest of the charges alternated between the sisters, all racked up in Las Vegas, just as Laura Smith had said. Additional fuel, food, cosmetics, substantial charges at the Venetian that approximated the hotel's rate for a deluxe room plus some room service.

Milo said, "Escaping to Sin City. Hopefully it's actually them and not someone with their plastic."

I said, "They can't be thinking too straight. Even if Ursula paid the charges before, Richard would get them now."

"Ah, impetuous youth." He called Brenda again, confirmed that a request had been made to mail the bills to the condo in Oxnard.

"Is there any way to block that temporarily?"

"Why would we do that, Lieutenant?"

"Between you and me, that's their father's address and he's who we're worried about."

"Oh . . . sorry, officially there's no way without a court order."

"But," said Milo.

Click click click buzz buzz. "Now we're not being recorded. At least on my end."

"Not on mine either."

"All right," said Brenda. "Here's what I think: We're a big company with excellent technical support. But glitches do come up. Though they tend to get fixed pretty quickly."

"Maybe one glitch could be replaced by another?" said Milo.

The woman laughed. "You're a demanding fellow."

"Truth, justice, blah blah blah, Brenda. Seriously, these are scared kids and they're in danger."

"From their father. That's horrible. Okay, I'll see what I can do."

"Thanks a ton."

"My brother's a cop. Indianapolis."

"That's great, Brenda."

"Thought you'd see it that way."

28

Richard Corey proved to be a creature of low activity and even lower sociability.

He remained inside his condo except for a noon trip to buy beer and a solitary evening walk along the waterfront.

"The kid I put on him said he acted kind of weird," said Frank Gonzales. "Kept his eyes on the ground, didn't pay attention to anyone, even his tenants. Younger couple, they met him walking, Corey passed right by. But the kid's greener than lettuce, could be dramatizing. Today I'll check on Corey's boat."

Milo said, "I found it. Cracked engine block, dry-docked in a boatyard near the Ventura harbor until Corey gives the okay to repair. Meanwhile he's paying storage fees."

"Good for you," said Gonzales. "Does the yard happen to be Harvey's Boat Haven?"

"As a matter of fact."

"I know Harvey Milner. I'll have him call me if anything changes."

"Thanks, Frank."

"I should be thanking you, sunny day on the water, fishing's been not bad, mostly smelts, but one nice rock cod. You cook?"

"Not much."

"Me neither, but my wife does. In her hands, smelts is gourmet."

Milo phoned Deputy D.A. John Nguyen and asked if Richard Corey's prior permission to examine his financial and phone records still applied.

Nguyen said, "Probably not."

"It was pretty open-ended, John."

"This ever goes to trial, you want to blow it on something stupid?"

"Damn."

Nguyen said, "Maybe . . . I guess a case could be made either way. Theoretically. But you didn't learn anything the first time, so why bother?"

"We think this guy had his wife killed and did three other women by himself. Now we're concerned he'll go after his daughters. He sold their horses for slaughter and emptied the ex's house."

"Making a big change," said Nguyen. "A John List thing?"

"Could be."

"Horses, huh? Sounds like parent of the year. Where are the daughters?"

"On the run. But Corey's super-rich, can move fast, John. Anything we can do to get a handle on his behavior could be useful."

"Bastard ends up killing his kids, wouldn't that be a headline? Okay, have your way with his paper trail. You need backup from some white-collar droid, give 'em my number."

"You bet, John." Milo grinned at me. He'd already begun scouring without authorization.

Nguyen said, "Any idea where the girls are?"

"Their credit cards have them in Vegas yesterday, checking out of the Venetian and returning to California. Gas and munchies in Barstow, then Bakersfield, then to Carmel, where they rented another hotel room. If they've moved since, I don't know about it yet."

"Which hotel in Carmel?"

"Seaview Lodge."

"You're kidding," said Nguyen. "Took a chick there couple of years ago, we're talking high-end girlie-spa. These kids are scared but they're getting hot-rock massages and salt rubs? Daddy paying those credit cards?"

"Yup, but I blocked his access to charges and if he tries to cut off the accounts it won't go through."

"How'd you pull that off?"

"Gentle persuasion and a bit of . . ."

"Say no more," said Nguyen. "Even so, the girls don't know he's been blocked, so what, are they stupid?"

"They're not geniuses, John, but maybe they're just doing what they know."

"Which is?"

"Living idly and well."

"Run for your lives and take a cool road trip? At the risk of emptying my bladder on the winning float in the Rose Bowl Parade, I'd be remiss if I didn't raise another possibility."

"What?"

"They're not rabbiting, my friend, they're pulling a Menendez. Remember how the brothers traveled and partied right after they blasted Mom and Dad?"

Milo looked at me. The same question had come up early.

He said, "There's no evidence these girls have done anything criminal, John."

"So far."

"They definitely didn't kill their mother and I can't see them involved in the others."

"You're the detective," said Nguyen. "I'm just saying keep a corner of your mind receptive to bad news."

"John, my entire damn *brain* is a satellite dish aimed at bad news. Failure and rot is what I'm thinking about at this very moment and it's giving me a damn headache."

"Price of doing business," said Nguyen. "For me, Advil is an *hors d'oeuvre.*"

Milo passed the phone receiver from hand to hand, stared at the wall, drummed his desktop for a while, finally faced me. "Menendez gone femme?"

I said, "I don't think it's any more probable. Corey would have no reason to include two kids in his plans and Laura Smith seemed credible."

"A luxury hotel in Vegas, then a spa?"

"Just what you told Nguyen. Not too bright and sticking with the familiar."

"Even if they're traumatized."

"Maybe especially if they're traumatized. Also, they could be getting back at Daddy by spending his money while they can."

"Brat One Oh One." He knuckled an eye. "Show up to ride your horses, find out they're gone. Guess I can't blame 'em."

I said, "The horses and the entire contents of the home where they grew up. Which raises an interesting point: Corey would've had to hire an equine transport company and a sizable moving van. Maybe the guardhouse recorded the names of the companies."

"Assuming there was someone on duty with a functioning brain." Cursing under his breath, he found the number of the Rancho Lobo guardhouse and called.

Monte's Moving and Storage in Canoga Park had sent two vans paid for by Richard Corey to cart and transport household goods to a downtown warehouse leased by RC Enterprises. That company turned out to be a newly registered business owned solely by Richard Corey. No time lost replacing Urrick, Ltd.

Milo said, "Out with the old, in with the new."

I said, "Like we thought, this is all about Corey starting a new life."

He rubbed his face. "Nothing like a renaissance of blood."

The horses had been picked up by a Lancaster outfit named Equi-Trans, specializing in "humane transformation." The company's website was thin on specifics but Milo finally pried out the cold facts from a "representative."

Unwanted steeds were shipped to a pet-food slaughterhouse in Roswell, New Mexico.

He hung up. "Roswell. Coupla gorgeous animals turned to kibble for space aliens? Jesus."

Shoving his office door open, he charged into the hallway, stalked up and down a few times, returned. "Here I am with a bunch of murders and *horses* are getting to me."

"Animals can do that."

"Sydney and Jasper." He shook his head. "What the hell did they do to deserve being turned into pet chow? All right, enough sentimentality, onward."

He sat back down, waited.

I said, "What?"

"Help me define 'onward.'"

If I'd had anything to offer, I'd have told him.

The next forty-eight hours revealed no contact among Richard Corey, Grant Fellinger, and Flora Sullivan. After two nights of Fellinger and Sullivan returning dutifully to their spouses, enthusiasm for either lawyer as a suspect waned. The watch on Sullivan was lifted, surveillance on Fellinger limited to after dark.

Two additional days passed with nothing to report and Milo stopped calling me to pass along failure. That left me nothing to do but think and imagine.

The same questions kept spinning in my head.

If Richard Corey had hired his ex-wife's executioner and had worked solo on the other murders, why the dinner-for-two tableau? I'd explained it as a control-freak production. But there were all kinds of ways to assert dominance and Corey's condo had offered no signs of interest in culinary matters. Just the opposite, it was Sad Bachelor Central.

Had food and death somehow pushed an *accomplice's* buttons? The obvious candidate was Darius Kleffer, a man who made his living cooking and had been dumped by one of the victims. Kleffer had been in New York during Kathy Hennepin's murder but that didn't absolve him of the other killings.

Could Kleffer and Corey have met up somehow and devised a homicidal tit-for-tat?

I carve up your girlfriend, you shoot my wife.

And let's toss in a couple of other women just for laughs.

But so far no link had arisen between Kleffer and Corey and there didn't seem to be an avenue to search for one. Still, I wrote down Kleffer's name followed by a chunky question mark.

Flora Sullivan had dined out in style with her husband and her boyfriend. On the face of it that meant nothing. But she was Frankie DiMargio's link to a building that was looking more and more like a death-trap. Was *she* the link to the dinner scenes? Malignant foodie with a hobby other than pleather? Had we been too hasty eliminating her?

Next: the Corey sisters. Recent expenses placed them clear out of the country, in Vancouver, Canada. They'd purchased only small stuff, nothing close to the cost of a room. Crashing with friends?

If they were worried about their safety, why hadn't they contacted the police? Could they have been criminally involved? Professing love and grief for their mother but secretly allying with their father?

Had he used them, only to turn?

Bad man seeking a new life. Did that include a new love slave? Another victim already culled from the herd?

One thing seemed certain: Richard Corey *was* at the hub of all this evil. If nothing else proved it, the horses did; there *was* something about cruelty to animals that alerted you to a psychopath on duty, and Corey's casual dispatch of his daughters' beloved pets spoke to a special brand of callousness.

That fit the exploitation of Kathy Hennepin and Frankie DiMargio. Shy, withdrawn women vulnerable to the advances of even an awkward man like Corey? But Corey as a lothario was hard to picture.

That brought me squarely back to Grant Fellinger, a man able to overcome homeliness and bed a beauty like Ursula Corey. Smooth and aggressive and willing to use his legal training to battle a mentally ill homeless woman who'd yelled at him.

Bringing about her terrible death. Because killing was fun.

Maybe we'd been right about Fellinger from the beginning.

Food and death.

I looked down at my notes.

One name stood out: Darius Kleffer.

I tried to reach Milo, got voice mail everywhere, left multiple messages but didn't hear back until he texted me that evening:

thanks for the 💡. boo hoo, dk alibied on everything.

Advil was starting to look like a dandy appetizer.

Eventually, I cleared my head and focused on a limited issue: Why hadn't Frankie DiMargio been spotted at any tattoo parlors near her home or her work?

Maybe because my circle had been too narrow. Using my phone and the Internet, I expanded by several miles, composed and printed a list, left and began dropping into establishments staffed by people with high pain thresholds.

Smelling enough blood and electricity and rubbing alcohol to last a lifetime.

The prevailing attitude was surly mistrust of anyone with unbroken skin. Some of that receded when I explained that Frankie was a murder victim. But no one recognized her or the inkwork visible on her DMV photo.

I asked several artists about the quality of the work. Quick consensus: the kind of stuff anyone could achieve with stencils.

A couple of needle-wielders thought it likely that she'd frequented more than one source. I took that as a positive: more shops meant a higher probability of success. But a full day of searching proved futile.

I returned home and used my phone.

Clara DiMargio answered. "You found something!"

Feeling like a jerk, I said, "We're moving along, Mrs. DiMargio."

"Oh." Deflated.

"Could I ask a few more questions?"

Long sigh. "Sure."

"Did the money you and your husband give Frankie pay for her tattoos—"

"No way," she said. "Even if I agreed to that, which I wouldn't, my husband would have hit the roof. We paid her rent and her utilities—her phone when she still had one. Would there be enough left over for *that* garbage? I don't think so."

"Any idea how Frankie did pay?"

"You're saying someone else gave her money? Maybe the same person who . . . oh my God, why didn't I think of that? Where *did* she get money for *that*?"

"How recent was her last tattoo?"

"Well, I wouldn't know—hold on, maybe I do. A couple of months ago she came in with an especially ugly one, a snake around her neck, just crude and nasty and ugly. Bill got mad and asked where she was getting the money to waste. Frankie turned around and left."

Muffled sob. "I'd baked peanut butter cookies, Frankie loved them when she was a little girl. They went untouched. I tossed them in the trash. Oh, sir, everything just fell apart."

29

A control freak financing fresh ink might want to be on the scene to supervise.

I printed an L.A. street map and plotted, marking the epicenter between Frankie DiMargio's rented garage in Mar Vista and Even Odd, then radiating outward.

Plugging in the locations of tattoo parlors I'd already visited was discouraging: I'd covered more ground than I thought, with only a narrow band of untraveled territory remaining.

But that blade-shaped bit of terrain included a cluster of ink shops on or near Fairfax Avenue.

The fourth one I visited was called Tigray Art set between two Ethiopian restaurants and my hopes rose when I spotted an antiques shop called Nocturna sharing the space.

The room was divided by a waist-high partition of plywood stapled with sheets of black velvet. To the right were jumbles of junk, including some mangy-looking stuffed birds in cheap cages. To the left an old barber chair, porcelain chipped, steel oxidized. An ominous-looking needle replacing the dental drill dangled overhead.

The wall was papered with patterns and stencils. Monsters, demons, African animals, space aliens, nothing that matched the ink on Frankie DiMargio's DMV shot.

No customers in either side today. The proprietor was a huge black man wearing a red jersey tank top, green lederhosen, and knee-high riding boots. His own body art was done in an iridescent pale blue that created a head-to-toe brocade over dark skin. The effect was like viewing him through lace.

His earlobes were stretched to three times their normal size by studs and chains and a pair of rings pierced his septum—doing Bekka from Even Odd one better. Both eyebrows were paralleled overhead by seams of tiny diamonds embedded in his flesh. His welcoming smile flashed upper incisors filed to points.

Gesturing to the chair, he reached for the needle.

When I showed him Frankie DiMargio's picture both movements froze. "You want low-level like this? Don't do it, man."

I said, "Not up to your standards?"

"This is mundane, brother."

"Any idea who—"

"Don't waste my time." He turned away.

"This woman was murdered."

He stopped. Metal clanked. "You a cop?"

Pondering truth versus falsehood took less than a second. I flashed my useless consultant badge. Most people aren't attuned to details. He didn't even bother to look.

"Well, I don't know her, man."

I stepped forward and held the photo closer to him. "You have any idea who inked her?"

One of the diamond trails above his brows arced. The effect was a burst of miniature fireworks in a starless sky.

"Maybe."

"Maybe or definitely?"

"Yeah," he said. "I'm talking my brother."

"A colleague?"

"No, man, my brother, like he's Cain to the Abel."

"Your real brother?"

"Same mommy, different daddy. I taught him everything and he goes off on his own and does *that*?"

"He opened a competing business."

"Competing? I don't think so, man. That's like finger-painting competing with Michelangelo."

I glanced at the junk-pile portion of the store. "Does he also do antiques?"

"He does crap is what he does." He took Frankie's photo from me, studied, sneered. "Yeah, he did a lot of *this* crap. Like, that butt-ugly snake. Ever seen an asp looks like that? More like a toad with anorexia—this, too."

He pointed to a row of dots diagonally sectioning Frankie's chin. "And look at that bug, that qualify for Egyptian scarab? More like a cockroach. That over there is Khepri." Pointing to a design on his wall. "Mofo tries for scarab, ends up with a diabetic cockroach. He's got no visual perception, man, couldn't draw a scarab if you held a gun to his head."

"Where can I find your untalented brother?"

"Where else?" he said. "The Valley. He's 818 consciousness from the get-go."

"Could I have his name and address, please?"

"She really died? Huh. Well I don't think *he* killed her." Laughing. "He's too chicken-liver for that, his work's like . . ." jabbing the photo. "Look here, all wispy, no meat and potatoes. Too scared to dig in and get *down*."

"See what you mean. His name—"

"I called this place Tigray, know what it means?"

"Tiger?"

"No, man, that's Spanish, with an 'e.' This is with a 'y,' *that* my tribe. Tigray nobles from Eritrea. All my life I've had lucid dreams informing me I'm from the union of Sheba and Solomon."

I nodded.

"You don't believe me," he said, "that's *your* problem. The day will come when monarchs arise and the truth blinds."

"Hope it helps with the traffic problem."

He stared at me. Cracked up. "Okay, you're a comedian, I like comedians, did a few in my day." Rattling off a series of names, some famous, others obscure.

"Mostly," he said, "they do it hidden. What I call MBA ink."

"Like a mullet," I said. "Business in front, party in back."

"Mullet's for rednecks." He poked Frankie DiMargio's photo. Her image rippled. "Sorry for her, she looks like she was a serious chick. Good bone structure, I could've done her proud. Tigretto wasted her time."

"That's the name of your brother's shop."

"No, man, that's what he calls himself. Tigretto aka Little Tigray. Like we're Italian or something. The shop is Zanzibar. Like he's *from* there." Laughter. "He's from Pasadena."

Thirty-five minutes later I was facing a soft-bodied, light-skinned black man with a baby face. A shaved head helped foster the image of an overgrown infant. So did his voice. Michael Jackson in a hurry.

His layout was identical to his brother's, tattoos plus random junk. When he saw Frankie DiMargio's picture, he said, "Oh, sure, the quiet one. She send you?" Looking me over. "You want MBA ink?"

"Unfortunately, she's dead," I said. "Murdered." Anticipating his next question, I flicked the consultant's badge. He gaped, paid no attention to my insufficient qualifications.

"Murdered? Oh, no, by who?"

"That's what we're trying to figure out."

Tigretto's eyes moistened. "I'm so sorry for her, she was a great customer." Pointing. "I did that and that and that."

"Who did the rest of it?"

"No idea."

"How long has she been coming in?"

"A few months."

"Did she ever come in with anyone else?"

"With a guy," said Tigretto. "Her boyfriend, he knew what he wanted for her. Him I knew before because he came in with another chick. Total virgin, she was going to make the plunge but wimped out."

"When was that?"

"Hmm . . . I'd say maybe . . . a year ago? Less, six, seven months. Then he came in with Frankie and she went all-out. I figured maybe that's why he found himself a new chick, the first one didn't cooperate."

"Can you describe the first one?"

"Hell, yeah, I got great visual perception and memory. White, straight, not bad looking. Quiet. She never argued with him and she actually got in the chair but then, just as I was about to start, she just up and split."

I said, "Stay put," left his shop, hurried to the Seville, and found Katherine Hennepin's photo in the pile of case material I kept in the trunk.

Tigretto said, "Yeah, that's her. No reason for her to wimp, I use topical numbing cream. Except for people who come in not only for the art but also for the pain."

"Was Frankie like that?"

"You know," he said, "she was. She said the pain made her feel real."

"Tell me about the guy with her."

"Knew what he wanted."

"How so?"

"She's the one getting inked but he's directing. What to draw, where to put it, what color. And unless he's MBA'd under his clothes, he's got no ink of his own. I asked him if he wanted something for himself, doing a couples thing, some people find it romantic, you know? He shakes his head and points to Frankie and tells me she's the canvas."

"That's the word he used? 'Canvas.'"

Nod. "Like he thinks he's the artist when I am. But he had the money so I got going. It took time, that Nile asp was big and complicated, Cleopatra would be proud."

He beamed.

I said, "Frankie tolerated it well."

"She just sat there, no topical, not moving a muscle. Like a dog on tranqs. I've seen it before. I see all kinds of things. Psychology, you know?"

"Describe the guy with her."

He did.

Everything changed.

CHAPTER

30

Another shift of a mad prism, a new paradigm.

I dialed Milo's mobile frantically. Voice mail; same for his desk phone. I tried the landline at his house, got Rick's grave rendition: *If this is an emergency for Dr. Silverman . . . if you're trying to reach Detective Sturgis . . .*

"It's me, call me back, A-sap." Swinging away from the curb, I sped back to Laurel Canyon. Two blocks in, my cell chirped.

Milo said, "Glad I reached you."

"You got my message?"

"What message? No, I've got one for you, guess who just called? Grant Fellinger. Sounding scared as hell and asking to meet sooner, not later. I'm on my way over right now. Feel free to join the party, maybe he'll validate parking for both of us."

Click.

I caught up with him in the reception area of Grant Fellinger's law firm. Pocketing his badge as the receptionist said, "This way," and rose to escort him.

New face at the front desk: a fuzzy-bearded boy-man around five four in place of the pretty young Latina who'd been there the first time. Milo's long legs outpaced him and after struggling to keep up, Fuzzy said, "I'm just a temp," and returned to his post.

Like the first time, Fellinger was waiting out in the hallway. The moment he saw us, he ducked into his office.

When we entered he was behind his desk, sitting up straight, trying to look calm and authoritative. Futile attempt; he'd sweated navy splotches all over his pale-blue shirt, his tie hung off center, and patches of his hair had come unslicked.

An empty Old-Fashioned glass sat at his elbow, next to a fifth of Johnnie Blue.

"Thank you for responding quickly. I hope I'm overreacting."

Milo said, "To what, sir?"

"Merry's disappearance," said Fellinger. "Maybe it's nothing, I hope it is, but this isn't like her."

"Merry being—"

"Meredith Santos, our receptionist."

"Pretty girl—"

"*Gorgeous* girl," said Fellinger, eyes sailing to the right.

More than professional feelings? Catching himself, he looked directly at us. "By that I mean gorgeous inside as well as out. She's a real class kid, terrific worker, military vet, never took a sick day. You don't see that often. I try to reward exemplary employees by taking them to dinner, just did that for Merry."

"The problem is—"

"She hasn't shown up for work for three days running and no one can reach her."

Fellinger kneaded some of the extra flesh beneath his ears. "Maybe that doesn't sound like a big deal, Lieutenant, but as I said, you'd have to know Merry. Calls, texts, nothing. It's just not like her."

"Does she live alone?"

"No, in Venice," said Fellinger. "Oh. That was a non sequitur, wasn't it? Sorry." Deep breath. "She lives in a house in Venice with two roommates, girls around her age. Problem is, they're both traveling, couple of weeks in Europe. This morning we called Merry's folks in Phoenix. Her parents were getting worried, too, and I'm afraid we did nothing to calm them down."

"Has anyone been by her apartment?"

Fellinger blushed. "I did. On the way home from work, last night. I knocked, rang, no answer. Looked through her mail slot and saw mail on the floor."

A fresh coat of sweat glazed his forehead. "You probably think I'm overreacting. But here's the thing—and this is going to sound strange, particularly in view of what happened to Ursula—as if we're some sort of . . . we're just a boring law firm, nothing out of the ordinary occurs here . . . I'm sure this is irrelevant but the timing . . . maybe I shouldn't even open up this Pandora's box, if I'm wrong and frankly I hope I am, it'll turn out irrelevant. Because this person's already unhappy with the firm and the last thing we need is complications."

"Which person is that, sir?"

Fellinger pinged his empty glass with a fingernail. Long, deep breath. "Recently, we let an employee go. A couple of days before Merry disappeared. I'm sure there's no link, but . . . Merry had problems with him. Other people, as well."

Milo said, "Other women?"

Fellinger poured himself scotch, tossed it back. "Several female employees were made to feel uncomfortable, so we were forced to take action. He didn't take well to being fired, not well at all. In fact, he showed me a different side of himself. Nasty. We confronted him and the day he left I noticed him passing Merry's desk and giving her a look. I'd have to call it rage. Cold rage. I forgot about it but then Merry didn't show up and by the third day—" A second quick snort. He burped. Grimaced.

"Lieutenant, here's where it's really going to get dodgy, but I might as well . . ."

Rolling the glass between his hands. "Not only did I get to thinking about Merry, I also began wondering about Ursula. Because this person *was* with Ursula shortly before she died. Walked her to the elevator, for all I know he rode down with her. By itself that means nothing, if he hadn't showed me that other side of himself, I'd never have given it a second thought. But the look he gave Merry plus all the other complaints. And now no one can find Merry—I just don't *know.*"

I said, "What was Jens Williams accused of specifically?"

Milo's head whipped toward me.

Fellinger blinked. "You already had him on your radar? Oh, God."

Still studying me, Milo said, "How about we start at the beginning, Mr. Fellinger?"

"The beginning was nine months ago when we hired Jens. My previous assistant left to have a baby and I happened to be talking to a colleague and she said she had a cousin who'd fit the bill perfectly."

"Which colleague was that?"

"Another attorney in the building," said Fellinger. "We've worked together, there was a trust level and this cousin sounded ideal. Yale graduate, had worked as a playwright, smart, industrious. He interviewed fine. A bit on the wimpy side but that's okay, I don't need attitude. I even paid him a bit more than I might normally because of the Ivy League thing."

"Give me the name of Williams's cousin, Mr. Fellinger."

"She needs to be involved? You're sure it's relevant?"

"I'm not sure of anything."

"All right . . . her name is Flora Sullivan but I can't believe she'd have anything to do with something . . . unsavory."

Tall, lanky woman. Bird-like, myopic. Same body type as Jens Williams. A pair of storks.

Once you knew, the family resemblance was obvious.

I said, "Williams ended up being a disappointment."

Grant Fellinger said, "He was no great shakes as an assistant, but adequate. It wasn't until a couple of weeks ago that other attorneys in the firm began to take me aside. Their staffers had started complaining about Jens. Had been feeling uneasy for a while but no one came forward because no one knew it was more than an individual issue. But once women began talking to each other, a pattern arose. Not something you could really sink your teeth into, no inappropriate touching, not even remarks. He'd just begun to bother female employees by looking at them. By being there when he didn't need to be."

I said, "Showing up and creeping them out."

"Exactly. The complainants—there were seven of them, all younger women—would find him staring at them. The adjectives they used included lascivious, sly, weird, spooky, stalky. Even rapey, which is a new one on me. In any event, you get the picture. So how do you deal with something so ambiguous? There were certainly no legal grounds but I met with the partners and we agreed we'd have to do something."

He looked back at the bar. "Here's where it gets sensitive. I absolutely need you to be discreet."

We waited.

Fellinger said, "Well . . . what we decided was that we'd try to find something else about Jens that was objectionable and use that to get him out. And he made it easy because his work had begun to suffer. Tardiness, lack of focus, downright apathetic toward the end. I began wondering about some sort of emotional issue. Particularly in view of the complaints."

I said, "Inhibitions breaking down."

"Here's an example," said Fellinger. "One of the partners has a crackerjack assistant, she's been with him for years. One day she exited the ladies' room and found Jens right outside the door. Lurking, as she called it. He didn't move when she saw him, just stayed there. Smirking. We're not talking the main lav which is out in the open, men's and women's side by side. This was a smaller unisex bathroom in the storage room. She was searching for files but Jens wasn't. I know because I didn't assign him to look for anything."

Milo said, "See what you mean. So the firm looked for dirt on him."

Fellinger frowned. "I'd prefer to call it constructive research. I assumed the primary responsibility because I'd hired him. I went over his résumé with a fine-tooth comb. Which, I'm embarrassed to say, I *didn't* do the first time. He was Flora's cousin and she gave him high accolades. Turns out he fooled everyone *including* Flora. At first when I told her we'd have to let him go, she wasn't pleased, we actually had words. But then when she learned the truth, she understood. And called me later that day to apologize, turns out he's only her third cousin, she didn't know him that well."

Tense chat in the parking garage.

Milo said, "What truth did she learn?"

Fellinger threw up his hands. "He lied about everything. He did attend Yale, but only for a semester, he flunked out. Playwriting was total b.s. No productions, no credits, nor did he work for any of the firms he listed."

"What kind of firms?"

"A theatrical publisher, ad agencies. Even the law firm in New York where he'd claimed to work knew him as a client. They defended him in a battery case."

Milo said, "A defendant who uses it for his bio. That's pretty nervy."

"I guess if we'd done due diligence it would've ended before it began. But now my main concern is Merry Santos."

"And maybe Ursula Corey."

"Oh, Jesus, I hope not."

I said, "Given all his lies about employment, any idea how he's supported himself?"

"The only bona fide job he listed," said Fellinger, "the only one I could confirm, was—get this—cooking. He worked as a chef in a New York restaurant. Not a full chef, some sort of assistant. I talked to the manager but he wasn't helpful beyond 'personal issues.' But I can guess."

Another toss of hands. "Idiot couldn't even hold on to a kitchen job!"

31

We remained in Fellinger's office as Milo worked his phone. John Jensen Williams's phone account had been disconnected weeks ago.

I thought: disposables. His and hers.

Maybe his his and hers, if you factored in Richard Corey, a man who'd used untraceables for years.

The home address Williams had given the law firm traced to a body shop in East Hollywood. The proprietor, one Armand Hagopian, had never heard of Williams nor had he ever worked on the six-year-old Ford van Williams had registered in Connecticut.

Learning all that turned Grant Fellinger a sickly shade of gray. "How the hell did we pay him?"

Milo said, "That was going to be my next question."

A race-walk through the suite brought us to the desk of a woman in her sixties named Vivian who handled purchasing for the firm and doubled as the bursar. She said, "Oh, him. He picked up his check in person. Like clockwork."

Fellinger said, "You didn't find that odd, Viv?"

"I found *him* odd, Mr. F."

I said, "How so?"

"I don't know, just a little . . . removed? Like he was in another world? I didn't mind the check, though. Saved us postage and an envelope, save some trees, huh, Mr. F.?"

Back in Fellinger's office, the three of us remained standing. Fellinger kept eyeing the booze, grew fidgety, laced his hands together as if imposing external restraint.

I said, "How exactly did Williams react when you fired him?"

"At first he said nothing. Stared at me—glared at me. I kept waiting for him to say something but he didn't so I asked him if he had anything to offer. He didn't even shake his head, just kept glaring, like he was trying to bore into my brain with his eyes. I've been to court and seen enough mind-games, it didn't bother me. But objectively, it *was* creepy. I really understood what our gals had been going through."

"He had a way of being intrusive without actually doing anything."

"Yes. But let me reiterate: This was a totally different person from the one I hired."

Milo said, "So he just glared. That was it?"

"No," said Fellinger. "That changed when I began walking away and he said, 'Just deserts.' Which I took as a threat so I faced him and gave him a bit of stink-eye and he slinked off."

"Just deserts," I said. "A chef using a food analogy." Aiming that at Milo, not Fellinger.

Fellinger said, "Not even a full chef, he's obviously a loser."

Milo said, "How, specifically, did Meredith Santos say Williams bothered her?"

"Same as the others. Hanging around—she called it an incursion into her personal space. And one time she also found him loitering outside the bathroom. But the main head, so a men's room next to a women's wasn't overtly weird. What really bothers me about Merry is she was one of the last to complain about Jens."

I said, "Engaging him at his angriest."

Nod. "And now he's gone and no one can find her."

He turned to Milo. "Please. Do your utmost. If something happened to Merry, I'd never get over it. She wasn't on my personal staff, she worked for the entire firm, but we were—I suppose she considered me more available than the other partners. More prone to offering positive feedback. And Jens would know that, so if he's trying to get to me—I don't even want to think about it."

"Any special perks for Ms. Santos beyond merit dinners?" said Milo.

Fellinger blinked. Thick shoulders gathered around his bull-neck. "If you're implying some sort of inappropriate relationship, you're way off base, Lieutenant."

"Doing my job means asking questions, Mr. Fellinger."

"Fine. And the answer is no."

"So there'd be no reason beyond your getting along with Ms. Santos for Williams to use her against you."

Fellinger looked down. "Perhaps he resented—look, Lieutenant, I'm a red-blooded American guy but I understand boundaries."

I thought of his hand on Ursula Corey's ass. Maybe Milo was thinking the same thing when he didn't respond.

Fellinger said, "Why in the world you'd want to waste time attacking me—"

"Richard Corey told us you and Ursula were—"

"Having an affair? Nonsense."

"Corey's totally off base?"

"About a romantic affair? Absolutely."

Milo stood there.

Fellinger scratched the side of his broad, flared nose. "Were we screwing occasionally? Yes, we were. But that was pure recreational sex and it only happened after Ursula and Richard were separated irrevocably. In my mind, that doesn't violate any boundaries whatsoever, because there was no power inequality between Ursula and myself. If anything, she had the upper hand."

"The checkbook."

"No need to be vulgar, Lieutenant. But yes, she was the client and I served at her convenience. So we had sex, big deal. I'm assuming we're all adults here."

"Last I checked, sir. But you can see why we'd want to clarify."

"I'm afraid I can't." Fellinger huffed. "If that idiot said Ursula and I were romantic, he was being delusional. Ursula was a red-blooded woman and I saw no reason not to indulge her. Frankly, if Richard could get it up in the first place, Ursula wouldn't have been compelled to look elsewhere. I've worked on their case for five years and, to be brutally honest, Richard's a washout in every way you can imagine."

"When we spoke to you the first time, you seemed less disapproving of him."

"I was being gracious," said Fellinger. "Being professional. There was no reason to—in any event, what does any of this have to do with the issue at hand? I called you here about Merry. You need to look for her."

"How did Richard and Jens Williams get along?"

Fellinger's eyes widened. "I'm not aware of their getting along in any way—oh, no, you can't be . . ." He backed behind his desk, began sitting down but was inches from the chair and had to catch his balance.

His second attempt succeeded. "Richard and Jens? You have to be—Richard was an occasional presence here. How in the world would they ever develop any sort of—"

"You never saw them together."

"Well, of course—I mean . . . Jens was my assistant, we had meetings, he'd obviously be in the same room during some of them."

He mopped his face with his handkerchief. "You really think the two of them had something to do with—they somehow colluded to kill Ursula?"

Milo said, "We're not even close to that, sir, and we'd appreciate you not suggesting it to anyone."

"Then why bring it up? You need to tell me—"

"With all due respect, Mr. Fellinger, we're not your employees."

"No. You're not. Sorry. I'm simply worried about Merry and you keep hopping from topic to topic—let me say this. Much as I think Richard's a wimp, I can't see him wanting her dead. The entire crux of the negotiations was the interdependency of their relationship."

"Meaning?"

"Without both of them, there's no business, so why would Richard jeopardize his financial stability?"

Milo said, "Let's talk about Deirdre Brand."

"*Her?*" Fellinger paled. "You're researching me? Why the hell would you—"

"Ms. Brand was murdered—"

"Nonsense. That's ridiculous."

"Nothing ridiculous about it, sir."

"No, no, I didn't mean it that way, no one's death is . . . trivial. What I'm saying is I had no connection to her, my lawsuit was discontinued because I was informed that she'd left town, hadn't responded to subpoenas, couldn't be located. I figured I'd done what I set out to do, put the matter out of my mind."

"What did you set out to do?"

"Isn't it obvious, Lieutenant? I wanted to teach her a lesson. Even crazy people can't be allowed to overstep."

I said, "Civics lesson for a schizophrenic."

Fellinger said, "You weren't on the receiving end of her insanity, Doctor. But murdered? I was never told *anything* about murder. So let me go on the record: I'm sorry that happened. Yes, she was nuts and abusive but I certainly didn't want to see her murdered."

"Who informed you she'd left town?"

"The court informed me she couldn't be found. I assumed she'd run away."

Milo said, "Learned her lesson and left."

"Obviously you people don't grasp my situation with her. Put yourself in my shoes: A total stranger with a disturbed mind takes an inexplicable, pathological dislike to you. Every time she sees you she comes over, stands over you when you're simply trying to eat your lunch. She rants and raves and shakes her fists and behaves in an overall threatening manner. All because one time she panhandled you and you had the temerity to refuse her. It got to the point where I was looking over my shoulder every time I went over to the mall for coffee or lunch or whatever. I had no choice but to try to have her put away."

"You were aiming for involuntary commitment," I said.

"Good luck with that, the system stinks. So I figured a civil suit might help lay some groundwork. Or maybe she'd get nervous and leave me alone."

I said, "To sue her, you had to serve her with papers. How'd you pull that off?"

"What do you mean?"

"I'd think someone like that might be hard to get hold of."

Fellinger's mouth dropped open. "Oh, God! Now I see where this is going. Shit."

Milo said, "Sir?"

"Where was she killed, Lieutenant?"

"A park in Santa Monica."

"No, no, no. I can't *believe* this!" Fellinger poured a double, tossed it back, placed his hand over his chest. His color had gone bad, pallor and flush combining in a sickly mottle.

Milo said, "You all right, sir?"

"No, I'm not all right. This is too damn much." Pressing his hands to his temples, he breathed heavily. "It's nuts, no way."

"What is, sir?"

Fellinger looked at me. "You're right, serving her proved to be a giant hassle. I went out-of-pocket for several professional processors, including county marshals. No one succeeded in finding her. I brought up my frustration with Jens. He said, 'No problem, Mr. F., I'll take care of it.' A few days later, he reported that he'd served her. I asked him how he'd pulled it off and he said he'd observed the mall until he spotted her but instead of confronting her, he kept an eye on her. Eventually, she left and boarded a bus that he got on, as well. She exited at a park in Santa Monica."

Fellinger wiped sweat from his brow. "He was quite proud of himself—said he went to a nearby liquor store, bought a forty-ounce bottle of malt liquor, and taped the papers to it. The minute she took the bait, she was served."

Shaking his head. "I thanked him. And now she's been murdered. Jesus. When was she killed?"

I said, "Couple of months ago."

"Oh, God, please don't tell me that woman died because some psycho misinterpreted my intentions."

Milo said, "No reason to blame yourself unless you got specific about hurting Deirdre Brand."

"Of course I didn't! All I wanted was for her to be served."

"So maybe Williams is just a guy who does favors for those in authority."

"And now he *hates* me for firing him," said Fellinger. "So he's punishing me by taking Merry? Can you start searching for her instead of all this talk?"

"We'll try, sir."

"That doesn't sound encouraging."

Milo walked out. I followed.

We met back at his office. During my drive, I'd called and texted Darius Kleffer. So far, no reply. Milo shoved papers off his desk, including flyers for restaurants near the station.

"Food," he said. "Used to think I liked it."

He ran John Jensen Williams through NCIC, found the New York battery conviction as well as a voyeurism case in New Haven when Williams had been an eighteen-year-old freshman at Yale. Caught peeping through the dorm windows of female students, he'd received a suspended criminal sentence and had been expelled. The battery case—slapping a line cook at a Midtown restaurant—had been dropped for lack of evidence.

Milo said, "Lucky boy. Unlucky society."

I said, "Maybe not quite so lucky with being forced out of Yale."

"No jail time for a guy we're assuming is ultra-twisted sounds like lucky to me."

"That and he's learned to be careful."

"Showing up outside the bathroom and creeping out women ain't careful, Alex."

"I'll amend that. Careful until recently."

"He's falling apart? Great. Think he took the Santos girl?"

"My guess would be more likely than not, but at this point I don't trust my instincts."

"Why not?"

"From Fellinger to Corey to Williams? I've been wrong about too damn much."

"Makes two of us. How the hell did you guess it was Williams? And why didn't you tell me?"

"I called to tell you before we met up at Fellinger's but you had your own news and hung up. I'd just found the tattoo parlor where Frankie was most recently inked and talked to the owner. Every time he worked on her, Williams was there, taking charge of the situation. Frankie was extremely submissive, sat there like a zombie, turned down a topical anesthetic, because pain made her feel like a person. Months before that, Williams brought Kathy Hennepin to the same place and tried to get her tattooed. The artist said she was uneasy but was on the verge of doing it. Then she burst out of the chair and split. Shortly after, she was dead and Frankie had taken her place."

"She tells Williams no and dies?"

"A boy and his slaves."

"Jesus." He pinched his nose, breathed out noisily, seemed amused by the sound-effect and sat back with his feet up. "So Williams was the evil wizard running Frankie's life. Still see her as a possible button-woman for Ursula?"

"Doesn't sound as if Williams needs help killing anyone, but who knows?"

"Kathy dies because she defied him, and he bashes in Deirdre's brain in order to kiss up to the boss?"

"His real motive is he enjoys stalking and destroying and defying authority. Which leads us all the way back to Richard Corey: an even richer man in need of a favor. Earl Cohen just told us he hated Ursula. The girls said the same to Laura Smith. Psychopaths are gifted at sniffing out need so that it wouldn't have escaped Jens Williams's attention, sitting in all those negotiation meetings, taking notes. Richard might as well have been spraying pheromones in Williams's vicinity."

"Who do you think made the first move?"

I said, "Definitely Williams. People like him are good at creating needs their clients didn't know existed."

"He convinced Corey?"

"More like insinuated himself into Corey's consciousness. Maybe on a day when Richard looked particularly troubled. He was the perfect client with the perfect alibi. And no reason to connect him to Williams."

"Corey begins his new life and Williams gets to do what he loves most."

I said, "Williams has no criminal record, and who'd suspect someone working for Ursula's lawyer? On top of that, Williams belonged in the building and Ursula knew and trusted him. He escorts her to the elevator, keeps going—maybe making up a story about having to run an errand in his own car. Or the conversation just kept flowing and Ursula thought nothing of it. Williams walks with her, then positions himself behind her, calls out her name, and either he pops her or Frankie emerges and does it. Back to the office, wait until the cops arrive, feign shock."

Milo thought for a long time. "How do I find this bastard, seeing as his own boss has no idea where he lives?"

"For a start, I'd put the watch back on cousin Sullivan, in case she's sheltering him, wittingly or otherwise."

"Pleather Flo," he said. "She's who got Frankie to the building. Maybe I'll luck out and they're kissing cousins."

He phoned Reed and Binchy, informed them of the change of plans, then turned to me.

"Kathy Hennepin got snagged the same way. Doing a damn delivery."

"Maybe her involvement wasn't quite so random," I said. "Williams worked as a chef in New York, we have to consider that he might've known Kleffer."

"Oh, man, what you said right at the beginning—Kleffer got a buddy to do Kathy."

"Or Williams hated Kleffer and targeted Kathy because of it. The restaurant scene is competitive. What if Williams and Kleffer vied for the same job and Williams lost out? Or Williams developed a grudge against Kleffer for another reason—he *was* arrested for battering another kitchen worker. Either way, he seduced Kathy as revenge."

"And she just happens to deliver to his building?"

"Maureen Gross told us she *volunteered* to deliver those papers. What if she was going with Williams by then, saw the address on the documents, and took the opportunity to combine business with pleasure?"

"When Kathy dumped Kleffer she told him she needed someone more stable. What, Williams convinced her his cuisine was more haute?"

"More likely Williams conned her the same way he conned Fellinger."

He frowned. "Yale, playwright. Yeah, that would work."

"For all we know he had her believing he was a bona fide attorney. Working at the firm, Williams would've picked up more than enough jargon to be convincing. We need to talk to Kleffer again. I just tried to reach him, no success. But let's give it another shot."

This time, the chef answered and I asked if he knew Jens Williams.

"That fucker, that fucking asshole *fucker*! Tell me before *you* find him, give me fucking five minutes alone with him in a fucking locked room, I bring my Japanese *cleaver,* I turn him into fucking *paste,* I grind his bones in a fucking *duck* press, I—!"

I held the phone out to Milo.

He took it and said, "Darius, when's your next break?"

32

Kleffer met us in the cut between Beppo Bippo and the furniture store. We found him smoking and stamping each foot in turn. His back was to us. One palm was pressed to the wall, pushing stucco hard enough to raise sinews on his arm. Dime-store Samson out to topple the world around him. When he saw us, he shoved his phone at us. "Look!"

The tiny screen shook in his grasp, a rectangle filled with movement and sound. The scene was white-garbed people, slicing, sautéing, deep-frying. The soundtrack was clatter.

Kleffer jabbed the mini-movie. "See?"

Milo said, "See what?"

"Shit—look—shit, I lost it, hold hold—shit okay, here, this is me. With the sausage. And over there, in the back—what the fuck—okay . . . *there*. That's *him!*"

Enlarging a corner of the image, he indicated a tall, thin figure behind a stainless-steel counter. Dark hair streamed from under the man's snood. Heavy-rimmed eyeglasses stood out against pale skin but even at max size, features weren't discernible.

Hands worked fast. Chop chop chop.

Milo said, "That's Jens Williams?"

"Yeah, yeah," said Kleffer. "He was called J.J. A better name is Asshole."

"You worked together?"

"The New York food scene, people move between the same places."

"Which restaurant is this?"

"No, no," said Kleffer. "This is no restaurant, this is a show. *Mega-Chef Slice-Dice.*"

"For TV?"

"Yeah, yeah, The Gourmet Network. This was the pilot, it didn't get picked up. I got on the A-team because I was already sou-ing for Mr. Luong, he knew I had talent. *Asshole* got on Billy Slade's team, wanted to sous but only got prep."

"Prep being—"

"You slice raw vegetables over and over. That's like you suck."

"Meat woulda been better?"

"Protein?" said Kleffer. "What do you think? The more up in front you are, the more you get to transform protein. I got sweetbreads, Mr. L., he knew what I could do with them. I made sausages with a chestnut sauce, judges came in their pants."

Milo said, "Meanwhile, J.J.'s chopping lettuce."

"Kale. Swiss chard. Carrots." Kleffer laughed raggedly. "Got so pissed he cut himself, bled all over the *mise en place,* everything ruined, he got kicked off the show in the middle. Like a fucking exile! He was just a prep slut, anyway. Meanwhile, I'm doing my sweetbread with the chestnut sauce, must have drove him nuts, he hated me."

"Because of the sweetbreads."

"More than the sweetbreads," said Kleffer. "My team won. And he was a fucking loser."

Milo had him email the video to the desktop at his office and to his cell phone.

"Anything else, Darius?"

"I know he hurt Kathy, you just told me on the phone."

Milo said, "Not exactly—"

"You hand him to me, I give him mega-pain slice-dice."

"Let's take it slow, Darius."

Kleffer smoked, kicked the ground, slapped a wall.

"Darius?"

"Yeah, yeah, I'm mellow."

"You think Williams would've killed Kathy to get back at you because he was upset over a cooking competition?"

"When he fucked himself up by bleeding on the *mise,* everyone was talking about it, Billy Slade fired his ass from Inca Grill. Last I heard he was making burgers in a dive-bar on Delancey Street."

Kleffer laughed again, tilted his hand back and forth. "Sear, flip, sear, flip. That'll melt your brain. Asshole *deserved* it, he was a shithead from day one, even unloading on the Guatemalans."

"The Guatemalans?"

"The prep guys, they're like the backbone of the kitchen, you don't piss them off. Asshole actually hit one in the face, claiming the guy was messing him up on purpose. Which is stupid, the Guatemalans are professionals. You can get away with a lot of shit in a kitchen but you don't mess with the Guatemalans, they know more than you. That was his problem, thinking he was smarter than everyone, going to Harvard."

"We've been told Yale."

"Same difference," said Kleffer. "So what if you took Persian fucking philosophy? Can you conceive a badass sauce? Can you marry flavors? The kitchen is the ultimate test, Asshole couldn't stand up to it. He never liked me because whenever we ended up in the same place, I was higher up. That's why he stole Kathy from me. *I know* it was him."

He stubbed out his cigarette, lit another. "I leave New York and come here. So guess who shows up? It's like, you've *got* to be kidding."

"J.J. showed up at Beppo—"

"No, no, a place in the Valley, fusion Italian Japanese, I'm not working, I'm *eating*." Kleffer's eyes narrowed. "I'm having dinner with Kathy, the relationship's going good, I'm thinking we're solid, everything's copa. All of a sudden, who's standing at the table? I say hi but I don't invite him. He sits down anyway, like we're bros. Real friendly, smooth, like a different person than an asshole who'd hit a Guatemalan. What am I going to do, kick him out and look like a dick in front of Kathy? So he has a couple of drinks with us, soon he's talking more to Kathy than me."

I said, "Talking about what?"

"Basically how fucking great he is. Harv-Yale, whatever. How he used to be a chef, the culinary world had its 'charms' there's nothing better than feeding human beings, one day he's gonna tackle world starvation, but now he's moved on, time for a change, he's working in law. I knew it was bullshit but who cares? All I wanted was to get rid of him, get Kathy home and . . . he leaves, gives me a bro-hug, I never see him again."

He smoked greedily. "I never think anything about it, why would I?"

I said, "You never connected him with the man you suspected Kathy of seeing."

"The bastard she cheated on me with?" said Kleffer. "Why would I think it's him, he's a *dick*."

"How soon after he showed up—"

"Maybe a coupla months." Head shake. "She *drops* it on me. You're out, Darius. Not saying it but I know: Another guy's in. It fucking *broke* me." Patting the left side of his chest. "Why would I think it's him? She said she was looking for stability."

"Working in law," said Milo.

"Yeah, yeah, but that didn't register because I knew it was bullshit. Asshole's chopping vegetables, now he's a lawyer?"

"He said he was an attorney?"

"Working in law, what the fuck does that mean? You really think it's him?"

Milo said, "We don't think anything yet, Darius. We're collecting facts. Anything else you want to tell us that would help find J.J.?"

"You *do* think he did it," said Kleffer.

Milo moved closer. Kleffer's back was to the wall. "Darius, I'll repeat myself this one time—"

"Okay, okay . . . no, I don't know where he is. Didn't hang out with him in New York, don't hang out with him here."

"Who did he hang out with in New York?"

"Nobody, that's the point," said Kleffer. "Like after hours, we'd all go drinking, chefs, the Guatemalans, sometimes servers. We're tired and hyped and hungry, looking for a great beer, a nice sandwich."

"Not Williams."

"Not him never."

I said, "Did he have any girlfriends in New York?"

"Nah," said Kleffer. "Hope to hell he didn't." He rocked on his feet. "If what you're thinking is true."

He returned to work.

Milo said, "Stealing another guy's girlfriend to make up for poor knife skills."

I said, "His knife skills failed on TV but they're good enough for his extracurricular interests. And Kleffer could be wrong about Williams not having any girlfriends in New York. There could be a crime scene or two in Manhattan—"

"I checked for similars."

"You know as well as I do that NCIC doesn't catch all the relevant details. In an isolated case, why would dinner for two be seen as important? All it would imply is a killer the victim knew well. Even if investigators did find it interesting, they might want to hold it back."

He thought about that, produced his cell. "Sean, how's your time situation? . . . good, I need you to call every precinct in Manhattan, nothing shows up there, try Brooklyn. Find out if they've got any unsolved murders with our dinner-for-two angle. Not just food at the scene, a table actually set up . . . because we got a new suspect who lived there for a few years . . . Fellinger's assistant, Williams, I'll tell you about it later . . . try Connecticut, too—specifically New Haven."

On the way back to the station, he checked the Corey sisters' latest credit card activity. Still in Vancouver, one purchase: tampons.

I said, "They're not spending big so they're definitely staying with someone. Maybe Ursula has relatives in Canada."

"Maybe, but I'm sure not gonna ask Richard. Speaking of which, what do you make of the dinner scene at Ursula's house? She wasn't one of Williams's slaves. She was a contract hit."

"Williams sees himself as an artist, so he signs his creations."

"Sick bastard," he said. "And now he probably does have the Santos girl . . . or had. Apart from BOLO'ing his van, if he's even still driving it, what the hell else can I do?"

I said, "Williams is gone but as far as we know Corey's still in his condo in Oxnard. Give Nguyen the new facts and get him to say Corey killing the horses and terrifying his daughters is grounds for a search warrant. Then toss the condo for Corey's cash-stash and anything that links him to Williams. Same for the warehouse downtown where he trucked the contents of Ursula's house. With evidence, you can leverage him for info on Williams's whereabouts."

"Assuming he knows."

"All we can do is assume. You search and find nothing, you can always beat the truth out of him."

He laughed and got Nguyen on the phone. The deputy D.A. said, "I like horses as much as anyone but that ain't even close."

For the next hour, Milo did all the right detective things: instigating the BOLO on Jens Williams's van and the ten-year-old Lexus registered to Meredith Santos, then diving into government paper.

Social Security finally offered up the tidbit that Williams had re-
sided for nearly two years in Miami prior to New York. Milo back-
traced his employment records: working as a buffet chef at two resorts.

Both hotels had Williams leaving of his own accord, neither had
anything notable to say about him. He'd been driving the same van,
hadn't even racked up a parking ticket.

At Miami PD Homicide he spoke to a lieutenant named Abel Sorriento and inquired about homicides with a culinary aspect.

"Food? Everything's food here," said Sorriento. "Plenty of nonsense goes down outside nightclubs and restaurants, but almost all of
it's one idiot shooting another, nothing psycho like what you're saying."

"Okay, thanks."

"Bon appétit."

A check-in with Sean Binchy revealed nothing encouraging at the hand-
ful of New York precincts the young detective had reached.

"There seems to be this general suspicion thing even when you give
them a badge number, Loot. A few times, they actually called to verify
me."

"Overcrowding, Sean."

"Pardon, sir?"

"Urban living," said Milo. "Put too many rats in a small cage, they
get protective of their pathetic millimeters."

"Ha," said Binchy. "I'll remember that the next time Becky gets on
one of her I-want-to-travel kicks. You ask me, nothing beats L.A. on a
warm day."

Just before four p.m., Milo tried Frank Gonzales.

The Oxnard D said, "Back on dry land for the rest of the day, had
to clear some papers. Corey's in there, all right, one of my rookies spotted movement behind the drapes. Also, the next-door neighbor stopped
by with an envelope, probably the rent check, and got let in."

"Thanks for taking the time, Frank."

"No prob. I've been thinking about Corey. Guy kills a bunch of women but has no history at all? Just decides to start in middle age?"

"The situation might've changed, Frank." Milo updated him on a possible link between Corey and John Jensen Williams.

Gonzales said, "Corey contracted his wife but this other dude did all the work?"

"Looks that way."

"Any indication Corey and Williams are still interacting?"

"Not so far."

"If this Williams got paid, no reason for him to show up," said Gonzales. "You still see Corey as high priority?"

"You bet."

"Okay, we'll stay with him."

Moe Reed, watching Flora Sullivan, had managed to make it up to her firm's entrance without being noticed. No sign of Cousin Jens. Same for the parking tiers. Just to make sure, he'd asked Al Bayless to check the new tapes. Zilch.

Milo said, "Any new impressions of Sullivan, Moses?"

"Just saw her in passing. She walks fast but not due to nervousness, if that's what you mean. More like it's her normal pace."

A few moments later, Grant Fellinger rang in, wanting to know if any progress had been made locating Meredith Santos. When Milo said, "Not yet," Fellinger said, "You really need to be taking this seriously," and gave him the Arizona home phone number of Santos's parents. "Obviously you're going to want to touch base with them."

Muttering "obviously," Milo reached the Santoses, did a lot of listening and torturing his necktie. He hung up saying, "Nice people in a terrible situation—okay, time for a beer. Or six. I need to get outta here. You with me?"

We were walking to the stairway when Sean Binchy phoned, excitement making him sound like a birthday boy. "Nothing in New York,

Loot, but I talked to a captain at New Haven and he referred me to a city nearby called West Haven and they connected me with their chief. He had something *just* like it. Same year Williams was a student at Yale. Fantastic, huh?"

Milo whipped out his pad. "Good work, Sean. Go."

"Victim was Loretta Sfiazzi, twenty-five, waitress at one of their better seafood restaurants. She didn't report to work, was found by her landlady in her apartment, laid out on the floor, no sexual assault but strangulation and multiple stab wounds just like Ms. Hennepin. Dinner for two on the table, but not fancy like ours, just canned chili and an unopened bottle of red wine. A couple of ex-boyfriends were questioned but they alibied out and after that no suspect was ever developed. What he—Chief Donald Molinaro—thought was strange was the chili. Loretta worked at a high-level restaurant, it didn't come from there and when she entertained she was known to take food home regularly, all the employees were allowed to. Her folks said she never ate chili and her table was set with nice dishes and flatware—they'd belonged to her grandmother. The wine fit, though. Parents confirmed it as a Christmas gift from them, Loretta was saving it for a special occasion."

"He comes with a can in his pocket, borrows the rest," said Milo. "Premeditating at eighteen."

"That's what I figured, Loot. Anyway, West Haven had no idea what to make of it, they were shocked to hear what I had to say. Not that I could tell them much, just that Williams was our prime suspect."

Milo filled him in.

"Bizarre," said Binchy. "I asked Chief Molinaro if Williams could've worked at the same restaurant as Ms. Sfiazzi. Unfortunately the place closed down, everyone's gone or dead. But I did compare the date of the murder with Williams's peep bust and it happened real soon after— ten days."

"Expelled, so he takes it out on a woman."

"Not exactly, Loot, he was still enrolled, they took their time kicking him out. Chief Molinaro said it's always like that, Yale tries to cover up everything. He also said the toughest part about the place is getting admitted, after that you coast. But I guess Williams was feeling unhappy."

CHAPTER

33

The beer break took place at a tavern called Doc of the Bay, a block and a half west of Café Moghul. I'd never been there but the bartender greeted Milo like an old friend. I thought I knew all his haunts. Learn something every day.

Getting there was interesting, a quick walk prolonged when Milo crossed Santa Monica Boulevard and continued past the tavern before recrossing.

I said, "Why the mini-hike?"

He pointed to the Indian restaurant. "Don't want to hurt her feelings."

"You guys are going steady?"

"Hey. Stardom has its responsibilities."

"Do you know her name?"

"Bear in the zoo, does he need to know anything about his keeper except grub gets tossed in on time?"

"But if he's smart, he doesn't growl."

"Exactly."

◆

The bar was small, stuffy, hung wall-to-wall with sports jerseys in plastic boxes and a single white physician's coat displayed in the center of the memorabilia.

I said, "Doc of which bay?"

"What do you think? The sick bay. Owner's a bone-setter named Schwartz, worked as a team physician for the Rams."

"Rams in L.A. is ancient history."

"So is Schwartz."

A plump young barmaid came over. "The usual, Lieutenant?"

"Thanks, Samantha."

"For you, sir?"

"What's the usual?"

"Carslberg Elephant chased with Miller Lite."

"Do you have Sam Adams?"

"Sometimes," she said. "If we don't, I'll bring you something else."

Mugs arrived, along with wasabi peas and cheese crackers that resembled tiny, flattened basketballs. One long swallow and a mouthful of carbs later, Milo said, "What do you think about having another chat with Corey?"

"Good idea but I wouldn't confront him."

"What, be his pal?"

"Stay low-key, business-like, try to work his daughters into the conversation."

"How?"

"You're a bit perplexed because they seem to have left town, can he help you locate them. He'll lie but maybe he'll give off a tell."

"How much should I say about Ursula?"

"You're now wondering if someone in the building was involved. Again, does he have suggestions. Once you've planted that seed, you can see if he tries to reach Williams. No sense subpoenaing his phones, both of them will be using prepaids. But maybe you'll get lucky and they'll do a face-to-face. Either way, keep an eye on his movements."

He finished the Elephant, let out a huge gust of beery breath.

"What's the alcohol content of that stuff?" I said.

"Seven point two, less than wine." He lifted the bottle. "Think of it as Chardonnay for the workingman."

Loosening his belt, he announced, "Time for dessert," and turned his attention to the light beer.

I said, "When are you planning to revisit Corey?"

"Tonight, soon as the traffic eases up, say seven thirty, eight-ish."

"In the meantime, we could try for face-time with Cousin Flora. Maybe you can get something out of her that'll help you find Williams."

"His psychological makeup?"

"That would also be good," I said, "but I was thinking last known address."

Back to Century City. Might as well buy a permanent parking space.

We reached Flora Sullivan's suite at five thirty-two p.m. Her firm sported a roster of partners that spanned three feet of black granite wall. As the workday drew to a close, lawyers and their staffers exited through three sets of glass doors set on separate walls.

The directory listed each partner as N, E, or W. Sullivan was W. The woman at the front desk of that section was large, white-haired, and imperious and locking her desk as we arrived. The first tip-off that she took herself far too seriously was her nameplate in oversized faux gold mounted on a beefy walnut stand.

ROSE MARIE GRUHNER

The second was her ignoring us completely.

Milo waited for a lull in the foot traffic before identifying himself as LAPD, no specialty cited, and asking to see Flora Sullivan.

Rose Marie Gruhner dropped keys in her purse. "She's busy."

"For how long, ma'am?"

"For as long as she chooses."

Milo said, "I'm with the—"

Gruhner said, "I got it the first time, makes no difference."

He edged closer to Gruhner's desk and stood there. Gruhner finally looked up. "Sir. We get law enforcement all the time, the rules don't change. No one without an appointment."

"Cops all the time?"

"Frequently," said Gruhner. "This is a real estate litigation firm, claims and counterclaims are the nature of the business."

I said, "Process servers are always trying to con their way in."

"Including marshals in uniform, sir. I tell them what I just told you two: No one gains entry without a prior appointment. We'd have chaos."

"I'm a detective, ma'am, not serving papers on anyone."

"I don't make the regulations, sir, I only enforce them."

I said, "Tell Ms. Sullivan that Leon Bonelli sent us."

"I won't tell her anything of the sort because she gave clear—"

"Trust me," I said. "She'll want to know. Leon Bonelli." I spelled it.

Gruhner said, "Sounds like a tall tale."

"It's an extremely short tale."

"Ach." She punched an extension and relayed the information. As she listened, her face blossomed pink around the edges. "She is *not* happy. See yourselves in."

As we walked past her, she called out, "Don't you want directions?"

No need; Flora Sullivan was waiting in the middle of the corridor, arms crossed. Same pose Grant Fellinger had assumed. Maybe they taught it in law school.

She had on a black pencil skirt and white silk blouse with a Peter Pan collar. The heels on her red shoes put her into NBA guard territory. Dark curls were drawn back tight. Silver-rimmed eyeglasses dangled from a chain around the long stalk of her neck.

The resemblance to Jens Williams was hard to avoid.

She watched our approach, blank-faced. The trek to her door was longer than to Fellinger's, offering a sideshow of abstractions in pastel tones. Hidden speakers streamed a soft-strings version of "Eleanor Rigby." Scary song, when you thought about it.

When we were twenty feet away, Flora Sullivan swung into action like a bronco released from a pen, race-walking toward us on stick-limbs, face splotched salmon-pink.

A flamingo who'd imbibed too much rosy plankton.

She planted herself in the center of the hallway. "Who do you think you are to bandy about personal information to my staff?"

Milo said, "Ms. Sullivan, I'm Lieutenant Milo Sturgis, LAPD—"

"That is not an answer."

"Sorry, ma'am, but the moat was deep and we needed to lower the drawbridge."

Flora Sullivan blinked. Her eyes were dark blue and wide. The miserly mouth I'd seen in her photo was glossed crimson. Not a pretty woman by a long shot, but she had presence.

"I am not interested in medieval architecture, Officer Whoever You Are. Now you answer me: What gave you the right to lie your way in here by referencing a dear friend of mine?"

"Your personal life has no concern for us, Ms. Sullivan. We need to talk about your cousin John Jensen Williams."

"Jens? What in the world about? He's a distant cousin, I barely know him."

"You knew him well enough to get him a job in this building."

"I did him a favor—oh, *that.* I was assured that once J. J. was gone the matter would be resolved."

Milo said, "This is about homicide."

"What?" she shrieked. A tide of noise rolled behind her and caused her to shut up. A group of well-dressed, tired-looking people rounded a corner and headed our way. One of the men gave a finger-wave. "Flo."

"Mark."

The group passed. Lots of quizzical over-the-shoulder looks.

Flora Sullivan said, "Shit. Let's talk in my office."

Size- and layout-wise, her work space was a near twin of Fellinger's, softened a bit by more pastels and blond furniture. Only two photos, both of Sullivan and her husband, headshots offering no hint of disability.

She unfolded her long frame behind her desk. "Before I hear any more nonsense about homicide, you're going to give me a straight answer: What does Mr. Bonelli have to do with your business?"

"Nothing," said Milo.

"You lied in order to con your way in here. Is that proper police procedure?"

"Ms. Gruhner was a bit of an obstacle."

"Ms. Gruhner does her job properly. Without her, this place would be a zoo." Sullivan looped the eyeglass chain over her head, placed the specs on the desk. "I'm not satisfied with your answer. What's your interest in Mr. Bonelli?"

I said, "None other than he's your friend."

Some of the salmon spots deepened to crimson. "He's a dear acquaintance, from all the way back to college. So?"

"When we Googled you, Mr. Bonelli's name came up in conjunction with yours several times. Charitable fund-raisers, that kind of thing. We really need to speak with you so we grasped at straws. Sorry."

Giving her an out; I doubted she'd prolong the argument.

Another finger-jab. "Why are you nosing around me, period? And don't try to weasel out of an honest answer."

Litigation 101: Take control of the situation.

Milo said, "We're here because you're J.J. Williams's only local relative and he's a person of interest in several homicides."

"That's ridiculous." Sullivan laughed, finished off with a snort. The equine comparison grew stronger. "You're wasting your time and, more important, you're squandering mine." She stood. "Now it's time for you to exit these premises."

"We need to locate Mr. Williams—"

"Need what you want but I can't help you."

"You knew him well enough to recommend him to—"

"I was being nice! And look where it got me. They're the ones who hired him. Ask them for an address."

"The one he gave Mr. Fellinger's firm was bogus."

Sullivan blinked. "Really."

"Really. Where can we find him, ma'am?"

"I have absolutely no idea."

"Even though—"

"He's a distant relative who I helped get a job. That's something I'd do for a nonrelative if they were qualified."

"Mr. Williams's qualifications were—"

"He went to Yale," she said.

I said, "You're close enough to know that."

She glared at me. "It wasn't exactly a family secret."

"J.J. was known in the family as bright."

"Bright enough . . ." Deepening her tone for dominance. But then she ruined it by blinking and glancing down and fooling with her glasses.

I said, "He told you he graduated Yale."

"And?"

"Actually he left after a year."

A sleek red fingernail pinged the top of her wedding picture. "Obviously, I'm not privy to his life history, it was a long time since I'd seen him."

I said, "He called you when he arrived in L.A.?"

"He phoned out of the blue and told me he'd moved to L.A. We hadn't spoken in years. You're positive about his leaving Yale?"

"No doubt about it," said Milo.

"Hmm," said Sullivan. "Well, that's a shame, but no way for me to know that. If my mother was lucid, I suppose she might've known. She and J.J.'s mother grew up together, more like friends than cousins. But

Leticia—his mom—passed years ago and there's not much left of my mom, mentally."

I said, "Did you and J.J. grow up together?"

"Not at all, he's from Connecticut, I was born in L.A., my father moved here to work for Lockheed—who cares about my life history? Now, if you'll excuse me—"

Milo said, "So J.J. calls out of the blue, saying he needs a job—"

"He asked if I knew any openings for a paralegal, any kind of assistantship in the legal field. It just so happened that I'd been talking to Fellinger and he mentioned he was looking for someone. I thought, perfect match."

"Because J.J. was smart."

"Smart and experienced," she said. "He'd worked at Skadden in New York, which is white-shoe, heavy hitter."

Milo and I said nothing.

Flora Sullivan played with her glasses. "Did he lie about that, too?"

"We'll look into it," said Milo, "but almost certainly."

She sighed. "What a mess. Still, homicide? This has nothing to do with the family. Nothing at all."

"You have no idea where he could be."

She shook her head. "When he called the first time, I asked him where he was staying. He said he hadn't settled yet, would let me know. He never did."

"You never pursued it."

"There was nothing to pursue. The extent of our contact was that single call. I tried to be social, offered to get together once he settled but he never took me up on it. Since you've poked around, perhaps you've learned that my social life is rather constricted."

"We wouldn't know about that."

Sullivan's stare was long, searching, angry. "Well, I'll take you at your word on that. The occasional fund-raiser, yes, and I try to get in a round of golf once in a while. But my focus is my husband. He's para-plegic. Drunk driver."

"Sorry, ma'am—"

"What's done is done, one soldiers on." She sat back. "Now please, let's end this. It's been a long day."

Milo said, "We'll be out of your hair in a sec. Do you have a phone number for J.J.?"

"I keep telling you—hold on . . . you know, I think I might. Only because I'm compulsive, when I get a call, I log it."

Flipping open an iPad, she scrolled and read off seven digits.

Milo said, "That's the one he gave Fellinger, Ms. Sullivan. It's been disconnected."

"Oh. Then I guess you're out of luck."

I said, "Working in the same building, you'd have to see each other occasionally."

"Not as often as you might think," said Sullivan. "Over the past few months I'd estimate J.J. and I have bumped into each other four or five times, tops. Always on the elevator, where else do people mix in an of-fice building? We exchanged smiles but obviously one doesn't converse in a compartment full of strangers. Now, if—"

I said, "Your father worked in aerospace. What did Jens's father do?"

"That's relevant to his alleged murderous behavior? Which I still find hard to believe, would you care to give me some details?"

Milo said, "Sorry, can't."

"One-way street?" said Flora Sullivan. "Then again, you're men."

I repeated the question.

She said, "I didn't answer you the first time because I don't know what J.J.'s father did and I wouldn't be surprised if J.J. didn't, either, because the bastard abandoned Leticia when J.J. was a baby. Mother was always talking about how she had to struggle just to get by."

"No sibs?"

"No."

"When did she pass on?"

"Hmm . . . a long time ago, she wasn't that old. Heart attack. She smoked and drank and her diet wasn't great. She worked in a diner—greasy spoon, you know? Probably ate the crap they served."

I said, "She was a cook?"

"Short-order," she said. "Poor Leticia spent her life literally slaving over a hot stove."

34

The elevator we boarded was packed. I thought of John Jensen Williams using the compartment as a stalking ground, wondered how many other women had qualified as prey.

We got off and walked to where Ursula Corey had met her death. Just another patch of concrete now. Milo stared for a while then we took the stairs up to where I'd left the Seville.

"What'd you think of Sullivan?"

"Probably clean but that doesn't mean Williams won't try to contact her again."

"That's why I told her he was suspected of homicide. He does call or show up, I want her to be scared shitless and rat him out."

A block later: "Nifty how you used Bonelli to gain entry, then finessed the issue."

"I hoped she'd appreciate the discretion."

"She must've, because you also pried out that recap of Williams's blighted childhood. Mama working the griddle."

"Mama with a drinking problem," I said. "Maybe angry and bitter about being abandoned by Papa."

"Tsk tsk," he said. "Toss in poor nutrition and it's all explained."

Stalled in a queue of cars snailing up the exit ramp, I phoned Robin and told her I'd be heading for Oxnard.

She said, "Now? You'll sit on the freeway."

"We'll grab a bite first."

"Come home, I'll cook for both of you."

"Love to see you but don't bother, I'll pick something up."

"No bother, I'll do a one-dish," she said. "How about pasta with leftovers? Those *bigoli* things you liked the last time and whatever I excavate in the fridge . . . okay, here we go, there's some pastrami from the weekend. I'll toss in eggs, a little bacon, do a riff on carbonara."

"My bella signorina. If you're up to it, sounds great."

Milo said, "What does?"

"Homecooked meal."

"Yes yes yes."

Robin heard that and laughed. "Darling, I talk to *wood* all day. Your handsome face combined with his appetite will make me feel valued. Plus I'm celebrating."

"What?"

"I just spoke to you-know-who, told him I wouldn't be making replicas for him or anyone else. Surprisingly, he was a gentleman. Maybe it's 'cause he's just out of rehab. And uncharacteristically lucid. Whatever the reason, I'm feeling free."

The food was on the table when we arrived. Huge batch of spaghetti, three times as much as we usually prepared.

Robin drank wine, Milo and I stuck with water followed by coffee. Blanche positioned herself strategically to the right of Milo's chair, just out of Robin's view, sucking up the not-so-occasional strands he dangled near her flews. Anytime Milo reverted to feeding himself, her head rubbed against his leg. If he rubbed back, she did her cat-purr thing.

Robin said, "Intense goings-on under the table."

Milo said, "Animal magnetism."

Over a final dose of coffee, she said, "May I ask what you guys hope to learn up there?"

Milo said, "At this point, anything." He summed up.

She said, "This Williams character did his own killings for fun but Corey's wife was a business deal?"

I said, "More like mixed media. He got paid but she was his biggest trophy because she was out of his league."

"Stealing the boss's bit-of-fun? That and getting rid of an ex I can see," she said. "But a father going after his own kids?"

Milo said, "They stand to inherit Ursula's half of the business."

"He's big-rich already, he would murder his only children for more?"

I said, "In this case, more means huge money but it's beyond that. The girls represent his old life and he craves a new one. In a single day he had their childhood home stripped bare and shipped their horses off to slaughter. Luckily for the girls, he lacks subtlety and acted strangely enough to scare them clear up to Canada."

"Taking a girl's horse," she said. "That's sure letting her know her fantasy is over."

"At this point, his fantasy is all that counts."

"What a bastard. Two bastards. You think they just happened to get together?"

I said, "More like puzzle pieces fitting together. Williams is attuned to weakness, Corey is emotionally unstable. During the divorce negotiations, Williams sniffed out Corey's mounting rage when no one else did. When the time was right, he made himself available. Unlike Corey, he *does* know how to be subtle, probably raised the subject in a way that wouldn't incriminate him if Corey balked. That's why I think his acting out at work is significant. He's stopped pretending to be normal."

Milo said, "Maybe because Corey paid him big-time for the hit and he no longer needed the job."

Robin said, "But the big picture is hatred of women."

I nodded.

"It always comes down to that, doesn't it?" She touched my face. "Talking to wood doesn't seem half bad."

We set out for Oxnard just before eight. Smooth sailing all the way to the 101 and we were well into the West Valley when Milo's phone burped a few digitalized notes from Brandenburg 6, Movement 1. Shame to do that to a masterpiece.

"Sturgis . . . who? Don't know anyone—oh, yeah, I do, put her through . . . this is Lieutenant Sturgis, what's up . . . really? From where did they . . . all right, I'm listening."

He'd neglected the hands-off and all I could hear was a female voice chirping nonstop.

When that ended, he said, "Anything else you want to . . . yeah, sure . . . tell them I'm available if they want to speak directly . . . I understand that . . . pardon? Oh, sure." He laughed. "But let's hope it doesn't come to that . . . yes if it does happen, I'll vouch for you, promise."

He stared at the silent phone. "You won't believe who that was. Sassy little Laura Smith, Ashley and Marissa just phoned her, she wouldn't say from where, but we already know. The main thing is they wanted her to pass along a message to me, even though they don't generally trust the police. They're scared for their lives, want their father 'busted.' Sooner rather than later."

"Putting in their order."

"Poor spoiled kids, reality is not going to be kind to them. Their story is they learned he was the one who'd stolen their horses so they drove to his condo and confronted him. Really unloaded on him, like they were used to. This time instead of sitting there and taking it, he grabbed both their wrists and squeezed hard enough to hurt them.

With a 'maniac look' in his eyes. When the girls tried to break free, he shoved them hard enough for Ashley to fall down. Marissa tried to help her up and all of a sudden Daddy's in their face again, blocking the door, and now he's got a gun in his hand. They both started crying, Marissa admitted wetting herself. They started begging but Corey just stood there with a crazy smile on his face, like he was a stranger. They really thought they were finished. Fortunately, someone knocked on the door and that seemed to snap him out of it and while he was distracted, they pushed past him and got the hell out of there."

"They didn't think to call the cops."

"Like I said, they don't trust the cops. Also, they were probably too freaked out to think about anything but escape. They're not geniuses to begin with, Alex. Look how they've continued to use their credit cards, thank God I got the accounts blocked."

"Daddy with a gun," I said. "He's dissociating in order to accomplish things he wouldn't ordinarily dream of."

"Like killing his kids. And paying to have his ex murdered."

"Ursula cheated on him, the girls gave him attitude, finally he reached his limit."

"Lunatic with a gun," he said. "That changes things. Let me inform Gonzales."

He made the call to Gonzales's home. Gonzales said, "Thanks, we'll be ready for anything. You almost here?"

"Ten minutes."

"My wife claims she'd still love me if she could remember my face so it'll take me twenty, maybe twenty-five, to remind her. But my rookie will greet you, name's Sheila Entell. The gun change *your* plans?"

"Hell, yeah," said Milo. "I figured to drop in on Corey, play nice, see what I could pry out of him about Williams."

"And now?"

"Now, I'm not sure, Frank. Okay if I call Entell directly?"

"Guess so," said Gonzales. "No, scratch that, I'll get there sooner, have to make it up to the wife but so be it."

"Don't want to sow discord, Frank."

"One sec." Silence on the line; Gonzales came back on, speaking softer. "Moved to another room. Yeah, my princess will be discording plenty, she cooked homemade tamales, all steamed and ready to go. Beef, chicken, these sweet ones she does with dried fruit. But she also invited her mother, catch my drift?"

Milo laughed. "Happy to oblige."

"One thing," said Gonzales. "Dropping in this late won't ring any of Corey's bells?"

"I was figuring to pour on the charm but let's talk when I get there."

"Hmm," said Gonzales. "Charm, I'm trying to imagine that."

Milo hung up. I said, "What quid pro quo did Laura Smith ask for?"

"If she gets busted again, I get her out of it. Totally."

"Such faith. Touching."

"No sense disillusioning her," he said. "Being young's hard enough."

35

Gonzales's extended-cab GMC pickup truck was parked half a block from Richard Corey's condo, taking up a whole bunch of red-zone. Gonzales wore sweats and a zip-up jacket, held out a sheet of aluminum foil.

"Tamales, she let me bring some of the sweet ones, here."

We ate. I said, "Delicious."

Milo said, "You're married to the perfect woman, Frank."

"So she tells me. Nice old Caddy. Impound?"

Milo said, "His."

"Really. Original engine, Doc?"

I said, "Third rebuild."

"Nothing like loyalty—okay, Sheila's waiting up there." Pointing to a side street running perpendicular to the harbor. "Corey hasn't left, his lights are still on, you can see the TV blinking behind those drapes. We got a lucky break, the next-door neighbor left a couple hours ago, so if it does get weird, less risk of innocent bystanders."

Milo said, "No reason for it to go weird, Frank."

"I know," said Gonzales, "but you know."

◆

The building slipped into view under a nearly starless sky, dark bulk checked by amber rectangles of curtained windows. Gonzales whistled softly and a woman in her early twenties stepped out of the shadows. A blond ponytail poked from the back of her baseball cap. Her face was finely boned. She wore a leather motorcycle jacket, jeans, and running shoes. The jacket looked too large for her; ample room for a shoulder-holstered 9mm.

"Officer Entell," said Gonzales. "She's been doing a great job."

"Thanks, sir," said Entell, looking past us at the condo. "But nothing really to do."

Milo said, "We call that a good situation, Officer." He told her who I was. She said, "The subject's a nutter?"

Gonzales said, "Nutter with a gun, like I told you. They don't think there's going to be any problems, this is just a social call."

"All right," said Sheila Entell. "Social call this late?"

Milo said, "It'll throw him off but I'll take the soft approach. Starting by phoning him right now to avoid too much surprise."

He called. No answer. Rechecking the number, he tried again.

"Maybe he's in the bathroom," said Gonzales.

The four of us headed toward the condo. Neighboring houses were unlit in both directions. Weekenders. Up close one of Corey's front windows was flicked with strobe-like flashes of light and color. TV on in the living room, like Gonzales had said.

Milo tried calling again. Same result.

Gonzales turned to Entell. "You're sure he's in there."

"Sir, I am sure. I've never shifted my attention from that side of the residence. And I don't think he jumped off that two-story deck in back."

Milo said, "He could still be in the bathroom, Frank."

Gonzales said, "And my mother-in-law could be my best friend—okay, try him again."

◆

Two more attempts; nothing.

Gonzales said, "I'm heading out to the harbor-side, see if I can spot him in there." Glancing at Entell.

She said, "I'm sure he's there, sir."

"Hell," said Gonzales. "Maybe he did jump off the deck, he's one of those, what do you call 'em—rappellers." He mimed a hand-over-hand routine. Scowled. "Or someone helped with a ladder."

"Williams," said Milo.

"For all we know they're still asshole buddies."

Unzipping his jacket, Gonzales exposed his own service gun, keeping it holstered but touching the weapon as if for reassurance. "I'm going back there, check out the walkway. You take Lieutenant Sturgis with you and do the easy part, Sheila."

Entell said, "What's that, sir?"

"The front door. I'm thinking no one's going to answer it."

Entell led but as we neared Corey's door, Milo insinuated himself in front of her and motioned for me to stand back. He rang the bell. Repeated. Knocked, did it harder. His third knock was enough to ease the door ajar. Vertical light slashed the darkness, clean and bright as a scalpel. Televised blather filtered through the crack.

A sultry woman's voice bandying words like *"performance"* and *"enhancement."*

Milo stepped back and took out his Glock. Faint snap as Sheila Entell freed her weapon.

Milo said, "Just stay there, Alex." He toed the door open another inch. "Mr. Corey? Lieutenant Sturgis."

More light, more throaty salesmanship from the woman on TV. *"We love you guys, but we really love you bigger."*

Milo pushed the door another few inches. Waited. Got the opening wide enough for entry. Staying Entell with a palm, he went in, gun-first.

Seconds later: "Oh, damn."

◆

Richard Corey slumped on his sofa, facing his flat-screen TV. Bowl of popcorn to his right, five empty beer bottles arrayed neatly near his feet.

He wore a gray terry-cloth robe and nothing else.

The top of his skull was caved in, more damage to the back than the front. Diagonal wound. I pictured a full-force swing from above. Someone behind him.

Bone fragments created a jagged halo. Brain matter was a pied clot of rust and white.

His mouth gaped. Any skin free of gore resembled gray plastic.

A retractable, black polycarbonate billy club, the kind police departments call batons and order in bulk, sat on the kitchen counter, caked with dry blood. The weapon was laid precisely atop a dish towel, displayed proudly. Blood stained the sofa and the carpet, spattering and splotching the ceiling. Lots of fine-spray castoff on the ceiling. Red in some places, browning in others. Jackson Pollock gone murderous.

The woman smiling from the TV screen wore a bikini and a gold chain around her hips, and pointed at a line-drawing of a phallus the size of a small car. The organ was filled with ducts and channels ("the love canal," "the pleasure trough") that had eluded the anatomy texts.

She said, "Guys, make us happy. Get in touch with your hugeness."

Patrolwoman Sheila Entell clamped a hand over her mouth and began making little gagging noises. She'd turned a bad color. Her gun-hand dangled, 9mm arcing wider and wider.

Placing one hand on her wrist, Milo used the other to gently uncurl her fingers and take the weapon. Turning away from the corpse, she began breathing rapidly.

Milo said, "Got your radio with you, Officer?"

Dull nod.

"Call Sergeant Gonzales."

Entell reached under her motorcycle jacket. Her eyes drifted back to the corpse on the sofa. "That's him?"

"That was Mr. Corey."

"Oh, God! I *watched* him but I've never actually *seen* him? How could it happen when I was right here?"

"It probably didn't," said Milo. "From the looks of it, he's been here awhile."

"But how?" she repeated.

I said, "The next-door neighbor. What did he look like?"

36

Sheila Entell had been concentrating on Richard Corey, hadn't paid much attention to the visitor when he exited and drove away.

But her sketchy description was sufficient: tall and thin, probably not an old guy. And oh, yeah, wearing glasses, you could see the shine.

Milo said, "When exactly did he leave?"

"Like an hour, hour and a quarter before you got here. I'm sorry, I can't tell you an exact time, maybe it was forty-five minutes. Give or take. I don't *know,* sir. He was the *neighbor.*"

More assumptions blown to bits.

That was the point.

Milo said, "Tell me about his departure, Officer."

"He came out and got in his car and just drove away."

"You saw him at the wheel?"

Entell bit her lip. "He went over to the driver's side, sir—did I totally screw up by not paying more attention?"

"You didn't, Officer, I'm just trying to get some facts and I'm going to ask you questions and if you don't know the answers, that's okay. How was he dressed?"

Blank stare from Entell. "I think he was wearing a jacket—I honestly can't be sure."

"Color of anything he had on?" said Milo. "For purposes of an APB."

Entell shook her head.

"Anything stand out about him?"

"No, sir, that's the thing! I mean there was no reason to consider him at all, I never even saw him go in, that was Ottmar and he didn't report anything weird to me and while I was here nothing changed, nothing indicated trouble or struggle or anything, sir. The TV even kept going. And when he came out and got in his car he seemed normal."

"Normal, how?"

"Not jumpy, not looking around like he'd done something wrong, sir. He just drove away."

Her lips quivered. Milo patted her shoulder. "You did fine, don't beat yourself up."

Frank Gonzales entered and took in the corpse. "Our Mr. Corey."

"None other, Frank."

"Well, this sucks. Okay, got a call in to a righteous judge for a victim's warrant, got all the other usual stuff in motion."

Sheila Entell's shoulders rose. "Sirs, I just thought of something. When he left wasn't the only time I saw him. Shortly before, he came out and put stuff in his vehicle. But, again, normal, I really wasn't—"

"What kind of stuff, Officer Entell?"

"Boxes, bags—" Entell's body went rigid. "I might be able to give you details, sirs! The vehicle. First off, the make: gray Corolla, sirs, of that I'm sure. I also remember some of the tag numbers, not all, really really sorry, but some, maybe that'll help a little?"

Milo whipped out his pad. "Go."

"Okay," she said, inhaling deeply. "I want to make sure I get this

right . . . okay . . . first an 'S' then two 7s. No, no, wrong, just the opposite, sorry, okay, this is it: two 7s first, then the 'S.' "

Milo said, "So, 77S and four digits you didn't see."

"Yes, sir. Only reason I noticed the 7s was there's this old TV show
my grandpa used to work on. *Seventy-Seven Sunset Strip,* he was a cam-
eraman, always talks about how his old shows were better than the crap
on today. He also worked on that other one, Rockford, whatever, anyway when I saw it, I thought 77S, like 77 Sunset, you know?"

Milo said, "Good work, Sheila."

Sheila Entell stared at him. "Really?"

"Really. Anything else you remember?"

"No, sir, like I said, he walked away normal and later he drove away
normal. He *always* looked normal." Her eyes dared a peek at the corpse.
"You really think it was him?"

"We don't know. Did he leave alone?"

"I didn't see anyone else."

"No woman."

"Not on my shift, sir, just him. Brian and Ottmar never mentioned
a woman, either. But maybe they wouldn't. He was just the neighbor,
they were watching Corey."

Milo said, "Could you check on that, Frank?"

Gonzales was already on the phone.

Rookie patrolman Brian Sweeney had never seen anyone enter or exit,
period, including the tall man wearing glasses.

Rookie patrolman Ottmar Buenavista's account kept Gonzales on
the phone longer. When he hung up, anger tightened his voice.

"Man and a woman, she was young, dark-haired, could be Hispanic but maybe a dark-haired Anglo." Gonzales frowned. "A 'killer
body. Like a dancer.' "

He shook his head. "*That* he paid attention to."

Milo said, "A young, attractive Hispanic female who worked with
Williams has been missing for three days."

"Oh, fantastic. We got a Bonnie-and-Clyde thing or a captive thing?"

"Either way, it doesn't look good for the girl. Williams isn't much for long-term relationships."

"Damn." Gonzales plucked his mustache. "You know him to drive a Corolla?"

"Only registered vehicle we have for him is an old Ford van."

"So maybe the Corolla's hers."

"No, she drives a Lexus."

"So maybe one of them has two cars. Or it's stolen or the plates are, let's see what we can dig up."

Cross-referencing partials with makes and models would take time and have to wait until morning when DMV offices were open for improvisation. But Meredith Santos's registration info was available now and Milo ran her through DMV again.

Only the Lexus.

Gonzales said, "We got a serious GTA situation in Oxnard, let me check the hot-sheets."

Milo said, "Meanwhile, can I talk to the rookie who saw her?"

"Be my guest." Gonzales redialed Buenavista, handed his phone to Milo in exchange for Milo's, and reached a colleague at Oxnard auto theft.

Milo said, "Officer, this is Lieutenant Sturgis, I'm working with your sergeant and need to ask you a few things. Anything else you can say about the female living next door to your subject? . . . Sergeant Gonzales has related that. Anything else? . . . all right, now describe the relationship between the male and the female . . . what I'm getting at is how they acted in each other's company . . . did she at any time look tense or frightened of him? . . . okay . . . any physical contact between them . . . just a hug . . . all right, good, call me immediately if you think of anything else."

He clicked off. "The additional wisdom is boobs that big are probably fakes, we should try topless clubs." He smiled. "Lad has a bright future as a Sherlock."

I said, "Silicon. There's something you can put on the APB."

"Chesty girl. That sound like Santos? I can't say I was studying her that closely the time we saw her but nothing stood out. Pardon the expression."

"I didn't notice it, either. But she was dressed for office work."

"Suit and pearls," he said. "Women can do that."

"Do what?"

"Camouflage themselves."

I eyed the condo. "So can men."

Gonzales returned. "No stolen Corollas that match but it takes time for victims to report, so it may show up yet. Buenavista have anything more to say?"

Milo said, "No sign of fear or tension on the female's part."

"Bonnie still thinks she's safe with Clyde."

"God help her," said Milo. "Or she's in on it. Santos's boss said she was the last to complain about Williams's stalking behavior but maybe that was a ruse."

Gonzales said, "You know how it is with pervs, they start with peeping, some of them move on. But why would she lie about being bothered by him?"

"Good question—so maybe she is in trouble, they had a thing and it broke up nasty. Their getting together in the first place would be understandable. They worked in the same place for months, plenty of time to develop chemistry. But I didn't pick up any tension between them the brief time I saw them. You?"

I shook my head.

Not that I'd been looking.

Guided somewhere else by a psychopath.

Sheila Entell would be flogging herself for a while, thinking she'd screwed up due to inexperience. But it could happen to anyone because by nature we expect the usual and it's not that hard to fool anyone with minimal misdirection.

Achieving dominance by sticking it to authority.

To the world.

37

The "good judge" called back twenty minutes later, agreeing to sign a warrant for the next-door unit. Agreeable jurist, but a stickler: telephonic wouldn't cut it, everything had to be on paper, to satisfy those "ACLU types who've been major pains in the asses lately."

Part of that attitude might've been due to being woken up and hell if he'd leave the house. He had a home fax, would wait but not for too long.

Frank Gonzales ran off to call someone at his office and get the process going.

As we waited outside the condo, vehicles converged from the east. Uniformed officers to tape and guard, techs toting forensic luggage.

The last to arrive was a coroner's investigator who looked as if she'd seen it all twice. She examined the body quickly, emerged, saying, "Kind of obvious," and released it for further examination.

Moments later, a tech stepped out and said, "Okay, you can come in."

Milo and Gonzales returned to the death scene. I waited outside, the conspicuous civilian with no role, and used the time to phone Robin.

She said, "Oh, no. What's going on?"

"We were right about Williams and Corey colluding. To the point of Williams living next door. But Williams decided to dissolve the partnership. Lots of reasons to do that—covering his tracks, enjoying it, and, probably foremost, making off with Corey's cash-stash."

"Right in front of the cops."

"That's part of what I meant by enjoying it."

"What a monster," she said. "When are you coming home?"

"Up to Milo, he'll need me to drive him back. Don't wait up."

"I won't," she said. "But I probably won't sleep too deeply."

Twenty minutes after he reentered Corey's condo, Milo emerged, brandishing a clear plastic evidence bag and waving me over. Inside the bag was a single piece of U.S. paper currency, wilted around the edges.

Legal tender but it was hard to make out the denomination through the mist inside the bag.

Milo said, "You can touch it."

Cold. "The fridge?"

Milo said, "Wedged in back of the vegetable bin, I was lucky to spot a tiny corner sticking out."

I said, "A stray that fell unnoticed. From the big cash-stash Corey kept there."

"Nothing there, now. Williams scored a big haul." He exhaled. "Idiot Corey couldn't use a bank or a brokerage account because he'd been evading taxes for who knows how long. So he cooled his dough. Literally. Must've taken up a lot of space, there sure wasn't much else in there."

"Not a food guy."

"Yeah. I know."

"Any wisdom from the scene? To me it looked like a sneak attack from the rear."

"From the rear and above, the amount of bone damage says a hefty swing—going for the outfield. Corey's position suggests he was couch-potato-ing, no indication he had any idea what was in store."

"Trust thy neighbor," I said. "He pays Williams to shoot Ursula, tosses in free rent."

"Double-barreled idiot. Letting a guy he knew to be homicidal live next door, and get behind him with a baton. Entell said Williams was wearing a jacket, so easy enough to conceal."

I said, "Interesting choice of weapon."

"What do you mean?"

"Using police equipment."

He ground his jaws, slapped hair out of his face. "Corey was smart enough to make a fortune, what the hell possessed him?"

His eyes shifted to Frank Gonzales a few yards away, talking on the phone. "Damn paper warrant for both units, it was me, I'd just go next door because Williams was seen with a woman but no one noticed her leaving and if that ain't grounds I don't know what is."

Gonzales saw him scowling, held up a finger. Milo pulled out a panatela, lit and smoked and paced and fidgeted for the fourteen minutes it took for Gonzales to say, "Okay, it arrived in my office."

We followed him to the unit where John Jensen Williams had possibly lived with a young, dark-haired, huge-chested woman. Milo's head lowered for battle, as he struggled not to take the lead.

Gonzales gave the door a token knock, called out, "Police, open up!" and when that brought no response, ordered a uniform to get a ram.

Clearing the place didn't take long. No one inside, dead or otherwise, the only furniture two futons, a folding card table, and two matching chairs.

Chemical smell of recent cleanup.

No clothes in the closet, no obvious sign of habitation until Milo gloved up and examined the kitchen.

This refrigerator was crammed tight with food.

Plastic-wrapped Wagyu steaks, ducks, and veal sweetbreads. A similarly wrapped goose, two disarticulated quails, three packages of ground venison. All the labels from a yuppie market in Brentwood that pulls off price-gouging by sheathing it in eco-religion.

Local and sustainable, indeed. The goose looked past its prime, and abandoned long enough, all this flesh would soon be rotting. The bottom bin of fruits and vegetables had already taken on a rancid odor. Unaffected were a bottle of Laurent-Perrier Brut Champagne and a six-pack of "organic gourmet" water "harvested" from an obscure island in the South Pacific.

Gonzales said, "Looks like someone was planning to stuff their face."

"Probably not," I said.

"Why not?"

"He knew when he'd be leaving. This is all about advertising."

"Advertising what?"

"Himself. As a man of elevated taste."

The big puzzle remained: How could the woman Patrolman Buenavista had seen with Williams disappear without being spotted? But a third call to the rookie, this time from Gonzales, produced a prosaic downer of an explanation that left him punching his palm and shaking his head.

"Fool's a green-bean," he muttered. " 'Oh, yeah, Sarge. She did leave in another car. A van, actually.' "

Milo said, "Williams's Ford."

"They traded cars, huh? Or the Corolla was stolen and Williams had her take his drive, maybe meet up with him so he could ditch it."

"Sounds like a plan, Frank."

"Damn . . . at least this chicklet left alive."

"Don't write her an insurance policy."

"That's for sure," said Gonzales. "He took Corey by surprise, probably has one planned for her. You say this girl was in the service?"

"Yup."

"You'd think she'd have some smarts."

"He's got a way with women, stomach the direct route to the heart and all that."

"He cooks for them?"

"Sets a lovely table," said Milo. "Then everything turns to garbage."

"Clever," said Gonzales. "The cooking part, I mean. Before I met my wife I had the basic crazy girlfriend, used to make dinky tostadas for her, didn't take much more than that."

His smile spread under his mustache. "Not the wife, though. Can't fool her, she's got taste buds."

Forensics completed, body transported, resumption of quiet. No neighbors had come out to watch, not even a light switching on.

Just before midnight, Milo yawned and said, "Let's get the hell out of here."

I raced back to L.A. One mile into the fifty-mile journey, Milo's eyes were closed. By mile two, he was snoring.

Hard to say if that indicated uncanny relaxation in the face of evil and frustration or just escape. Either way, the soundtrack he provided was thunderous and steady, sibilance broken by random gasps and the occasional infantile squeak.

When my cell phone beeped, he continued the serenade.

My answering service. I triggered the hands-off.

The operator said, "Oh, Doctor, I didn't think you'd answer, was just leaving you the message so you could get it tomorrow morning."

"Might as well tell me."

"It was the police," she said. "I know you work with them but it wasn't that lieutenant who's always calling you, this was someone else. He said it wasn't an emergency."

"What's his name?"

"Let's see . . . a Detective Bamburger? Just like Hamburger with a 'B.' From Valley Division."

I thanked her, switched back to manual, and punched the number.

"Bamburger, Homicide."

"This is Alex Delaware."

"Who? Oh. Didn't expect you to call back so soon, Mr. Delaware."

"What can I do for you?"

"Oh," said Bamburger. "Says here Ph.D.—that's a doctor, right? Sorry, *Doctor* Delaware. Anyway, reason I phoned is this business card of yours that I'm looking at right now was found at the scene of a crime and I wanted to check a few things with you."

"Who got killed?"

A beat. "Says here you're a psychologist."

"I am. I'm also an LAPD consultant and I happen to be working on a multiple murder case with Lieutenant Milo Sturgis from West L.A. Division. He's sitting right here, if you'd rather talk to him—"

"You know," said Bamburger, "that sounds like a good idea."

I nudged Milo's arm. He snorted, gulped air, rolled away and faced the passenger door. A second prod, harder, got his eyes fluttering. "Huh?"

I gave him a moment to regain focus, told him about Bamburger.

He said, "Don't know him . . ." Then: "What the—"

Sitting up straight, he snatched the phone. "Sturgis."

He listened to Bamburger, turned to me. "You know someone named Alvin Brown?"

"Nope."

"He says no." Back to me: "Black male, thirty-one, runs a tattoo shop in North Hollywood—oh, shit."

My turn to jolt into hyper-alertness. "A shop called Zanzibar?"

Milo verified that.

I said, "Oh, shit, indeed. Brown called himself Tigretto. He inked Frankie DiMargio. With Williams at her side."

Milo returned to Bamburger. "You're not going to believe this, Lloyd."

The cop-to-cop exchange that followed took up a good chunk of the ride and I was transitioning to the 405 by the time he handed the phone back to me.

I said, "When do they think Brown got shot?"

"Sometime last night. Williams goes in and out, in full view of surveillance, doing his murder thing."

"Didn't notice the shop hours when I was there. Is it open late?"

"Officially it closes at seven. What it looks like is Mr. Brown came in after hours to do a tattoo and ended up shot in the back of the head. On the surface, a robbery gone bad, the register was cleaned out, but right away Bamburger had his doubts, why would someone operating a cash-business in a so-so area leave the register full overnight? The scene had a staged quality to it—a few drawers opened but no serious scrounging, plus a healthy Baggie of weed and some pills were left behind. The murder was one shot from behind, no binding or submission. Your basic surprise execution. Sound familiar?"

I said, "Brown was aware of Williams, knew he was dangerous. He promised to let me know if Williams showed up again."

"So Williams set up the appointment using another name. Or Busty Bertha did. She comes in, sits in the chair, in walks Romeo and boom."

My stomach knotted. "I hope my card wasn't what got Brown killed."

"That was the case it wouldn't a been found in his pant pocket. Williams and his girlfriend concentrated on killing and staging, no reason to frisk the victim."

"So why make a new victim?"

"Same as Corey," he said. "Tying up loose ends, they've got to be planning a serious escape."

I said, "Wonder if any tattooing actually got done. You find new skinwork on either of them and match it to a bloody stencil, you've got nice evidence."

He redialed Bamburger, got the answer quickly.

"A stencil was left on the chair. But no bloody tissues, no bottles of ink nearby, so looks like it didn't actually get used. And guess what the design was: miniature horn of plenty, kind of girlie. Sparkly rays, twinkly little stars, a whole bunch of nature's bounty tumbling out."

"More culinary art," I said. "He considered branding his new friend, decided not to risk it, but killed the messenger anyway."

Both of us reluctant to tag the friend as Meredith Santos. Because she'd served her country, was, by all accounts, a class act.

Not that either of us was willing to trust our instincts.

I drove, hands riveted to the wheel.

Milo stared out the windshield and went mute but didn't fall back asleep. When I pulled up to the West L.A. station, he got out without a word.

CHAPTER

38

I slept poorly, watched the sun rise as my brain channel-surfed between fatigue and restlessness.

Thinking of John Jensen Williams. Knowing he could be anywhere. Everywhere.

Instant mood-disorder mix, just add failure.

When I got to Milo's office at eleven a.m. he acknowledged me with a two-finger salute and kept typing.

NCIC on the screen, followed by a statewide site that concentrated on recent felonies. Running Meredith Santos through all the databases, still not knowing if she was a victim, an offender, or both.

She was a decorated army veteran. Administrative specialist—ordering supplies—in the thick of battle, a base near Fallujah.

Honorable discharge three years ago. Pure as milk.

A greasy box sat next to Milo's computer. "Want some brunch?"

"No, thanks."

He fortified himself with a cruller, a donut, and a bear claw. Wiped his chin and announced, "Now the fun part of my day," and phoned Santos's parents in Arizona.

Her mother answered and he said, "It's Lieutenant Sturgis from L.A., again," and labored unsuccessfully to avoid frightening the woman. When he finally worked in John Jensen Williams's name, she said, "Never heard of him, sir." A gasp. Tears.

A new voice came on, sharp as a box cutter. Captain Henry Santos, U.S. Army (ret.), taking the phone from his wife. "What's that name?" he snapped.

Milo repeated it. "He could also be going by J.J. or Jens—"

"Negative on all counts. Not known to the family. You're saying he did something to Merry?"

"We don't know that, sir."

"But you suspect or you wouldn't be bringing him up."

"We're not sure but it's possible, Captain Santos."

"None of this makes sense, sir. I trained the girl in self-defense, she knows how to take care of herself."

I thought: Martial arts takes on a black-belt in psychopathy? Don't get your hopes up.

Milo said, "For all we know she hasn't—"

"This is going to be bad," said Henry Santos. "I can feel it."

A check of the APBs and BOLOs on the van, the Corolla, and the Lexus produced no leads.

Milo said, "Wonder if the Corey girls knew Williams was living next door, maybe they can identify the woman with him . . . I'm groping, but let's give it another try."

The sisters had stopped using their credit cards.

I said, "If they're staying with relatives in Canada, maybe you can find out who. What was Ursula's maiden name?"

He flipped through the Corey murder book, shook his head. "Her middle name on her license, ready for this: Gladys." He logged onto county tax records. Nothing.

I said, "May I?"

"May you what?"

"Type."

A civilian using a police computer is a big no-no. Every day Milo and I spend working together probably breaks a dozen rules.

I sped straight onto the information highway, plugging in *ursula gladys british diplomat,* hoping the combination of keywords would narrow things down.

It did.

A single hit, but the right one: eleven-year-old obituary from *The Times* of London.

Lionel P. L. Overland, a retired foreign service official who'd been posted to Bangkok, Singapore, and Hong Kong, had passed after a long illness. Eton, Cambridge, London University, faithful service to the Crown, et cetera. Retirement enriched by a love for orchids originating during his years in the Far East.

Preceded in death by his wife Gladys Mae, survived by his only child, Ursula Gladys Corey.

Ursula overland paired with *bangkok* and *singapore* produced nothing. But *hong kong* coughed up the website of Gilbert Overland, Ltd.

High-end antiques shop in Ocean Terminal, Kowloon.

The island was sixteen hours ahead of L.A., making it just after eight a.m. I emailed.

Seconds later, I received a reply.

Gilbert Overland, Proprietor, responding with surprise but no dread.

The Los Angeles police? Ursula's murder?
Yes.
Dreadful. Still reeling.
How'd you find out?
Her ex told me.
You're her cousin?

Yes.

Were you in regular contact?

When she came to HK, she'd visit. Why are you emailing me?

We're trying to locate any other relatives.

There are none, U and I are both singletons, the Overlands weren't much for breeding. Why not simply ask Richard?

He wasn't aware of any relatives besides you.

Well, that's true.

No family in Canada?

None. Why?

Searching for information.

That doesn't really answer the question Mr. Sturgis.

At this point, more questions than answers.

I see. Do you know about the divorce? Lots of animosity.

Ursula told you about it.

Often. Especially during her last visit.

How long ago was that?

A year. What do you think of him? Richard.

I turned to Milo.

He typed in

Interesting guy.

Urs made him sound quite dull.

I signed off and relinquished the computer.

Milo said, "Good try. At least we know not to bother looking for family. So maybe a Maple Leaf pal."

He phoned Laura Smith and asked about friends in other cities. Sounding groggy, she said, "No way, everyone's here."

"Thanks again, Laura. You haven't heard from them?"

"Uh-uh." Yawn. *Click.*

I said, "If they're scared enough they might turn to an adult, not a peer."

"Friend of Mommy's," he said.

"The only one we know is Phyllis Tranh."

"If she's still a friend after dating Richard."

"Don't imagine that would change things," I said.

"Why not?"

"First off, Richard and Phyllis didn't last long. More important, Ursula would've been happy to have Richard occupied."

Googling *phyllis tranh* produced the California business registration for Diamond Products and Sundries, Inc. The company was a sizable concern with additional locations in Las Vegas and New Jersey.

Plus a "storage facility" in Vancouver.

"Makes sense," I said. "It's a trade outlet to the Far East."

Milo punched in Albert Tranh's home number in Beverly Hills.

Tranh said, "You'd need to talk to my daughter about that."

"Please, sir, if you know anything about the girls' whereabouts, it's important to let me know."

"Of course, Lieutenant."

"You have a warehouse in Vancouver. Do you also keep a residence there?"

"I do not."

"Does Phyllis?"

"My daughter's an adult, I don't snoop into her personal affairs."

"Where can I reach her?"

"She's traveling."

"Where, Mr. Tranh?"

"I'll have to check."

"You don't know?"

Pause. "As I said, Phyllis is an adult and she's extremely active and mobile."

"Is she traveling alone?"

"She usually does."

"I'm going to ask you a direct question, sir, and you need to answer truthfully: do you know where the Corey girls are?"

"No, Lieutenant."

"It's important that I reach them, Mr. Tranh."

"May I ask why?"

"Their lives have taken another unhappy turn. Their father was murdered recently."

"Really," said Albert Tranh. "Who by?" Even voice.

"Unknown, sir."

"I hope it becomes known. Good day, Lieutenant."

Milo stared at the phone. "Real choked up, huh?"

I said, "Un-dearly departed."

"Not a popular guy. It's like when you split with someone and everyone starts telling you what a jerk he always was."

He wheeled away from his desk, stretched his legs. "At least the girls are safe with Daddy out of the way. If Tranh does know something, my informing him might bring them back." He sat up. "Williams would have no interest in them, right?"

"Not unless they witnessed something."

"Like what?"

"Seeing Williams at the condo, overhearing something. Come to think of it, if Richard suspected they knew of his deal with Williams, that could explain his threatening behavior toward the girls."

"More than just being fed up with their attitude? But then why would Corey move on them with that gun? I want to snag someone, I put them at ease. Like our bad boy."

I said, "You're rational and Williams is an experienced psychopath. But Richard was a social klutz and whatever little interpersonal judgment he began with was diminished by fear and rage."

He shook the bakery box. Crumbs rattled. "Okay, so we leave the girls in peace until Williams is out of the picture. Hopefully in this millennium."

He cracked his knuckles. "Bastard could be anywhere . . . you're right about his being motivated by the thrill. If it was the money he was after, easy enough to sneak it out and split. Any more thoughts about his psyche?"

I said, "He thinks he's unique but it's the same old story: a chronic washout with a grandiose sense of himself. Could he actually work at something and succeed? Sure, but he never will, believes he deserves the goodies just for being Mr. Wonderful. Like most psychopaths, anxiety's not a big part of his life but he's not immune to tension and once in a while—when he lets himself think about the difference between his goals and his reality—it gets out of hand."

"So he hunts for a slave."

"Someone he views as inferior, allowing him to feel superior. He stalks, seduces, captures, controls, and when the thrill ebbs, he destroys. But unlike some serials, he's not locked into a tight script. He'll kill for money or as a jokey favor."

"Jack of All Nasty," he said. "Meredith Santos doesn't sound like a submissive, but who knows?"

"If we ever get to meet her, we'll see."

"If?" he said. "Where's the old optimism?"

I didn't answer.

He frowned. "I thought you might say that."

We left the station and took a walk up the block. Neither of us said a word.

Fresh air did nothing to unclog my head and Milo's expression said it hadn't helped him, either. As we began the return trip, he said, "This case, the damn food angle, has screwed up my digestive system. I can't even *think* about lunch."

I thought: three pastries an hour ago.

I said, "Time heals."

CHAPTER

39

As we climbed the stairs back to Milo's office, he said, "You're right. As usual."

"About what?"

He touched his belt buckle. "I can imagine feeling better in a couple hours. Say, Italian."

He spent time making sure the BOLOs had gotten to airport cops at LAX, Burbank, and John Wayne. Moments later, Frank Gonzales phoned.

"Our CS-eyers got semen and other stuff from the futons in Williams's unit, there'll be plenty to DNA. No gun there or at Corey's so whatever weapon those girls saw is gone, I'm figuring Williams took it."

"That's how I see it," said Milo.

"Too bad they can't describe it so we know what to look for."

"Maybe eventually."

"Not that Corey used it on anyone. Sounds like a nutcase, brandishing at his own kids."

"He wasn't a paragon of mental health, Frank."

"Anything from the Valley guy on that tattoo artist?"

Milo said, "Not yet."

"I followed up on the alerts right before I called you. Still zero."

"I know, Frank."

"I'm boring you," said Gonzales. "Boring myself."

Milo phoned Lloyd Bamburger.

The Valley D said, "Hey, just about to call you. Bullet from Mr. Brown's head is a 9mm. That match yours?"

Milo said, "My vic Corey was a .25 but it could match my vic DiMargio."

"The slug from Brown is at the lab, where's DiMargio?"

"At the crypt, I'll get it sent over."

"Anything on your alerts? Haven't had time to check, I'm assuming nothing."

"You're assuming correctly, Lloyd."

"You find something, I know you'll tell me."

"You'll be among the first to know."

"Among?" said Bamburger.

"Figured I'd phone my family back in Indiana first, Lloyd. Prove to them I really do have a job."

Bamburger laughed and hung up.

Cradling the phone, Milo rubbed his eyes, then his entire face, played with an unlit cigar.

I said, "Just thought of something. Williams has been cleaning his plate. We need to warn Kleffer."

The cigar snapped between his fingers. He tossed it in the trash. "Hates the guy enough to steal then off his girlfriend . . . oh, man."

No answer at Kleffer's home. A call to Beppo Bippo produced an officious host.

"Chef is *cooking*."

"Tell Chef Lieutenant Sturgis needs to talk to him."

"That's not possible—"

"Make it possible."

A stretch on hold was rendered less endurable by brain-stabbing techno music featuring the same two bars beaten senseless.

The snotty-voiced man came back on. "He is creating a mussels *soufflé,* it's *fragile,* he can't be *interrupted.*"

"How about his life? That fragile, too?"

Noise in the background. A beat. "Did you say something, sir?"

"Never mind."

"I gave him your *message,* sir. He didn't *care.*"

Milo stared at his phone.

I said, "There's survival, then there's mussels soufflé."

He broke into laughter, was still convulsing as he collected his gun, keys, radio.

I said, "Where to?"

"Moron doesn't deserve it but c'mon."

CHAPTER

40

We drove past the restaurant, cruised neighboring streets looking for J. J. Williams's Dodge van, the Lexus registered to Meredith Santos, a gray Corolla tagged 77S XXXX, owner unknown.

During the fourth circuit, Frank Gonzales checked in again and cleared up one third of the vehicular mystery.

"Toyota just came in stolen. Woman parked it near a seafood place on the Ventura harbor. She went in for takeout, left the keys."

"Again with cuisine," said Milo. "Ever have mussels soufflé, Frank?"

"Sounds gross," said Gonzales. "Top of that, I got a shellfish allergy."

"So Williams switched cars but no sign of his van."

"Not yet, Ventura PD's checking the harbor, asking around at the tourist shops. They've got whale-watching going on, maybe the bastard hopped on a boat and jumped off somewhere, good riddance."

"God forbid, Captain Ahab."

"No, I'm Ishmael," said Gonzales. "The good guy."

◆

I circled three more times. Satisfied that none of the vehicles was parked nearby, Milo had me pull over a block north of Melrose.

He unlatched his seat belt. "Okay, National Geographic fans, time to explore the world of lusty gustation."

I said, "Maybe I should go in alone?"

"Why?"

"Williams saw both of us but I might be able to slip in easier, avoid attracting too much attention."

"You think Williams could be in there?"

"Just covering bases."

"Why would you have it easier?"

"I don't look like a cop."

He scanned my clothes. Black turtleneck, jeans, brown deck shoes. He was wearing a gray suit that had long surrendered to gravity, a wash 'n wear shirt that could've been off-white or just overlaundered, and a skinny tie made of something.

"What, I can't pass as a hipster gourmet?"

"Place like that," I said, "it isn't about the food."

"What's it about?"

"I'm not sure."

He thought for a while. "Okay, but don't stay in long, keep your phone on with my cell on the screen. Let me know if you see anything remotely interesting."

I stepped into a room full of noise and aroma. Squarely in the lunch hour, the restaurant's waiting area was jammed with skinny people craving small plates at big prices.

I peered through the crowd and caught a glimpse of the open kitchen. Just like the first time, frantic activity.

Unlike the first time, Darius Kleffer wasn't part of it.

I spotted him sitting at a table-for-two against the left wall of the restaurant, his back to me. But recognizable because of his Mohawk, his inked arm, his black chef's togs.

His companion was a woman in her twenties with long, lustrous black hair. Diagonal bangs sliced through a section of her longish face. Gigantic gold hoops dangled from her ears.

Serious eye makeup and cheek-rouge. Big dark eyes.

She wore a sleeveless red jersey top, silver jeans, gray suede knee boots with half-foot heels. Tattoos on her flesh, too, a blue-and-maroon sleeve on her left arm. The rest of her was fish-belly white.

Pleasant but unremarkable face.

Remarkable body.

Her chest was monumental, heralded by the scoop neck of the red top. The blouse was cut low enough to barely skirt nipples poking through jersey. A central cleft was deep enough to conceal a paperback book.

Kleffer was doing all the talking. She was doing all the hair-flipping and the lash-batting and the smiling.

Both of them leaning in, faces inches from the bottle of white wine set between them. Glasses one-third full. Unidentifiable tidbits on the plates.

A voice at the head of the queue said, "Sor-ry, nothing ye-et." The same snotty voice as over the phone. No regret at all, just a gloating drawl.

More people squeezed into the waiting area. The host took that as a signal to ignore everyone as he pretended to peruse the reservation book.

Seeing him gave me a start. At first glance, he bore a striking resemblance to Jens Williams.

Second glance modified that: This prince was slightly older and six inches shorter. But the overall look was the same: longish, greasy, calculatedly messy dark hair, heavy-duty nerd-specs, cheap sharkskin suit tailored too-short and too-tight, black shirt, pink string tie.

I realized that Williams's hipster cliché style would work in the city—in any good-sized city—enabling him to blend in and seek new venues.

The host kept fake-reading.

The crowd of aspiring tapa-istas closed ranks in front of me. Someone elbowed my ribs. Someone else had the temerity to grumble but that protest died quickly under the glare of disapproving conformity offered by the rest of the crowd.

In this world, waiting in line was a badge of honor and griping was politically incorrect.

Maybe the mussels soufflé really was amazing.

I got shoved again.

Turned and made my exit.

Someone scolded, "You can't do that, you'll lose your place."

Back behind the wheel, I described what I'd seen.

Milo said, "Busty lady."

"Breast reduction would leave her busty."

"You think she's the one Williams was shacking up with next door?"

"Or he found another like her."

"So, not Santos. Is that good or bad?"

I didn't reply.

"Damn . . . or maybe it's a coincidence and Kleffer's just hanging with his new flame."

"Maybe," I said. "But the interaction I saw was more flirtation than comfortable relationship."

"So he just met her, is wooing with his cuisine. No sign of Williams?"

"Nope."

"If Ms. Bosoms is keeping house with Williams, he's using her as lure to draw out Kleffer."

"Whatever she's selling, Kleffer's buying."

His lips vibrated like a trumpeter's. "Okay, let's find parking across the street—near one of those other restaurants. Somewhere we can keep an eye on that cut between the buildings where Kleffer goes to smoke and wax dramatic."

Three other eateries with similar clienteles. Every inch of curb the dominion of private valets.

I eased the Seville behind a Bentley coupe that shouldn't have been painted orange, and cut the engine.

Perfect view of the cut. Milo said, "Now we wait."

A red-jacket ran over and tried to open the driver's door I'd kept locked. He squinted. "Ah teck it forrr you."

High-pitched, eager, Mideast accent.

Milo said, "We'll just stay here."

"No, no, rrrestorant awnly."

"No, no, us."

"Sirrr—"

"Come closer, my friend."

"Huh?"

"C'mere."

No reason for the man to comply but Milo's curled finger drew him in as if the digit were magnetically charged. Flashing a twenty, Milo unfolded the bill and revealed what he had wrapped underneath.

The valet's eyes caromed from the cash to the gold shield.

"Huh?"

"This is your lucky day, friend. Money for nothing and we stay here for free."

The valet blinked. "Det's a song?"

"No, just reality."

41

L.A.'s not known for wearing out shoe leather, especially when the sun shines and sitting around beckons. But the stretch of Melrose where Beppo Bippo and a slew of other eateries sat boasted an intermittent but healthy parade of pedestrians.

Some of the foot-traffic veered to sample Darius Kleffer's cuisine. Others kept going and made different choices.

The cut between the buildings remained empty. Kleffer back to his knives or still enjoying the company of the woman in the red jersey.

Milo said, "She look like a stripper to you? 'Scuse me, a dancer."

I drew back in mock outrage. "A girl's curvy, she can't be a neuro-surgeon?"

"Curvy with tattoos?"

"Actually," I said. "I gave a lecture to a bunch of med students a couple of months ago. A few had been inked."

"Changing world." He yawned. "Not really. Not where it counts."

The valet he'd paid off took keys from an Audi, sped off, and returned to drop off a Mercedes. A second man joined him at the booth. Heavyset mustachioed Anglo wearing a black sport coat, red slacks and bow tie.

The head valet. Did he get to play with the Lamborghinis?

He looked at us, said something to his colleague. Brief chat, then Bow Tie rolled over like a tank on treads.

"I'm afraid you'll need to move."

Milo repeated the money-wrapped badge routine. Bow Tie grinned. "Thanks, guys." Examining the bill, he rolled away.

I said, "What was that?"

"The rhythm of life."

Forty bucks was enough for the valets to work around us, as we sat for half an hour. Twenty-five minutes in, Frank Gonzales reported more good news: the discovery of John Jensen Williams's van.

"Right there at the harbor, he didn't even try to be subtle."

"Took a while to find it."

"It's a big place, he left it out on the north end, near one of the boatyards. No, not the one where Corey stored his tub, that's still in dry dock. And no one has Williams renting any kind of watercraft."

"Anything interesting in the van, Frank?"

"Nothing obvious, let's see what the scrapers pull up. I asked for it to be towed to our lab, Ventura had no problem with that. Anything on your end?"

Milo told him about the woman flirting with Kleffer.

Gonzales said, "Sounds like the one got my rookie's pulse throbbing. So not Santos?"

"Nope."

"That could be too bad for her. I'll keep on the alerts, results are supposed to come straight to my computer, but you know how it is."

"I do, Frank."

"Look at us," said Gonzales. "We can send a man to the moon but we can't find squat."

◆

Thirty-four minutes into the surveillance, the head valet began to approach us a second time, smiling hungrily.

All that nothing hadn't done much for Milo's mood and the warning look he shot was enough to send the man scampering away.

"Greedy fool," he said.

I said, "Look."

Darius Kleffer and the woman in the red top had exited the restaurant and turned left. Toward the cut. Kleffer already had his cigarettes out.

Even with the giant heels on her boots, the woman was petite, not much over five feet tall. That and a tiny, tight waist and first-rate posture made her chest seem even bigger.

She carried a small purse covered in some sort of white-and-black fur. Her gait was pride epitomized, flaring hips rolling as if on ball bearings, each buttock cheek functioning independently.

Great muscle control. Accustomed to flaunting her body.

Maybe a "dancer," indeed.

Walking next to her, Darius Kleffer's slouch was sad.

He stopped at the same spot he'd chosen when we'd talked to him, pressing his back to the brick wall and facing the woman. She edged closer.

He offered her a cigarette that she accepted. He lit up both of them.

They smoked and flirted some more and a couple of times the woman's mouth opened wide with glee and she threw her head back and set off a brunette tsunami, finished the mini-production by touching Kleffer's arm.

The badinage continued, interrupted in spurts by passing pedestrians.

"Ah, true love," said Milo.

A few more minutes of clear view, more passersby. Milo tapped the dashboard.

I said, "What's the song?"

" 'Colonel Bogey March.' " He shut his eyes.

I kept watching. More pedestrians.

One of them had stopped a couple of feet shy of the cut.

Tall man in a black baseball cap and long black raincoat.

Illogical choice for a warm, clear afternoon.

Just as I nudged Milo, the man turned into the cut, hand reaching under the coat.

I swung the driver's door open. Milo was already out of the car, running across Melrose, dodging traffic in two directions, setting off a storm of honks and curses. I hurried to catch up, caught my own share of hostility.

Maybe it was the noise, maybe not. The man in the baseball cap turned.

Long, bony face.

Wide, black-lensed sunglasses.

A perfectly square dark soul patch bottomed a thin lower lip. The portion of scalp visible beneath the cap was shaved clean. Fingernails were polished black.

But no mistaking John Jensen Williams. The knife in his hand.

A sudden thrust toward the interior of the cut.

Milo neared the curb, gun drawn. Pedestrians screamed, scattered. Someone shouted, "Dial 911!"

Williams waved the knife. Long, curved blade. Like the one Robin and I used to gut and bone fish.

Inches of metal glazed crimson.

Darius Kleffer lay on the ground, clutching his abdomen.

The woman in the red jersey stood between him and J. J. Williams, expressionless. Unsurprised.

Then, spotting Milo and his gun, she began fake-crying.

Hnh hnh hnh.

John Jensen Williams looked at his knife. Turned back to Kleffer, now moaning in agony.

Milo said, "Drop it! Now! Drop it!"

Williams said, "You bet, this was self-defense," in a mild voice. He lowered his arm. His fingers loosened. The knife dangled.

"Drop it!"

"I'm trying to, I'm a little nervous." Williams smiled shyly. The knife canted downward.

His fingers tightened. Now the blade was tilting up.

He lunged at Milo.

Milo shot him, center of body mass, just like they teach you at the academy.

Williams, the rip in his raincoat barely noticeable, remained on his feet.

"Aw," he murmured, looking steady.

Protective vest?

Milo must have wondered the same thing. He shot again, creating a noticeable hole in John Jensen Williams's smooth, pale forehead.

Williams said, "Wow," and dropped hard. Nearly landed on Kleffer, who was mewling and losing color.

The woman in the red top flipped her hair. "Oh, thank you, sir! You saved my life."

Not a glance at Darius Kleffer, now screaming in agony, blood leaking around his fingers.

I went to tend to him.

Milo cuffed the woman.

She said, "Sir. I'm the victim."

"Of your own stupidity."

"*You're* stupid. Fat and ugly, too."

"Sticks and stones," said Milo, dialing 911.

CHAPTER

42

She called herself Kashmeer Katte, had fake I.D. to prove it. The same bogus document listed her age as twenty-five. The card shared scant space in her rabbit-fur purse with four hundred dollars in cash, two condoms, two plastic-wrapped nuggets of cocaine and one of methamphetamine.

Her real name was Agnes Brzica, her actual age, thirty-one. No sense disputing that, she came up five times on NCIC. Arrests for solicitation and drugs and once for assault.

Despite being found out, she lied about everything, starting with how long she'd known J. J. Williams.

"Just a couple weeks, sir." She'd managed to cadge a jail uniform one size too small, setting off a power struggle with the silicon implanted in her chest.

Milo said, "A girl who dances with you at Black Velvet says Williams has been coming in for months, lots of times you two went home together."

"Which girl?" said Brzica.

"That matters?"

"Some a them lie."

He waited.

"Okay," said Brzica. "Yeah, I partied with him, I just didn't want to get in trouble."

"I see."

"Honest, sir. I had no idea what he was."

"You thought he was a wholesome guy."

Long pause. "He was okay."

"He used you to lure Darius Kleffer outside so he could kill Kleffer."

"No way, sir."

"Yes way, Agnes."

"Uh-uh. It wasn't like that, sir."

"What were you doing in Kleffer's restaurant? Don't say eating."

"Eating." Giggle. Hair toss. "Okay. I just went in 'cause he said he was a friend, wanted to surprise him."

"Williams said Kleffer was a friend."

"Uh-huh."

"So he did use you to lure Kleffer?"

Silence.

"Agnes?"

"Not really, sir."

"If all Williams wanted was to surprise Kleffer, why not just bop in himself?"

"Hmm."

"Hmm?"

"You'd have to ask him."

"Kinda hard, Agnes."

Big smile. Hair toss.

"Why'd Williams use you if it was just a surprise?"

"I guess I was a bigger surprise."

"Kleffer said you worked at getting him out of the kitchen. Sent three compliments-to-the-chef messages, nagged the server."

"He's alive?"

"No thanks to you, Agnes."

"Wow, that's awesome, sir. I was surprised when that happened. Really. He's got really stinky breath."

"Kleffer or Williams?"

"The German. Really stinky."

"He's lucky he's got any breath at all, Agnes."

"You can call me Kashmeer, I like it better."

"Fair enough, Kashmeer. What else are you going to tell me?"

"I didn't do nothing, sir."

"Sounds like you actually need to believe that."

"I don't need, I know, sir."

"Okay, Kashmeer. Let's talk about Richard Corey."

"Who?" Exaggerated innocence.

Milo smiled. "Kashmeer, Kashmeer."

"What?"

"Your DNA came up in the apartment next to Richard Corey's. It's not exactly a huge complex."

"All right," said Brzica. "J.J. said he was a friend. Also."

"All those friends. J.J. was a popular guy."

"Yeah."

"Just a regular social butterfly."

"I guess. He did live next to him, said he wasn't paying rent. That's what a friend does. Right? They help."

"When did Williams tell you what he planned to do to Corey?"

"Never, sir. I didn't even know until you told me, sir. Honest."

"Williams goes into Corey's place, comes out with bags of money, you didn't wonder."

"If I knew, maybe."

"He never showed you the money."

"No, sir," she said. "I'd a liked that."

"Liked what?"

Big smile. "When they show me the money." Dropping her hand to her crotch. "When it drops into the g-string. The greatest feeling, sir."

"Okay, let's move on, Ag—Kashmeer. Meredith Santos."

"Who?"

"A girl who used to work with Williams."

"Don't know her. I'm sorry, sir."

"For what?"

"Calling you fat and ugly. I was scared."

"Hey," said Milo, "reality is reality."

"No way, sir. You're muscular and masculine."

"Gosh."

"Can I go now? It's almost time for lunch."

"Not quite yet, Kashmeer. We need to talk about Meredith Santos. She's disappeared."

"Okay."

"Williams never mentioned her?"

"Uh-uh."

"Meredith Santos, Kashmeer."

"Nope."

"Hispanic, a little younger than you."

"Never heard of her."

"Gorgeous girl," said Milo. "I'm talking beauty-queen caliber."

Anger striped Brzica's face. "He didn't need that."

"Didn't need what?"

"Fancy *pussy*. He had *me*."

He spent another two hours with her, gave me a try, allowed Frank Gonzales to have a go. By the time she asked for a lawyer, all of us were tired but Agnes Brzica remained full of energy and refusing to say where she'd lived before meeting Williams.

Hard to say how much of that was temperament, how much a residual effect of the meth she'd smoked.

Left alone in the interview room, knowing she was being video-taped, she danced and sang and shimmied and fluffed her hair and her breasts. Removing her jail slippers, she waved them like cheerleading props.

When her public defender arrived, she was standing on her head and wiggling her toes.

Her legal representation was a twenty-something named Ira Newgrass. He forbade her from saying another word, assured Milo he was wasting his time, anyway, "nothing is going to stick."

The Oxnard deputy D.A. assigned to the case, a woman named Pam Theroux, agreed privately. "All you have her on is flirting with Kleffer."

Frank Gonzales said, "C'mon, we've got her living with Williams right next to Corey, leaving before Corey's murder, waiting at that motel and meeting up with Williams and then coming to L.A. to abet a homicide."

"Residing and waiting aren't crimes, Detective."

"She's evil," said Gonzales.

"Evil isn't my business," said Theroux. "The penal code is."

"You can't do anything?"

"The most we could attempt would be conspiracy and that's a stretch. We're not wasting time on something that isn't winnable."

"What about the dope in her purse?"

"Oh, sure," said Theroux. "We can get her a couple years on that, some of it'll probably be suspended. I thought you were talking a serious charge."

Milo said, "I'm less concerned with punishing her than finding out where Meredith Santos is. If we can't hold anything over her head, there's no leverage to get her to talk."

"So dangle a totally suspended sentence on the dope and see if she bites."

Later that day, Milo called Newgrass and made the offer.

The PD said, "I'll ask her."

An hour later: "She says she'd love to make a deal but she really never heard of this person. How about you don't file on the drugs, anyway?"

"Why not?"

"She's being sincere."

"Just like you," said Milo. He slammed down the phone.

When Frank Gonzales heard the news, he said, "That's the way it goes. Cookies crumbling all over the damn place. No, forget that. No more food analogies."

Three days after the death of John Jensen Williams, Milo called Albert Tranh.

"It's safe for the girls to come home now, Mr. Tranh."

"Why's that, Lieutenant?"

"The bad guy's out of the picture."

"Arrested?"

"Six feet under."

"Oh," said Tranh. "I see. Well, that's good but I'm not sure why you're telling me."

"If you find yourself in a situation where you can pass along the information, I'm sure the girls will appreciate it."

"I'll bear that in mind, Lieutenant."

A day later, Tranh phoned. "Ashley and Marissa are appreciative, though obviously there's a lot else on their minds."

"When are they coming back?"

"I've been informed that they may remain where they are."

"In Vancouver."

"Apparently," said Tranh, "they've found employment. Seem to be learning responsibility."

"Good lesson for rich girls," said Milo.

"All the more reason," said Tranh.

"Any horses up there?"

"The topic has come up."

Eight days after the death of John Jensen Williams, the combined force of Milo and Frank Gonzales finally convinced one of Kashmeer Katte's fellow dancers to spill.

Kashmeer had sublet off the books, scoring the converted garage of a dingy bungalow in East Hollywood rented by three of the other strippers.

"Another back house," I said.

"Unbelievable," said Milo. "We're talking carbon copy of Frankie's place. No taxidermy, this place yielded better treasure. Three handguns, including the .25 used to kill Ursula, the 9mm used to shoot Frankie, and another 9mm with both Williams's and Richard Corey's prints that had never been fired."

"The gun Corey waved at his daughters."

"Brand-new, not loaded. Idiot was a paper tiger to the end. We also found the cash Williams took from Corey. Hundred and eighteen K, Williams didn't bother to hide it, just kept it in bank bags under the bed."

"He was living there with Kashmeer?"

"Since leaving Oxnard. I informed her PD, he calls back an hour later, his client is now ready to 'discuss.' I told him my priority is finding out what happened to Merry Santos, she doesn't give that up, she bores me. Nothing from him since. We'll see."

I said, "Williams leave behind any souvenirs?"

"Best I can say to that is maybe. There was a jewelry box on Brzica's nightstand with some interesting contents. Starting with a Lady Patek with a dead battery, way too classy for Brzica."

"Ursula was taking two watches to be fixed?"

"I called her jeweler, and he never sold her a Patek, but she could've picked it up somewhere else. The other stuff is trinkets, no reason for

Williams to have them unless they meant something to him. I've sent photos to Kathy Hennepin's family, they think one pair of costume earrings *might've* been hers. What was more probative was—get this—a stuffed baby owl that had to come from Frankie."

"Trinkets," I said. "That poor woman in Connecticut couldn't have afforded Tiffany. Maybe something will come up."

"I'll try, but good luck after all these years. Sean did find one strong possible in New York, two and a half years ago, when Williams was living there. A Japanese woman named Yuki Yamada here on a work visa so she could be a sous-chef at a fancy fish place in Midtown Manhattan. She was found strangled and stabbed in her Lower East Side apartment. Dinner for two on the table—sashimi, et cetera—but no one made anything of it because she was a pro, the assumption was she'd set up a meal. No sexual assault, no DNA. NYPD didn't sound fired up. The new mayor's prioritizing traffic fatalities."

He rotated his mouth. "There have to be others but I'm gonna concentrate on sweeping out my own stables."

Horse analogy.

I said, "Makes sense."

Ten days after the death of John Jensen Williams, Al Bayless called. The cameras we'd installed in the building had nabbed one would-be car thief and "a pervy-looking dude hiding behind an SUV. Any way we could hang on to the gear?"

"Sure," said Milo. "Consider it a gift."

Bayless said, "Two offenders. And that's just a couple of weeks, no telling."

"Bosses happy, Al?"

"Wish I could say they cared, Milo, but I'm happy—that steak'll be on me."

"Sounds good."

"I mean it, man."

"I know you do."

◆

Fifteen days after the death of John Jensen Williams, Milo and I were at Café Moghul celebrating the return of his appetite.

Agnes Brzica continued to profess ignorance about the fate and whereabouts of Meredith Santos.

"Idiot's holding out, for what I don't know, but her lawyer's even a bigger cretin, it's like talking to a stain."

He forked, chewed, and swallowed a massive chunk of tandoori lamb.

"Yum—think of this as therapy, Alex."

"Eating?"

"It's not merely ingesting, my friend, it's therapeutically recontextualizing the whole food thing."

"Self-help," I said.

"Is there any other kind?"

The previous night, he'd treated Robin and me to dinner at a Beverly Hills steak house. Two nights before that, he'd dragged Rick out for Mexican, and twenty-four hours before that Al Bayless had treated him to "a T-bone the size of Argentina."

I watched him make his way through the lamb and the lobster and the snow crab. Big bowl of rice pudding waiting in the wings, he had only to blink at the woman in the sari to summon more.

He was chewing hard—tough piece of lamb—when his phone rang.

He swallowed. "Sturgis."

What he heard made him smile. He said, "Yessir!"

I reached over and triggered the hands-off.

Captain Henry Santos's voice, sharp and clipped as ever, said, "Okay, here she is."

A woman said, "Lieutenant Sturgis? This is Meredith Santos. I hear you've been looking for me. So sorry if it's been a hassle."

"No hassle at all. Glad you're okay."

"I'm better than okay, I'm great!"

"May I ask—"

"Where was I? Hold on . . . I'm in a different room, Dad's kind of a . . . he's kind of conservative."

"Parents can be that way."

"Especially parents who've careered in the military. Where've I been? Traveling with a friend. A doctor. Also a dentist. He's both, an oral surgeon. We met at a party and just hit it off and decided what the heck, both of us had been working way too hard for way too long, why not? So we flew to Maui and—hold on, I think I hear Dad . . . no, it's fine . . . where was I?"

"Maui."

"Oh, yeah, we went to Maui and had *fun*."

"Fun is good," said Milo.

Merry Santos said, "Honestly, sir, it's been a real long time since I had any. Same for Darren—that's his name. He was in Iraq and so was I. He spent two years doing field surgery, came back and now does reconstruction at the Westwood V.A., plus he moonlights to work off his school debt. I've been grinding, too, sir. Lawyers can be real jerks, they think keeping you late and taking you out to dinner makes up for treating you like a peon. But no complaints, you do what you have to do."

Milo said, "See what you mean about fun, Meredith."

"Bet you do, sir. Being a homicide lieutenant and all that. Anyway, I wanted you to know that I appreciate the time you put into trying to find me."

"Happy endings make it worthwhile, Meredith."

"Well, then, this was super-worthwhile, Lieutenant. Anyway, Darren and I just went!"

Soft laugh. "We played, Lieutenant. We did nothing but play."

ABOUT THE AUTHOR

JONATHAN KELLERMAN is the #1 *New York Times* bestselling author of more than three dozen bestselling crime novels, including the Alex Delaware series, *The Butcher's Theater, Billy Straight, The Conspiracy Club, Twisted,* and *True Detectives.* With his wife, bestselling novelist Faye Kellerman, he co-authored *Double Homicide* and *Capital Crimes.* With his son, bestselling novelist Jesse Kellerman, he co-authored the first book of a new series, *The Golem of Hollywood.* He is also the author of two children's books and numerous nonfiction works, including *Savage Spawn: Reflections on Violent Children* and *With Strings Attached: The Art and Beauty of Vintage Guitars.* He has won the Goldwyn, Edgar, and Anthony awards and has been nominated for a Shamus Award. Jonathan and Faye Kellerman live in California, New Mexico, and New York.

jonathankellerman.com
Facebook.com/JonathanKellerman

ABOUT THE TYPE

This book was set in Garamond, a typeface originally designed by the Parisian type cutter Claude Garamond (c. 1500–61). This version of Garamond was modeled on a 1592 specimen sheet from the Egenolff-Berner foundry, which was produced from types assumed to have been brought to Frankfurt by the punch cutter Jacques Sabon (c. 1520–80).

Claude Garamond's distinguished romans and italics first appeared in *Opera Ciceronis* in 1543–44. The Garamond types are clear, open, and elegant.